EWERTON DEATH TRIP

Borgo Press Books by A. R. MORLAN

The Amulet: A Novel of Horror
Dark Journey: A Novel of Horror
Ewerton Death Trip: A Walk Through the Dark Side of Town
*The Fold-o-Rama Wars at the Blue Moon Roach Hotel and
    Other Colorful Tales*
One Degree Above Hell and Other Stories

EWERTON DEATH TRIP

A WALK THROUGH THE DARK SIDE OF TOWN

A. R. MORLAN

with James B. Johnson and John S. Postovit

THE BORGO PRESS

MMXI

EWERTON DEATH TRIP

FIRST EDITION

Published by Wildside Press LLC

www.wildsidebooks.com

DEDICATION

This collection is dedicated to **Ardath Mayhar**, without whose extensive efforts this work would not have become a reality—I cannot thank her enough for all the time she invested in getting this work brought before a publisher, and later on, in scanning and preparing this manuscript for digital publication. Without her, these stories would remain buried in yellowing pulp magazines, unremembered and unread. It is through her interest and encouragement that they have been reborn.

CONTENTS

ACKNOWLEDGMENTS

THESE STORIES WERE previously published as follows, and are reprinted (with minor editing, updating, and textual modifications) by permission of the author:

"Night Skirt" was first published in *The Horror Show*, Winter, 1987. Copyright © 1987, 2011 by A. R. Morlan.

"Four Days Before the Snow" was first published in *Night Cry*, Summer, 1985. Copyright © 1985, 2011 by A. R. Morlan.

"The Holiday House" was first published in *Night Cry*, Spring, 1986. Copyright © 1986, 2011 by A. R. Morlan.

"Simon Says" was first published in *Night Cry*, Winter, 1986. Copyright © 1986, 2011 by A. R. Morlan.

"Garbage Day in Ewerton" was first published in *Night Cry*, Summer, 1986. Copyright © 1986, 2011 by A. R. Morlan.

"When the Bad Thing Comes" was first published in *Eldritch Tales* #22, 23, 24 & 25, 1990-91. Copyright © 1990, 1991, 2011 by A. R. Morlan.

"Street Coffins," with John S. Postovit, was first published in *Bone-Chilling Tales*, Li'l Demon Press, 1988. Copyright © 1988, 2011 by A. R. Morlan and John S. Postovit.

"Trick or Treat" was first published in *The Horror Show*, Fall, 1986. Copyright © 1986, 2011 by A. R. Morlan.

"Scrap When Empty" was first published in *Night Cry*, Winter, 1985. Copyright © 1985, 2011 by A. R. Morlan.

"Does it *Ploop*?," was first published in *Night Cry*, Fall, 1986. Copyright © 1986, 2011 by A. R. Morlan.

"The German Lady" was first published in *Smothered Dolls*,

AUTHOR'S NOTE

THE TITLE OF THIS collection is a reworking of that seminal 1973 book, *Wisconsin Death Trip*, by Michael Lesy. I have also taken inspiration from the arrangement of his book (a collection of photographs and newspaper articles from Black River Falls, Jackson County, Wisconsin), specifically his division of the material involved into what he called "five primary sequences," when grouping the stories in my collection.

If the reader is interested in seeing a work which has had a strong influence on my own work, I would highly recommend that he or she seek out this volume.

PART ONE
CHILDHOOD AND ITS AFTERMATH

NIGHT SKIRT

LUCY'S BARE FEET MADE soft slapping sounds on the dusty plank floor as she made her way down the upstairs hallway, heading for the staircase. Her cotton nightgown brushed against her calves, almost making the little girl giggle, but she curled her lower lip in between her teeth and bit down hard, telling herself, Gramma doesn't giggle when her night skirt brushes on her legs...she just lets it trail out like twilight, all dark and deep and...wide behind her.

Lucy always tried to be like her Grandmother, even though her blue serge middy skirt only came down around her knees, and the blue wasn't blue enough...not that rich, plum-like blue-black of Gramma's night skirt, with that star-like twinkle of lacy petticoat peeping out from under the thick hem when Gramma walked. Once Lucy had tried tying her winter coat around her waist, using the sleeves like apron ties to keep it around her body, but even though the coat was blue-black wool, it just wasn't the same as Gramma's night skirt. The ripple of the material wasn't there, and neither were other things...but hadn't Gramma laughed when she was Lucy strutting around in her thick ersatz skirt, bending over to scoop up Lucy in her plump arms, then whispering in her ear, "Is my Lucy trying to wear a night skirt? Oh Lucy, Pumpkin, Gramma's night skirt is very special...not for little girls. Oh no, no, no," only when Gramma said No, no, no it didn't sound like it did when Mother said it (as Lucy slapped down the uncarpeted stairs, her small mouth twisted like she'd just tried to eat a peeled lemon), oh no, not at all....

Gramma was everything to Lucy, for all of Lucy's six and a half years on earth, just as Lucy was everything to her mother's mother. Ever since Gramma's big house with the gingerbread trim on the roof overhang and gay red shutters and big curved porch was taken away by the county (Mother said it was all President Hoover's fault for getting us into this mess, but Lucy didn't think that her Gramma even knew the president), Gramma had lived in Lucy's house Downstairs, because climbing the stairs was too hard for a woman with too-white hair and soft puffy dotted arms and teeth that could pop out of her mouth. But Gramma's age wasn't the only reason she slept downstairs.... Lucy wasn't supposed to know any of this, but like Aunt Dora said, little pitchers have big ears, and Lucy couldn't help it if her room was next to Mother and Daddy's room—

"Couldn't she live somewhere else—anywhere else?" Mother had said to Daddy many a time after Gramma swept into their house and settled down in the sewing room off the kitchen, and Daddy's answer was always the same, "She's your mother, you're her daughter, and you happen to be an only child. Where else is she supposed to go?"

And Mother's reply was always the same—never answering Daddy's question, she'd almost sigh, "I wish Lucy hadn't attached herself to her like a barnacle on a barge...it isn't... healthy—"

"Your mother did all right by you—you turned out so well. Why shouldn't Lucy be fine?"

"But those were different times.... When I was small *every* mother wore long swishing skirts and tucked lace handkerchiefs in their sleeves. It's 1931—she shouldn't be dressing like that that.

"And don't tell me we should buy her a dollar cotton pongee dress from Sears and burn her old things. Oh I know that's what you were thinking—and it wouldn't work. My mother's worn a long black skirt for ages...since before Poppa died. And I do believe that she will *die* in that awful thing. What's that Lucy's taken to calling it? Night skirt? Some such silliness...and *she* fosters it. I won't stand for it, the way she addles poor Lucy's mind. It's bad enough *we're* old—"

"Old? *I* feel pretty fit for—"

"Fifty. And I am forty-five...perhaps having such a late baby wasn't the ideal thing to do—after all, my mother is in her seventies—"

"Oh you worry too much," Daddy would always end up saying, before turning over in the bed and making the old mattress creak and groan like a withered tree in a thunderstorm. And Lucy could almost feel her mother's anger seething out of her, through the wallpaper and plaster of the wall between their bedrooms, and into Lucy herself....Lucy imagined her mother's displeasure being something cold-bright and pulsing, like the full moon swimming in a foggy sky. And as she lay in her too-short bed, her feet poking through the white enameled spindles at the foot of the bed, Lucy wondered if Gramma could feel the seeping anger dripping down on her through the floor to the sewing room below. Gramma often told Lucy that Grammas have a way of knowing things, all sorts of things, and since Lucy's other Grandmother (and both her Grandfathers, for that matter) all died back in 1918 during the influenza epidemic, Lucy took her Gramma's word for it.

After all, Grammas wore the night skirt with the star-sparkling white petticoats, and Lucy's mother only wore a rayon slip under short cotton and pongee dresses—and didn't Gramma sit Lucy on her big lap and whisper in her ear that short dresses were bad? That they weren't—couldn't be—special like the rippling and soft and oh so dark it sucked in all the light night skirt? And hadn't Gramma shown Lucy how special her long blue-black-purple skirt could be? There was a time in the front yard, in winter (the most special secret time, while Lucy swore on her heart and hoped to die that she wouldn't tell Mother and Daddy what she'd seen) and the other time when Lucy had scooted along the floor while Gramma was napping and lifted up the hem of the night skirt and curled up in a little ball under the heavy fabric.

Lucy remembered, as she made her way down the stairs in the darkness of evening toward Gramma's room, that she had been able to see only a faint haze of light, like trying to look through stacks of screen windows resting alongside the house on the day Daddy changed the windows in early summer. And the more she'd looked, the better she could see...only through the cloth of the night skirt, things looked different. Colors changed, and shapes of things, too...at first Lucy hadn't recognized Mother at all—for seen through that night-dark fabric, Mother was a horned, angled creature, all hard surfaces and spikes....

That was when Lucy whimpered, and Gramma nudged her out from under the night skirt and had Lucy on her lap before Mother could open her thick lips to scold or complain...but Lucy saw the *look* in her mother's hazel eyes, and almost imagined the horns again. And for many a night Mother told Daddy in the half hour or so before sleep overtook them that she ought to take Gramma's "damned skirt" out and *burn* it, just toss it on the trash-heap and *incinerate* it, and Lucy wondered why Mother didn't just suggest giving the skirt to the rag man who came around each week, but every time Mother mentioned the night skirt, all she could seem to think of was destroying it.....

Lucy was careful as she went down the stairs not to make the treads squeak, even though she could hear the loose flutter and harsh *blap-blap-blap* of both her parents snoring up above her, and she held onto the big thick railing which was almost level with her shoulders, her slightly damp hand sticking in places to the somewhat gummy old varnish of the wooden rail. Down below, the light came through the shaded and curtained windows in hazy patches of light, just like the way light had been filtered by Gramma's night skirt, only sort of *different*, too. It was hard for Lucy to put into words, but the mind-pictures came easily enough...along with other pictures, from other times with Gramma. Like last winter.

Reaching the cool first floor, her bare toes feeling cautiously for any sharp things like pebbles or splinters on the varnished wood surface, Lucy made her way toward Gramma's room, and as she slowly walked, the memory of *another* walk, this time over snow and cold concrete, came back to her....

Gramma said she didn't like going outside in the snow—said she might slip, said she might fall and break old brittle bones—but Lucy's birthday was coming up next week, and Daddy forgot to mail the invitations for her party when he left the house that morning, and Mother was busy ironing clothes, making puffs of whitish steam come up with a hot, fabric smell off the ironing board set up in the kitchen, so Lucy begged and begged, until Gramma said she'd walk down the street with Lucy to the mailbox, and drop the tiny stamped envelopes into the slot that Lucy couldn't reach herself. But Lucy could tell that Gramma wasn't too *keen* on the idea, but she said nothing to Lucy as she held the little girl's hand, which poked out of the coney fur trim of her winter coat, and Lucy was so happy to have her invitations mailed that, at first, she thought Gramma would get over being upset. And maybe Granma *would* have been just fine, but Lucy shook her hand loose from Gramma's kid-gloved grip and began walking *backwards,* like Effie Nemmitz in school could do at recess time, and Gramma began to cluck and scold softly, telling Lucy, "Oh Pumpkin, little *ladies* don't walk like that!" but Lucy was thinking that *she'd* show old Effie come Monday that she could...and then Lucy looked *down*, at her faint foot-prints in the sugary dusting of snow, and at the foot-prints of her Grandmother...and that was when she stopped in her tracks, one tiny gloved hand *pointing,* just pointing down at what she saw.

That was when Gramma reached down and took her hand and steered her back to the house, leaning down every once in a while to whisper something fast and quiet to the little girl, until Lucy began to nod in awareness, and near the front porch Lucy solemnly crossed her heart and hoped to *die* rather than *tell anyone*, even Effie Nemmitz at school, what she'd seen in the fast-melting snow.... Other grandchildren might have been *scared* after seeing what Lucy saw, but she loved her Gramma, and the deep, pitch-black secrets of the night skirt, and in return for promising never, never to tell, Gramma had made a promise to Lucy, too. Her breath billowing out in small semi-transparent white clouds before her gently, slightly sagging face, Gramma had whispered, with soft popping clicks of her false teeth, "Someday, my little Pumpkin, you'll get to wear the night skirt, too...not your Mother, but you, my girl."

And even though Lucy didn't understand everything, just yet, she'd nodded in agreement and a few weeks later she'd tried making her own night skirt out of her coat, making Gramma laugh. That was when she'd said the night skirt wasn't for little girls...at least not yet.

But as Lucy made her way toward the doorway of Gramma's room, keeping her arms out at her sides so she wouldn't knock over any of Mother's bric-a-brac stands with a thump and a crunch of delicate shatter, she told herself that now, now she could wear the night skirt, that Gramma would surely understand...even if she wasn't alive any more.

Lucy had been what the neighbors called "a brave little girl" when the doctor came out of Gramma's sewing room-cum-bedroom yesterday, closing his black leather bag with a snapping-fingernails click that made almost everyone in the parlor jump in place and twitch their closed mouths before they cast their eyes to the floor and began to pat Mother on the back with gentle fingers and closed hands. Even without being told, Lucy knew what had happened...and without asking she knew that the night skirt was now hers. Gramma had said so, hadn't she? That day, when Lucy had seen the footprints that weren't always foot prints, trailing out behind Gramma, even though her Grandmother had been careful not to step on snow, if she could help it, instead searching out the bare spots on the cold concrete...but in some places there was nothing *but* snow, and *there*—there Lucy had seen the rounded arches of hooves, and the five-toed round pads of cat paws, only really *big*, and the thin skitterings of bird claws, and here and there a regular shoe print…but *only* here and there. And all the funny prints in the snow trailed out behind her Gramma's wonderful, terrible, oh-so-thick-and-*dark* night skirt, dusted here and there by the sweep of the trailing skirt, but *not* obliterated.

And Lucy had been a good girl, keeping the secret she'd X'ed into her breast with trembling fingers. And without being told she'd kept secret what she'd seen through the night skirt, that angular place that *wasn't* Gramma's room anymore, peopled with that horned, strange thing that was but wasn't her own mother. When Gramma nudged her out from under there, Lucy had felt the sharp claws of the five-toed paw at her back, poking through the wool jersey of her dress, and felt the lashing curl of a tail whip around her arm—but Lucy hadn't told about *that* either, for even if she *hadn't* liked her Gramma, and had run screaming to her Mother, begging her to look, Gramma would have had normal feet tucked in normal dark stockings and sensible leather shoes for that was part of the mystery of the night skirt, that keeper of the dark, and all that crept or crawled or prowled under cover of darkness. The mystery and magic of the wonderful night skirt, the secrets that Gramma promised to tell Lucy, "later, when you're a big girl, and can wear the real night skirt," only "later" never came, but Lucy was a big girl, almost *seven,* so she figured that that was old enough to wear the night skirt, to use it like Gramma had *used* it. For hadn't the men from the county who took away her house gotten all tumbled and broken when their Ford went into that ditch last fall? True, Gramma's big fancy house was sold by then, to those nasty Parks people, but hadn't Gramma had a smile on her weathered face while she rocked and rocked after hearing the news about the car accident from Daddy?

Even though Mother and some of the other ladies from the neighborhood had come into Gramma's room and washed her, before setting the damp cloths on her now slack face and folded hands, they hadn't taken away the night skirt, hadn't thrown it on the trash heap and burned it to a cinder, like Mother kept saying she wanted to do, even though the night skirt was

Lucy's now. *Maybe Mother didn't want the other ladies to see her do that,* Lucy said to herself as she paused at the closed door of Gramma's room. The fact that her Gramma was dead didn't bother Lucy overmuch, at least not in the way it might have bothered *other* little girls who loved their Grandmothers. Because *her* Gramma had told her things, oh *lots* of good stuff when *Mother* wasn't listening...and even though Gramma had been caught by surprise when the men from the county took away her house, and hadn't been able to make the night skirt *work* for her then, she'd gotten something called "revenge" on them all, and she'd chuckled and hugged Lucy tight when she said that, and all Lucy could think was, *When* I *get the night skirt, first I'm gonna show old Effie some really fancy walking, and* then *I'll....*

But up until last night, when Gramma's lower tummy got to feeling bad, and Mother all but tore the night skirt off of her, *saying* it was so she could get a nightgown on Gramma, but Lucy knew what her Mother was *really* thinking when she took the skirt off the protesting old woman. Lucy had always thought of "and then" as being a long, long time away. Like next year, or longer. But when Lucy had heard Gramma whimpering under the closed door, while Daddy rang for the doctor then rang up the neighbors, Lucy had realized that the time of the night skirt flapping and flowing and dragging around *her* legs had come at last. And as much, as losing Gramma hurt, Lucy was all antsy inside during the rest of the evening, until the time when she heard her parent's last faint words coming through the wall ("And first thing tomorrow, that *skirt* goes out the door, you hear me, Alvin?" "Uh huh....") and then heard only raspy warbling breathing...and now, she had her small fingers wrapped around the door knob, the metal slightly cool and just the faintest bit greasy, and slowly she turned the knob, until the door swung inward onto darkness even deeper, and thicker and softer than the night skirt.

Gramma was there, in the almost solid blackness. Lying on her bed, a now drying cloth over her face and hands, even though it wasn't warm enough to start worrying about *that* sort of thing. Lucy was glad that Mr. Byrne and Mr. Reish were *both* down with the grippe, otherwise the two undertakers might have come and taken Gramma away, and maybe Mother would have tossed out the night skirt—*Lucy's* night skirt, now—into the back yard trash can, where any *animal* might have slithered or crawled into it...and Lucy didn't want to think about what might happen *then!*

Her eyes were more and more accustomed to the dark now, and Lucy could *very* faintly see the two whitish places where the damp hankies rested on her Gramma's face and hands. Which meant that if the bed was *there*, the rocker where Mother had placed the folded night skirt had to be right *here*—Like a slumbering animal awakened by the gentle, loving touch of its owner, the night skirt rippled under Lucy's small fingers. Darker than the surrounding darkness, the night skirt felt as warm to Lucy as if her Grandmother had just removed it only minutes before, and feeling for the opening with her hands, Lucy opened up the waistband and after tucking her nightgown around her legs (it would make a good, if makeshift slip) Lucy stepped into the night skirt, rolling the fabric up and up until the hem of the skirt dusted her insteps. Feeling around on the rocker, Lucy found Gramma's belt and tightened the strip of excess cloth around her waist, her arms hampered by the thick roll of excess cloth scrunched up under her armpits. But Lucy didn't mind that at all; like Gramma had told her, she was going to be tall someday.

Feeling the heavy swish of fabric around her thin legs as she walked, Lucy paused by her Gramma's bed, whispering, "I'll come and make you better in a little while...after I come back from their room. Then we'll play, okay, Gramma?" and after giving the still hands a cloth-screened pat, Lucy left the room, heading for the staircase.

The cloth of the night skirt made a faint, susurrus noise that almost masked the delicate click-click of claws and scrabbling scritch of talons as Lucy made her determined way across the carpetless floorboards.

FOUR DAYS
BEFORE THE SNOW

BABIES, THEY CLAIMED, were a blessing. But not the crawling things that inhabited her dreams and that turned her waking hours into a nightmare.

She was covered with them. Dozens. Their pudgy legs dug hard into her belly and breasts as they inched up her prostrate body. Finely fleshed palms traced the contours of her face. *Try to move, Can't,* Too many of them, Too much weight pushing down her arms, her legs. No good—even if she could move, could throw off the covers, they'd fall to the floor and break. And how could anyone get up and walk across a floor of broken babies? *Better feign sleep,*

More babies coming. Thumping sounds against the metal legs of the daybed and base of the couch, shockingly hard noises for such soft, malleable little bodies. Surging against the bed, *thuwunk, thuwunk....*

Maureen opened her eyes. Faint daylight made the window a luminous rectangle in the wall before her, a shape which hung, disconnected, before her line of sight. Worming a hand out from under the covers, she rubbed it across her eyes, hard, until an eyelash got caught under the lid. Maureen closed her eyes tightly, until the tears came. When she opened them again, the rectangle was softer, more washed-out. Soft was better this early in the morning—oh God, those soft babies. They were still *on* her, she could see them faintly, and feel their oppressive weight.... With great trepidation she inched her hand down toward her chest—and came in contact with soft fur. Pooter-kitty let out a trilling *purrupt?*—and stretched out a dainty paw toward Maureen. Of course. What with Pooter and Digger and Smoo sleeping on her all night, she was bound to dream about babies. Sometimes she and Larry even joked about having three furry kids.

Relaxing with that thought, she moved up in the bed until her shoulders were resting against the back of cushions. Pooter rode up on Maureen's chest, digging in with her claws, and hung on. (One was painfully sharp and stuck in Maureen's left breast.) Digger was a dead weight across his mistress's pelvis, and Smoo-boo discovered that two wiggling feet equaled one mousie-under-the-covers. The other half of the bed was empty: Maureen almost called out "Larry?" since the digital clock next to her read 6:45, and it only took him ten minutes to get ready for work and another minute to get there for the seven-to-three shift, but she remembered him telling her last night over supper (Banquet Western dinners, his favorite) that Steve and Julie's van had broken down and that he'd been leaving early to give them a ride. Which meant that he'd taken the Pinto, which in turn meant that she could just forget about going uptown today for some eggs and hamburger. Walking a mile and a half in five-below weather was out, and she'd be goddamned if she'd ride the Ski-Doo even if it was legal in the city limits; no way was she going to give those polyester princesses in the parking lot with their Mark V's and station wagons a chance to flash the old half-smile and turned-up eyes at her. It was bad enough waiting in the checkout line with a cartful of generics and store-brand groceries, and having some former classmate of hers from EHS trot up with *her* cart full of Libby's, Hunt's, and Campbell's goodies, which would lead to the inevitable "Is your Larry still working at the mill? Oh, my Bryan? I guess you didn't see the article about his Jaycee award in the *Herald*. Well, it's on page…." No, if Larry didn't leave her any wheels, Larry didn't get his scrambled eggs tomorrow morning. As if he couldn't get them himself.

She hoped that Steve and Julie would have enough sense to take the van up to Miller's Auto *now* and get the stupid clunker fixed; Maureen could just imagine them letting it go because Larry was giving them a ride. A free ride, probably; he couldn't ask his ice-fishing buddy to pay for a little thing like $1.10 a gallon *gas,* now could he?

Sighing, Maureen closed her eyes and tried to snuggle back under the covers *(no use getting up, just have to turn up the heat),* but as soon as the covers touched her chin, the baby feeling came back. The pressure and heat from all those bodies made her skin ache. That had been one awful dream. No, strike that—nightmare. Nothing *bad* had happened, nothing horrid, but something that real and (her flesh rippled with the tactile memory of it) so *suffocating* had to be a nightmare. Which was odd, because no one would believe that dreaming about babies, sweet-breathed, cooing, tiny *googoos,* could be so repulsive.

It was useless. She had to crawl out of that warm, comforting bed and get dressed. After those babies, it was no longer pleasant to lie there (and she was never going to get used to the metal bar under her back). Reluctantly Maureen rolled Pooter onto Larry's half of the bed and threw back the covers. The rush of cold made her bladder ache. She searched the carpet with her feet for her slippers. Gone. With three cats around the house and nothing to occupy them for eight hours besides digging the litter out of the pan and clawing the drapes, it wasn't surprising. Her blanket-cloth PJs had attached footies, not that they'd be much help on a morning like this. Larry had probably turned the heat down too much last night. Funny, those babies had been so hot, even though they were naked…. Even the cats didn't generate that much heat, not even in summertime. The skin under her top felt hot. *(Oh jeeze, Maureen, of* course *it's hot, Pooter was sleeping there, you idjit!)* Maureen's head felt like someone had tilted it and poured a bottle of Elmer's down her ear until her brain was a sticky, solidifying mess. Shaking it, she thought, *That was one hell of a bad dream, nightmare, whathaveyou.*

She got up, stretched until some bones in her spine popped,

then hunkered down to look under the daybed for her slippers. Abruptly Maureen let out a hollow moan and sank to the floor in a graceless sprawl. One of them was under there, a vague pink shape huddled next to the base of the couch. A baby. That's where they had come from, the babies were hiding in the hole, in that empty gaping space where the bed folded into the couch during the day, only now it was filled with hiding babies, dozens of soft babies crammed together while Larry slept with her, only to stir and stretch and creep out after he left, clambering onto the bed to pat her face and bruise her body, dozens more of them bumping up against the bed….They had hurried up and crawled away to hide when she woke, but one of them straggled, maybe lingered for a last gawk at her, and didn't make it back into the hole. She wasn't sure, but something shiny and round was glinting down there, waiting for her to reach under the bed: *Please put your hand under this bed, just hold out your hand.* Her full bladder began to let go, slowly, a few drops slipping down her thighs, but if that baby moved….

Smoo-boo jumped off the bed with a *purrupt!* and scurried under it. White body faintly luminescent in the darkness of the room, Smoo made a beeline to the baby. Maureen tried to cry out—babies can hurt little kitties, Mom had told her so many years ago, or was it the other way around? Surely something would hurt something—but no sound would come out of her open mouth, and Smoo (butt wiggling, tail twitching) pounced on the baby and dragged his prey proudly out to *her.*

"Oh, *Smoobie*...." Her voice was as thin as a newborn's cry. Smoo *purrupted* in reply and dragged Maureen's pink, button trimmed slippers onto her wet lap. Pressing his furry body against hers, *tight,* she giggled nervously into his pink-lined ear, "Come on, Smoobie, Momma's gotta get up and clean herself off."

After turning on the radio (WIFC out of Wausaw—"Where the *music* does the talking") and throwing her soggy pajama bottoms in the bathtub, Maureen pulled on Larry's brown robe and walked the few steps into the kitchen. The floor was hop-scotched with a grid of wet paper towels. Attached to the refrig-erator door with a photo-magnet (Maureen holding Digger up-side down on her lap) was a note in Larry's handwriting—*Don't blame me if Smoo smells like a baby. "Daddy" spilled the milk on him. Sorry bout the mess.* Maureen sopped up the excess liquid on the floor with the towels before wadding them up and pitching them. The three cats followed her into the kitchen; Maureen took her first good look at Smoo and said, "You poor thing, you look like Billy Idol," while rubbing down his spiky white fur with a fresh paper towel. He did smell milky, a lot like a baby.... Her stomach did a flip-flop and she decided to skip solid food this morning. She poured a cupful of cider into a small pot and set it on MED.

Padding back into the living room (a whole ten-foot walk), Maureen carefully folded the blankets and top sheet in toward the middle of the mattress—the folding mechanism chewed up the bedding—before taking hold of the far end and lifting it. From this vantage point the bed, with its pink top blanket, looked like a tongue sticking out of a brown tweed mouth. Sort of like a man with a beard and mustache around his lips, or a guy's whang going in.... She shook the thought away, that was too close to her nightmare. "Shit, how silly can a person get?" she mumbled, pushing the bed back into the yawning cavity between the arms of the couch. Imagine, *babies* living in there.... Where would they all go when she put the bed back in? Besides, no way could you fit that many little babies in that space, it was only a double bed. Not enough babies could ever squeeze in there, certainly not enough to come pouring out in masses like that.

Maureen threw the cushions back onto the couch, then covered it with the throw, an old ripcord brown bedspread. Not that it did more than just cover up the damage; the cats could, and did, crawl under it and claw the fabric until the sides of the piece were the consistency of angel hair. Periodically Larry would look under the cover and yell, "Fer Christ all Friday, Maureen, either get those cats declawed or I'll never buy you another piece of furniture again, whaddya think I'm *working* for?" and she'd continue to sit there eating or sewing or watching TV, not saying anything, but knowing he was right, that he had a point, but also knowing that declawing was so cruel (even Larry felt that way), and so expensive.... Besides, what did he expect her to use for money at the veterinarian's office? Maybe he expected her to take the operations out in trade. That thought made her laugh out loud; sorry, but the vet wasn't her type. If she was lucky, she wasn't his type either!

The couch finished, Maureen crossed the room to the thermostat and turned it from fifty-six to sixty-two. It came on with a muted purr. Whenever she heard people (especially those polyester princesses) in the bank or the IGA talking about how they made the Supreme Sacrifice in the name of Conservation by turning the heat *down* to sixty-five at night, Maureen had to stifle a laugh and the question, "What would you gals do at *my* house?—freeze your cunts off?" Alone, she could let out a sour laugh over the irony of it all.

The silver pot was jiggling on the burner when she reentered the kitchen. Silly little aluminum two-cup pot with a bent handle. Part of her wedding stash. Some bonanza of goodies *that* was, she thought as she poured the bubbling cider into her cold mug, which she then carried to the table. A four-slice toaster, two jelly roll pans (who the fuck made *jelly rolls* anymore?), a set of cheap pots and pans, five sets of towels in five different colors and patterns, a blender that broke, and one set of flatware. Whoopie ding-dong. And a whopping seventy-five dollars in cash, mostly fives. That had gone for the second-hand daybed.

Warming her cold fingers by wrapping them around the white china mug, Maureen read the words surrounding the blue windmill which decorated its front: *OLD DUTCH FOODS Northeast Distributors Wayne and Ruby Mesabi Ewerton WI* 561-7968. Larry had worked for the Mesabis for six months after their wedding, delivering chips to the bars, the high school, the IGA, Applebaum's and the bowling alley, and getting to take home the stale bags of snacks because Ruby and Wayne felt sorry for him and Maureen, living in the shitty part of town as they (still) did and being newlyweds and all. She wished she had a dime for every bag of barbecue and onion and garlic chips she'd eaten for lunch in that half-year. Not with lunch, but *for* lunch. That was before the opening at the paper mill three years ago. Steve and Julie had clued Larry in on that one, before the notice appeared in the paper, so Maureen supposed that Larry did owe them a free ride this morning, and every other morning. The pay at Old Dutch was a lot less that he was getting now—a *whole* lot less—but at least his hours had been regular, none of this changing-shifts-every-two-weeks shit, and they had been able to *do* things together, even if it was only playing marathon games of 500 or sitting on the hill behind the drive-in and trying to lip-read a movie. Now they'd listen to the rock radio until five thirty, then they'd turn on the TV, usually with her watching and him dozing in his chair by the window, and eventually she'd end up watching him snore softly through his open mouth and wonder what kind of chemicals he was breathing in at the mill, or what he was absorbing in through his skin. Sure, they said it was safe, but how come Steve had those boils on his face (and he'd never been a pizza face in high school)? And as for Larry—well, they never discussed it, but there was a tacit nighttime agreement that if she asked and he refused, it wasn't because of not *wanting* to…. Oh sure, the working conditions were safe all right, isn't that what they told those people in *Silkwood*? Conditions there were really hot, all right.

Maureen sipped her breakfast slowly, swirling the hot liquid around in her mouth before swallowing. The mug was about as ridiculous as the pot with the bent handle *(his side gave us that)*; the mug's handle had an opening just big enough to accommodate her forefinger, and she wore a size six ring. Larry didn't try to fight it, he just held his like a tumbler. That worried Maureen; china conducted heat like something else, and Larry never seemed to feel it. Probably those goddamned chemicals….

thuwunk

Maureen slammed her mug down on the table so hard that the amber liquid sloshed over the rim, leaving a large puddle on the Formica top. The ersatz wood paneling pressed in around her as she waited, not breathing, until the sound came again (they're outside, they're waiting for me outside, all those cold little babies, milling around—) *thuwunk...thuwunk....* (The noise was coming from outside the house, probably the front porch. Throwing her parka over Larry's robe, Maureen ran to the front door.)

The frigid air felt dry and hard in her mouth and nose, stinging her forehead and cheeks. The sky was a malignant opal; washed out blue, faint gold, and grimy white, overlaid with dirty swirls of smoke from the rows of unpainted houses across the street. Blackened tree branches, coated thickly with frost, etched jagged chiaroscuro lines across everything, giving her neighborhood a shattered, broken look. No one else was outside, not even the bent old man from Crescent Street, walking his shaggy black mutt. No kids, none at all in the neighborhood, not since the bottle blonde bitch from upstairs had moved out—skipped town, to put a fine point on it—with her four rug rats. The apartment to the back of the house had been empty for going on three years now, ever since that night when old lady Winston had the stroke and the ambulance took her and her husband away. Palmer Winston had come back long enough to throw his clothes into a battered gladstone and his few belongings into a Lux detergent box, and after the funeral the Winstons' son had cleaned out the rest of the furniture.

Maureen leaned against one of the five wooden uprights which held up the porch roof, looking down the street both ways. No snow last night, so no snowplows to make a strange noise. The grey house on the corner showed some sign of life, or movement at least; the car was idling in the driveway, sending fragile plumes of grey exhaust into the icy air. She didn't know the name of the people who owned the Volvo; had never seen them up close, or talked to them. Maureen didn't know any of her neighbors by name, which was the way she and Larry liked it—most of the time, anyway. They had been on a first-name basis with the Winstons, out of politeness, and sort of knew the shrew upstairs, but only under duress. (Even if the bitch's hair was bleached almost white, Maureen didn't think that white was what the woman put down under "race" on her driver's license, but she couldn't figure out whether her ex-neighbor had been passing; Amerindian, Hispanic, or what Larry's family called "Eye-tailian." Whichever she was, Maureen always thought that dark-skinned women got kind of homely once they hit thirty, and Ms. Bleach Blonde was at least thirty-five.) The blonde bomber and her brood had blown the neighborhood after Larry called the cops out after her kids last July; they'd been letting the air out of the Pinto's tires. Once Social Services had gotten wind of it, she'd been asked to move somewhere else in town, but she'd beaten them to the punch by loading up her Scout (paid for with our tax money, Maureen thought bitterly) with her few trashy belongings and runty brats. She did leave her roaches, as well as several unpaid bills...which the county had picked up. Funny, Maureen couldn't remember the tramp's name, but she couldn't forget her hands. Her fingernails were long and always filthy, which was strange, considering that the only manual labor she ever performed was picking up her food stamps and welfare checks. A week after she'd moved, when the landlord's wife cleaned out the apartment, the Orkin truck from Wausau had pulled to a stop in front of the house, and Larry had rechristened their dear departed neighbor La Cucaracha. Maureen had only stopped looking for the little brown buggies last month, when it got good and cold. No one had come by to look at either apartment. Sometimes, when she was just about to fall asleep, Maureen would hear Ms. La C. shrilling, "You'll pay, you sonsabitches!" at their locked front door before trotting off in her miniskirt to her Scout and driving away into the hot July night.

Yes, it was worth it to be reclusive. Even if it meant that she only had the cats for company on most days, it was still worth it. However, it was *not* worth being the only person standing outdoors today; not in January, and certainly not while she wasn't wearing any pants—*thuwunk*

She spun around so fast that her slippers almost lost purchase on the slick porch floor. At first she didn't see it. Then she looked down and saw it at the edge of her vision, rolling around on its side next to the front wall of the house. A baby-food jar.

Maureen had put the jar in the garbage and taken it out again twice before two o'clock that afternoon. She knew it would sound silly, and the very silliness of it all nearly stopped her, but she finally decided to show it to Larry when he got home. Maybe he'd even get a laugh out of it, out of the coincidence of her dreaming about those babies (*funny, we weren't even talking about kids, not even Steve and Julie's, I wonder what made me—*) and being wakened by the sound of this baby-food jar rolling on the porch, Stranger than the coincidence was the fact that it was on the porch in the first place, what with no kids in the neighborhood of any age, and garbage day being Monday, three days ago, much too long for a jar to lay low without being seen, Weird, how she personalized the jar, gave it a life and will of its own, just because it had a cute baby face on the label; but the circumstances aided her fantasy. What else could she think about a supposedly inanimate object that just happened to find its way onto the porch (up three steps, no less) when it had no business being in this part of town in the first place? Now if there were kids living on the block, or if La C. the Blonde were still in town, just looking for ways to make trouble, Maureen never would have given the appearance of the jar another thought. But, damn it, there wasn't so much as a dog running around their street.... Whether it was spooky or just a fluke, it would be worth talking about over their dinner, something besides Larry's litany about how he hated this job. Besides, Larry loved that "Believe It or Not!" kind of shit.

She picked up the jar and studied it. The label was red, with the oh-so-cute Gerber baby on the front (Larry's mom had told her once that Humphrey Bogart was the model for the baby, but Larry's mom bought the *Globe* and the *Enquirer* with religious punctuality every Monday, so Maureen was a *teensy* bit skeptical about that information), and stated that this jar, when full, had contained "Junior Strained Potatoes." The label wasn't a bit dirty or torn. Inside, the jar contained the moist residue of whitish strained potatoes. *Somebody must've put this on the porch,* she decided. *It would've shattered if it had been thrown* or *even rolled at the wall.*

No animal could've done it, and there was just no way the wind could've picked it up. Placing the jar on the counter, Maureen thought, *If it's a joke, I'm not laughing. Folks,* then turned her attention to picking out a frozen dinner for each of them tonight. She hoped Steve got the van fixed.

Maureen waited until after Larry assured her that the van was indeed fixed to tell him her story and show him the jar. But telling it made it seem so trivial; her reactions were so personal, so wrapped up in her own private observations and reflections, that her recitation became banal and flat. Not even all those speech and creative writing classes she took at EHS helped. Her fear seemed so small, unimportant. She smiled weakly when done.

Larry pushed his chair away from the table, shook a cigarette out of his hard pack, lit the match on the sole of his shoe, and blew out a grey cloud which hovered over their empty metal dinner trays like a frown before it drifted into the living room.

"You mean to say that this baby-food jar here woke you up? Jeeze, that does beat all." He took another puff, and exhaled, "'S a good thing you weren't dreaming 'bout a Mack truck rolling over you, or 'bout getting blown up by a——"

"That's not funny."

"True. Now peeing yourself when you thought your slippers were a baby, *that's* funny." He blew his smoke at the ceiling, tilting back in his chair.

Maureen got up and took the dirty tray over to the sink. "Next time you piss up the bed after downing a six-pack," she said over her shoulder, "I'll have to remind you how funny it is." She threw the jar into the trash bag.

"What's got you pissed off?" Larry took his coffee mug into the other room, trailing ashes on the carpet. He sat down in his chair, and Pooter jumped on his lap. He stroked her tabby fur with his free hand, having balanced his mug on the arm of the chair. Maureen placed an ash tray on the other arm, then slumped into her usual spot on the sofa.

"I said, what's got you pissed off? It was kinda strange, but you gotta admit, after eight hours at that place"—he jerked his cigarette toward the mill—"I'm not about to jump up and down over a coincidence. Hell, the only reason you dreamed about babies was 'cause the cats was on top of you, and the jar was just…just…." He fished around for the word, lost the bait, and then went on, "Pooter's got a nail needs clipping."

Maureen took that for a truce. "Yeah, I noticed this morning. She nearly took my boob off with it."

"Then why didn't you cut it?" Larry looked at the un-vacuumed rug at his feet.

"The way she claws and bites? No thanks. Here, you do it."

She threw him the nail clippers.

Flipping the protesting cat onto her back, Larry pushed out her claws one by one until he found the offending nail. "You didn't have a minute to do this, but I see you had the time to do your nails up red. Must've taken all day to do that."

She curled her hands and hid them under her armpits. Faking a shiver, she asked, "You think we should turn the heat up?"

"It's only my money." Pooter jumped off Larry's lap, shook her hind foot at him, and scooted off. Smoo woke up and took off after her. Larry watched him. "Forget it, Smoob, she's spayed. You're not her type anyhow."

Maureen thought of the vet, and of taking it out in trade. "What are you giggling about? I thought you were so cold." She got up and turned on the TV, WGN. "I'm all right, forget it."

They watched *WKRP in Cincinnati,* the one where Jennifer and Herb get stuck in the elevator together. Having seen it several times, Maureen and Larry talked during the dull spots, stopping only for the funny lines they knew were coming.

"What was so bad about having babies on you? They don't bite, y'know."

After a bit: "I just don't like them."

"Why?"

"Come on, Larry, let it go. She shrugged. "I dunno. They stink, make a mess."

"And these guys don't?" He pointed his cigarette at the cats, now curled up in a huge furry mass in front of the register by the TV. Keeping her eyes on the tube, she shrugged again.

They watched a little more of the show in silence (Herb was telling Jennifer that his wife didn't give him "num-nums" unless he mowed the lawn first; Larry snorted, "Is that all you got to do?" until he suddenly asked, "How come we ain't had a kid yet?"

"What?" The popping sound her neck made when she turned her head was stunningly loud.

"You heard me. Why not?" he asked in a too-casual tone.

"We can't afford to turn up the heat and you want a kid?"

Make it light, Maur.

"I didn't say I wanted one, I just asked why you didn't get yourself knocked up right after we got hitched, like all your girlfriends did."

Feeling shaky, Maureen kept her voice light. "They didn't get p.g. by themselves, asshole. Using your own finger just doesn't work."

"Don't make a federal case outta it, I was just trying to pay you a compliment." He lit another cigarette and resumed watching the show.

Waiting until the Jello feeling in her guts subsided, Maureen asked, "I must be a dumb shit—how was that supposed to be a compliment?", fighting the part of her mind that kept yelling (no, screaming), *Let it go, don't pry, don't....*

"Y'know, I drove Steve and Julie home after work, like I told you before, only they invited me in for a while after the baby-sitter went home, and what with those rug rats running around, screeching and crawling all over the place, we all got to talking about how expensive it is to raise up kids, and Julie said they needed new shoes for—" Larry put his hand about three feet from the floor—"the middle one, whatzisname?"

"Clark," Maureen whispered.

"Him, Clark. And that the bigger one, Andrea, needed a bottle of that kind of cough medicine that makes you spit up that shit in your lungs—"

"Expectorant," Maureen added automatically.

"Yeah, that crap, but Julie said if they bought one they couldn't get the other, and while she was tellin' me that, Steve starts bashing Clark for dropping the crusts from his sandwich on the floor, and I just couldn't *wait* to beat it out of there." He took a deep drag and let it out very slowly. "I mean, we went to school with these people, we were friends, and now it's like they're from another planet or something. Y'know, I felt like I was still a kid and they were my parents. I mean it was just like being home and seeing the squirts climbing all over Mom and Dad again, the way they'd talk through the kids' noise, and on top of it they had on that country crud on WAXX. I remember when Steve got caught lifting a Kiss record from Gambles' and I wondered when they got on one track and left us where we are. On the way home I got to thinking that maybe having kids *does* something to you or whether it was having them when you couldn't afford them that makes people act funny. I just got to thinking that I wouldn't want to change that way. Hell, twenty-four is too young to be trapped like that, I've got things to—"

Maureen remembered listening to Julie and women like her, people she had grown up with and experienced things with, actually saying, "I'm glad they play KEEY in the IGA now, I couldn't stand that kids' music," and "Those punks should have to roll up their windows when they have their radios on, who wants to listen to that junk?" and remembered thinking, *Are you all so old, or didn't I grow up yet?* It was so hard to listen to her former friends now, those old mother hens...

"—mean, we ain't got it that good yet, but what we got's paid for—oh, d'ja know, Steve had to take out a second loan on the van?—I mean it's just us and the cats, and I don't have to buy them shoes." Larry opened his mouth to say more, but settled for a shrug and a mumbled, "Thanks" before getting up and heading for the bathroom. Passing by the couch, he pressed his hand, palm down, fingers spread, lightly on the top of Maureen's head. After he left the room, Maureen hid her trembling hands between her thighs and rocked gently back and forth on the couch.

They were back. The babies. Dozens of them, all softly naked and smelling of burped milk and Johnson's Baby Powder, jostling each other for purchase on the blanket, making cooing, burbling sounds. She could see them through the narrow space between the top of the blanket and the lower fringes of her bangs: pink moon faces, wandering eyes, moist sucking mouths, and bloated, pudgy hands reaching for her hidden face, hidden breasts. Scrunching up her eyes, she watched them through the rainbow of her lashes. They looked like the Gerber Baby under stained glass: pink, green, violet, and blue babies, but moving, not flat and static like the baby on the label. Maureen could feel their warm, moist breath on her forehead. A pair of damp, soft hands pushed aside her hair, gooey lips made contact with her skin

Thrashing her way out of the covers, Maureen beat at her face, her head, falling to the floor in a tangle of blankets and sheets. *Oh God*, she thought, *the cats, I've hurt the cats, I've fallen on*—but as she looked about the semi dark room, she could see Digger stretched out across the back of Larry's chair, Pooter curled up in Larry's place below her brother, and Smoo pressed against the register. But *I felt them, I did*, her mind protested, *there was something all over me.* Dazed, she stumbled over to the window, and yanked up the shade. Larry had taken the Ski-Doo to work; the Pinto was parked where Larry left it yesterday afternoon, cardboard held in place over the windshield by the wiper blades so she wouldn't have to scrape ice this morning. Larry was no prince (not even a Polish one), but at least he thought of her once in a while. The sight of the car was both comforting and reassuring; it was hard, black, and solid, and pushed away those baby thoughts until she backed away from the window, and saw the jar.

Turning the jar endlessly in her hands, Maureen felt its coldness invade her entire body. She wasn't going to show it to Larry, oh no, no, *no,* not after the way he'd praised her last night, how he'd thanked her for their childless state. She was certainly the one to thank, all right. And she wouldn't tell him about this latest dream, either. No baby talk. No mentioning babies. Maureen pressed the jar, lid first, into the soft part of her guts, level with her womb, until she bared her teeth in a soundless grimace from the sheer cool pain of it. Funny, when she had aborted herself, she didn't recall that it had hurt this bad.

She had confirmed her pregnancy a little over a month after their honeymoon. Every since her first period eight years before (it had come on her birthday, her eleventh, and Mom took one look at the rust-colored blight covering the blue roses on her flannel pj bottoms and yelled to Dad as he ate his breakfast of hash browns and scrambles, "Our 'Reen's a woman now," while Maureen wondered glumly if it would always feel that *sticky),* she had never been more than a day late. Neverneverneverne. And now, two and a half weeks late….

She had spent the first two weeks telling herself that it was only the newlywed jitters, just stress making her so *damned* late, and spent the past four days downing three aspirins every four hours, an old trick she and her friends used to play on their bodies when they wanted to get their periods over in three days instead of five or six. Yesterday she had forced herself to go upstairs and ask Ms. Welfare Bitch if she'd mind picking up an *e.p.t.* kit when she went shopping. When La C. held a grimy red-nailed hand out in front of her own flat belly and flashed a questioning smile, Maureen cut her off with a curt, "I think the cat is pregnant, and I don't feel like driving ten miles to the vet, okay?" Her neighbor said she'd do it; then, just as Maureen was heading for the stairs, she added, "If you ever want to knit something, I've got some really big needles." When Maureen spun around, flaring, the Blonde Bombshell smiled and went on, "They're really great for knitting up things like cat blankets fast." Maureen told her to keep the change from the kit, and ran all the way up to the front door. The next morning, Maureen crawled out of bed early, carefully deposited her sample in the tube, and hid the kit before Larry got up. After he left, she spent nearly an hour just staring at the dark brown ring in the bottom of the tube.

Good going, she thought, *you've just proved Mom right... like it or not.* At their reception in April, Mom had solemnly predicted over her Cold Duck when it seemed like everyone was within earshot—even the frigging *band* was taking five—"I'll be a gran'ma 'fore this year is out," and *everyone* had listened, just like one of those damned E. F. Hutton commercials, and Maureen had whispered to the nearest honeycomb paper bell on the wall, "Oh, *thanks* for the vote of confidence in me... *Mother.*" And they hadn't gone beyond third base before the wedding rehearsal last night.

Maureen had sat at this very table, in this very apartment, staring at the six-board repeat in the very same fake wood paneling. Their third of the house had only three rooms plus a bath, and the bedroom was so small that only a nightstand and single bed might fit, so Larry parked his Ski-Doo in there.... Certainly a crib would never fit, let alone a changing table, bassinet, high chair, potty, and whatever else a kid had to have so that he or she wouldn't yammer later on, "I wuz *deprived!*"

Larry wasn't making diddly-doo yet, and considering how depressed the job situation was in Ewerton, she and Larry agreed that it would be unfair for her to work too, not as long as they were scraping by on his salary alone. For two people, "scraping by" meant living on generics and lots of unsweetened tea, but damn it, where do you buy generic baby food, or baby tea? For a moment, Maureen tried to picture Larry's face when she'd tell him; he'd probably try to smile and have the motion get strangled on his lips as he said something like, "A googer? Great, Maur, but that'll mean WIC food stamps and I'll have to look into overtime...."

No thanks. Maureen wasn't going to become a self-satisfied *taker,* like the Blonde Bitch ("I've got some really big needles"), or a welfarette, lumbering around the IGA behind a shopping cart full of plastic gallons of milk, King Vitaman cereal, and cans of o.j.; one kid sitting in the cart, kicking sneakered feet, the other still in the oven; pushing stringy hair out of her eyes as she fumbled in her purse for the requisition slip from social services—just another warm-milk baby machine, shitting out a new one every two years to keep her WIC qualification. *No way.* Maureen already balked at the thought of food stamps, even though she and Larry were both eligible for them. Larry scorned those thin booklets of stamps and those signs taped to the cash registers in all the Ewerton stores—"Please tell check-out this is a FOOD STAMP order"—but not for Maureen's reasons. Unlike her family, his had been on welfare for years: free cheese, stamps, WIC fuel assistance, the works, and once, only once, while they were dating, he told Maureen how ashamed he felt every time his mom pulled that book of yellow-and-blue stamps out of her purse and he'd catch the girl behind the counter, and the people standing behind his mother, giving the both of them the fisheye. Maureen never wanted to see his eyes water behind his lashes like that again. Their being on the dole, for whatever reason, would kill him. Not literally, of course, but there were worse ways to kill a person....

Yet here she was, the killing knife in her belly: p.g., knocked up, a bun in the oven, in a delicate condition, in a family way, heir-conditioned, preggie, you *know* what. And damn it to hell and back and *back,* she didn't *want* a frigging kid, didn't want to be fat, bloated, and brown-blotched, didn't want it crawling out of her in a slimy mass, trailing a pulsating rope…. It wasn't fair, fer Christ all Friday, she'd used her diaphragm and made Larry put on a rubber whenever she thought she was in her fertile time, but *damn*, this had to happen! Wait and see, not "this," but *he* or *she* had to happen. Somehow, Maureen couldn't stomach (haw, haw, *stomach*, wasn't that a riot?) the idea of having a tiny human being bottled up inside her; better to think of it as a blob of tissue, a few cells cobbled together, no different right now than a starfish or a puppy or a salamander. Once she saw a special on TV that said how a starfish and a human looked the same shortly after conception, like a few misshapen beach balls clustered together in a huge, huge ocean.

That was more like it. Think of it as a starfish, an itsy-bitsy starfish that got started in the wrong momma. Maureen could handle that. For a second, a cartoon she'd seen in one of Larry's skin magazines popped into her head; a nurse was carrying a blanket-wrapped bundle to the startled father, saying, "Here's your baby…tongue," which is what it was all right, a big wet-looking bouncing baby *tongue,* and the cartoon had grossed her out when she first saw it, but now she thought, *No chance that this'll be a tongue, but it's still gross-looking right now…. It'll be ukky and soft and shapeless for a few more days, not looking much like anything human. Didn't the biology teacher say that the sex doesn't show up for months on an embryo, or something like that? So it's still an it.*

Clinging to that thought like a lover, Maureen scurried around in the boxy apartment, rifling through the few Ewerton High School textbooks Larry'd swiped before graduation, opening and shutting cupboards with sharp *bangs,* pouring and mixing and running water. When she was done, she carried her book, bottles, and long tube into the bathroom, the door of which she locked. (Larry wasn't due home for five hours, but she had to be alone, as alone as a pregnant woman could be.) Completely disrobing, she propped the Health 102 textbook up behind the bathtub faucets—the book was bent open at the *Female Reproductive System* chart—crawled into the empty four-foot-long tub, the clammy ceramic surface sending tingles of cold up through her bare soles into her entire body, making her nipples grow hard and raisin-like, hung the full enema bag and extra-long nozzle-tipped tubing on the shower head, then lay down, legs bent up sharply at the knees, and, after consulting the line drawing in the battered textbook, thrust the blunt end of the nozzle deep within the soft folds of her lower body, until she reached what she thought was her cervix. While trying to judge just how high up her uterus was, a wisp of regret brushed her mind, but she pushed it away brusquely. This was not something to be compared with lovemaking; it had to be separate, something cold and impersonal. After a time, she slowly retracted the tubing, then tilted her body upward, where it shone pale green in the filtered light of the green curtained window across the room. She let the saline solution do whatever it was going to do inside her for at least another ten minutes.

That done—it was just a "that," nothing specific, just another douche...and if it did get bad, she could lie, "Sorry, Doctor, I grabbed the salt when I meant to pick up the baking soda," and pray that she looked innocent and repentant enough—so, *that* done, she dressed, and swallowed four aspirins followed by a shot of Larry's carefully hoarded, special-occasion Jack Daniels, and stretched out on the living room floor, a throw pillow under her head. The cats (only Pooter and Digger back then, still kittens) had curled up next to her, and she didn't wake up until the bad cramps and nausea came, and the dark blood had soaked through her panties and jeans, right through to the maroon carpet beneath her.

She wasn't any of those things she had been that morning, things like knocked up, p.g., with child. Later she realized just how lucky she was that her salt douche hadn't burned out her uterus, or that she had stopped bleeding after only eight days, and within a couple of months she seldom thought about what she had done. Maureen hadn't felt especially guilty; after all, it could have been a false reading on the test, and if it hadn't been, the thing inside her had been so tiny, so amorphous, not much of anything, really. And it wasn't as if Larry had been panting for her to have a kid.

"This would be its third birthday." Maureen heard the words, but couldn't understand why she'd uttered them. No one would ever know when its birthday would have been; it could have been premature, or late…. But it was dead, history, with no one to mourn or miss it. And wasn't Larry happy that they didn't have a child or two by now? At least he was able to set aside five bucks a week toward The House with a Garage, which was the only reason they hadn't moved into the five-room apartment in the back (or into the Roach Motel upstairs, with its six rooms)— so they could save on the rent, toward the better house. Larry didn't want to live on Welfare Road forever. With a three-year-old, they'd both be working, they'd have to move into a higher-rent place, and the five bucks would be spent before it was made.

Larry had actually said "thanks." Damn it, wasn't that something? Didn't that make that morning spent in their icy tub worth it? Her Larry, who thought that no visible holes in his t-shirt meant he was dressing sharp, who spent whole free weekends polishing and waxing his Ski-Doo in the bedroom, had thanked her for not burdening him with a kid.

Sure, it would've been three; they had been married over three years. So what? Maybe in another couple of years, they both might think differently about having a baby. But what would make that baby, or the one after that, any better than the first? The thought came unbidden and unwelcome, as did the next: *I wonder what it was?* Maureen pressed the jar—this one was Junior Beans—into her guts, again and again, trying to blot out the thought.

"Run it by me again why we're always eating something out of a metal tray." Larry was testy; the machine he worked on at the mill required three people working in continuous shifts to operate properly, and if your replacement didn't come in with the new shift, you had to stay until someone showed up. Which could mean waiting for your replacement's replacement. While that happened to Larry early on in his first year there, tonight he'd only had to work almost two extra hours (the guy on the three-to-eleven shift had had a flat), and even though the two hours were double time as far as pay went, Larry was still in a bitchy mood.

"'Cause of days like today. If this had been a pot roast, it'd have been ruined." Keeping her eyes aimed at her Taste o' Sea haddock dinner, she speared a 'tater puff and put it in her mouth.

"Might have been ruined, but it still would've been pot roast."

Larry blew a cloud of smoke at her, breaking their unspoken rule that he not smoke until they were both finished eating.

"Next time, I'll make a pot roast."

Larry's blue eyes opened in amazement. "Since when do I like pot roast?"

Maureen finished her meal in silence. She didn't look up when Larry trotted off to the living room, turned on the set, and sat down. Just in time for *WKRP*.

Not for the first time, Maureen told herself that she could tell the day of the week not by the calendar, but by the TV. Sunday was *Ripley's Believe It or Not!*, some MTV, and then the *ABC Sunday Night Movie*. Monday through Friday was *WKRP, Barney Miller, Entertainment Tonight*, followed by either an hour or so of MTV or whatever prime time show they currently liked. Maybe a movie if a good one was on TBS or WGN. Saturday, *Sneak Previews*, more MTV, *At the Movies*, and *T. J. Hooker*. Sometimes the *CBS Movie* or *Love Boat*. If something was preempted or rescheduled, the whole week was thrown off kilter. After the TV was shut off for the night, they'd feed the cats (*she'd* feed the cats, Larry had the morning honors), wash up, and go to bed. It didn't even matter if Larry was on the eleven-P.M.-to-seven-A.M. shift, or the seven-to-three or three-to-eleven shifts; Larry told her, "No sense both of us being screwed up." So when Larry slept odd hours, she'd watch with the earphone in, sitting on the floor so he could keep the bed unfolded. She didn't know why, but she never sat on Larry's chair.

Every day, every week, has been the same, Maureen thought, as she rinsed off the metal trays before placing them in the rack, then ran the dishrag over the table. *Like a bucket full of water that you can swing around, with the momentum keeping every- thing inside. I can't pick out a day in the last month—shit, in the last year—that's been radically different.*

They no longer went to the show, that would be taking money away from The House. Bar-hopping was out, too—not that she missed it, but at least they'd see some new people once in a while. Maureen dropped the wrung-out rag into the sink, dried her hands on the slightly grimy towel (Larry eschewed the bar of soap next to the faucets), then made her way into the living room, passing by the garbage bag, which contained the latest jar, camouflaged as wrapped-up cat droppings.

I can count on the fingers of one hand how many different people I've talked to this week. Wonder if Larry can say the same? She curled up, feet tucked, on the far end of the couch. Her husband blew some smoke her way, until she coughed despite herself. "Your babies leave you another present this morning?"

For a second, Maureen debated about answering. Pretending to be engrossed in a show she'd seen three times before, she said "No," as noncommittally as possible. She felt as if someone were winding her intestines around a stick, like pasta on a sharp fork, tighter, tighter, just pulling them out of her inches at a time. Just what in hell was so damned fascinating about a crummy baby-food jar? A jar that probably fell out of a grocery bag (*empty*, Maureen?) or got separated from the rest of the junk in the garbage truck (*twice*, Maureen?) or something, anything, *Just let it go, Larry, or I'll ram your cigarettes pack and all up your frigging* nose.

The commercial came on, for a lanolin-impregnated toilet tissue. Reaching for a nail file and an orange, Maureen said, "Larry, we need more t.p. Are they still selling the cases of seconds to you guys?" Using the point of the file like a knife, she scored four lines from pole to pole before peeling the orange. The feel of its skin beneath her nails nauseated Maureen.

"Yeah. You want one case or two?"

"We could stack the boxes in the bedroom, if we can afford two."

Larry ground out his cigarette and lit a fresh one. "I suppose we could. You want anything else? I might as well put it all on one check."

Maureen swallowed the orange segment she had been chewing. "They got more seconds for sale now?"

"Paper towels, disposable diapers, tissue, and paper napkins, I think that 'bout covers it. I can ask how much you gotta buy."

She crammed three segments into her mouth, so she wouldn't be able to reply right away. The s.o.b. knew that they didn't need or want diapers; what made him even mention them? Maybe he was making fun of her baby dream. Larry was never the subtle type. When a long enough time had passed, Maureen said, "See how much a case of paper towels is. Don't buy anything until I check the price at IGA and see if it's a buy."

Larry stiffened the fingers on his right hand and brought them up to his forehead in a brisk salute—"Yes, Mother! Orders received!" then relaxed and turned back to the TV.

Pretending she hadn't heard his witticism, she placed the peels on the end table, then curled up more tightly, knees touching her breast, arms crossed high above them under her chin.

It didn't make sense. When you saluted, you never said "Yes, Mother!" you said *"Yessir!"* or "Orders received!" or "On the double!"—but not "Yes, Mother!" This had to be her fault. She had to go and show him that blasted, fucking *jar*, after her intuition had made her throw it in the trash. But how was she to have known that a second one would appear? It had seemed funny for a short time, but twice in two days wasn't humorous, it was sick. And she had never told anyone about the abortion—*I've got some really big knitting needles*—leastways no one still here in town, not even Mom or Dad. Not that she was close enough to her shadow-behind-the-newspaper father to confide in him, but anyhow, no one here in Ewerton knew, and she had cleaned up her jeans and the rug before Larry came home that day, so he wouldn't suspect

Larry knew. Somehow, without her telling him, he had psyched her out, keeping quiet about it until yesterday. He resented her not asking him permission to salt baste their kid. So that was it. He knew…but how in hell? Maureen had never discussed her periods with him (Larry, who averted his eyes from the Kotex and New Freedom and Stayfree boxes on the store shelf, wasn't into discussing female troubles), and he hadn't been home on the morning when she whoopsed her breakfast and spent the remainder of the day glued to a spinning couch; he had been too worried about bringing home the bucks to notice that his new wife looked much too pale and whacked out. And she had prided herself on her perfect composure, on the way she never let any key words slip during their meals or lovemaking.

But he must have known. Some little word or glance or licking of the lips at the wrong moment must have tipped him off, setting off *his* intuition. What else explained his sudden interest in babies, her not being a mother yet, those disposable diapers (he had no reason to mention those, none *what* so *ever*!), and those goddamned baby-food jars. Maureen felt crawly little baby fingers ripple along her skin, tiny fingers connected to sucking, drooling babies….

The show broke for a commercial. An actress they both disliked came on, making a smarmy plea for sponsors to take on poor kids overseas.

"Christ, don't that beat all. There's ghetto kids and kids down in the sticks down South going hungry, and she's asking us to feed the brats in some country we ain't even friendly with." Larry shut up for a few seconds, then resumed his monologue. "'Only fifty-two cents a day, the price of a cup of coffee.' Lady, I ain't *got* sixteen bucks a month to go giving to some South American brat. Shit, can you figure what that comes to for a fuckin' *year*?" He took another puff and turned to Maureen. "Can you, huh?"

"I'm no good at math," she whispered, staring at the bloated babies and toddlers on the screen, while the actress said something abut "a small hand reaching out."

'That's almost two hundred bucks a year, just so all these Third World rug rats can grow up big and strong and whip our boys' asses come World War Three. Aw, look, they send you pictures of the little pissers along with your sponsor kid, so you feel real sorry and adopt two or three more—Lady," he addressed the TV screen, "you should see how I live, then maybe you'll send me fifteen-sixty, huh, Maureen?"

Larry couldn't be the only one who knew. She felt as if what she had done was cosmic knowledge; as if every person would slowly turn around when she went outside and point an accusing finger at her, maybe wag it back and forth, or make "shame, shame" gestures at her from behind their car windows. She hadn't realized before that one baby, one blob of tissue smaller than the nail on her little toe, for crying out loud, could come back to haunt her like this. (*Oh, Maureen, don't be an ass about this*, a tiny voice said, but she ignored it.) The next thought made her stiffen: suppose she hadn't aborted the baby that morning. Sure, she'd probably killed it, but that didn't mean she had expelled it. When she had wakened after doing…it…she hadn't studied her clothes for any tiny nubbin of dead flesh or anything else. After she'd shucked off her clothes for the second time that morning, she'd stepped into the bathtub to shower; there *had* been bright reddish brown twisting DNA spirals of blood flowing down and around her white legs, but no clots and no embryo, at least none that she'd noticed. If anything slid out of her after she turned the water on, it had gotten sucked down the drain, unnoticed and unmourned.

Once she'd gotten the blood off her legs and washed the residue out of the tub, Maureen had dressed, cleaned the rug, changed the napkin she'd put on minutes before, scooped up her dirty clothes and washed them uptown, then had come home in plenty of time to fix dinner. Just an average day, a little cleaning, a little cooking, and a little abortion, no sweat. Better buy a new box of Morton's, though.

The rest of her period had been heavy, but she downed lots of One-A-Day plus Iron tablets, and soon it was all over, and later on she was careful, oh so careful from then on.... Besides, a year or so later she had read that home abortions are usually botched; the knitting needle goes through the wall of the uterus, or the chemicals burn out the tissues but leave the scalded embryo, and there were usually complications, and sometimes legal action if you happened to get a goody-two-shoes doctor— so if hers was so easy and uncomplicated, wasn't that a sign? If that baby (*my* baby) had been meant to live, to make it, her home-made saline solution wouldn't have worked so well. But suppose it had been only partially successful? That would mean that she had a dead bit of tissue firmly embedded on the wall of her womb—a minute bump, true, but nonetheless a *something* inside her, just...just what? Waiting? No, that couldn't *be*; she'd had dozens of periods since then (and they'd all been on time), so there was nothing inside of her but...insides. She hoped.

These dreams are only guilt, she told herself during Barney Miller. *And the jars—they're just jars. Remember when you read* Ring of Bright Water, *how all that shit washed up on the guy's beach?* So *a lot of garbage must roll up onto people's lawns. Even up the three steps of our porch. That must be it. And the baby...well, sorry, kiddo, but you're dead. That's all she wrote. The Blob is dead.*

Forcing herself into a better frame of mind, she watched *Entertainment Tonight* and didn't wince during the Huggies commercial (now wasn't that being a good girl?). And after the show ended, Larry switched on MTV, just catching the shot of the hourly rocket blastoff, When Martha Quinn announced that Michael Jackson's "Thriller" was going to start off the hour, Maureen headed for the bathroom; she'd seen the short feature four times this month alone.

Once she attended to business, she stood in the doorway and asked Larry, "Want anything? I'm going in the kitchen."

Michael was sprouting long whiskers while his cute girl-friend in the poodle skirt screamed. Larry said, "Yeah, half of the bucks *he's* got—ah, guess I'll have a beer and some of those taco chips—"

"Can't. All gone."

"Shit. Bring the crackers and the cheese crock, or didja eat that too?" On the TV, Michael was eating a box of popcorn, chewing with his mouth open; his girl was cringing in the movie seat next to him. Taking her eyes off the screen, Maureen shot back, "No, I didn't, and the taco chips weren't good after December second." By the time she made her sandwich and got out the beers and the cheese crock ("Season's Greetings from Lowell Paper Co."), the undead were chasing Ola Ray into the haunted house. Larry opened a beer, slurped down a good swallow, burped, and said, "After seeing that special about how they made this, it isn't as much fun. Oh, thanks, Maureen. You bring a knife for the cheese?"

When she returned with the knife, Michael was telling Ola, "Come on, I'll take you home," then turned to the camera wearing a big grin and yellow sclera lenses. Maureen handed her husband the knife and said over the credits, "You know, that ending is kinda cruel. I mean, after telling her that it's going to be okay, it turns out that he's gonna kill her or something." She settled down in a corner of the couch to eat her sandwich.

"'Aw, it's only a movie!'" Larry mimicked, then laughed. "Really, you don't *know* that he's gonna off her."

The baby didn't know either—*stop it!* She took another bite of her turkey bologna on white and gulped it down. A Miller beer commercial came on, and Larry grandly tipped his can of white and black generic beer at the screen. She swallowed and said, "I guess I just expected more for a million bucks, that's all. I suppose it's all right, but I've seen better."

"Like what?" Larry was throwing broken bits of cracker to the cats. She'd have to vacuum tomorrow.

"'Billie Jean' was good, and that 'TV Dinner' one that ZZ Top did—"

"You're the expert on those things."

She overrode him. "—but I like 'Owner of a Lonely Heart' best."

"Yech! That Yes thing where the guy's got worms and

spiders and scorpions on him? You, who didn't like the end of 'Thriller'?"

"You forgot the black cat and the lizard. Anyhow, it's Kafkaesque. You know, the guy who wrote—"

"*I know* him, I *know* him, I'm not a total idiot, y'know."

"Who's saying you are? I just wasn't sure if you had—"

Larry snapped the lid of the crock back on and shot back, "Yeah, sure. Nobody's supposed to know death anything but you. If I was home all day, I'd read Kafka too."

"Last time I read him was high school. High school!"

"Nah.... I thought it was kindergarten." Larry slurped some more beer before continuing, "I'm not really as dumb as I look. I can read when I get the chance."

Finishing her sandwich, Maureen took the plate back into the kitchen. First thing tomorrow, she was going to fish those jars out of the garbage and throw them in the back dumpster at the IGA when she went shopping. They were malign. She wasn't sure what it was about them that was so bad, but it was something. Best to get them out of the house entirely. The garbage wasn't good enough. Maybe then she and Larry would stop this backbiting, this bickering about utterly stupid things like stray garbage on the porch and what they saw on TV at night. Things that never bothered them before. She had read about things giving off bad vibes when she was in junior high, back when she and the friends that weren't her friends anymore used to read *Linda Goodman's Sun Signs* and Joyce Jillson's daily column religiously, in the days when whether or not one's slave-bead necklace was jinxed really mattered, those good old days when the kids pretended that they could see each other's auras, and faithfully wore necklaces of little plastic beads strung on elastic, until suddenly it wasn't the thing to do anymore. Those days were dumb, juvenile, but maybe the "vibes" psychobabble wasn't too far off the mark. No matter what she thought about the jars that someone (*something?* now, now, Maureen....) had dumped on the porch for a joke, it wouldn't hurt to get rid of them.

After finding a clean tumbler in the cupboard (how Larry could drink it straight from the can she didn't know), Maureen rejoined her husband in the living room. "Crumblin' Down" was playing; the video was up to the point where John Cougar Mellencamp was vaulting over the parking meters, then landing in a split. (Larry grumbled "cheater split" to no one in particular.) Looking from the set to Larry, Maureen remarked, "You look a little like him," as she poured half the beer into her glass and waited for the foam to go down.

"Who, him?"

"No, the parking meter."

"You think so?" he asked in a peeved tone.

"What's wrong with him?"

"Nothing, but...." Larry sighed. "But he's wearing an earring."

"So? One of the guys in Def Leppard has about five in one ear." She drained her glass.

"But *I* wouldn't wear one of *those*." Now he started to pout.

"I just said you *kind* of looked like him. Around the eyes and mouth."

They watched the end of the song in silence. Then, finally: "I wish I had his money." *Typical, Larry, very* typical.

The beer made her feel giddy. "So go tell 'em you're his long lost brother and maybe he'll give you some."

Larry threw a cracker at her; she picked it up and lobbed it back, blowing a wet raspberry at him. Feigning great anger, Larry growled, "Them's fighting words," and, after getting up, threw himself on top of her. They rolled around until she slid off the couch in a giggling heap. Reaching down, Larry grabbed her under the armpits and pulled her back on the couch next to him. It felt nice. They hadn't sat on the couch together since... since she couldn't clearly remember when. Sometime when Jimmy was still in the White House, or was it after he left? The beer was making her mind fuzzy. *The hell with it,* Maureen thought, as she finished the rest straight from the can, *it doesn't matter when we were here together—we are here now.* Maybe they might forget about the tacit nighttime agreement once they unfolded the bed. Maybe they might…. She dozed, snuggling in deeply against his shoulder.

Suddenly Larry nudged her awake. "Now *that's* who I look like, and he ain't wearing an earring, either." Groggily she turned her head to the screen. Some guy was playing the electric piano, a blonde with long straggly hair and gold granny glasses. The song was vaguely familiar. She looked at Larry.

"*Him?* What you been drinking?"

"No, no, no, wait…*him.*"

Jim Morrison came on, singing "Gloria," a version that Maureen hadn't heard before. Morrison's satin shirt glimmered under the bright lights onstage.

"You're nuts. He's got your hair color, but that's about it. Besides…." She buried her head behind his back, her face brushing the couch cover.

He pulled her out and asked, "Besides what?"

Maureen shuddered. "He's dead. Don't go saying you look like a dead guy, it gives me the creeps." She felt soft warm skin touch her all over, her face, her breasts, and felt the beer-bile backing up her throat.

"He wasn't dead when he made this, stupid. Besides, we're all dead, if you think about it. Right from the time we're conceived we're goners. Just a matter of when, that's all. Nothing to get all riled up about. Hell, it's the only big surprise we got to look forward to."

For Larry, that was heavy. And morbid. She forced herself to swallow the bitter liquid rising up her throat, making the skin ripple on her thighs and arms….

Maureen got up, got the rest of the six-pack, and helped Larry kill it. If she got bombed, maybe she'd sleep like a stone.

Saturday morning. Larry had the day off, so he was still curled next to her when the latest baby dream woke her. Only this time they had been crawling, newborn and really tiny, out from *under* the covers, but she couldn't remember birthing them, they were covered with bits of blood and sticky residue and trailing their umbilicals like raw tails behind them, making sucking, mewling sounds, eyes aglaze.

Thank God Larry slept hard after a drunk. Carefully she slid out of bed, keeping the covers tight to the bed against drafts, and peeked out the window. The jar was perfectly centered, right on the windowsill, so that the sweet, bloated, glassy-eyed Gerber baby was staring at her. She stuffed her knuckles into her mouth, but a high strangling sound came out anyway. Larry slept through until ten-thirty, long after she had hidden the jar in the trash and had drunk a fast breakfast with Mr. Jack Daniels.

On Sunday morning, the jar was on the doorstep. It fell off and shattered when she opened the storm door, staining the porch floor with residual beet juice. Larry turned over, mumbled, "Tryin' t' get some *sleep*," while Maureen ran quietly for a broom and dustpan....

That afternoon Maureen treated Larry to a steak, not chopped and covered with gloopy brown gravy in a metal tray, but fried in a pan (okay, the hash browns were frozen, but Larry loved it anyhow), so Larry took off for town and came back with a six-pack of Bud and a thank-you treat for her: a whole box of her favorite I'll-kill-for-it junk food, Twinkies. Maureen felt giddy, like when they used to date years ago; so to hell with who (what) ever was playing Mickey Mouse games with empty jars. And as for the dreams.... *Sorry kiddo, I did what I hadda do. No hard feelings, s'right? S'right.* For the first time in days she felt good, really good, despite this morning's dream (sticky lines of dried blood where they passed over her) and the broken glass all over the porch. She had a decent guy, a little security, and a whole box of Twinkies. She was actually looking forward to watching TV and not having to go into a panic when a Pampers commercial came on.

Before they turned the radio off, the weather report promised a break in the numbing cold and *snow* for tomorrow; soft, shimmering snow that would cover up the hard pack and show footprints, prints of dogs, people going to their cars, and people who left little gifts on their porch.... The voice on the radio sounded like a benediction. Her bad mood was going to leave with the cold snap. *Amen.*

There was an old rerun on *Ripley's Believe It or Not!,* but they both liked Jack Palance (Maureen found his voice to be utterly sexy), so they watched anyway, talking over the noise of the TV about little things: Steve's new carpeting in the van, their folks, what kind of cat food made Digger sick that morning. Halfway through, the show broke for a commercial and Maureen got up, only swaying a bit on her feet. "I've got to go use the litter pan." Even three beers hit her hard, otherwise she never talked cutesy like that. Larry had Digger on his lap and was busy tickling the neuter's soft reddish belly.

When she returned, the commercial was over and Palance's daughter Holly was hosting a segment about water therapy. Digger jumped off Larry's lap and onto hers. Looking down at the cat, she cooed, "Doesn't Daddy rub you right, Digs?" and when she looked at the screen, there was a hugely pregnant woman, naked, in a tank of cloudy water, giving birth to a baby, only the baby was expelled right into the water, where it bobbed about like a cork in a wine bottle, a pale pinkish cork in murky white wine, and Larry was going, "Bleh! How can her old man watch that? I'd be barfing my guts out on the floor—" while Digger kneaded her belly; his blunted claws felt like the baby hands, soft with crescent-shaped hard tiny nails, digging into her face, her breasts; then they were showing lots of babies shooting through the water, as if through a clear womb, just propelling through the watery void, so silent, so fishlike, funny she didn't remember this from the last time they watched the show—odd that it hadn't bothered her then—but they seemed to have purpose, a direction which you wouldn't expect at *all* from dumb, pink little babies, babies with someplace to go, something to accomplish.

The Twinkies came shooting back up her throat, hot and

bitter, fueled by the Bud. The bile was pressing, pressing, even behind her nostrils. The yellowish, foaming mass came shooting out of her mouth and nose just as she threw the toilet lid up. Maureen held her hair back in a crude ponytail with one hand and hung onto the rim with the other. She tried to shut the door with her foot from where she knelt on the floor, but no go. She could hear Larry anyway.

"Didn't you just go to the can? Maureen, you all right? O.D. on Twinkies? You knocked up...? Okay, don't chew my head off, just asked." A merciful pause, as the segment on the show changed. "Hey, Maureen! Remember this? You *gotta* see! They got all these naked Japanese guys running around in the snow, oh you gotta see this—"

After wiping off her face with a cold washcloth, she flushed the toilet and walked back into the living room. This she did remember, a little bit, and it *was* a "gotta see," all these men scurrying through the snow in what must have passed for loincloths in Yotsukaido, Japan—they didn't cover *much* loin, though—during something Holly Palance called the "Muddy Naked Festival," and Maureen started laughing so hard the tears kept flowing (she'd been crying as she puked), until the announcer said something about how part of the festival was meant to bless children born that winter, and then Maureen remembered seeing this before, and remembered the babies, little Japanese babies, true, but still babies with those little grasping hands and sucking mouths, and the camera showed a guy carrying one into a rice field.

"Maureen! You're missing this! Slippin' around in the mud, drunker than skunks. Whoops! There goes one, right on his ass.... Maureen, you sure picked a dumb time to get the barfs— whoa, there goes another one, now they've all fallen down—"

The babies were dying. She wouldn't let them have any milk, so they were getting thin, thinner, sticklike bones were poking her body, and the flesh didn't just smell milky anymore. Their umbilicals were dried and rough as rope, and they were crying; thin firesirens from far, far off. Then that sound ended, too. All she could hear was the dry rasp of their bodies moving slowly away from her across the blanket. Whispery sounds, followed by the plops of their bodies as they fell off the bed like overripe spoiling fruit from a withered tree. They landed, one and then another and another, for the cats to fight over, making low growls....

Maureen woke slowly this time, the dream reality still superimposed over the real. Next to the bed, the cats were still growling. Slowly she looked over the edge and saw that they were gnawing on the smooth round buttons which decorated the tops of her slippers; nearly eyelike round buttons....and she hoped it had snowed.

Damn it, the radio had promised her snow, and she wanted it. Then she'd finally see the footprints of her mysterious admirer, the bringer of her bad dreams. Maureen had to know right *now* if it was a child from another street who thought that the nice young couple with the black car should have a baby that it could maybe baby-sit for in a few years, a kid just having innocent fun, or if it was Mom, Mom who'd been so disappointed when the end of year came without a "visit from the stork," as she'd so coyly put it, Mom, who'd been proved wrong for one damned time in her life. (And even when Mom would've been right, Maureen had been able to prove her wrong through just a little cheating, an especially satisfying win over Mom—hadn't the pain and the bleeding been worth it just to foil Mom's plans, for once?) And if it wasn't Mom or a little kid (maybe the Blonde Bitch had blown back into town), Maybe then she'd worry a little—no, *really* worry, but please, please let the radio be right let it have snowed.

Throwing back the white top sheet, she hurried to the window. The shade flew up and smacked around the roller. Maureen let out a tiny squeal of joy, a Christmas morning sound, when she saw the feathery white flakes floating thickly down. The wind angled the snow across the floor of their porch, where it made a coating thick enough to show Larry's single line of footprints, going straight across the porch and down the sidewalk to the car. She could see every footprint clearly under the ten—no, a dozen at least—baby-food jars, all of them shattered, the paper labels torn and curled with age, the lids strewn about like a huge child's tiddledywinks game.

Just Larry's footprints, no others, only his on the porch, and on the sidewalk.

Except for the small, fluttery marks. They could have been birds, or the fragile legs of a starfish in the wrong kind of water.

When Larry came home that afternoon, Maureen hadn't taken the mail out of the box, nor did she answer his repeated knocks. The shade was up, so she had to be up too. Digging through his pockets for his keys, Larry noticed that the floor of the porch was coated with shards of broken glass under a thick batting of snow; it crunched unpleasantly under his boots. He could dimly make out the skid lines where the mailman must have slipped on it. Muttering "What the fuck's go in' *on!*" he fitted the key into the lock.

The unmade bed nearly touched the open door. The cats were huddled together on the end table, staring at his wife. Maureen was curled up on the floor, knees touching her breasts, under the TV. She was still in her soiled pj's, matted hair covering her face, just staring at the unfolded bed. All she'd say when he kept shaking her and begging her to tell him please tell him what had happened was, "Issa empty, jawr all *empty*," as she kept staring at the dull silver lid pressed tightly in her bloodied fingers.

THE HOLIDAY HOUSE

"AM NOT." GEOFF tried to put some distance between himself and his pals, but his Air Jordans weren't much help this afternoon, no matter what the ads on the TV promised.

"Am *tooooh*," Tony sing-songed right behind him, with Adam bringing up the rear. The pair stopped abruptly when Geoff wheeled around in mid-stride, arms crossed, a wild squint in his eyes which didn't come from the glare of the descending sun behind them.

"I. Am. Not. Chicken," he spat out in a flat, even voice which sounded uncomfortably like Police Chief Stanley's did the time he warned them all about riding their bikes on the sidewalks, *again.*

Not willing to be beaten that easily, especially with his tag-along fourth-grader cousin in tow, Tony stuck balled fists under his armpits, flapping his elbows up and down.

"Paw-wuk-wuk-wuk," he cackled, scratching at the cracked pavement with a duct-tape mended sneakered foot. Adam hung back, giggling. *Jeezus,* Tony wondered, *did I sound that dumb when I was his age?*

Refusing to give in, Geoff simply stood there, moving only when a Wisconsin state bird (AKA the mosquito) landed on a tanned forearm. His slap rang out with dry clarity in the nearly deserted old residential section of Ewerton where the boys had been wandering around for the past hour or so, just hanging out. Most everyone who belonged on Roberts Street was inside watching television, or fixing dinner, or at work; visible were an elderly couple sitting on the screened-in porch of their yellow Victorian, and the Happy Wanderer, slowly shambling off to the half-way house on Crescent Street where he lived with the rest of Ewerton's semi-trainable mentally disabled, or coo-coo-boos to Geoff and Tony's crowd at school. Mentally disabled or coo-coo-boo, the Wanderer ignored Tony.

"Maybe he's a ding-a-ling like the Happy Wanderer," Adam chipped in during a lull in the clucking. That worked.

"I ain't no coo-coo-boo!" Geoff shot back before he could help it; instantly he wished he had a lip zipper, or at least a Velcro yap-flap.

Tony let his arms drop. Pulling loose threads off of the bottom of his faded cut-offs, and hating Adam for beating him to the punch like that (*wait till I get that snot-brain home*), Tony casually wheedled, "At least the Happy Wanderer ain't scared to go up to the Holiday House. 'Course if *you* are, *we* understand, don't we, cuz?" The younger boy started to shake his head *no* but Tony overrode his mom's sister's dumb bunny kid's lack of comprehension with the capper, "'Least the Wanderer don't say he's not a chicken and then turn around and act like one."

"The Happy Wanderer don't even *talk*," Geoff retorted, "he's so dopey all he can do is shuffle-butt around and walk up to people's kitchen windows to smell what's cookin'. He eats with his fingers, *fer* cryin' out loud. All that moron knows 'bout chicken is eating it."

"And even *he* ain't been by the Holiday House since—"

"Shutya *trap* already," Tony yelled at his cousin. Placing his hands on his hips, Tony spread his bare legs until he looked like a four-foot-seven copy of the Colossus of Rhodes transplanted to the river of asphalt between the sleepy rows of towering, slightly decayed Victorians, ancient swaying elms, and rusted-out late model cars. Glancing behind him up the street, toward the Holiday House in all its sage-green and warped-siding splendor, Tony asked, "Are you more of a *man* than the Wanderer?"

A pause, then, "Well, *sure.*" (The Happy Wanderer started

roaming the streets of Ewerton back in 1967, fresh from fifteen years in Special Ed classes.)

"You got more guts than the Wanderer?"

"Yeah!"

"You gonna go up to The Holiday House?"

"Shit, no." With that, Geoff spun around and headed for home, toward the part of town where the sprawling split-level ranch homes were surrounded by manicured turf, all the trees were uniformly under seven feet tall, and the polished cars still had the showroom smell inside....

"Paw-wuk-wuk-wuk-paw-wukwukwuk—" Now the old couple in the butter-colored-gingerbread-and-stained-glass confection craned their Q-Tip fluffy heads in Geoff's direction. The Happy Wanderer was long gone....

His pace slowing, Geoff thought, *Aw, what the* H, *it's just a frigging* house—

Black and red Air Jordans beat a light tattoo on the uneven street below. Stopping just a step short of Tony's face, Geoff warned in a Bubble-Yum scented whisper, "Don'chew say *nuthin'* 'bout this to my folks, you hear? You know how they feel 'bout B and E, even if the house is empty."

"'Cept for the ghost," Adam piped up, but Tony cuffed his shaggy head.

The three boys ran up to the overgrown lawn of the Holiday House—when the grass got to be *too* long, the city sent over some men from the City Crew to mow it down to a militaristic stubble—stopping short of the curb.

There was no sidewalk in front of the house, unlike its neighbors. Old Man Holiday's wife had been a Crescent (as in Crescent Street and generations of Crescents in Ewerton since the glaciers), so when the Sidewalk Ordnance went into effect back in 1949, the city fathers kindly turned their heads and looked over their collective shoulders while everyone else's lawn got dug up. Hence the Holidays, Wilbur and Hortense, didn't have to shell out the hundred and fifty dollars that it cost to have a sidewalk put in if a homeowner didn't have one in front of his house already.

Nobody was supposed to notice the gap in the ribbon of concrete that ran past the rest of the homes on Roberts Street, and if anyone sent a letter of complaint to the city councilor or the Ewerton *Herald,* it would conveniently get lost in the mail. A lot of letters vanished that way in early 1950.

So there the trio stood, sneakered toes touching the sprouting cracks in the curb before them, holding grimy hands over their eyes against the glare of the sunlight behind the crumbling chimney which topped the gingerbread, spindles, and column-covered stale cake of a house like a melted candle. Without the traditional decorations in the windows and on the porch, the house hardly looked the way it used to when the old coot Holiday was alive.

True to his name, Old Man Holiday (Geoff and Tony and Adam's grandparents used to call Wilbur H. "Old Man Holiday" when they were not much older than the children of their future offspring) always made a big to-do about decorating his house paid for with Crescent money—for each and every holiday, be it Flag Day, Easter, Halloween, or National Secretaries' Week. From the time anyone could remember, decades before the Great Sidewalk Hoo-Ha, Old Man Holiday could be seen festooning his wrap-around porch with appropriate colors of cloth (later crepe paper) bunting, hanging seasonal doo-dads and cut-outs behind the window shades, putting things like painted wooden Easter eggs or tiny flags on the shrubs in front of the bird-bath, and just driving poor Hortense absolutely bananas with his obsessive zeal. Unfortunately for her, she happened to die around Halloween in 1972, so she didn't even rate new decorations for the occasion of her demise. He just left on the black bunting (and whatever orange he couldn't reach after the snow-fall made the ladder impractical) until New Years.

After his wife died (croaked, to the boys' crowd) Old Man Holiday really went slap-holiday-happy; like the time he covered the whole lawn, front and back, with cones of corn stalks for Thanksgiving, or the time in '76 when he paid Tony's dad three hundred dollars to paint his chimney red, white, and blue for the Bicentennial. Later Tony's father said that the old codger wanted to paint the entire house red, white, and blue, a different band of color for each story, but Mr. Wilkes convinced Mr. Holiday that it would take at least three coats of the white and two each for the red and blue to properly cover the sage-green of the house, and Holiday was reluctant to cough up *that* much baloney, so he settled for his usual tri-color bunting and two dozen slightly yellowed wedding bells bought for half price at Clausen's Hallmark and Gift Shoppe.

By the time Labor Day rolled around, Tony's dad had had to climb back up on the roof to restore the chimney's original brick red color, after which he refused to paint it again, so 1976 marked the first and final appearance of the Flag Chimney.

All the paint—both tri-color and brick red—was peeled off of the chimney now. Not that Geoff and Tony were old enough to remember how it had looked during that long-ago summer, but that Bicentennial chimney had passed into the popular history of Ewerton, just like the time the county ambulance had to come out to the shitty section of town, past Crescent Street to Larry Kominski's apartment to cart off his wife who went so nutty two Januaries ago. It was destined to be talked about and mulled over at church pot-luck dinners and graduation day picnics for years to come. (Adam's dad's brother, Steve, worked at the paper mill with Larry, and Steve said Maureen sort of reverted back to her infancy, and spent her days at the nursing home sucking on the comer of her bedpillow like it was a big teat. Adam's and Tony's families agreed that cabin fever can get to a body that way.)

Anyhow, it was a shame that the chimney paint was gone, and that there were no faded Fourth of July decorations covering the house, because the dwelling seemed so...defenseless without them. Red, white, and blue paper buntings would have been so appropriate right now, even though the Fourth was nearly a month gone. There being no holidays in August, Old Man H. always left the July things up until the summer thunderstorms did the removal job for him. (Like the letters of complaint regarding the Missing Sidewalk Link, those protests over the piled up bunting and soggy honeycomb bells stuffing the rain gutters managed to get nicely lost in the mail.)

Without its gaudy seasonal clothing, the Holiday House was a naked old man, its pitiful bumps, popped veins, and sparse tufts of hair showing obscenely in the harsh light of the sun. Not that the house had ever been handsome; it was a bit too fussy around the eaves, and too massive around the bottom columns for that, but at least the decorations gave it a false life, not unlike the clownish make-up the stiff-picklers smeared on their clients' unprotesting faces. Unadorned as it was now, as it had been for the last two years—ever since Tony and Geoff were pulling their sleds past the House on their way home from the hill by the drive-in, and they saw the Reish-Byrne Funeral Home's head people-pickler (Mr. Reish to their parents) and Police Chief Sawyer coming out of the Holiday House bearing a white-wrapped figure on the stretcher they carried between them, and the two men refused to acknowledge Tony's query of "He dead?"—there was something else about the house that the boys hesitated to put into thoughts, let alone words, something that formed the faintest image, the softest murmur of...*wanting.,..* As in, "Please fill me, dress me. Lonely. Naked. Empty."

Silly notions, of course. All unoccupied houses looked that way. In Tony and Adam's part of town, the freshly slapped together two-piece homes which found their way to Ewerton on the backs of trucks had that lonesome look, until there was a station wagon parked in the garage, some My Pretty Pony curtains in the back bedroom windows, a turtle-shaped plastic wading pool on the lawn and a lone size-one thong lying next to the garbage cans. The *only* difference with the Holiday House was that it could never hope for the station wagon, My Pretty Pony curtains, turtle wading pool, or even a battered old thong to keep it company. Roberts Street was strictly senior citizens and students' apartments territory.

"—and who cares if a lot of pets are reported missing in this part of town, that don't mean that this place is haunted," Geoff explained, ignoring the fact that he hadn't seen a squirrel or a bird or even a stray cat roaming around since two blocks ago.

Tony shook his head. "My dad says that he found a mess of dead birds clogging up the top of the chimney when he painted it, and he should know—"

"That was ten years ago. 'Sides, a cat probably hid 'em there."

"Crows and raccoons hide stuff. Cats eat what they catch."

"Don't mean nothing. Don't mean that the place is spooked." Geoff could hear the wind beat the unlatched screen door against the front wall of the house. He knew without touching it that the front door would open at the slightest turn of that huge domed knob....

"—or that Andersen guy who blew town on his lunch hour last June, left his car and keys right in front of the tracks up by the—"

Tony could be a *real* A-hole sometimes. "What *about* him? He was two miles away from here. Old Man Holiday's place couldn't have gobbled him up. *Pleeze.*"

"But his wife was a Holiday, few times removed—"

"So *what?*"

"That means the place can get you wherever you are—"

"Bull-sheet." Geoff stepped onto the unkempt lawn, near the huge elm with the Hudson Realty FOR SALE sign and the tattered remains of a yellow cloth ribbon clinging to the bark. Even the hostage crisis rated a decoration in Holiday's eyes.

Really, that Tony *could* be such a woman when it came to the wild stories, and when he was dragging along his cousin, AKA babysitting, Tony would just shovel it on higher and deeper for the kid's benefit. Not that it hadn't been creepy, though, hearing about that empty Subaru just sitting there by the tracks, key in the ignition, doors unlocked, just waiting for someone to start it up, waiting for somebody like Holiday's great-great grand nephew by marriage (as in shotgun) to drive that car back to the sash-and-door factory, then back home to Andersen's house out past Crescent Street, in the shit-ball side of town. Over where

Maureen Kominski went nutso one snowy January day—that it had been snowing was also duly noted in town lore. Just as the official word of mouth would state forevermore that it was a warm June day when Sam Andersen—Paul to some folks—skipped town without benefit of car, spare change, or so much as a pair of spare undershorts, leaving a wife and bunch of toddlers in a lurch.

And according to the word of Ewerton, the kind of word spoken only over late-night cups of coffee long after the kids are asleep, or over the *slug-slug* of the washers at the Super-Suds Launderette on Sixth Avenue, the consensus was that not having a sidewalk wasn't the only...*different* thing about the Holiday House. But the adults, having shed their imaginations, were content—or simply opted to settle—for that fact. Their kids took it one, or maybe two or three better.

Standing now on the porch of the house—warped boards above and below him, thick spin of cobweb covering the yellow bulb next to the front door, and piles of molded leaves huddled in the far comers of the porch—Geoff tried to look through one of the misty windows. The bottom of a scalloped, fringed, and water-stained shade, pull-ringed string hanging straight down, was even with his eye level; beyond that he could make out only thick, overfed dust kitties curled up in the faint light which slanted from another window across the wooden floor. No ghosts—not that anyone had ever actually reported seeing one here anyhow—but, more importantly, no missing pets or great-great grandnephews. Some lines through the dust that may have been animal tracks, though. No biggie.

"Still chicken, big man?" Tony yelled from next to the elm tree. Adam was pushing an empty Skor wrapper around the pavement with his foot.

The lingering heat made fine trickles of moisture run down Geoff's armpits under his Nike sleeveless t-shirt. Even the fact that the sun was dropping fast didn't make a difference. Geoff wished that he had a Pudding Pop, a Kool-Aid Ice Cup from the fridge at home, even a lousy old piece of ice. Didn't those guys realize that it was going to be like a frigging *oven* in there? Holiday's relatives left up most of the shades after they took out the furniture, and the sun had been beating in there all day long.

Well, he'd show those dipdongs. When Geoff came out of there, all sweating and parched, he'd beat a box of Jello Pops out of that Tony. Geoff knew which pocket old Tony-Baloney Wilkes kept his spare change in.

Without a word, he went up to the door, turned the hot knob, and went in, making sure that he slammed the door behind him *hard.* Geoff thought that he heard Tony say something, but the drumming silence of the house rang in his ears, drowning out much of Tony's voice.

The place was humongous. Inside it seemed even bigger than it looked on the outside, but Tony's dad said that dark paint does that to a house. The dust kitties clung to his red and black shoes with invisible claws, refusing to be shaken off. Geoff balked at reaching down and pulling them off with his fingers. At least they'd prove that he had gone in, looked around.

Dark wood doors, over eight feet high. Door frames six inches thick all around each door, and deeply carved. Massive cabbage roses on the walls, water-stained dark brown along the outside walls. Pale memories of the oval and square pictures which once hung on the walls. A curved staircase in the hallway, faded flowers underfoot. His scalp itched from the excess wetness under his hair.

Pantry so empty it swallowed all sounds of footfalls. Rusted hulk of a woodstove in the kitchen, greyish powdery logs scattered about the dusty floor. Brown flutterly rings of rust stain under the pump in the sink. And *hot,* like the room was in the oven and not the other way around. A forgotten shriveled sprig of mistletoe hung above the door to the cellar.

Up the stairs. Happily no squeaks or groans from under his feet. Sweat ran down from the back of his neck, paused at the elasticized waist of his shorts, then continued down to the split between his cheeks. Like walking into the bathroom after his sister Julie had taken a shower and forgot to open up the window afterward, only *dry.* Same amount of heat, though.

Bedroom, bedroom, bedroom. Not that the beds were there anymore, but the outlines of the head boards were there, like when Geoff stared at something brightly lit then closed his eyes, the image burned on the underside of his lids. Geoff's feet were sticky under his socks, and the backs of his calves were damp. He was within mounting distance of the next flight of stairs when he saw the door. Unlike the others, it was shut. Tucked partway under the curve of the staircase, it almost blended in with the deep brown wallpaper covering the hallway.

Under the bottom of the door the floor looked slightly whitish. Probably mold. Geoff remembered the time when his mom left a loaf of Ewerton Bakery bread, the kind with no BHT in it, in the kitchen cupboard for a week last July. Mold just loved days, places, like this.

But he was pleasantly surprised when he touched the knob. It was cool, almost cold. If he had been younger, he would have been tempted to try that dumb tongue-on-the-pump-handle trick that Granpa always teased Geoff and his sister about during Christmases at the farm. He and Julie never took Gramps up on his dollar wager to do it, though. But this, this unexpected pocket of relief, of *cool,* was better than a won dollar bet; it was like wishing on the birthday cake candles before blowing, then managing to snuff all of them out in one breath, and forget about the cheater puffs. Even the wood felt chill, almost moist. Resting his sweaty cheek against the door, Geoff turned that wonderful knob and entered the cool.

The *room* was the cool. Shimmering ribbons of rippled ice—sweetly slick like the sticky hunks of ribbon candy Granpa would pass around at family gatherings—adhered to the faded trellis wallpaper all around him. Beneath his Air Jordans the wood floor was crunchy with frost, a November morning lawn stretching out in untrod purity for yards before him. His soft soles made eager smacking noises with each step.

Dim sunlight filtered in through the north window, the only window in the room. A tacky melted-bead plastic Santa, the kind that folks in Tony and Adam's part of town put on their garage doors come Christmas time, obscured the lower half of the window. Flanking the decoration, the flimsy lace curtains were frozen to the window frame. Geoff tried to move one; the brittle fabric broke under the tips of his now-cool fingers. Likewise, the glass itself was frozen, swirled, really, with dainty curlicues of ridged frost. Geoff in his wonder did not notice the fine threads of sweat that covered his body solidifying into similar delicate raised patterns of ice.

Old Man Holiday had hung his plastic Santa in between the storm and inner windows. His mom did the same thing with her suncatchers so the cat couldn't swat them off the window and onto the kitchen floor. The overlay of frost dimmed the bright colors of the waving Santa. Geoff remembered Granpa's bet about sticking his tongue on the pumphandle; Granpa would tease them and tell Geoff and Julie, "Betcha *couldn't* do it and not get stuck there....If you kids get stuck, you can't holler for help without a tongue." About then Mom or Dad would tell him to quit saying stuff like that, scaring the kids, blah, blah, blah... what the heck, Geoff thought, an old window can't be like a pump handle. Granpa wouldn't pay him for taking up the bet here, with no one watching, but either way, he had always wondered how it felt...it couldn't hurt as much as Granpa claimed it did. So intent on sticking his tongue as long and as flat as he *could* that he didn't notice how white *everything* looked through the window, Geoff knelt down and let his head incline toward the window, tongue out and ready.

"Tony, our moms are gonna wonder where we are," Adam whined, hugging his scabby knees with brown arms. Getting up from where he had been sitting for the past three hours under the elm tree, Tony felt the sting of hot pins and needles in his calves and feet. Sitting down next to the Royal Pain in the Ass, he assured the smaller boy, "Our moms will think we're at Geoff's."

"But they'll *call* and we won't be there, or his mom will call our moms and either way well get our butts kicked."

'They'll think we're on the way home." Tony looked up at the house, hoping for a moved shade, a flicker from Geoff's Bic—Tony knew that his friend sneaked his dad's cigarettes—*something* that proved that Geoff was still in there.

"But then our *dads* will drive around looking for us, and when they find us *they'll* kick our—"

"Cram it." Tony got up and began to circle the house, not right next to it, but along the edges of the grassy lawn. Afraid to stay by the curb alone, Adam tagged along at a distance behind Tony. Both looked, saw nothing. Adam's snuffly breathing sounded disproportionately loud and wet in Tony's ears. He was tempted to give Adam a smack upside the head; sure as shit that *would* be when Dad or Uncle Jim would be making a pass of the neighborhood, car lights on high beam, and he'd be in for an ass chewing, while the runt got off scot free.

Itching the mosquito bites on his arm, Tony craned his neck up, up, to try and look into the second and third floor windows. On the north side, near a corner of the second storey, was a single window which looked like it did back on that sub-zero day when Old Man Holiday kicked the bucket. One of those cheap plastic bead Santas waved down at Tony, through a string of Christmas lights tacked around the inner outline of the window. The edges of the shade looked different, too. They were white, not the yellow-tan of the others. *The old fart probably sprayed on that white crap that's supposed* to *look like frost*, Tony told himself. Not that many people in Ewerton, or much of northern Wisconsin, had a dire need for that stuff. Mother Nature would do the job for free when the temperature dipped below zero.

The street lamps sizzled on, cold greenish-tinged white. The sprayed-on frost glittered delicately in the light, which was kind of weird, since the stuff the merchants sprayed on the store windows always looked flat and dull....

Tony broke into a run, slapping Adam on the arm as he passed him by. "C'mon," he shouted, "Beat'cha home."

"But what about Geoff?" came the wailed question, followed

by the pound of feet on pavement.

"Probably snuck out back and went home," Tony puffed. "Probably eatin' ice cream at home and laughin' at us," Tony shot back before he pulled ahead.

Tony didn't want Adam to see that he was chicken.

SIMON SAYS

CHUCKIE TRUNDLED BACK into the living room, gave an exasperated snort and shrilled at Andy, "I *Hid.* You dint *Seek* me" before slop-slop-slopping all over in his Big Bird slippers to the easy chair where Andy sat. Without bothering to look up from the textbook which he was reading (*Your American Heritage*) Chuckie's big brother mumbled, "*You* said we were playing hide-and-go-seek. *I* said I was going to finish this *home* work first. So beat it, Chuck-a-Puck."

Chuckie hated being called Chuck-a-Puck, even though it wasn't as bad as Uppie-Chuckie, or Puck-Cherry, or Slime-Face, or other "or" names, but something told him that they were all equally noxious, as well as something else that Chuckie couldn't quite get a handle on in terms of *words*; but even though *analogies* were beyond him, he did know that Andy's name-calling made him feel inside the way undercooked scrambled eggs—the way Daddy usually made them when Mommy was off visiting Gramma or "sick" in bed upstairs with the flu—felt sliding down his throat in slurpy, snotty clumps because taking the time to *chew* that runny yellow mess would have only prolonged the agony of having to eat it in the first place because Daddy would be watching him to make *sure* he ate it all up, and if Chuckie dawdled over them, the plateful of oozing yellow eggies would get cold, then—*then* swallowing them would be *exactly* like gulping down nose drippings on a cold day because otherwise he'd have to take off his mittens in order to blow his nose properly (*only* pigs *rub their noses on their* mittens) and

Mommy had warned him *never* to take off his mittens outdoors in the winter, so Chuckie would end up enduring that ucky, slimy taste in the back of his throat, because if he *did* let his nose run Andy would be right there to whisper, "Snot-brains, Snot-brains, lookit them dribble out, Snot-brains...," when Mommy and Daddy weren't around to hear it....

Chuckie had that gloopy-mess-going-down-the-hatch feeling now, even though there were no eggs in sight, and the really cold weather was a good month off. Andy made him feel that way a lot; whether he was calling him Chuckie, Uppie-Chuckie, or by his real name, Charles. (Oh, that Andy had a way of making *Charles* sound bad too. He'd make his voice sound like something all rotten and crumbling, and probably smelly if you poked it with your finger, sort of a garbage-sucked-down-the-disposal *sinking* "Chhhaaarlesss—" especially late at night when Andy would pass by Chuckie's room on the way to or from the bathroom; Chuckie would be fast asleep, only to come to abrupt, heart-pounding wakefulness, hearing this raspy, drawn-out voice at his door intone "Chhhaaarlesss...," ending with that slithering hiss and—this was the *worst* part—that short, snorting *laughter* afterward.)

Chuckie plopped down in front of the TV and switched on Nickelodeon, "The Channel for Kids Only!" *Lassie* was on; Chuckie liked the show yet was saddened by it, all at once. He enjoyed the people, but the pretty doggie reminded him of Scooters (Andy untied him, I saw—but Andy told Daddy that Scooters broke free and the lady in the car cried and cried when she saw Scooters under the car) so Chuckie started switching channels. Some of them were blocked out by that dingus that the man from cable place installed (all the good ones...gone," Andy had bitterly complained. "Those shit-brains think I'll go blind if I watch the Playboy Channel and MTV...what *dorks*"... and then he warned Chuckie that if he "ever told Mommy and Daddy that Andy had called them shit-heads and *dorks* Chuckie would "really" have something to "Uppie-Chuckie" about; whatever *that* meant) and the other TV shows were either soaps or exercise programs, so with a prolonged sigh (Andy could have played at least one crummy game with him) Chuckie switched off the TV and wandered off toward the hallway. As he passed Andy and his stack of school books (*Family Guide Emergency Health Care*, *Law and History of the Middle East*, *Cavalcade of Literature*, and some *Cliff's Notes*) Chuckie pretended that he didn't hear the sepulchral hiss "Chhhaaarlesss" which wafted up from the depths of his brother's opened book.

Once he was in the hallway, Chuckie was faced with a choice of rooms to explore. To his left was Mommy's sewing room, a No No Room because of the Sharp Things in there. Still on the left was the bathroom, further down the hall. Boring. He didn't need to weewee just yet. On the right, Daddy's study, not quite a No-No Room, merely a Don't Touch Room. Just wandering around in a Don't Touch Room was okay, he supposed. Wasn't the kitchen mostly a Don't Touch Room, too? Very quietly, so as not to disturb Andy's studies (long overdue studies, judging from the shouting match Andy and Daddy had last night and which woke Chuckie up with Daddy bellowing that "Three 'effs' wasn't up to snuff" and Andy yelled back that Daddy could "stuff the 'snuff'" and then Daddy shouted "No fifteen-year-old punk is going to get away..." "I'm almost sixteen—" "*Oh*? How about almost grounded?" "Still almost *sixteen*, old man—" "*Oh? Really?* Well, *young* man, make that *almost* sixteen and *definitely* grounded!" and at that point Chuckie pulled his blankie tip over his head and squished his eyes tight and the next thing it was morning and suddenly Andy wasn't going along on Mommy and Daddy's business trip to Madison anymore and his usual sitter Stacey from the college didn't come and Andy wouldn't play *any* games). Chuckie let himself into the study and shut the door behind him.

It should have been his nap time, but Stacey would usually play games with him to tire him out, and since she didn't come, Chuckie hadn't played his usual Hide-and-Go-Seek, so he wasn't the least bit tired. And Andy wouldn't let him call Sara and Jason from next door, or let him go to their house. "You're my *re-sponsi-bility*," Andy had snapped at him after lunch, "And I'm not about to look after any more rug-rats." Therefore, Chuckie tried to *be* extra quiet, tried to be extra good. He stuffed his little hands into the side pockets of his Oskosh B'Gosh bibbies, the hickory-stripe ones Mommy had ordered for him from the Miles Kimball catalog. She had written "From Santa" on the gift tag, but Andy told him that Santa had died from frostbite up in Michigan during his midnight sleigh ride ("—and then his fingers and toes curled up and turned black and dropped off—") so Mommy had had to phone up the Miles Kimball people real fast and place a rush order for Chuckie's gift *pronto*! And then she *forged* the old fart's name on your gift tag. Know what they do to *forgers,* Slime Face? They get locked up in *jail*, and hafta live in a little room like the broom closet with a toilet with no seat and a hard metal bed chained to the wall, with no *sheets*. Know why there's no sheets? When they get a sheet, they rip it into tiny strips, then tie and braid all the strips into a long, white rope...a real *strong* rope. Then they tie a loop in one end, and put the loop over their head, and then they tie the free end of that long white rope to the top of one of the bars of their cell— did I tell you that one wall is all bars, and people can look in while the *felons* take a piss and do their poopers and brush their teeth?—and once the rope is tied good and tight to the bars, they jump down off of the hard bed where they was standin' to tie the rope and *then* the loop on their throat goes tight, real tight, like this..."—all this time Andy had his hand resting on Chuckie's pajamaed thigh as he tucked him into bed, but all of a sudden Andy's big hand was in Chuckie's PJs wrapped around Chuckie's pee-pee, squeezing it hard—"and *then* their eyes go big and bright red, and the tongue pops out like an old soft banana, and then the whole face goes *purple*..."—and at that point Chuckie began to squeal, and as the footsteps down the hall began to pound as Daddy ran for Chuckie's room, Andy let go and began to tickle Chuckie's softly protruding pink belly, until Chuckie began to giggle helplessly as Andy said *loudly,* "How's that, Chuckie? Huh, Chuckles?" stopping only, when the footsteps slowed and reversed, then faded away, and *then* he continued, in a low whisper, "and after their faces go purple, the *felons* piss and shit up their pants, just like *babies,* so they stink while they hang there in their cell, and finally they go all soft and squishy like a moldy grapefruit, so the guards have to cut them down and haul them off to the *morgue,* where they get a tag put on their big toe sayin' who they were and what they did only Mommy would get that *forged* tag with Santa's name on it so *everyone* would know that she wrote a dead guy's name on your tag—and *that's* what's gonna happen to *Mommy*—" he spat out the word in a bubble-gum scented spray of spittle, close to Chuckie's face—"if you tell her that I told you how Santa died."

Digging his baby fists deeper into the pockets of his bibbies, Chuckie remembered with satisfied pride how he had torn up the pretty tag with the stocking on it from his package, and thrown the pieces into the kitchen garbage can. No one was gonna stick his Mommy in a room with no sheets or potty seat! Even if Andy turned her in, it wouldn't matter. The tag was gone, or like Andy often said, it was *history.* Chuckie wasn't sure what "history" *was*, but it sounded important. And *big*, like the way Andy was big. Almost as big as Daddy, and bigger than Mommy already. And of course, much bigger than Chuckie.

Chuckie had to go up on tippy-toes to see level with the flat top of Daddy's desk, but what he saw up there made him climb onto Daddy's green swivel chair to get a better look. Oh *boy*, now he knew why Daddy's room was a Don't Touch Room. Daddy has his *stickers* stored here, not in a nice book like Chuckie had (*My Sticker Book* across a background of parachuting Teddy Bears, rainbows, and stars) but just tossed in an old tumbler with a chipped rim (a Don't Drink Glass). Daddy's stickers looked a little like the ones Chuckie got once in a box of rice cereal, the square ones with the little holes poked around all the edges so you could rip them apart, only Chuckie's stickers said things like I'M WAY OUT, AWESOME, and SUNSATIONAL! over neat pictures of worms and fishies and butterflies. Daddy's stickers said things like USA 22¢ and LOVE under a cartoon brown doggie (Scooters, lying under the car, and the thin red dribbles went down the asphalt into the gutter), and RACHEL CARSON USA around a woman's green face. Not that Chuckie could read all of this; but he did know his ABCs. Chuckie also knew that he took better care of his stickers than Daddy did of *his*. Maybe it was because Daddy didn't have a *My Sticker Book.* Maybe Daddy would be happy if Chuckie put these stickers into the *My Sticker Book,* in a place by themselves. They'd be safe there, safer than in the chipped Don't Drink Glass on his desk. Later on, maybe he and Mommy, or he and Andy (the gunk-down-the-throat feeling quickly came and went) could go halfsies on a sticker book for Daddy.

The folded-up stickers fit nicely in the top pocket of his bibbies. Chuckie was careful when he took them out of the chipped glass, mindful of the small jagged spot on the rim of the container. Didn't want an owie, no Sir! Chuckie then put the chair and glass back just the way they were. No one, not even a mouse, could have heard him as he shut the door of Daddy's study. The hallway looked the same, only now the bathroom door was nearly shut. Chuckie could hear the gush of water being passed into the toilet bowl. Andy and Daddy made lots of noise when they tinkled; Andy said it was because their "things" were bigger, and then would call Chuckie "Teenie-Weenie," which was one of the really bad names, one that made his whole body feel full of gloppy junk. Andy didn't just peep—or poop—in there, in the bathroom; sometimes he'd close the door all the way until the lock clicked, and do stuff. Funny stuff, things Chuckie didn't understand. Once, when Chuckie opened the bathroom door after knocking and knocking for ages (Mommy was already using the upstairs bathroom) until he just couldn't hold it any more, and when he walked in Andy didn't have time to pull up or zip up and Chuckie got scared because Andy's pee-pee was big, real big, and stuck straight out and then Chuckie got so scared he wet himself after Andy pushed him out in the hallway and slammed the door shut again....

Maybe Andy was doing *that* in the bathroom right *now*. Chuckie made tracks down the hall to the living room, where he squatted down in front of Andy's books. Big pages of long, long words stared back at him, and Chuckie began to flip the pages of the nearest book (*Law and History of—*), searching for pictures. He found one, but it wasn't bound into the book. The slick magazine stock was white-whorled with the ghosts of sweaty thumb-prints, forming a hazy nimbus around the peachy-pink body of the naked lady pictured there. Frowning to himself, Chuckie was just about to cover up the lady's exposed No-No Places with his pudgy hand when the low rumble started up behind him

"Ch-chhhaaarlesss—"

He tried to cry "Andy!" but all that came out was a weak "aaaahnd—"

Andy was smiling, very wide, not seeming to be mad at Chuckie for pawing through his school books. Hunkering down before the toddler, Andy said, in-between snaps of his bubble-gum, "How's 'bout we play a game, just you an' me, huh?" Since there was no one else *in* the house, something about the unnecessary "just you and me" gave Chuckie that good ole slippery throat feeling, but since Andy wasn't 1) pinching him, 2) squeezing Chuckie's pee-pee, or 3) caught by Chuckie in the act of making his own "thing" get all big and hard, Chuckie relaxed a little, figuring that maybe all Andy wanted to do *was* play a game.

"'Kay." Chuckie was about to ask if he or Andy should be "it" when Andy asked, "How 'bout 'Simon Says,' Huh?" Andy worked the gum furiously in his mouth, and bounced up and down on his heels.

Despite his usual innate caution around Andy, Chuckie's eyes lit up. His favorite game! *Andy must like me,* the little boy thought, *Maybe he's not mad 'bout the fight with Daddy no more.*

Andy pushed over the pile of books next to his chair, saying, "Simon Says take these books and pitch 'em in the kitchen trash." Giggling, Chuckie complied, lifting one book at a time (the first aid one was easy, but the *Middle East* tome was a two-armer), slop-slopping in his Big Bird slippers to the kitchen and the big green trash can, dumping in each book before trotting back to the living room. Once all the books were gone (history!) Andy—who by now had moved over into Daddy's chair—drawled, "Now dump out the coffee grounds over them."

Chuckie started to move, but caught himself before Andy could reach over and administer the usual "Simon Didn't Say!" tap on his knuckles. There was a slight edge to Andy's "Damn, you got me," as he retracted his own hand, before Andy, no, *Simon* gave the order again. Chuckie had to climb up on the step stool to reach the counter, and the Mister Coffee, with its filter paper full of this morning's grounds. Soon moist brown clots of smelly grounds lay over the big words across the covers of the books, seeping into the cloth-covered paper....

Back in the living room, Chuckie stood panting, waiting for Simon to "Say." Leaning back in Daddy's recliner, Andy thumbed on the Magic Vibra-Fingers. Coldly eyeing the tot, Andy whispered, "Simon Says empty all your pockets."

Chuckie was puzzled. This wasn't *fun.* Dutifully, he turned out his side pockets, leaving the white cotton linings sticking out like tiny fingers, and poked around in his flat back pockets. Empty. Just as he raised his hands to check out the big double pocket across his bib top, he remembered Daddy's stickers. Carefully, he fanned his hand inside the pocket, so as not to bring the stickers back out with his now damp palm. All pockets checked, he stood before his brother. Waiting, Andy sat silent, eyes slitted nearly shut, back pressed against the softly humming Magic Vibra-Fingers. Chuckie knew that only Daddy was allowed to turn on the Magic Vibra-Fingers, but maybe people who were *grounded* could use them too.

Fingering the light dusting of acne on his cheek, Andy murmured, "Undo your bibbie buckles, and let the bib flop down."

Trying to look unconcerned, Chuckie waited for the dread

"Simon Says undo—"

"Charles, I *said*, 'Simon Says undo your bibbies and let the....'"

Chuckie was halfway up the stairs before Andy could worm his way out of the recliner. Running into his room, Chuckie dove under the Care Bears comforter. Now it was nappy time, snore-foo, snore-foo, aw, lookit, Chuckie's beddie-bye—

"Chhhaaarlesss—"

Chuckie stopped saying "Snore-foo," stopped breathing, simply lay there in stiff animal terror. Slowly, Andy lifted up the comforter, chanting, "*Peek-a-boo, I see* you." And descended.

There were no pounding footsteps coming down the hall to stop Andy this time.

After Andy was through; and had the stamps in his own pocket, he marched Chuckie down the stairs, past Daddy's big recliner—the back rippled slightly under the oxblood leather-ette; Andy'd forgot to shut off the Fingers—down the hall, to Daddy's desk, where Andy triumphantly dropped Daddy's stickers back in the Don't Touch Glass, then, with his hands clamped tightly on Chuckie's tiny shoulders, marched the little boy—stubby white pocket flaps bobbing with each step—through the hall, living room, and into the kitchen.

"Simon Says sit on this stool and don't move." It hurt down there when he sat, but Chuckie complied, not daring to quiver, not wanting to blubber again.

Chuckie watched as Andy stalked the kitchen, considering, choosing, and assembling many of the Don't Touch kitchen things on the counter in front of Chuckie.

"Know what Dad'll do when he finds out you touched his stamps? Huh, Slime-Face? He's gonna send you to jail, the bad place where *felons* who forge Santa's name on little snot-nosed *brats*' Christmas tags go. And you'll get the cell next to Mom's. Oh *yeah,* only she won't be able to come when you call for her. 'Cause she's gonna be hanging like a kite in the power lines, hanging from the *bars,* her face all purple and black and oozing pus like a big fat zit, and she'll be staring at you with busted-out red eyes, staring at her *baby* boykins while you tinkle, Teenie-Weenie, and soon she'll smell ripe and...."

"NO! She's *not!* Ripped it up! Nobody's gonna take her. I threw it out! It's *gone,* an...."

"Ohhh...Uppie-Chuckie, I *found* the pieces...taped them back together. It's *her* writing on the tag. Her *for-gery*, Chuckles. Just like its *your* finger-prints all over those stamps. Dad's stamps. And the cops, they can *see* them. They just love to throw little shits like you into cells, all alone in a smelly grey cell, with no cute little plastic potty chair, just a big bowl so you'll fall in and get flushed down like...."

"Nonononono.... NO!"

"Simon Says shaddup!"

Chuckie shadduped, but Simon Didn't Say not to shake, not to start to slowly tinkle into his bibbies. Simon hadn't said anything about that.

Andy stood across the wood counter from him, one of Mommy's big sharp Don't Touch kitchen things in his hand, staring down at the can full of wet books and coffee grounds. Gradually, light came into his eyes, and the corners of his mouth jerked up. Just a little.

"Yo, Uppie Chuckie, mebbe I can fix it for you...fix it so Daddy won't have to call out the *police* on you, fix it so they won't have to see your finger-prints all over the stamps. Interested? Huh?" Leaning over, Andy rubbed the broad flat part of the silver Don't Touch Thing across Chuckie's warm cheek. The metal felt cold, and more wee-wee seeped into his bibbies. Chuckie waited for Simon to Say "talk," but Andy went on:

"I can fix it so Dad won't whip *your* ass for dumping my books and throwing Mom's coffee grounds all over 'em like a *bad little boy*—" he ignored Chuckie's frantic head-shaking "—and I can fix it so's the school won't come and make the cops throw you in the slammer for mutilating school property. I learned how to fix it from one of those books you *ruined,* that you *demolished,* that *you* trashed. Wanna get out of it, Teenie-Weenie? Wanna let me handle the punishing for Dad, for the coppers? Wanna get off easy? Wanna let *Mommy* get off easy, too? I'll even flush that tag. Huh? How 'bout it? Dad punishes mean, and the cops are even *worse*. You wanna get the *old* treatment for thieves? Once you get it," Andy's voice teased seductively, softly, "you'll never have to get punished again…. Mommy, neither." Taking in Chuckie's wary yet scared look, Andy continued in a contrite, hushed tone, "*Really*, Chuckles, and I'll even say that *I* dumped my books, how 'bout that?" Jerking his head back toward the can full of coffee-soiled books, Andy added, "It's all spelled out in there, in that textbook. No more spankings for stealing, no more yelling, no cell, no seatless toidy. One little…thing and then your off the hook. How 'bout it…? Simon Says talk…!"

"Pleeease, Andy, don't wanna go jail, don't wan' Mommy go jail, pleee…!"

"If you give me a 'pretty please' I'll take care of it right *now*…," and Chuckie (fighting back that cloggy-throat feeling) could hardly get the words out fast enough, "Pritypleeese Andy, pr'pleee."

Andy's smile was big, bigger now, smearing across his face. "Okay…. Simon Says put your right hand on the breadboard."

Snuffling, Chuckie started to place his hand on the big blond wood board, until words that Mommy had once yelled rang out in his mind: "Chuckie, I don't *ever* want to see your fingers anywhere *near* this cutting board when I'm doing up a chicken, do you *understand*, young man?" Mommy might be a forger, and maybe even a *felon*, but Chuckie knew that Mommy wouldn't *let* him hurt himself. Really pee-peeing into his bibbies now, Chuckie sat there, hand held up above the bread— no, *cutting board*, staring at Andy's frozen smile, his throat full to bursting with that *gunky* feeling. The big silver Don't Touch Thing *(Cutting* Thing, Chuckie remembered, along with a sudden, pinkly bloody image of pale raw chicken parts strewn across that same lightly oiled board) in Andy's hand was poised above Chuckie's tiny wrist. Andy was breathing hard, not even chewing his gum anymore, and his eyes had the same wetly bright look they had had when Chuckie caught Andy doing bad things to his big pee-pee in the bathroom.

"Simon *Says* put your *hand on the*—"

(Another picture formed in Chuckie's mind, only this time it was his *hand* lying on the board, dribbling pinkish watery chicken blood all over the counter...the drops running down the sides of the cupboards below, and the worst part was that the tiny curled hand wasn't *his* any more...it was just an old hand, bloody and cool and slippery with thin skin that moved loosely over the fragile bones, and maybe Andy would pick it up and throw it in the trash with the books, and cover it with stinky brown coffee grounds, so Chuckie couldn't find it—)

"NO!" The word was almost too big for Chuckie's throat and mouth, his whole head ached from the uttering of it. He started to retract his outstretched hand but Andy's left hand darted out across the wide counter, made barest contact with the soft tips of the little boy's fingers, and held on tightly. The pain was almost as bad as when Andy squeezed too hard on Chuckie's pee-pee, but this time, Andy didn't have him pinned down in a bed. As Andy tried to force Chuckie's arm and hand back onto the board, Chuckie planted the soles of his Big Bird slippers hard against the cupboards which formed the base of the big counter, and then—pushing until his little legs felt like they might snap off at the knees—Chuckie flew backward so quickly that Andy was pulled halfway across the counter after him...so quickly that Andy's upraised hand, the one with the big silver Don't Touch Cutting Thing clenched tightly in it, came down hard and fast—right in Andy's left forearm.

Chuckie's backward fall was partially broken by Daddy's kitchen chair, but his side still hurt when he landed on it. Scrambling to his feet, finger-tips still tingling, Chuckie slipped once on the no-wax floor. Behind him, Andy, who was breathing very hard and loud now, great raging breaths that made the snot in his nose bubble in and out, pulled the now reddened Cutting Thing out of his forearm. It made a soft, "gooey, sucking noise when Andy finally yanked it out, and the blood that splattered over the white wood and gold-specked Formica counter, and even on Chuckie himself wasn't watery and pinkish and pale like chicken blood, but deep and red, redder than catsup or Mommy's nail polish, or the paint of Scooter's old dog house— and Chuckie imagined that his arm would have looked like that, flowing red at the end like a faucet, then a voice deep inside, said, "*You spoiled Andy's game. He was gonna* help *you, and* now *look*—"

Maybe. (oh *please* don't let Mommy go to jail and hang there) maybe, Andy wouldn't be mad if they played *another* game, no more Simon Says....

"Hide an' Go Seek! Hide an' Go Seek!" Chuckie cried, before he turned and *ran,* nearly falling again in his haste to get out of the kitchen.

As he ran, Chuckie could dimly hear Andy's ragged, sobbing breaths (instead of counting, like he was supposed to, Andy gibbered, "Fuck it, *ohhh fuck it!*"), followed by the dull clatter of the cutting board and the Cutting Thing falling to the floor. Chuckie made it to the living room, pocket flaps bobbing up and down, past the still vibrating recliner, and almost to the stairs before he heard Andy's now raspy "Chhhaaarlesss... Simon Says *get back* here!" behind him. Unable to look back, Chuckie screamed, "No—*Hide* an' Go *Seek,*" then bounded up the stairs, crawling on all fours, scrambling on the carpet, his sore side making his breaths hitch and burn, pulling himself up two and three steps at a time, his bibbies wet and sticky against his hot pumping legs.

Top of the landing. Chuckie heard the sucking drone, "Chhhaaarlesss," again, but it was still *below* him. As he ran along the hallway, Chuckie heard the shuffling footsteps begin. Hunkering down low, he ran into Andy's room (Chuckie wasn't *stoopid*: he knew from playing Hide an' Go Seek with Stacey that the Seeker never looked in the *obvious* places...like under the baby sitter's long coat—where it hung in the closet. Or in the Seeker's own bedroom...or so Chuckie hoped). Andy's big bed was unmade, the thick brown down comforter loosely flipped over on the bottom half of the bed. Chuckie crawled on the bed, and curled-up under the comforter. He didn't snore-foo this time, even though Daddy had told Chuckie that *everyone* went "snore-foo" when they slept, Chuckie couldn't *believe* him anymore. Daddy still believed in Santa Claus, too, and Chuckie knew that *he* was dead, so now, Chuckie knew that snore-fooing was a *lie* that Daddy told him.

His brother was upstairs. Andy's breath whistled in his nose, a high, quavery slurping sound that made Chuckie wince. Andy had the Don't Touch Thing again; every few seconds he'd slap it against his thigh, a flat swacking noise: in between groans, he said, "Simon Didn't Say to *run-away,* Chuck-a-Dead-Duck.... Simon Didn't *Say...,*" as he patrolled the hallway, waiting for Chuckie's snore-foo. Andy's voice grew indistinct when he walked into a bedroom, growing so soft that Chuckie could barely hear it, then it became loud again when Andy reentered the hallway. As he waited, his nose itching from the stale bed smell, Chuckie dimly wondered, where that taped-together Christmas tag was, the one that could send Mommy to jail now that Chuckie spoiled Andy's attempt to fix it for her, so she *wouldn't* have to go to jail. The *forgery* was probably in here, but Chuckie couldn't look for it just yet. Maybe when it was his turn to be the Seeker.

Once again, Andy sing-song-sobbed "Si-mon *Did-n't* Say to run *away, Uppie-Chuckie*" was growing faint, fainter.... Abruptly, instinctively, Chuckie rolled out from under the covers, down to the floor, where he scrambled under the bed. Dust kitties nested in his sweaty hair as Chuckie crab-crawled under the bed, over to where he could see part of the hallway through the open doorway. No Andy.

Quietly, *SOOO* quietly, Chuckie crept out from under the bed, and kept on crawling out of the room and into the hallway. A drop of blood glistened on the half carpet, winking at Chuckie under the muted glare of the lights high above him. Past Mommy and Daddy's bedroom, almost within a finger's reach of the first step down, Chuckie heard the junk-down-the-disposal, bottomless howl—"Chhhaaarlesss," and the sound was so cold, so rotted and crumblyugly that Chuckie felt as though he was being sucked, down into the icky, slimy depths of the disposal in the kitchen, falling down and down with no one to pull him out, and his pee-pee jerked in his bibbies from the effort of letting out the last of the panic-hot tinkle inside him. The pound of Andy's footsteps was different too; slow, heavy, and draggy, and he wasn't banging the silver Thing against his legs anymore.

As Chuckie scurried down the steps, his slippered feet slid across the low looped nap of the carpet, and he shot down the stairway like it was that big slide at the park, the high silvery one, only Chuckie wasn't laughing as he bumped down and down helplessly, Near the bottom, he spun around, and high above him he saw Andy, and his scream became so big that his jaw ached open to let all of it come out. Andy had pressed his arm against his chest, and now his white tee-shirt had a big blotch of red in the middle, and the red spread up to his neck and down to his belt and there were smears of blood in his hair and on his white face and his eyes were glittery with unshed tears and the white-lipped mouth was taut and closed, yet that *sound,* the *"Chhhaaarlesss"* noise, was still coming out, and in his free hand, Andy held the Cutting Thing in a white-knuckled grasp. Falling back first to the floor, Chuckie *knew* that Andy wasn't playing Hide-and-Go-Seek at all any more, Oh, Andy was Seeking, but it didn't matter if Chuckie was Hiding or not; all Andy wanted was to finish the game of "Simon Says" *in* the kitchen....

The footfalls loomed closer as Chuckie frantically darted around the downstairs. The bathroom? He didn't know how to lock the door. The kitchen—not there! Sewing room? "No-No-Chuckie!" came Mommy's voice. Daddy's—no, that's where his *fingerprints* were!

The footsteps were near the bottom now, and the sucking—garbage-down-the-sink-hole voice was loud and reverberating...,
"Siiii-mon Diidn't Saaaaay!" when Chuckie remembered the

Door. The kitchen (all the *red,* running down the cupboards!) door, the only one whose lock he *could* open, Stacey showed him how, solemnly telling him, "Only open this in case there's a fire or something and I can't open it for you, *okay,* Chuckie?" and making him cross his little chest with jelly-sticky fingers. Fighting the stoppered up throat feeling (Chuckie wondered if Andy with a Cutting Thing in his hand was an "or something") the little boy scurried across the living room. Behind him, he could hear the pound of feet, and the wheezing snuffle. Chuckie could almost *hear* the slow seep of blood entering Andy's shirt, could almost see it crawling, capturing the thin white fabric, painting Andy all bright red.

The no-wax floor sported an irregular red stripe near the counter, and Chuckie saw a half-print from Andy's tennis shoe, half-moon of zig-zag lines—

"Si...Si...Simon says st...stoppp—!"

—which he jumped over, landing on a clear patch of floor, only Andy didn't see the slick of wetness and slipped on it just as Chuckie reached the door, but his small fingers were sweat-slippery and the knob twisted uselessly under his grip, the big golden knob that was bigger than his fist, the knob with the little button in the middle—*the one that Stacey pushed,* in *to release the lock*!

Behind him, the force of Andy's fall had opened up what had started to clot inside his arm, and the spurting started again, but Chuckie didn't wait around to watch the blood jet out; he pushed the button with his thumb and *then* the big knob turned easily under his baby grip.

Andy's breaths—thin, reedy—sounded in Chuckie's ears as he pulled open the inner door, only to be confronted with the screen door. The latch handle nipped his tender fingers as he fumbled with the mechanism, but Mommy wasn't there to kiss them and make them feel better, and Andy was getting to his feet, so Chuckie braved the pain and let the screen door *thwack* shut behind him. The air was chilly, making his wet legs cold, and his side ache anew. Panting, Chuckie ran down the bricked-in path to the front of the house, rounding the corner just as Andy's red and gushing figure appeared on the back stoop. Leaving the path for the driveway, Chuckie headed toward Sara and Jason's house, but their mommy's big green car was gone and, since they didn't have a regular babysitter, Sara and Jason must have gone with their mommy. The rough gravel of the driveway hurt his tender feet, poking sharply through his thin slipper soles (the Big Bird heads bobbled crazily on each foot), and the cold air cramped his lungs, yet Chuckie continued to run, his legs pumping harder as he heard the splatter of gravel, displaced by Andy's bigger feet, the stray pieces hitting the backs of his calves, digging into the hickory-stripe denim. Chuckie raced down the graveled drive right up to the end, and onto the flat hardness of the sidewalk, the rounded curb (once he felt a brush of hot fingertips down the middle of his back, between the bibbie straps, and Chuckie forced himself to go fast, *faster*!) and beyond, into the street, the Don't Go Alone Place, the Look Both Ways *street*, where Scooters had run to when Andy let him go, left him to run off and get hit by the lady in the car—

—the sobbing rasp of Andy's breath behind Chuckie was drowned out by the steadily growing sound of tires gobbling up the smooth pavement, a rubbery sliding sound like Chuckie's toy truck rolling on the kitchen (blood!) floor, growing louder by the second, and Chuckie almost wound up standing there still and confused, like Scooters had been, but—unlike Scooters, Chuckie had a Mommy who would be going to *jail*, to a *cell* unless he could make Andy play another game of Hide-and-Go-Seek with him, and let Chuckie Seek this time, so he could find that *forged* tag and—.

—Chuckie ran to the other side of the street, not looking back, even when he heard the brakes of the car screech uselessly, or heard the people inside the car scream…or heard the dull squishing *thump* of Andy hitting the rushing hugeness of the car. The silver Cutting Thing clanked harmlessly on the hood of the car a second later.

When he heard that, and *only* after he was sure that the "Don't Touch Thing" was out of Andy's hands, did Chuckie turn around.

The people—two girls and a boy, all of them much older than Chuckie—were out of the car, next to Andy. The boy in the blackand-gold jacket with the big EHS on it was uppie-chucking all over the yellow center lines, inches from Andy's head. The vomit steamed in the brisk air. The girls were hugging each other, sobbing and gibbering, not wanting to look, but looking regardless. At Andy. Chuckie padded, Big Bird heads wobbling, over to his brother, and looked at him too.

Andy didn't look *too* different; redder and more twisted, but not much worse than before. His eyes were still open, only the blue part was rolled up high and there was lots more white showing. Scooters had looked worse, Chuckie decided, and while he was tempted to ask, *Is this how Scooters felt?*, all he said was, "Who's gonna play with me *now*?" Andy didn't answer him, didn't say "Chhhaaarlesss,"…didn't do anything but leak redly on the pavement. Chuckie remembered that Daddy had to lift Scooters up off the road, that Scooters didn't get up. Chuckie didn't think that he could pick Andy up, but maybe the three kids could, after they stopped crying and uppie-chucking. He didn't think that Andy was going to get up by *himself*. Chuckie decided that he had better wait until Andy was brought back to the house, maybe when Andy was better he could Hide and Chuckie could Seek him, only Chuckie would Seek for the *forged* tag first and flush it down the potty before the police came to the house to take Chuckie away for stealing the stickers. They would take *him* because Andy was going to tell Daddy what he did, tell Daddy because Chuckie wouldn't let him fix it for *good,* like it said to do in the book under the coffee grounds in the garbage, but (Chuckie swallowed down a clog in his throat) he didn't care if he went to jail. He didn't care if people watched while he pee-peed, didn't care if he didn't have a nice Care Bear comforter at night. Once Andy was home again, Chuckie would Seek the *forged* tag, so Mommy wouldn't have to go to jail with him, to wind up hanging from the bars in that little room with the hard bed and no seat on the potty. Or have the Christmas tag tied on her toe in the morgue.

Chuckie's *Mommy* was a *forger* and a *felon,* but he still loved her.

GARBAGE DAY
AT EWERTON

SPIRALS OF CIGARETTE smoke did a languid death-dance over the shade of the Strawberry Shortcake lamp before dissipating into the stale air which filled Jennifer's bedroom. Whenever Monica happened to glance her daughter's way between paragraphs of *The Adventures of Strawberry Shortcake and Her Friends*, Jennifer would roll her pale blue eyes up toward her reddish bangs and part her lips in a noiseless sigh.

This time, Monica ignored her. Other nights, during other story hours, they would do that old "But the TV said smoking's no *good* for you, Mommy" / "Did I *ask* you to tell me what's good for me?" two-step, but tonight she hadn't *told* Jennifer, that would have spoiled the plan that Jennifer didn't—*couldn't*—know about; but tonight, *tonight*, it just would have seemed wrong to fight with Jennifer....Even if Jennifer's argument—damn, *she's only six*—against smoking was right, hashing over the subject just wasn't proper tonight. Not that she wasn't tempted to do so, no matter what Dave had said about this being *the* night to go through with it, but giving in to her temper, especially under the circumstances, would be an act sure to haunt her even more than she knew she was going to be haunted later.

The next time she looked up from the page she was reading—and dropping stray ashes on—Monica avoided Jennifer's white second-hand Sears canopy bed. Instead, her eyes were drawn to the window, where, on this hot July night, the combination storm/screen window was opened just a crack. The lowest automatic setting on the window was notched for a four-inch opening, but now only a one-and-a-half inch slit admitted warm air into the room. Dave had propped up the window with a couple of Miller High Life matchbooks.

Monica stifled a bitter, ironic laugh over the printing on the matchbooks; they had such a "high life" here in good old Ewerton, Wisconsin, living on one minimum-wage paycheck. If life got any higher.... Best not to think about such things on a half-empty stomach. She and Dave had let Jennifer eat the lion's share of the canned ravioli tonight, and now the only thing Monica could do to fight off the hungries was smoke them away. Looking at the propped-up window, she remembered how Dave had had to use Jennifer's new Garfield ruler, bought especially for Jennifer's first-grade pencil case, to make sure that the opening would be just wide enough when he brought it up to the window later tonight. Staring at the window, she struggled to remember whether or not she had kept the sales slip from the IGA. The ruler still had the price sticker on the back.

Her eyes darted over to the bed when Jennifer rolled over. The suddenness of Jennifer's move, coupled with the fullness of her yellow checked nightie (wryly, Monica remembered that she had bought it in the next largest size, so that Jennifer would get at least a couple of years' wear out of it) left Jennifer tangled tightly between her Care Bear sheets and gingham gown. Dimly, Monica knew that she should wiggle out of the white child-sized Bentwood rocker in which she was jammed and walk the short distance to Jennifer's bed to untangle that mess of tangled fabric, but she continued to sit where she was, mindlessly sticking her generic menthol cigarette into her face at measured intervals, simply watching the little girl struggle. It was so hard to believe that a body so small could move independently; her child resembled one of those baby dolls that flails its arms and legs when you pop in the Duracells and flip the hidden switch. Strange to think of such a being as a thinking, feeling, hurting person...try as she might, Monica could not remember ever being so tiny (and still so alive) when she was only six years old. Not that she didn't remember her childhood. Why, she could rattle off the names of all her dollies, both store-bought and homemade; Moonbeam from the Dick Tracy comics, her favorite Chatty Cathy, Samantha from *Bewitched,* Betsey Wetsey (who did just that for a week after taking a bath with Monica), Molly made from men's "Monkey-socks," and the soft Alice in Wonderland Mom made from a mail-order kit. And moments from first grade were also there, dried flies embedded in the soft slush of her mind; how she cried when the little boy next door told her she looked like a pig in her new glasses, her first crush (his hair was dark brown and his name was Mike) and the Valentine's Day party when she kicked up a stink because Joey Carlson gave Valentines to only half the kids in class, plus one for the teacher, and she was one of the kids who didn't get one. All that really important shit.

But she couldn't remember how it *felt*, how it *was.* To be little and alive and taking life in in huge unfamiliar doses while she grew bigger and bigger, and suddenly the world was old and familiar, and she was starting over again with Jennifer. Her Jennifer, when she had been longing for a Jason, or a Jamie.

True, Monica's childhood was still there, a shriveled seed tucked deep in the soft folds of her self, but her present state of adulthood impinged on the purity of those days, those memories. She wished that she could ask Jennifer, "What's it like, huh? Is it scary, or neat, or just…what? I can't get it back anymore, the way I was, the way you are now. Can you clue me in, before it's gone for you too?" Perhaps, if things were different, she might have actually done just that; a good way to get close to your child, to establish emotional bonds that last a lifetime, all the *Family Circle* and *Woman's Day* kind of parent-child advice column gibberish that seemed a billion miles away from tonight, and from what she'd have to do later....

Showing Mommy how smart, how self-reliant she was, Jennifer wormed her way out of the tight wrappings then settled down on her belly under the gaily printed pastel sheets. Lately Jennifer had been eager to show Mommy and Daddy how smart she was, how she could open up her own can of spaghetti, how she could break up the dry lumps of Quick in the bottom of her glass all by herself, how she could write her name in a sprawling left-handed scrawl across the discarded envelopes from the many bills her parents got in the mail. Not that she could read the words "Final Notice" or "Please Remit Late Charges" printed on the bills inside, but wasn't that what school was for, to teach her how to read?

This morning, Jennifer had told her Daddy how she was going to go look "for a overtime job" to help out, so Mommy could "buy real Quick again." Monica had wondered when Jennifer would catch on to her refilling the old Quick can with the generic kind of chocolate drink mix. All Dave could do was say, "Daddy's girl is really gonna make her old man proud," then leave the table quickly, mouth working silently. He had really wanted a girl—Monica suspected him of *wishing* her unborn baby into a girl, especially after she followed the "recipe" in the womens' magazine for conceiving a boy.

Funny, after all his talk about "Daddy's girl" this and "My girl" that, guess who Dave appointed to actually spend tonight with Jennifer, up here in her room? As if Monica wasn't capable of turning a key in an ignition.

Chickenshit Dave couldn't even face up to Jennifer after coming to his decision. Typical, Dave, typical. Touching the end of her spent cigarette to the tip of a fresh one, she mused that maybe it wasn't so easy, what he was getting ready to do outside, but *damn,* all he'd actually done before that was to weather-strip the frame around Jennifer's door and haul up a bundle of newspapers from the basement, so she could fold them into tight strips while Jennifer played outside this afternoon, just in case the weatherstripping wasn't air-tight enough. A bag of neatly folded strips sat outside Jennifer's room.

Dave didn't have to sit in here, choking on the smoke build-up but unable to stop adding to the miasma, reading drivel by the hour to a child who had heard the stories many times before, waiting. If it wasn't for the sheer numbing anticipation and helplessness of it all—it had to be done in darkness, but that darkness was so slow in coming—perhaps she wouldn't be so nervous. Granted, she could have done what she usually did whenever Jennifer raised a stink—like she did during supper when she found out that Daddy would be gone tonight, "working," when she pounded her plastic Mickey Mouse cup on the table, splattering the walls and ceiling with milk—which was to march the offender up to bed; no nighty-night kiss, no story, and no Snoopy night-light in the hallway. But tonight—tonight should be as good as possible. Or at least as bearable as Monica could make it for Jennifer, and for herself.

"Mommy, can I ask you somethin'?" This in the "I'm buttering-her-up-for-the-kill" voice, usually reserved for when she wanted Santa to bring her the newest gee-gaw seen during the Saturday morning cartoons. By accident, Monica ground out a new cigarette, swore, then lit up a fresh one. "What?"

Winding a wisp of fine red-gold hair around a pudgy forefinger, Jennifer went on in her best nonchalant voice, "I'm not sleepy yet, but I will be if we play annuder—"

"Forget it." Monica had given in to Jennifer earlier that evening, letting the girl play her Strawberry Shortcake video game, a morbid little musical bodyparts romp which showed the nasty Purple Pieman hacking up Strawberry and her pastry-named cohorts into a random field of wiggling body parts that didn't even shed strawberry blood, for Chissakes. The game was bad enough, but when it reminded Jennifer of the fact that there was an opened box of strawberry-filled toaster pastries sitting in the cupboard, Monica had to make a big show of how late it was getting, and how Jennifer needed lots of sleep. Little girls had to sleep a lot in order to be smart in school, Monica told her child, trying to make Jennifer forget about the lone box of food on the bottom shelf of the kitchen cupboard. Dave and Monica's breakfast.

Jennifer asked, "Are you mad 'cause I was winning?" and, after receiving no answer, turned over to stare at the latch-hook Smurfette rug Monica's mom made for Jennifer before

Mom died last year, the rug which hung on the opposite wall. Yesterday, turning under the covers would have left Jennifer facing the window. They'd moved the bed, to give better access to the outside.

Of course they weren't about to show *her* the article, tell her that somehow, she and Mommy and Daddy had managed to slip through the cracks again, only this time they were going to do something about that fact, sort of take advantage of the situation. Jennifer couldn't have known that the paper somehow forgot to print her parents' names under the "Marriage License" section in "Part 2" (following "The Sports Report") over seven years ago—so it was only a little less than six and a half, they were enaged, weren't they?—and likewise managed to lose that wallet-sized photo from their wedding and not print any story about their union. And Jennifer was much too young to recall that her grand debut in Ewerton was never mentioned in the paper. Sorry, kiddo, nowadays a person can't even count on the old saw about making the papers when he's born, married, and buried. What with adding new stories, correcting galleys, a line or two sometimes falls to the printing room floor. Nothing worth getting het up about.

And Monica and Dave couldn't be blamed if they missed seeing the article in paper about the final deadline for kindergarten enrollments last year, especially since the editor had to bump it to the classifieds so he could devote more space to that big pot bust out at EHS. Kids didn't learn all that much in kindergarten, did they? Have the kid watch a little extra *Mr. Wizard* and *Mr. Rogers' Neighborhood* to make up for it.

(Monica made a mental note to call back that woman about the video game machine; it was such a rarity to find someone in Ewerton, let alone this very neighborhood, who was willing to pop for something as frivolous as a video game system these days. Monica reminded herself to tell the woman that Dave had agreed to come down to the figure the woman offered; a buck was a buck.)

And Jennifer had been learning eye-hand coordination with

the video games since she was three, so missing out on kindergarten hadn't seemed like such a big deal, only Monica was slightly surprised to overhear a pair of women at the check-out counter in the Red Owl talking about getting letters from the school board encouraging them to send *their* kids to kindergarten this fall....Jennifer was getting set for the first grade, and the Ewerton school system hadn't invited her into the fold *last* year. It was then that she remembered Mr. Winston, the former elementary school teacher, who always made his way from house to house every summer when she was a kid, asking every family, "How many children? Any new babies this year?" Palmer Winston never missed a house, even those in the old people's section of town, with its row after row of declining Victorian homes. Until his wife died, and he started to cut down on the houses he'd stop at, out of both old age and boredom. Old peep's street was the first to go...her great aunt told Monica about that, rueful at the latest missed chance to tell her former classmate Palmer with a solemn face, "Yes, I had a baby. Five of 'em"—then Monica saw Mr. Winston pass her house last year, clipboard in mottled hand, as if he couldn't see the hitching post on the front lawn bearing the three wood-burned plaques reading DAVID, MONICA, and JENNIFER.

At the time she had written it off as forgetfulness on the old man's part. Or maybe—miracle of miracles—he had actually remembered from last year that she and Dave had a little girl, and decided not to bother them about it. Then they hadn't paid attention to the annual notice in the paper about the school census. This year they did.

Last year was Mr. Winston's final year as school census taker; a new science teacher at the junior high took over the job, and Monica's great aunt Vera got the golden opportunity to tell the young man that she had septuplets on her seventieth birthday, a act she related with glee over the telephone to Monica. That was the capper, even more so than the article in this week's paper about one hundred percent cooperation on the part of Ewerton residents in this year's school census, and how it made the new teacher's job so much more pleasant and easier, all that happy horseshit. If the new census taker went to Roberts Street, where Great Aunt Vera lived, he had had no idea of who in Ewerton had kids and who didn't. "100% cooperation," the paper had said. And the new man hadn't paid any attention to the number of names on the hitching post.

Later, Dave had taken the post down. It did need a new coat of varnish. And they could take it with them when they left town. The manager at the apartment complex in the Twin Cities said to Dave that they could move in next week at the earliest if they didn't mind the smell of new paint. Dave's homemade hitching post would look good in that narrow entry hall leading into the living room, or so he told her. She had stayed home with Jennifer while Dave went apartment-hunting with Larry Kominski, a former classmate of Dave's who had moved to the Twitties after divorcing his wife last year. Dave told her that Larry's wife was brain-damaged or something; the two men hadn't been in close contact for several years, even though they both lived in Ewerton after graduation. All Monica knew for sure was that Maureen Kominski was out at the nursing home on the other side of town, and that Larry Kominski now worked for Honeywell in Minnesota. Being newly single, he didn't have to worry about getting the highest wages right off. Supporting three cats wasn't as costly as supporting a wife, too. Something about Larry and his unseen wife—ex-wife—Maureen reminded Monica of that nursery rhyme in one of Jennifer's books, the one about Peter, Peter, Pumpkin Eater. Poor Maureen, vegetating in her pumpkin shell out at the nursing home. Still, it wasn't *that* bad, what Larry did. Might have been worse.

Across from Monica, next to the slightly opened door, was Jennifer's toybox, currently covered with her dolls. My Friend Mandy, a "feather-leather" E.T., a Miss Piggy beanbag with snarled hair, plush Smurfs, and Tenderheart Bear stared at Monica with flat, uncomprehending plastic and paint eyes. She was reminded of the highly gilded and jeweled animal and human figures the Egyptians used to seal in their pyramids. The kind those archeologists found in that boy king's tomb; the same ones she and her parents had driven down to Chicago to see a few years back. She had wondered then if they did the same, all the pomp and circumstance, for female royalty who died. Now she wished that she had taken the time to look up the answer to her mental question. Maybe E.T. and Tenderheart Bear would do in a pinch. They'd have to, now.

"Whatchew looking at, Mommy?" Propped up on one elbow, Jennifer watched her mother slowly flip the pages of the *Herald*. "Nothing. How bout if you get some shut-eye, Miss."

Jennifer rolled over onto her back, arms crossed behind her head. "Not tired."

"Who's not tired?" Monica reached for a new cigarette. *"I'm* not tired, Mommy." Monica chose to ignore the petulant undertone in Jennifer's answer. Jennifer, not taking her eyes off of the ceiling with its dense cover of glow-in-the-dark stars that were just beginning to show a faint pattern of luminescence in the gloom not touched by the light from the twenty-five-watt bulb in her bedside lamp, asked, "Whatchew reading?"

"The paper." Why lie about it? No harm done.

"This week's paper? The one with the picture of the kittens?"

"Yeah, Jennifer, the same paper." C'mon, kid, forget about the "Pet of the Week" kittens and fall asleep already.

Turning over to face Monica, Jennifer pleaded, "Read it to me, please Mommy, pretty please?" It usually worked with Dave, that "Pretty please" shit; a phrase enclosed in a pink glass box, next to the BREAK GLASS IN EMERGENCY sign....

Monica read. She read about the school census, the announcement that the Soo Line was pulling out half its runs through Ewerton, the words under the picture of the two tiger-stripe kittens who were scheduled to be put down if no one adopted them before next Wednesday. She read the single item under "Help Wanted," and the sixteen "Looking for Work" classified ads. She read the huge two-color "Going out of Business Sale" advertisement that the Red Owl store had splashed across the innermost two pages of Part 1. She read the Legal section; the

DWIs, the forfeitures, the DNR violations, the burglary arrests, the assault charges brought and dropped. Soon, Jennifer was nodding off for real, before Monica even got to the sports.

Monica stopped mouthing the mundane, numbing words when she saw Jennifer's eyelids stop fluttering and close for real. On the street below, a passing car ran over the lid of a garbage can, an echoing, tinny rumble. Three short taps on the horn of their car. Dave. Gingerly, she wormed her way out of the tiny rocker, her bare lower thighs making sucking noises as they parted from the painted seat. Quietly she made her way to the window. Pushing aside the limp pink curtains, she saw Dave fishing the extension hose and cleaning head—the wide, thin one Jennifer used to call "the mustache mouth" when she was tiny—out from under the bushes near the garage. It was dark outside, the dark that comes right before the street lamps sizzle on in lightning-bug coolness, so Monica could barely see Dave make the final attachments to the car. Having sat down there for the past couple of hours, his eyes were probably used to the dark. Good thing the extension hose and the house were almost the same color. (The better not to see you with, my dear, said the Big Bad....)

Dave had left the ladder standing against the house after cleaning out the rain gutters yesterday. Lots of people in Ewerton left stuff like extension ladders outside overnight, even though the unemployment situation meant that neighborly trust was occasionally violated lately. Anyway, they wouldn't be needing the ladder in the Cities.

Suddenly, she was glad that Dave had insisted on moving Jennifer's bed away from the window. She had argued last night that once it came up to the window nothing would matter anymore, but he was right; knowing it's coming is one thing, but having to *see* it come for you is another.

The sound of the duct tape unrolling made slight *snicking* noises; faint, but damn, Dave should have thought to unroll and cut off the necessary pieces while he was down by the car. Jennifer wasn't *that* deep in sleep yet. The stiff black brushes on the cleaning head scratched at the screen as Dave finished taping the head to the outside frame. They did not make eye contact through the film of curtain. She couldn't hear Dave go down the ladder, but she could picture every slow, backward step in her mind.

Not much time left. Now that the wait was almost over, Monica wished that it was five o'clock again, and that she and Dave were back in the kitchen watching Jennifer eat her chosen meal of Chef-Boy-Ar-Dee Ravioli, dry Cap'n Crunch, and ersatz Quick. They would even give her the last box of toaster pastries, if she wanted them. And Jennifer could splatter the whole house with chocolate milk, if she wanted to. Monica patted the curtains closed, not that it mattered, or made any difference. Gas could permeate cloth, and Jennifer's curtains were pink dotted Swiss, so sheer you could almost see completely through them. In her mind's eye, Monica could picture the sign in front of the apartment Dave and Larry found in the Cities: HUNTINGTON COURT—SINGLES—COUPLES—No   CHILDREN—No PETS. She was glad Dave had never invited Larry over. He didn't *know*.

Perfunctorily, she bent over Jennifer and made a smacking noise near her left ear. Monica was never much good at bye-byes. She looked at Jennifer, then at the guard toys who watched the scene impartially. Take good care of her, she mouthed silently. Monica could hear the faint, sharp, chitinous click of the car door opening, and she knew that she had only seconds to get out, shut the door, and start stuffing newspapers into the places the weather-stripping didn't block off.

Monica took a last look at Jennifer, who suddenly opened moist eyes and asked in a soft voice, "Will I be dead for a long time, Mommy?"

"Just a while, Jenny." Then Monica was on the other side of the shutting door. As her heartbeat slowed to a semi-normal rate, Monica rested her cheek against the doorjamb and stared at the open doorway of the master bedroom across the hall. Two large suitcases stood next to the bed, tightly packed. Running her fingers along the smooth wood of the frame, Monica thought about what she'd have to do later. The opening of Jennifer's door, the rushed fumblings in there with the big black plastic bag from under the kitchen sink, thick and dark enough to hide the Care Bear sheets and the lumpy bundled form, made lumpier by the addition of the guard toys. Monica had insisted that they buy bags big enough for the toys, too—a concession Dave made grudgingly..

Hearing the low rumble of the car's engine far, far below, Monica thought, *The gates of the town dump will be locked this late at night, but Dave knows the place where the chain-link fence has more than a few broken links. The* bag *will most likely be covered over soon. Tomorrow* is *garbage day in this half of Ewerton.*

They'd have time enough to eat that last box of toaster pastries—and throw the box out with all the rest of the trash, the boxes and boxes of it—before going to gas up the car for the trip to the Cities. To the janitorial assistant position at Honeywell that Larry promised to get for Dave. Twenty-five cents over minimum, for starters. The apartment. One small bedroom. In her mind's hungry eye she could see the milk, splattered on the kitchen walls, slowly running down. Still semi-moist.

Hearing Jennifer's muffled cough from behind the door, Monica began to reach for the cough drops she usually carried in her shirt pocket; instead she reached down to the bag next to the door.

Then she began stuffing the folded strips of paper into the cracks around the door.

WHEN THE
BAD THING COMES

"When the bogiemen get you...they'll eat you alive."

Oliver Hardy,
Babes in Toyland

CHITTERING, IT THUMPED *against the closet door, made the knob rattle, the hinges creak. He huddled the floor, wedged between a bowling ball and a cardboard box labeled* Stereo: Stack Five High *filled with Christmas ornaments which rattled glassily with each ragged breath he took. When the grinding drowned out the pounding bloodroar in his ears, he let out a hurt-dog whine and pressed his sweaty face against the worn carton.*

The hall light outlined the bottom of the door in pencil-point sharpness, save for the dark spot where the bad thing sat, worrying its way in. He squealed again, made the bad thing outside more anxious, more frenzied. Pressing slick palms against his ears, he thought, I didn't do it, why chase me? *The door rattled and, like a snake in the jaws of a ferret, as the teeth chomped away slivers of the protecting door....*

I. Toobie
October 1986

As Yul Brynner told the Mexican villagers, "men are cheaper than guns," Troy's phone rang. He tried to ignore it; turned up the volume on his remote, stuffed his mouth full of potato chips, crunched loudly, in time with Elmer Bernstein's rousing score.

The ringing quit for a few blissful seconds (bozo probably realized he had a wrong number), but as Troy lowered the volume, the infernal ringing started again. Thinking, *Maybe I won the Reader's Digest sweepstakes...first thing I'll do is get a damned unlisted number!* Troy pressed the "Pause" button. The screen changed from a scene of *The Magnificent Seven* (there were only five or six of them at that point) to a hissing field of grey static. Nearly upsetting his bowl of chips as he reached for the phone, Troy swallowed the mealy chips before saying, "'Lo?"

"Whatsamatter, you in the can before?"

Troy groaned, and nearly hung up. He would rather have received a call from the IRS, telling him that he was in for an audit, rather than hear from Toobie. Worse yet, Toobie sounded loaded. Troy's thumb hovered above the "Pause" button, ready to bring the VCR back to life—after he found out what Big Brother wanted.

"Sure, Toob, man's gotta go sometime." (*Jeezus, get to the f' ing point already.*)

"Don't go when I'm gonna call ya." Troy heard his brother chewing something, probably a handful of peanuts from the big wooden bowl on Toobie's home bar.

"You want something, Toob, or just gassing?"

"Yeah, I want you to commere. *Now.*" Troy heard him take a noisy slurp from his can of Walter's. Always a can, never a glass. Debi drank hers from a glass, poured it slow so that beer wouldn't foam over the side and onto her fake fingernails.

Troy thumbed the "Stop" button: a commercial came on, for a floor wax which would make his floor look wet even after it dried. Easing the volume down, Troy said, "No can do, Bro. There's a tape in the VCR, *Magnificent Seven, da-dumda-dah, da-da-dum-da-dah—*"

"Rewind the sucker. Play it later." (When, *Toobie?* Midnight? *I gotta sleep* sometime—)

"I rented it so that I'd have something decent to watch *tonight*. Not tomorrow *morning,* but—"

"This ain't gonna wait. You gotta come, *now.* Debi ain't home," he coaxed, knowing full well that Troy seldom visited Toobie's home unless Debi, of the Devout Order of Perpetual Cheerleaders, was out. Figuring that if he got Toob off his back he could be back home by 10:30 at the latest—enough time to watch the movie before he became too sleepy—Troy pressed the "Eject" button. He put the warm tape under the VCR, shut the door so his cat wouldn't get at the videocassette—Lenny Wilkes charged 50 cents if the tape wasn't rewound—Troy didn't want to know the charge for cat-damages.

Telling his dozing tom, "Be good boy, take care of the house," Troy threw on his jacket and pocketed his car keys. On his way to the car, he thought, *It better be worth it, whatever it is.* With Toobie, it was hard to tell sometimes.

During the trip from his cracker-box prefab in the Woodlawn Development, past the hospital, the four-way stop (red lights strobed in the fine mist, like glowing animal eyes), then the long stretch of Maple Road which passed through looming trees mottled red-gold-brown in his headlight's glare, Troy drove slowly, due to the conditions. Thus, he had time to think, to reluctantly remember *another* October, when he was a kid, and Toobie was in his early teens.

Not that things were *different* then, despite the passing of the years. For Troy, his times with Toobie all had a strange *sameness* about them: their ages never mattered. *Crazy* Toobie: so dubbed by the brothers' elder cousin Palmer Nemmitz, after the day when the Horaks visited Palmer and his wife Bitsy out at their farmhouse in 1956. Troy was five and Toby was five years his senior. After lunch Toby slipped down to the basement; no one noticed his absence until a harsh grating sound began. Palmer—never an even-tempered man—stomped downstairs: he came up cursing and hollering how "that crazy little bastard" was trying to saw down the two-by-fours which supported the first floor. But instead of "Two by Fours," Palmer sputtered "toobie-fours." From that day on, Toby was Toobie.

And Toobie *always* did crazy things; irrational, immature things, which Troy got blamed for...such as the fall of the year Toobie decided to be a Rock Collector, until he tired of his collection, and stashed the flimsy box of stones under *Troy's* bed....

Monday, October 13, 1961

Troy was carefully stacking cookies on a saucer—anything *over* half a dozen ruined supper—and pouring out a frothy glass of milk while Mom vacuumed the back bedrooms. She walked heavy, dragging the rest of the huge canister model behind her as she vacuumed under all the furniture, occasionally pausing to move aside a piece of dropped clothing. Troy placed his bubble-topped glass and small plate of cookies on a TV tray. In fifteen minutes it would be *Felix the Cat* time; his chair was already in place before the TV.

Troy loved Felix and his magic bag; when he was small, he learned to count by holding his forefinger and thumb in a rough approximation of "four-clock"—the time when Felix was on channel four. Mom would finish vacuuming by then, and would go to the kitchen to start supper.

Gingerly, Troy began to walk from the kitchen, loaded tray in both hands, when a rattling whine started. From the direction of the strangled sound, Troy *knew* Mom was in his room. Sick at heart, sick to his stomach, Troy returned to the kitchen, as the tortured squeal abruptly ended. The split second of silence was shattered by Mom's "Troy, get in here *now*. Hear me? *Now*."

Troy dragged his Keds all the way, he could just picture Mom; her heavy, thick legs straddled over the vacuum, eyes blazing, mouth a mottled pink-white line, cheeks so red Troy could almost see heat coming off them, like heat shimmers on a winter roof. But he had to go into his room and look at her, had to raise his eyes and look into *her* eyes. He couldn't cover his ears when her voice boomed out loud in the confines of his room—"Just *look* at what *your* rocks did to the vacuum. Think vacuums grow on *trees*? Will you *fix* this? Not sitting on your *duff* in front of the TV you won't. Quit simpering and clean up your mess." Mom lifted the side of his Roy Rogers bedspread for emphasis, revealing a scattering of pebbles, small stones and larger rocks which spilled out of the fragile box when the nozzle of the vacuum tore open the thin cardboard.

On his knees (*It's almost time for* Felix, Mom), Troy scooped handfuls of the stones into the remains of the box, tried to gather every last bit of gravel, while Mom intoned, "I *told* you about putting *junk* under your bed, but did you *listen* to me? *No.* You clean this mess up before your father comes home. Take it out to driveway, rake it in—"

Troy made the mistake of saying, "But Mom, *Felix* time—" He felt the vibration of her pounding feet as she stomped out of the room, then stomped back in. His coat, hat and gloves dropped to the floor next to him. "The rake is on the porch…maybe *Felix* will help you." She stalked out, dragging the vacuum behind her. Troy whispered as he pulled on his coat and hat.

"They're *Tooble*'s, not mine, *he* did it, not *me*. I didn't do it."

The rake was where Mom said it would be. After he carried the crumbling box and its heavy load outside, he had to go back in for the rake. Felix time came and, as he raked the mass of loose stones into the driveway, Felix time went. The air above him carried the signal of his favorite program; it mocked him by *being* there, unwatchable.

While he worked, fine mist plastered his sandy hair to his forehead. Troy thought. *Got a sliver, oh Toobie someday the bad thing's gonna getcha for this, not fair. I didn't pick up those stones…didn't put 'em under my bed, either. I wish something real bad would come and* eatcha *up, make you go away.*

But nothing "bad" came for Toobie. When he came home from Freshman football practice he told Mom and Dad he made the final team cut. Dad took Toobie out for a beer (Dad *knew* the bartender at the Rusty Hinge, and Toobie *was* a big lug of a guy), so Troy went to bed, disappointed. Not even his childish fantasy came to his rescue, and he nursed wounds that festered huge and deep.

Troy was so lost in thought he missed the second left-hand turn after making the right-hand turn where Maple Road met the middle of Aspen Dive. He wound up on winding Elmhurst Drive, which became Willow Street midway through and dead-ended on the other side of Willow Hill. Troy had lived in Ewerton all his life, yet the hoity-toity Willow Hill district (the grass was of velour height, and the trees stood no higher than a good-sized man) confused him in the daytime, never mind a misty fall evening.

Until now, the mist had been too fine to necessitate the use of his wipers, but now it covered the glass with a distorting pebble pattern. Reluctantly, as he approached the dead-end of Willow Street, and the mock-Tudor splendor of the Bettinger house (Cousin Palmer's step-daughter's family home: at least *they* could afford to live out here),Troy switched on his wipers. They rubbed smeary lines across the glass, and Troy cursed himself for agreeing to come see whatever it was his boorish brother wanted him to see.

As he made a U-turn. heading back down Willow Street. Troy wondered what couldn't wait. It seemed to be something pleasant. Toobie sounded up, more so than could be attributed to his can of beer. Could Debi be expecting? Was Troy supposed to stare in awe at the ring at the bottom of a urine tube? *No way, Debi's as fecund as an astroturf doormat. Besides, isn't the test done in the morning?* A raise, a bonus on his paycheck? Toobie would drive to Troy's house to show him that. Another picture for the puzzle book? That was more like it; the more he thought it over, the more sense it made.

As he crossed from Elmhurst Drive onto Aspen Drive, then turned onto Corduroy Drive, which became Vail Circle, then Wagon Road, before meeting up with Aspen Drive once again, Troy decided *Hell, that can't be it.* Why Toobie couldn't drive to Troy's to show off his latest masterpiece was beyond Troy; being drunk never stopped Toobie from getting behind the wheel, and he certainly knew where Troy lived.

Maybe he ran out of film, Troy reasoned as he slowed down, trying to figure out which overpriced home at the end of a long driveway *(not* fair, *I didn't pick up all these—)* belonged to Toobie. That made a *little* sense. Not wanting to run the risk of ruining the configuration on the Super-Cube by taking it for a drive, Toobie wanted Troy to baby-sit his latest creation while he took a run to the twenty-four-hour convenience store nearest the hospital to stock up on more film. Then, snap a shot of the "picture" on the front of the cube, then share a brew with Troy before Debi came home and bawled Toobie out for wasting more money on his pet project.

Toobie had gone through the whole rigamarole for the past two years, ever since Debi found a Super-Cube in the second-hand and new-but-chintzy shop on Wisconsin Street, a gift for Toobie's thirty-eighth birthday. Ewerton was always behind when it came to fashion, fads, what-have-you (last week they finally got a shipment of kiwi fruit, and there was talk that tofu might make it to the IGA); as far as Rubick's cubes and spin-offs went, Ewerton was still in the tail-end of Cube Fever, long after the rest of the world moved on to Rubick's Snake and Rubick's Magic. But Toobie believed that the market could use just one more great Cube Book—not a how-to, but an *artistic* endeavor. Or so he said it would be; a book showing people how to make pictures on any size of cube...including the Super-Cube Debi found. That cube made Rubick's Cube look like a pipsqueak, and dwarfed the four-squares-to-a row Son of Cube. It was the grand-daddy, no, the *great-grand-daddy* of all cube puzzles. That's what Toobie claimed, and, Troy decided, *Toobie should know...he's played with every one of those toys he can get his paws on.*

Troy wasn't sure when Toobie chose to ride that particular hobby horse (when he read about Uncle Toby and his "hobby horses" in *Tristam Shandy,* he laughed out loud—later, when he mentioned that Toobie's hobbies were "hobby horses," Toobie blurted, dumbfounded, "I don't play with no *horses!*"), but Toobie had been astride *this* particular hobby horse the longest of any of his mounts. The rocks lasted only a few months, and his base-ball card mania (taken up when he was too old for such things; he was in it for the power of having the best collection around) lasted nearly eighteen months.

When Toobie got tired of sorting the rubber-banded piles of cards on his desk, he shoved them off on Troy, who *tried* to divide them between himself and his best pal Brucie Sawyer, but the cards didn't lend themselves to a neat division. He and Brucie didn't speak to each other for three weeks. Later on came Toobie's crossword puzzlebook craze; he even invested in a dictionary that listed Egyptian sun gods and obscure abbreviations. Troy inherited the forlorn remains of that craze, too. He sold the dictionary at the U-W bookstore. The books themselves were useless; scribbled on, written-over where Toobie made mistakes, totally dog-eared. Crossword fever burned in Toobie for over a year, quenched only by the discovery of football pools and chicken-drop betting at rural taverns.

Toobie didn't attend college; when dad retired at the paper mill, Toobie stepped into his vacant job, despite his lack of seniority. The foreman at the mill was Mom's brother-in-law, hence, Toobie didn't need seniority (which he never could have *earned*).

For years, Toobie was content with his job, and his marriage to Our Lady of the Pep Rally, until the day when Troy (unmarried and liking it—when he and a pal double-dated, he overheard his date say to his friend's date, "Should I tell him 'bout Jim's kid? I'm not showing *yet*") came over for Sunday dinner and found Toobie sitting at his home bar, twiddling a newfangled Rubick's Cube.

From that time on, Toobie went Cube Crazy. Not long after he got the Super-Cube, he began work on his "book"—a step-by-step instruction guide for making "pictures" out of the color configurations on cubes. He went so far as to contact a vanity press outfit in the Twin Cities, and was in the process of negotiations—or so he told Troy last week. Toobie didn't care about the book's cost; he was sure it would sell in bars, bus-stops, anywhere Man searched for beauty, fun and a way to kill time. Troy suspected that Toobie saw his opus as a way to get rich quick; despite the times he had sworn to "get" Toobie for this or that transgression, dream-killing wasn't Troy's style. When Toobie sat amid piles of unsaleable, expensive books, he'd realize his project was an expensive bust. Then, *only* then, would Troy enjoy a silent laugh on his brother.

Troy snorted in disgust as he backed up and inched forward, trying to find the house. It didn't help that the homes on Corduroy Drive had fancy-schmancy decorated mailboxes, with the names hidden among cardinals, flowers and *naif* outdoor scenes. Come nightfall they were nearly unreadable. (*Maybe you don't* want *to remember where the Toober lives....*)

Troy recalled the fuss Mom kicked up when he tried *his* hand at a hobby—paint-by-number pictures. The paint *smelled* bad, he got a *spot* of it on his shin, and then—horror of horrors—he hung his "sloppy" pictures on his bedroom wall. By week's end, Mom was "tired" of dusting the frames; come garbage day, they were on their way to the dump, via the big white truck. But Mom never complained about the teetering piles of cards on Toobie's desk, nor did she care if Toobie ripped the comers off his crossword book pages and threw the ragged triangles of pulp paper on the floor—she had to vacuum *anyway*. And Dad—he had his drinkin' buddy, which was all that counted. Dad wasn't a bookworm; he wasn't interested when Troy wanted someone to read Whitman Little Big Books to him. Didn't Troy learn to read in *school*?

When Troy finally found Toobie's geese-decorated mailbox, he mused, *Beaver Cleaver never had it that bad...June never threw out the Beev's paint-by-number pictures,* as he made his way down the long, winding driveway which culminated by Toobie's unpaid-for house *(the crackerbox is* mine). Unable to let go of the painful memories, he remembered that every time Toobie found a new "hobby horse," he went ga-ga over it, sucked the pleasure, fun and worth out of his pastime until his mount was so dry, lifeless and boring he abandoned it without a backward glance. Toobie wouldn't look twice at a rock. He didn't even watch *real* baseball. Toobie didn't read, so he never did crosswords. *Granted,* Troy reasoned, as his tires crunched on the frosty driveway, *adults don't play with baseball cards, but who'll get stuck with Toobie's toys* this *time?*

As he got out of the car, Troy's feet slipped on the gravel. He remembered how his Keds slid across the wet, slimy leaves that 1961 afternoon; the damp cold didn't chill his hands or face *too* much, but gnawed deeper than the skin to lick his bones with a lizard tongue. As he had worked, he hoped that Dad wouldn't come home, because he *knew* what Dad would say when he saw the busted vacuum. Toobie's good news about football had saved Troy's butt (later, when *he* was in high school, Troy learned that final cuts were made in *September*; Toobie was bullsheeting the folks then, too), but Troy wasn't all that thankful.... Toobie got him in a jam and made him miss Felix in the *first* place.

Just as he was making Troy miss *The Magnificent Seven*, and Troy didn't know when he'd get another chance to rent it again; the waiting list was longer than his arm.

Toobie didn't lie: Debi's Rabbit was gone! (her bumper sticker read. "Don't laugh, it's paid for"). But his Pacer (the bumper sticker read "If you're rich. I'm SINGLE," and the little diamond shaped yellow sign in the rear window proclaimed "I Love Sex") was parked outside the garage.

The porch light was on, along with a lamp in the living room. Whether or not Toobie was actually in the living room was another matter: Troy couldn't tell after looking through the semi-opaque drapes. He tried the door...locked. No one answered the bell, or his knock. Troy rapped the windows with his car keys, then pounded the door. Troy checked the Pacer, which sat in a puddle of oil, but the engine was cool and no one was inside. The garage was also empty, as far as Troy could tell by peering through the uncurtained winlows.

Deciding that Toobie was either in the bathroom or getting a snack in the kitchen, Troy lurched around on the frosty grass, but was unable to see any movement within the dark and dimly lit room. The mist, delicate as spray from a perfume atomizer, felt like icy sweat on his face as he cursed Toobie.

His Mobil credit card did the trick. After opening the door, Troy carefully wiped his shoes on the rush mat—Debi would have a shit-fit if she found mud on her carpet—and stepped into the house. No radio, but the TV was on with the volume turned off. A video he hadn't seen before was on: Tom Petty, wearing a Mad Hatter outfit, chased a woman dressed as Alice in Wonderland. The action without music was surreal, eerie: when the band and three women dressed in body suits caught Alice, she turned into Alice-Cake, which they carved up and ate. Troy turned his head away, sickened. No wonder Toobie didn't bother with the sound.

Brass and linen table lamps cast a warm mellow light, to accentuate the amber walls, russet sofa and chairs, cream drapes and maple Early Sears Catalog American decor—which contrasted weirdly with Toobie's monument to the Great God of Schlock near the dining room. Toobie's cube collection shared shelf space with bottles of Jack Daniels, Korbel brandy, Lime-Flavored vodka. a dildo on a stand (a gift from his co-workers at the mill, an engraved plaque read "To a Real Upstanding Guy"), a watering-boy drink dispenser, the Jim Beam Upraised Finger decanter, false-teeth ice tongs, and a pair of pink golf balls adorned with painted red nipples. The base of the bar was a cooler that hummed; the liquid sound soon got on Troy's nerves.

Troy stood in the middle of the room, on the oval braid rug, listening. He wanted to yell, "Yo, Toob. *You* in the can?" but something—he didn't know what—made him keep his silence, Aside from the subtle hum of the cooler. Troy heard the steady drone of the electric clock over the mantle, the whoosh-whoosh of the fridge, and the slight whistle of breath in his own nostrils... that was all.

Toobie was a confirmed noise-maker. A beer-slurping,

burping, gas-passing, teethsucking. nose-blowing, lip-smacking, mouth-breathing, humming Noise Machine; it was a Horak family joke: if you *can't* find Toobie, hold a hand behind your ear and listen.

Reluctantly, Troy entered the kitchen. Every fiber in his body screamed, *Don't go in the basement*! *Norman Bates'* mother *is down there, Living dead, with trowels and* teeth! *Rats, big spiders*! *Golliwogs that were after good old Agent 86, Maxwell Smart*! *All sorts of bad shit*!, as Troy resolutely marched down the linoleum-covered steps of the half-finished basement. A wrapped water hearer, furnace (which let out deep clunking noises), a netless ping-pong table, the washer and drier, and empty cardboard boxes. No Toobie. Down there, Troy could have heard every step made above him, magnified with creaky accuracy by the floorboards above. Nothing. Nor a single creak or wooden whine.

Walking back into the kitchen. Troy wondered if Toobie had grown tired of waiting, and headed uptown…but Toobie never walked farther than the length between where he was and where the car was parked. When Troy returned to the living room, the 'fridge shut off. With the loss of its whooshing, Troy realized that he *had* to be the only person in the house. Toobie *couldn't* be here.

Taking a deep breath (the house smelled of a combination of Brut, potato pancakes, beer, peanuts and a trace of the mossy perfume Debi wore), Trov went over to the bar, and looked behind it, in the wastebasket Debi made Toobie use. Two empty Walter's cans, a scattering of peanut shells, and *oxblood* bits of plastic Troy couldn't identify off-hand (there was something vaguely familiar about them…something Troy thought he should know, yet it escaped him), nothing to get worried about. Next to the wastebasket were Toobie's thongs, deeply imprinted with the outlines of his heels and toes. The abandoned (abandoned?) thongs gave Troy a funny feeling. Toobie did keep the house so hot mold grew on the six-day-old coffee-grounds, so hot he could pad around in sandals at Christmas, yet Toobie never went barefoot....

Struggling to keep his breathing normal, Troy searched every room—kitchen, dining room, bedroom, spare bedroom, and bathroom—empty. He didn't call out; he was afraid that his voice would hit pubescent highs and lows, betray his feelings. Nothing to get ragged about. Tobie was only missing in a locked house. Not unusual at all, f-f-folks!

Troy's bladder was ready to explode in his lower abdomen; carefully shutting the door behind him, he stood before the toilet facing the humorous reminder Debi hung there, a duck (goose) stuck halfway in the, bowl under the caption "Bottom's Up!"

As Troy stepped out of the bathroom, he happened to look down instead of up as he zipped. It was then that he noticed the closet door....it had a *hole,* almost two, inches around, much bigger than a mouse would need to make, but with chewed edges a mouse *might* make. Wood shards were scattered outside the hole in the center of the bottom edge of the door on the tan plush carpet. Approaching the closet, Troy thought. *Toobie, if this is a joke. I'll kill you—*

—but someone had already done *just* that to Toobie. He was wedged tightly between his cased bowling ball and a cardboard box marked *Stereo: Stack Five High;* his bare fat feet stuck out. And, in the reflection of the hallway light, Troy saw the dark shimmer of fresh blood.

Closing the door, Troy backed away. He tried not to hyperventilate, tried to figure out whether to call 911 or the hospital or Coroner Lenny Wilkes (*Got to watch the rest of the movie, got to rewind it*) and above *all,* he hoped that wherever Debi was, she wouldn't come home until after they took Toobie away.

After a stammered phone call. Troy realized that whatever *did* that to Toobie might still be *in* the house. He waited outside, next to the Pacer with the silly bumper sticker and car window sign. Deep down, a part of him hoped that Toobie was scared shitless when it happened. Troy alternately giggled (*he looks so dumb, feet sticking out like Debi's barefoot earrings*) and sniffled (*Toobie won't put on thongs again*) as he watched for the flashing red lights in the thickening mist.

...as the teeth chewed, tore at the door, the man tried to back into the closet, but came up against hard wood. He whimpered again, which pleased the bad thing. It redoubled its efforts, gobbled the door with renewed vigor. He felt vibrations against his feet, and tucked his knees under his chin, like he did when he watched TV, but his knees didn't fit. *It didn't make* sense, *he was only a little* boy. *The bad thing was gonna get him if he didn't hide better. First it was gonna nip his toes, like it did with his finger, then, oh then it was gonna go for the* soft parts *he so desperately tried to protect. The hole was getting big, and the bad thing...."*

II. Debi

It misted the day of the funeral. Debi asked Troy, begged him, to *please* be a pallbearer, but Troy begged off with a phoney excuse about a sore arm. If he helped with the coffin, he'd keep seeing Lenny, as the coroner stood outside the closet and stared at Toobie and his bare feet (carpet dirt clung to the soles); Lenny kept rubbing his crew cut, muttering, "Why'd he go do that? Didn't have to go in the closet to tear out his throat." Troy had wanted to scream, *The hole, look at the* hole, *dumbshit! Something* did *it to him!* but all he did was nod dumbly as Sheriff Sawyer (Brucie's dad) told Troy that euphoria, of seeming to have one's life in order, was common with suicides. Toobie probably called Troy out here so *he* would find him before Debi came back. Stu Sawyer chose not to see the hole, after all, there was blood and bits of skin under Toobie's nails. The many tiny wounds (and the long big one) were crescent shaped, like nails...why mess up a neat conclusion with something as trivial as a freshly bitten hole in a closet door?

By the time Stu and Lenny and the volunteer ambulance attendants pulled Toobie out of the closet, the carpet was so matted with blood that the slivers of wood went unnoticed.

(Wayne Mesabi said, "I seen this stuff in Nam...bleeds like a stuck pig when the artery pops" and Troy had a sudden impulse to kick the Old Dutch Snacks Distributor right in the Beer Nuts.)

Troy pitied the men at the Reish-Byrne Funeral Home; if Toobie hadn't converted when he married the Patron Saint of Pom-Pom Girls, he could have been cremated, but then he wouldn't have been planted next to Mom and Dad in the Ewerton Cemetery, in the Horak plot....

Tuesday, May 21, 1974

"Mom, why aren't I a pallbearer *too*?" Troy asked as Toobie and the other five men put on their white gloves. Mr. Byrne stood off to one side, mortified, but unable to interfere. Mom kept her eyes turned toward Dad, who lay under a blanket of carnations and baby's breath. Finally, she said, "His *son*'s gonna carry him. That's that."

Mr. Byrne cleared his throat. Lenny Wilkes looked uneasy, as did Cousin Palmer, who shucked off his gloves. Feeling like a man before a firing squad who didn't receive a blindfold, Troy whispered, "Mom, I'm his son, too...or were you fooling around—" She started to raise her purse, as if to hit him, when Palmer snorted in disgust and tossed Troy his gloves before leaving. Mr. Byrne laid a hand on Mom's upraised arm, murmuring that it might be best if *both* sons carried their father. Mom snapped, "He said he don't want that pansy-ass at his side when he dies, and I don't want him there either."

At that point Lenny walked, too, as well as two of the men who worked at the mill. They had to wheel Dad into the church and down to the gravesite. Troy didn't see it first hand. Toobie told him about it...when they began talking again, a year later....

Troy was glad he was still Lutheran; he could be cremated. As the loudspeakers swelled with music from the tape in Mr. Reish's office, Troy thought it fitting that Mom died last year; otherwise, she'd be hogging the kneeling pad in front of Toobie's closed casket (topped by a studio portrait of him), wailing that God had taken away her precious baby, her only son.

The week they buried Dad, Troy was promoted to head of New Accounts at the bank, only two years out of college. When he called Mom to tell her the good news, she hung up after his first "Hello." But when Toobie won the "Safe Worker of the Month Award" at the mill, Mom took out an ad in the *Ewerton Herald* for him...

Now he was in line to be Vice President at the bank, Mom and Dad were six feet under, Toobie was in a wooden box—yet nobody gave two squirts *how* well Troy was doing. He would forever be Number Two Son, under the shadow·of undistinguished Big Brother. Troy could have understood his parents' slavish devotion to Toobie if *he* had been bright, college bound... but Toobie *wasn't*, which made Troy ache all the more. No matter what he did, it never measured *down* to Toobie's level—

"Troy? Troy? Mr. Reish says we have to...before he locks the—the, you know." Debi tapped his shoulder with her shield-like painted plastic nails. Her face was pinched under a coating of Cover Girl and pressed powder, her eyes red and black-rimmed like a kabuki actor's. She was swimming in a shapeless black jersey dress; Troy devilishly decided, *All she needs is black pom-poms and all black saddle shoes.*

They were alone in the visitation room (the one the Home reserved for important clientele); after Debi spoke Craig Reish walked in, and led them to the coffin. "I'm sorry, but state law...a relative has to view...the loved one. Debi, if you can't—"

She shook her head; her short curls flew. "I'm OK. I mean, I *should*—" but when Craig raised the lid, Troy noticed that her eyes were scrunched shut.

They didn't try anything heroic, per Troy's instructions. Except for his good suit, Toobie looked as he did when jammed in the closet, only the blood was gone. The red seamed lines were still there; just above the collar and tie Troy saw—

Instinctively, Craig shut the lid with a weak smile. A look passed between them: *Why torture yourself?*

All the way to the church Troy forced himself not to crack a smile (*You called them stiff-picklers when you were a kid...are you a dill or a sweet, huh, Toobie?*) as Debi snuff-snuffled her way through half a box of Kleenex.

Troy ignored the flower-blanketed casket to his left, and Debi's boo-hooing to his right; he concentrated on the flowers behind the altar, the spicy-stale incense, the droning Latin chant he couldn't understand. Troy dimly wondered if the priest would consecrate the ground as the priest said that the Lord works in mysterious ways to call his children Home. But all through the service, Troy saw—like an acetate overlay in a medical textbook—what was smeared all over the coats and boots in Toobie's closet, and saw how high up ("bleeds like a stuck pig when the—") the blood had gone.

That, perhaps, was the worst part of the funeral.

His vacation wasn't supposed to start until November, but they gave Troy an extra three weeks off, starting now. Four days after the funeral (that geek Mesabi slipped while carrying the coffin to the grave; Troy mumbled "Hope you fall in, *putz*," while supposedly bending his head in prayer), Debi pulled into Troy's driveway. He hurried out into the cold, to help her pull the carton from Green Giant Corn out of the Pacer. (Debi had removed the "I Love Sex" tag and covered over the bumper sticker with an Avon one.)

"Here, lemme take that." Troy hefted the box (Toobie's bowling ball had to account for most of the weight) and started for the house. Debi yelled, "Troy, wait up, I got some more stuff here." She sounded *almost* light and off-hand. She was doing better than he'd expected. The box she held was from Green Beans. The flaps barely covered what was inside; a paperback book could be seen. It had a cube on the front.

"No, Troy, Toobie would want you to have it...besides, it's only a two-finger ball." Debi finished her second cup of coffee, sucking the steaming brew past her dentures with an indelicate slurping noise. For no good reason, Troy remembered that when he first met Debi, she wore Old Spice, because she read that it was originally test-marketed for women, just as Marlboro's once sported lipstick-red tips.

The contents of the box Troy had carried in were spread across the living room in a macabre parody of Christmas morning. Here a bowling ball in a red case on the coffee table, there an instant camera on the TV, and scattered on the floor (to the delight of his tom Felix) were rumpled ties in ribbon-bright tones, baseball caps, boxed decks of poker cards, and the cream memo pads Mom had printed up for Toobie ("FROM THE DESK OF TOBY HORAK"only he didn't *have* a desk at work). Troy didn't need to look through the big box of ornaments Debi brought over ("I *insist,* I don't feel like Christmas...if I do, I'll buy new ones"), and as for the Green Beans box which rested by the closet door—they couldn't discuss *that* yet.

Debi's pale blue eyes kept flitting to the carton, as if she was waiting for Troy to bring up the subject. Her head turned slightly when she glanced over there, and her permanented curls bobbed. (Something Toobie said to Troy over a can of Walter's after Debi had her hair hacked off and tightly permed at the Last Wave Beauty Shop came back to Troy; Toobie leaned over the bar to whisper, "Now I don't know *which* damned end to fuck!") Remembering *that,* Troy had to either laugh or speak; he said, "Deb, what do you want me to do with that?" indicating the Green Giant box with his Morris the Cat mug.

"That?" She gave him a liquid glance, ripples of water spreading away from a skimmed stone. Chewing lipstick off her lips, she said, "Whatever...I thought you'd get a kick out of them. Think I should go through with his book?" Her eyes were eager, yet wary. For a moment, he felt genuinely sorry for her, and wished that he had stuck to his guns when they were kids, and not let Mom take Debi away from him...but Mom was desperate to get "her boy" away from the girl he was set to marry. Not Troy, but her "baby boy" *Toobie....*

Saturday, November 21, 1970

It started Friday night. Toobie came home from work and went back uptown after supper to put in the wedding invitation order at Hallmark's. No sooner had he left than Mom said to Dad and Troy (home from college), "Tomorrow, *you*—" she indicated Dad with a nod of her grey head "—take Toobie hunting. Make it a day. And *you*—" a nod to Troy "—help me here, OK.?"

"Mom, Debi's coming for supper tomorrow—what'll she *think*?" Debi West, a cheerleader for the football squad, Troy had been dating (a Catholic girl who took the pressure off him by insisting that she *couldn't* "you know" until she was married) was coming to Ewerton to visit the Horaks for a couple of days. He figured they'd end up meeting her *eventually*, so now seemed as good a time as any. But while he was at the U—W, he didn't know that Toobie had taken up with the town Spread-Legs... and popped the big question.

The name of the body to whom the spread legs belonged was Inez. Toobie was vague about her last name. Inez (small, dark-skinned, with improbable bleached hair, and a seemingly permanent line of dirt imbedded under her partially polished nails, a woman of undefinable age who wore ultra-short mini skirts and clumpy platform shoes) had only been in town less than six months, but she was *known*. Dad saw her cadging drinks at the Rusty Hinge, Mom heard her bragging in the supermarket about the buns she had taken *out* of the oven; after bouncing from bed to bed, she landed a job at the paper mill and caught Toobie's eye. She gave him hickies, he gave her *his* heart.

Mom and Dad (Troy learned later) made the mistake of telling Toobie Inez was no good, hence his trip to the Hallmark's. Toobie was twenty-four and *still* didn't know better; the good (if slightly road-tested) Ewerton girls only dated Toobie long enough to share a few beers, a few laughs, and a trip to the drive-in. Inez was thrilled; sleeping with the boss and *engaged* to him—she was in slut heaven!

Mom and Dad were each a heartbeat away from a heart attack. Having learned their lesson, they kept mum after Toobie announced his plans, but *nothing* would make Mom see the day when her Toby married a whore....

Saturday dawned crisp, cold, bright, a perfect hunting day. Dad made a pitch to Toobie, told *him* how a nice buck head, mounted on an oak plaque, would be a "great focal point" in his new home. Toobie bit, swallowed the bait; all Dad had to do was reel him into the station wagon and drive off with him for the woods.

As soon as the car was gone, Mom dialed the phone. Showing Troy her crossed fingers, she told Inez, "—thought we could have a cup of coffee, discuss the wedding—" (Mom all but choked getting *that* out) "—talk about flowers, our dresses." He nervously eyed the money Mom had fanned under the placemat on the table (which sported no coffee cups) and mentally added the worn fives and tens.

Inez blew in ten minutes later. Troy thought, *Roach, she has skin like the back of a roach. smooth and hard and* filthy—and *that* hair—he almost whoopsed up breakfast, when he shook her grime-rimmed hand. She noticed immediately that the coffee pot wasn't on the stove. Sitting down (her skirt rode up until Troy saw the dark top of her pantyhose) Inez said in a chirping, high-pitched voice that reminded Troy of Indians on the reservation up north, or the Mexican women he saw during his vacation, "Where's the coffee?"

Mom gave her a big smile. "Well some of it's in the *jar,* some is in my *husband*'s Thermos, and the rest is in *Toobie*'s Thermos. *You* don't get *any.*"

Troy folded his arms, to keep his hands from shaking. This was going to be worse than the time the rocks broke the vacuum cleaner. Oh yes, this was going to be so bad it was *good.*

Mom had an inkling that things between Toobie and Miss Roach-Face would get serious, why else would she go through so much trouble: write down so many names, so many motel rooms, so many doctor's appointments, so many *details*? Mom covered many pieces of paper with careful, sloping handwriting, neat as a shopping list, all ready to hand to Sheriff Sawyer (he was cousin to Palmer Nemmitz's wife Bitsy, and family is family, no matter how strung-out or distant). Mom reminded Inez, "Stu cares about public decency...he wants to protect this town from *sluts*." She spat the word out so hard Troy felt spittle fly.

That hard-planed face didn't move a muscle, but the brown eyes were sharp rocks, ready to be thrown to sting against skin. "Stu can't do nothing. I don't take no money...."

"I didn't say you were *worth* money."

Her over-painted mouth opened, then quickly shut (Troy saw that her teeth were mottled with grey, and thought, *Toobie, you kissed* that?)

"—but I think it'll be worth it for you to take money *this* time...provided you clear out—out of my house, out of my town, and out of my county. Remember, Stu's sheriff of all of Dean County. He likes to drive around, all over—he has a good mind for faces. And bleached hair."

Brown fingers darted out for the money. Inez was half-way to the door when Mom said, "I didn't say Stu still won't hear about—" The pieces of paper were snatched up and in Inez's bag before Mom closed her mouth. She waited until Inez had her hand on the knob before adding, "I didn't say I don't have *copies*—." When Inez raised her purse to swing it at Mom, Troy stood up (he was a foot taller than Inez, despite her heels) and caught the bag in mid-air, saying, "if you aren't out the door and heading out of town, I'll report you for assault and battery. Now *get*."

Inez didn't *get,* Troy did what he said he would (Mom held her while he dialed), by lunch-time Inez was in the county jail (later they learned that she somehow broke the sink off the wall of her cell—she earned an extra week in the Ewerton Hilton before she blew town), and by supper Toobie and Dad were home with a four-point buck strapped to the top of the wagon. Mom passed on Inez's message about having to leave town—

her mother was ill—and Toobie seemed relieved but didn't say anything. (Since he didn't read the paper he never saw the notice about Inez in the court-house news.)

Then Debi arrived in town, and Troy introduced her to his family—come suppertime, Mom seated her across from Toobie; he made eyes at Debi all night.

Eight months later, Debi quit school; in two months she and Toobie were off on their honeymoon, and Troy (throwing rice at their departing car with vengeance) wondered what in the hell *happened. Hope you can't get it up, Toob, hope it falls off. Too bad it didn't turn black like her teeth.... Toobie, how could you, she was mine....*

Wondering if Debi ever regretted saying "no" to him in college, Troy slurped down more coffee before saying, "I dunno. I think cube books have peaked. Of course, if you really want to, go ahead. Toobie put down a down payment, didn't he—"

"Refundable."

"Oh. You talk to the company, or do you want—"

"Would you—" The false nail from her pinkie was gone, Troy wondered if she had a spare in the box she kept in the bathroom (*"Bottom's Up!" Don't think she'll need a reminder for Toobie to put the seat down anymore...jeeze, she ever find that hole in the door?*) then wondered if she lost it while pulling the boxes out of the closet. He was glad that Lenny and his deputy coroner offered to clean up the closet after Stu took his pictures. At least she hadn't seen the closet, what was dripping there....

"Yeah. You have the number? I know the name of the company, but I'm not sure—" She fished a slip of paper from the outside pocket of her purse, and handed it to him. Her plastic nails felt strange (*as if you did up your own*) as they brushed his fmgertips, like the shell covering a tender-bodied sea creature.

As he read over the number, Debi said in a rush of words, indicating the box of cubes and cube books with the tip of her chin, "once you call, do what you want with the stuff, pitch 'em in the dump—" (*like my paint-by-numbers ?*) "—just do something with them. I can't *look* at them anymore."

Her voice verged on tears; they shimmered and hung in her eyes, trapped behind her varnished lashes. Unable to go over and comfort her, Troy was stuck by the silliness of her name.

Debi. Not Deborah or Debby, but an amputated fragment, a stump before her surname. *Debi* was a flick of pom-poms, short skirt billowing up to show matching sport panties underneath. Thirty-two (two birthdays in a row) with loose skin on pointy elbows and a pink china chopper-hopper on the commode wasn't *Debi.* Suddenly, Troy was thankful that he never went through life with her, to watch her at close range as she turned into St. Sis-Boom-Bah. Mom and Toobie took her away from him, but Troy still had the *old* Debi, the flicker of pom-poms in crisp football weather. Even Debi had lost that part of herself.

She pulled on her coat, bent at the waist to pick up her purse. "I've got to be going—"

"We should talk—"

"No." Hard and fast, like a slap on his cheek, then, softer, with submerged ice, "Everyone else has been doing the talking, remember? This is Ewerton, maybe you could stand it because you were born here, but with Toobie gone I'm on outsider status." She was almost at the door when she turned to ask, "Do you want all those...pictures he took? OK., I'll bring them over later...bye." Debi shut the door quietly behind her; soon Troy heard the muted rev of the Pacer's engine.

Picking up their mugs (Debi had left hers on the *TV Guide,* which now sported brown rings around the faces of the soap stars on the cover), Troy went into the kitchen, stepping through the mess on the floor. He put Debi's mug in the sink with the rest of the dirty dishes, and rinsed out his mug before setting it on the drainboard.

Yes, everyone *had* done all the talking for Debi and himself. The details of Toobie's unusual demise were hashed out in bars, stores, barber shops, beauty shops, right out in the street, fueled with nuggets tossed in by the ones who saw—as that dink Wayne Mesabi told anyone who *would* listen, he saw the *same* thing in 'Nam....

Troy walked back into the living room. He stuffed the clothes back into the box, threw the cards and note pads on top (*couldn't you have made some up for* me, *Mom?*) and carried the partially filled box—Felix had claimed the jersey ties for his own—to the hall closet. After stashing the box on a top shelf, he put the bowling ball on the floor, not far from the old stereo box of ornaments he had no intention of using. Troy didn't realize that this arrangement was identical to that in his brother's closet; he was musing that the camera which Debi had thought was Toobie's was really *his*—he had loaned it to Toob so many years ago that even *he* forgot whose it really was. It wasn't important any more, he decided.

What *was* important, at least to Troy, was that Debi would be bringing him the box of cube pictures—if his hunch was right, Toobie really *did* have something to show him that night...not his dead body stuffed in a closet. If Toobie was acting true to form that night, he took a picture, then automatically stashed it in the shoe box where he kept the rest of his "data." Once he had the pictures, then Troy might know just what it was that had been so important to Toobie, what he couldn't wait for Troy to see.

Troy wondered if it, *whatever* it was, might fit in a little hole chewed in the bottom of a closet door.

Debi *could* believe the death certificate ("death by self-inflicted means," the *Herald* hid the report about it among the county board minutes, and the obituary stated "passed away at home"), but Troy knew Toobie better. When you hate someone so much, you know *all* about them. Toobie liked Toobie too much to *kill* Toobie.

It wasn't until the following afternoon (no Debi, and no box of pictures; he decided not to go begging after them) that Troy was able to open up the Green Beans box. First he took out the seven paperback books (Toobie's entire library, titles like *The Simple Solution to Rubick's Cube, Conquer the Cube in*

45 Seconds, and *The Simple Solution to Cubic Puzzles*) and stacked them neatly. They'd go to the Ewerton Library, in Toobie's name.

He then took out the odd-shaped puzzles: pyramids, spheres and pointy things, and set those aside. Troy stacked the cubes like children's blocks, ascending with the decrease in size. If he looked at them fast, and didn't pay attention to the thin dark lines dividing the colors or patterns, they did resemble building blocks.

Toobie had each one in what he called its "*ally* natural" state; solid block of color or pattern on each side. Even the tiny gumball cube was put in correct order. No cube had its original wrapping, save for the jewel of Toobie's collection, the "SUPER-DUPER CUBE." (Toob was no nomenclator; that *was* the name of this particular cube, or so said the chintzy day-glo letters on the flimsy cardboard box.) Something about the Super-Duper Cube being *in* a box seemed strange, until Troy remembered the party....

Friday, July 13, 1984

Debi wanted to celebrate her husband's birthday at the Hole-In-One Club, someplace *refined,* but Toobie opted for the Rusty Hinge. All the place had was a pizza oven, so that's what they ate. The bartender stuck a candle in the middle of Toobie's, and Toobie acted as if manna from heaven had dropped before him from above. From the look on Debi's face, Troy was sure she wanted to shove Toobie's face into the pizza and grind it in for good measure. Troy thought, *Could've had me, Deb I* love *the Hole-In-One Club.*

They didn't have a private bar; all sorts of people sat near their table, blowing smoke, coming over to wish the Toob a happy birthday (and to mooch pizza). And pleasure of pleasures, those old gas attacks Dead Fred Ferger and Palmer Winston, plus Cousin Palmer Nemmitz (Troy called them The Three Musky Ears, although he liked his cousin) sat down at the next table. Dead Fred told them all how he won World War II and Korea single-handedly, prompting Nemmitz to lean over at a dangerous angle in his chair and whisper to Troy, "Fucking *file* clerk," then lean toward his table with a parting wink. If that wasn't bad enough, Mr. Winston kept giving Debi the eye (Troy remembered what a letch Winston was when he taught at EHS), but Toobie was too loaded to notice him.

When Debi couldn't stand Dead Fred a second longer, she reached into her cavernous purse and extracted a wrapped box the size of a slightly deflated basketball. From the way her wrist strained, Troy figured the box was heavy. (*Why don't you whomp him on the head with it?* he was tempted to suggest.)

Cutting into Dead Fred's monologue, she announced with a shake of her hoop earrings, "Happy birthday, hon!"

Toobie grabbed the box and shook it, rattled it, listened to it. On his way to the men's room, Mr. Winston leaned over to whisper to Troy, "Still the asshole, isn't he?"

When Troy turned back to his brother, Toobie had begun to rip off the paper, revealing the words "SUPER-DUPER CUBE" on the exposed side of the box. With a "*whoop!*" Toobie tore off the wrappings and box in one motion; an ape attacking an orange, only messier. Holding the monster cube in one pizza-stained hand, Toobie leaned over and gave Debi a wet smack on the lips. On his way back to his table, Mr. Winston nudged Troy and murmured, "Widdle boy *likeum* his toy"....

That was what was wrong with this box...it *was* a box, not part of 1984's landfill layer in the dump. Which meant, assuming that the el-cheapo novelty and second-hand store wasn't selling empty boxes, either Debi or Toobie bought a *second* huge cube... but there was only one left in the box. Then it hit Troy.

Toobie had duplicates of *all* his cubes. One to keep in its pristine, unshifted state (a point of reference), the other to twiddle around with and ultimately solve. There was only one cube of each size in the tower of balanced puzzles. Troy tried to remember if there had been two of each size on the shelves behind Toobie's bar, but couldn't. He had seen the contents of those shelves so often over the years that the content of a particular shelf was a blur to him.

Sighing, Troy decided that either Debi didn't bring the spares or Toobie had stashed them somewhere. That was it. For once in his forty years, Toobie Horak cleaned up after himself. (*Too bad he didn't live long enough for it to become a* habit....I *didn't put' em under my bed, Toobie* did.... *I hope something bad happens....*)

Leaning against his couch as he sat on the floor, Troy opened the huge cube box, dumped the mega-cube onto the floor, then balanced the box on his raised knees. The box was laughable; sleazy lettering, crude graphics, wonky orange lettering. He couldn't find the name of the manufacturer, or even where the hunk of multi-colored junk was made, just "Made with Pride by D. Fields & Crew" printed on the bottom (*guys, I wouldn't brag If I were you...*). And a price sticker, from that hole-in-the-wall dump on Wisconsin Street. Their window display of plastic puke, wind-up crawling hands and limp second-hand children's clothing had never lured him into the establishment. The price sticker read "$12.99+tx." *Way* too much.

Troy never saw a cube quite like it in any other Ewerton store, nor during his infrequent trips to Eau Claire or Wausau. Perhaps it was such a low-brow item no self-respecting store *would* stock it. Bored with the carton, Troy tossed it aside and picked up the cube.

Toobie had never let him work (play) with any of his precious cubes; when Troy hefted the thing, he understood why Debi's wrist looked as if it was about to break. The cube was extremely heavy, five pounds or so, which was odd. It was only, after all, made of plastic (*maybe it's SUPER-DUPER PLASTIC*), which usually wasn't *this* dense. Troy's vinyl trash can weighed nothing in comparison.

The cube was also large, six inches long and wide per side. Each individual square was about three-quarters of an inch long and wide, and there were eight rows with eight squares per row to a side.

The last time Troy took a close look at it was at Toobie's birthday party, and the light at the Rusty Hinge was poor (so customers wouldn't notice how dirty the glasses usually were). There, the whole thing had had a vague nicotine tinge. The photographs of the "pictures" on its sides were usually washed out because there was something wrong with the flash on Toobie's (Troy's) camera. In the good white light of his apartment, Troy finally saw that the colors on this cube were unlike those of any other cube in Toobie's collection.

Instead of the usual blue, yellow, white, red-magenta, green and orange combination, it sported off-tinges and strange hues. The white resembled old dentures, the yellow was oleo pale, the orange conch-shell pink-coral, the magenta was the shade of old bloodstains, the green was reminiscent of canned peas, and the blue verged on indigo, with subtle hints of black. Each color was so odd the cube was ludicrous.

Troy got up, eased the knots out of his calves, and took the rice-paper shade off his swag lamp, then held the cube next to the naked bulb. The lines between each square weren't black, but the grey-red shade of well-done steak, oxblood recliners, or the soft pads on Felix's paws. It was soft, and rubbery, he discovered, pressing one line with a thumbnail. The indentation sprang back edema-slow.

He gave the top row a turn to the left, then moved it back in place. The grating—somewhere on the aural pain range between fingernails on slate and teapot whistle—made his teeth ache. *How could you* stand *that, Toobie?* Maybe it loosened with frequent use. But the cheap imitation cubes Toobie had toyed with never stopped making noise (albeit a *softer* sound), no matter how long the Toober fiddled with them. But they hadn't produced that irritating, anguished screech, either.

He stood trying to imagine the effort it took to maneuver the cube into different configurations. At the very least, it must have given Toobie a good wrist work-out. (*The Cube-O-Matic! It dices, it chops, it tones your wrists! Only $12.99 + tx.!*)

Then Troy remembered that he was supposed to call that

vanity press, to cancel Toobie's book. After replacing the shade on the lamp, he gently put the SUPER-DUPER CUBE in its box, then searched for the number Debi left for him.

...would get him. It knew where to bite, oh yes, it knew how to bite him, not fast, but a little here and a little there. Just enough to pinch and hurt. He tried to curl up into a teensie tiny ball, 'cause he was a little boy and could do that. Roll up into a ball, tinier and tinier, until the bad thing couldn't find him...but the bad thing was tiny too. The spot at the bottom of the door, the dark place, *wasn't a spot anymore, but a* hole. *He saw light around the bad thing, as the door shook. The bad thing was chomping away the door, pulling slivers of wood away to make the hole bigger, bigger, and* then....

III. Palmer

"—boom in cube puzzles is over, so I was reluctant to undertake this project. Our function, however, is to provide a means for people to publish whatever they wish, as long as they pay for the finished product. But, Mr. Horak, I had a...*feeling* about this particular endeavor...your brother seemed to think that this book would catapult him into best-seller ranks. I explained that we only print books and provide *suggestions* for marketing them, but—"

"He was stubborn," Troy interjected. (*Tell the man what you mean....Toobie was* dumb, *he thought he* was *a hot-shot writer.*)

"-—is for the best, under the circumstances, that we abort this project. I *am* sorry, though, I'd like to extend my—"

"Uh, thanks. Appreciate it. And...thanks for understanding about Too-Toby. At least he was spared the embarrassment—"

"I understand. He didn't have a firm grasp on the purpose of our services. Most clients are interested in small projects, family reminiscences, poetry collections....I kept trying to explain to him that the marketing possibilities were limited—"

"Uh-Huh. Does he have a deposit coming back? Not to be pushy, but his *wif-widow* would appre—"

"The check will be in the mail. Again, I'm sorry—"

"Yeah, same here."

"Yes. Well, sir, I must be going—"

"Uh, thanks for your help, and goodbye."

Troy didn't notice if the man said goodbye or not. Walking away from the phone, Troy went over to the couch, where the box of pictures Toobie had taken rested. Debi dropped it off this morning, before he was up. It was on the doorstep, next to the morning paper.

The box was from Hush Puppies, wider but not higher than an average shoebox. It was clumsily tied with white string, creating a cross-hatch "cage" for the basset pictured on the lid.

Troy wasn't able to open the cache of photos; they were meant for the book which would never be published. If things had gone differently (*if you made it to Toob's house on time, instead of getting lost in your own damned home town*), that fellow at Jupiter Publishing would be looking over the instant photos, no doubt trying to decide whether to laugh or cry over them. Tugging at the taut string, Troy thought, *Needs a bow....*

Wednesday, December 24, 1958

"And which good little boy is *this* for?" Santa-Dad's beard kept slipping off, and the attached mustache got into his mouth, so his words sounded like, "Anf wh'ch gud wiffle b'h ith *ith* fr?" Dad-Santa didn't have to ask. Little Troy (Mom and Dad said it as one word, *Littletroy*) knew that the odd shaped package wrapped in snowflake pattern paper was for *him*. His microscope, the plastic one with the real lens he had pestered Mom and Dad for after Brucie Sawyer got one for *his* birthday in November.

Ever since the gifts were put out under the tree that morning, Troy had poked and probed the red and white papered gift. The tag said "*To* Troy," so he *knew* he was the "good little boy" Dad mentioned.

The microscope was in Dad's big hand, and Troy's fingers

were touching it, but in the split second before the gift was actually *given* to him, two things happened simultaneously. Toobie, who had opened his gift hand-knitted mittens—gave Mom his "I'm gonna have a shit- fit" look, and Mom silently shook her head, then made a sharp motion with her chin toward Toobie. Suddenly the magical microscope was out of Troy's grasp and up near Santa's eyes. Dad he-he-hoed and said, "Uh, oh, Santa made a *mistake!* This is for a good *big* boy!" and handed Troy's microscope to *Toobie,* whose puffy face under the out-grown crew-cut brightened. Mom let out a sigh of relief, and Dad-Santa gave Troy *another* box, but it only held a knitted muffler. Troy *saw* the tag which said "To Toby" before Mom thought to bend down and snatch it away when she thought Troy wasn't looking.

The microscope was in two useless pieces by evening. That night, after saying his prayers (he accidentally on purpose omitted Mom, Dad and Toobie, and instead asked God to bless Felix the Cat), Troy scrunched up his eyes and imagined a *bad thing* which would *get* Toobie, in his *bed* in the room across the hallway.

It'll be real little, *and* squishy, *like the crud Mom cleans out of the drain in the sink,* Littletroy assured himself in the cold darkness, and pulled his quilts and sheet up under his chin in delicious fright. *It'll have real* big *teeth, extra super big like* Grandpa's choppers. *It'll chew on Toobie from the toes on up, and spend a lot of time doing it, too, so he cries and cries, only I'll plug up my ears* (his fingers slid out from under the safety of the covers to poke into his small ears) *and stay in bed while it* gets *him. When it's done he's gonna make peepee in his p.j.'s and* croak. *When Mom and Dad wake up they won't know what happened to their "good big boy," 'cause the bad thing will hide and they won't find it 'cause it's little enough to hide* real *good.* Comforted by that reassuring thought, Littletroy drifted off to sleep...but the only bad thing there was come the next day was that Toobie was OK. Troy let his second beer slide down his throat without tasting it. Palmer was on his first can of Old Style, nursing the brew carefully because Bitsy wouldn't like it if he came home loaded before lunch. Troy was grateful that he had been able to find the old man; usually Cousin Palmer was with his cronies and couldn't be bothered.

They sat at one of the walled-in back booths in the Rusty Hinge. The Hush Puppy box was open; he and Palmer were looking at the rubber-banded piles of instant snapshots inside. They didn't bother to look at the ones under the first of the six photos in each set—the ones Toobie took of the other sides of each cube for reference after he came up with a pleasing design on the front—and worked quickly through the ones taken of the smaller cubes. With only nine or sixteen squares per side, it wasn't easy to come up with anything but geometries, so they only slowed down when they reached the SUPER-DUPER CUBE photos. Even Palmer admitted that those were interesting.

"Looks like what that robot Yul Brynner played in *Westworld* saw through his new eyes...everything all chopped up in bits and pieces," Palmer noted. Troy almost choked on his beer, thinking, *Geeze, even old Yul's gone now...oh shit, did I ever return that damned tape to Lenny?*

In the murky bar light, the over-exposed pictures looked professional: here a coral and bloody sky with a black bird flapping in the corner, there a green and yellow fish, and wasn't that a clown face?

"Nah, looks like a late-show monster. Ever see a clown with green lips?" Palmer burped lightly, excused himself, then asked, "What's under your skin? Blame yourself for Toby? When a man wants to go, there's no stopping him.... Didn't Stu tell you, when someone wants to...he acts as if he hasn't a care in the—"

"Toobie didn't tear his own throat out. I knew him. He didn't want to die...if he *did,* he would've put his toe in the trigger. Something *fast.* Not *that* way." Troy took a swig of the third can of beer which sat on the table. After wiping his mouth, he asked his elderly cousin, "Did Stu or Lenny or those boobs on the ambulance crew say anything about...that night? Aside from how he looked?"

"Mean 'I never saw nothing like it'? Lenny's god-damned broken record. I heard what everyone else 'round town heard. No use going into *that* can o' worms." As he folded his arthritic hands before him, his green eyes pinned Troy down like a moth on cardboard. Unable to avoid his eyes, Troy said, "There was a hole. Bottom of the hall closet door. That's how I found him, I *told* Stu but he didn't attach any significance to it, said the hole was there since kingdom come. 'Willow Hill's near the woods, small animals get in every house that way—'"

"Yeah, Bitsy's Angie and her family find critters all the time. Don't do any damage, used to shoo 'em out, before they bought that ultrasonic gizmo—"

"Toobie and Debi never had rodent problems."

"You ask Debi about the hole? Maybe *he* put it there...closets can mold up something awful 'less you have good ventilation. Bitsy's boots and my dress shoes turned green last winter, I had to put wooden blocks on the bottom of the closet and—"

"Can you ever remember Toobie doing anything he was *supposed* to do?" Troy looked through the pictures again; a red stick man on a green and yellow field, a green eye with a blue-black pupil, and a red and coral butterfly with a green square on each wing.

"Like sawing the two-by-fours in my basement? I could've killed the little brat on the spot, but your ma says, 'Oh *Palmer,* he's *expressing* himself, leave my baby *alone.*'"

"Jeezus-kee-rist! Is this what I think it is?" Troy held out the offending print of a skull-shaped whitish image against the blackish background as if it was swarming with stinging ants.

"Uh-Huh...rather prophetic—oh, sorry—"

"All right. That's why I called. I figured we could talk about this, that you'd understand."

Troy remembered how his cousin used to enjoy shows like *Thriller, The Twilight Zone,* and *Alfred Hitchcock Presents* (shows Mom never let Troy or Toobie watch). Sometimes when the Horaks visited the Nemmitzes and stayed until late at night, Palmer would excuse himself to go watch his programs.

Eventually Troy would drift over to him as Rod Serling invited them to travel to "another dimension"...most memorably, where a farm woman battled tiny, ray-gun toting aliens. Troy had to go to the bathroom, but he *couldn't* miss what happened to the lady in the farmhouse, so he stayed on the floor at Palmer's feet. Finally, the woman climbed to her roof after battling what seemed like dozens of puffy little men (Palmer assured Troy that there were only two of them, but Troy wasn't so *sure...*), and found a small white saucer. She hacked at it with an ax until a *voice* came out of it. Troy had to hold on with all his might to not wet his pants; he thought more creatures were going to come out and attack the woman, then—the voice said to go back, that the place wasn't safe...as the camera showed that the saucer was one of *ours.*

Troy let it go, his dark corduroy pants hid the wetness. It was so *unfair—our* guys were the *bad* guys! When he started to blubber, Palmer patted his shoulder, explained that the little men were scared, and didn't mean to hurt the woman. But Troy saw the big blisters on her hands, and heard her cries of pain; he knew that *she* didn't know they were our guys.

But for the most part, Palmer had *understood* things that Mom, Dad or Toobie only laughed at; in later years, after the good scary programs went off the air, he and Palmer would play the "Remember when the—" or "Did you see the one where—" game while Bitsy and Troy's folks played Uno or Scrabble in the kitchen.

That was why he had called Palmer, asked him to help him sort through Toobie's pictures (*if any bad thing was waiting me in there, I'd be safe*).

Troy knew he could tell the old man his half-formed suspicions and fears about Toobie (*It'll be real* little, *and* squishy...*the bad thing will hide and they won't find it...oh god, did it finally get you, Toob, after all these years?* Did *my wish come true?*), that Palmer wouldn't laugh when the little kid in Troy came out for a little while. Palmer wouldn't mind if Littletroy did something stupid, weak or yellow (*I'll stay in bed while it gets him*).

Troy counted on Palmer to say the right thing to that scaredy-pants kid before he hid again behind the walls of adulthood.

Yet, as much as he trusted Palmer, Troy wasn't sure if even *he'd* understand about the *bad thing*, the childish weapon Littletroy had fashioned, ready to sic on anyone who hurt him. Troy didn't understand it himself; he had never thought of it as magical, he didn't *really* believe in it—it never gave him nightmares or delusions come morning—yet. it never really *left* his mind, either. Like an appendix, it rested unused in his subconscious, until mental appendicitis set in, and there was no way to operate....

Chugging down his last beer, Troy told Palmer about Christmas eve of 1958, segued into the rock incident, and hit the high points of the Inez-Debi business. Palmer had been there before Dad's funeral, so he left that out. As Troy talked, the old man's gaze never left his face...until the part where he mentioned Toobie's bare feet against the closet door. Only then did Palmer avert his eyes for a second, before returning them to Troy's face. When Troy ended with his discovery of the boxed SUPER-DUPER CUBE, Palmer slowly nodded his head and upper body back and forth, as if to collect his thoughts. Finally, he spoke. in a tone which reassured Troy, let him know that his story *was* believed:

"First off, Stu Sawyer and Lenny Wilkes' brains would fit in a Cheerio and still leave room enough for an ant to use it as a hulahoop. Out here, imagination and belief in what you don't *know* aren't *appreciated.* You yourself had to leave town to get an education before anyone took note of you.

"Look at Toby. Didn't matter that he was a horse's behind. He was born and raised here, and related to half the town. Didn't make waves, just fit in.... His death couldn't be any different. What you think happened to him would mean *work* for the cops, the docs out here. *They* don't want folks knowing that they're just as stupid as the rest of us. So, Wayne Mesabi thinks he saw something "like" what happened to Toobie in Vietnam, presto, everyone dubs it a suicide. Not to doubt Wayne—although Lord knows, the man has mashed potatoes for brains—most likely he *did* see neck wounds, maybe even self-inflicted, like that in 'Nam. But never mind. He gave Stu and Lenny and all the rest an *out*, a way to make something strange all neat and tidy in a wooden box. I'm not suggesting it was negligence on their part, you said yourself the house was locked.

"Stu *did* check over the place when you left, told me so himself, so don't worry that we taxpayers are giving him a salary for *absolutely* nothing. Stu was satisfied that there was no foul play, least not the kind of foul play *he's* worried about. No psychos with sharp fingernails pushing grown men into closets and...you know. Far as Stu's concerned, his town and county are safe.

"Doesn't help Toby, but no loss, he was the town dumb-shit anyhow—don't give *me* that look, you said it yourself about him—so life goes on. No one pays attention to a chewed-out hole in the closet door because Toby *might've* done it himself. Even if Toby didn't, he isn't about to walk in here to contradict me, is he?"

"O.K., what *happened* to him? You watched all the scary stuff on TV, you're the expert—"

Palmer leaned across the scattered photos and cans of beer on the table, so close that his leaf-green eyes were inches from Troy's blue ones. His stiff grey hair touched Troy's sandy thatch as he said in a low voice, "Did your mother ever let you boys watch *Get Smart*? Good. Remember how every time Agent 86 was scared, or in a jam he'd protest, 'But the *golliwogs* will get me'? And the golliwogs never showed up, so you had to imagine them—"

Troy, hurt by the old man's levity, felt betrayed. "Are you suggesting that *the...golliwogs* killed him?"

What Palmer replied convinced Troy that his cousin *did* believe, and believe strongly, in the sincerity of Troy's account.

"No, Troy, not golliwogs, Something that makes the golliwogs seem—" he paused, with respectful awe, "—*nice*."

It wasn't until an hour later, while nursing a fresh beer in the back booth after Bitsy called the Rusty Hinge a second time and *insisted* that Palmer come home before she sent Stu out looking for him (Palmer patted Troy on the shoulder before he took off, saying, "You take *care,* hear, kid?"), that Troy realized that there was no way he could figure out which picture was the *last* photo Toobie took of the huge cube. He did feel better—albeit somewhat foolish—after telling Palmer what was on his mind, but still felt no closer to whatever it was that Toobie wanted him to see that night.

Troy fanned all the cube photos out in front of him (he removed the snaps of the other five sides of each cube) and tried to guess which one might have been spectacular enough to warrant his immediate attention, but all he could see was the utter waste of hundreds of dollars worth of instant film....

Sipping his beer, Troy figured that Toobie's waste of good money was par for the course. He remembered all the brittle, tasteless pieces of baseball-card bubblegum he chewed after Toobie cleaned out the shelves of the grocery stores (and incurred the wrath of the younger boys in town), then tossed the gum aside while he pored over his collection of cards. Troy recalled the cover prices of all those crossword puzzle books (*I got ten bucks; or the dictionary—used*); only the rock collection didn't cost Toobie anything, save for the rock collecting books he swiped from the Public Library. They sent the overdue notice to Mom, because Toobie took the books out in her name, and *she* paid for them, or something. But, come to think of it, that particular "hobby horse" of Toobie's wasn't without *cost....*

Thursday, July 21, 1961

It was the first day of the Ewerton Water Carnival, but Troy was hunkered down on his knees, rear end resting against the worn heels of his Keds, on the greasy garage floor, watching Toobie use Dad's carpenter's mallet to whack the big rock poised on the chopping block. Troy knew it wouldn't *work*; stones were harder than wood, rocks beat *everything* in fisties, but Toobie persisted, pounding the hunk of quartz with feverish abandon. Beads of perspiration coated Toobie's bloated sun-burned face, and moisture glistened in his summer bald cut.

Troy wondered why Toobie didn't take the ax; metal was harder than stone. Then Troy remembered, Dad used a chisel or wedge while using the mallet, but he debated whether or not to tell Toobie. If he didn't, Dad's mallet would be sawdust by the end of the hour. If he did, Toobie was bound to get mad at Troy for being smarter than him....Troy wanted to go to the Carnival, but Mom said that he had to go *with* Toobie.

So there Troy sat, legs cramping up (he was afraid to stand up while Toobie was swinging the mallet—suppose he cuffed Troy with it on the backswing?), watching his brother's useless efforts. Toobie picked *today* to whack at his stones (he saw pictures of the way rocks looked on the *inside*, after they were cut open and polished on professional equipment, and wanted to duplicate the results on his own...with no equipment and no idea of how to go about doing it) because Mom and Dad were out of town. So, Troy was *stuck*. If he went to the Carnival alone, someone was *bound* to tell Mom or Dad about it (you couldn't sneeze in Ewerton without everyone saying "God Bless you"), but if he stayed with Toobie, he'd be here until Mom and Dad came back...*tonight*.

Finally, Troy knew how to tell Toobie to try a wedge without *telling* him. Walking stiffly on cramped legs, he found the wedge on Dad's workbench. Troy pretended to pound it into a crack in the cement, using his curled fist as a mallet. After ten minutes, Toobie noticed what Troy was doing.

"Gimmie that."

"What?" Troy kept whacking the wedge. Toobie was sweating so much Troy smelled him over the gas and oil scent of the garage. "The thingamajig. I want it."

Knowing that he'd never get a "please" out of Toobie, Troy handed up the wedge. Things went faster after that; Toobie held the wedge over each rock with his left hand and swung the mallet against it with his right. One by one the rocks shattered; soon he had a pile of broken pieces, which were tiny versions of the big rocks. Whatever secrets Toobie expected to find inside (all pre-polished and shining) weren't there. Peering at each bit of rock in the warm, musty dimness of the garage, Toobie said, "Gimmie a cardboard box."

Thinking that his confinement was about to end, Troy hurried off to find one for Toobie, who sat next to the chopping block and stared in gape-mouthed disappointment at the unyielding chips. Troy found a box at the back of the garage (it was old, frazzled, but the only one he could reach) and brought it over to Toobie. He told Troy, "Put 'em in there," while he whacked a few of the bigger fragments into smaller fragments, which looked just like....

It took Troy *forever* to pick up the little pieces, as Toobie made *more* little pieces for him to pick up. Troy's Mickey-Mouse watch said it was past *lunch-time* now. Finally, Toobie demolished what he was going to demolish, stood up, dusted off his shorts, and announced, "I gotta shower. I stink. You take this in the house."

He took off, leaving Troy to cry silently as he tried to decide which would be easier—bring the heavy box into the house in one back-breaking trip, or carry handfuls of stones to the porch and fill the box up there? If he tried to carry the stones in the box it might break, and *then* he'd have to pick them out from in-between the blades of grass....

As Toobie entered the screened-in back porch, Troy yelled, "Hey, Toobie, when we going to the *Carnival*? Mom says I gotta go with you."

"She did?" *(You were sitting at the table when she said so—).* Fighting back tears, Troy said, "Mom said I could go if you—"

"I don't got no money, how can I go?"

Swallowing back the snot welled up in his nose, blinking back tears which burned his eyes, Troy said, "I got money...we can go halfsies—"

Toobie grinned. "Yeah!" He shouted, then ran in the house. Troy rubbed his eyes with a rock-dust coated fist, and his eyes stung more. Sighing, he scooped up handfuls of broken stones (he knew, he just *knew* that Toobie wouldn't bother with them again, Toobie had sucked them dry as dust, had leeched the last bit of interest from them) and began his first trip to the porch. *I hope the bad thing wiggles through the shower head Toobie... hope it eats out ears and nose and keeps on chewing on the way down....*

Troy turned the car from Aspen Drive to Corduroy Drive. The huge cube was on the passenger seat, belted in like a child. The box of pictures was at home; they *were* unimportant. What Troy was hoping against hope to find had something to do with the *cubes,* not pictures of them.

It came to him as he sat in the Rusty Hinge; one second he was reliving yet another bad home movie of the mind, and the next he was scooping up handfuls of instant photos and throwing them haphazardly into the Hush Puppy box, prior to bolting the bar.

Pieces. Bits. Odd-shaped fragments of oxblood plastic in the bottom of the Toober's behind-the-bar wastepaper basket. At the time, they had looked familiar, yet unfamiliar, too. Now, Troy knew what they were, and he could almost guess what it was Toobie had wanted him to see. Finally tired of his cubes, perhaps realizing that his book wouldn't be a best-seller, Toobie did a number on them. Took them apart, sucked the last drop of belated enjoyment out of them prior to chucking them. That explained the missing duplicate cubes. Using some tool, Toobie pried them open, exposed the unique mechanism which made the cubes work, leeched out the last iota of mystery, and then... what? Had Toobie deemed them so unique that Troy had to look at them before Debi came home?

It would have been more sensible to throw the pieces in a box and bring them over to Troy—so he could have the fun of disposing of them—unless (*"this ain't gonna wait. You* gotta come...now") there was some reason Toobie *couldn't* come over. Maybe whatever made this cube (the rest weren't oxblood colored) *go* inside was *of an impermanent nature*?

With trembling hands, Troy had picked up the cube (*why* is *it so damned heavy?*) and brought it outside. Before visiting Debi, Troy made another trip, to that novelty-cum-basement sale store where the cubes came from.

He hoped no one he knew saw him go in. The place was dimly lit inside; the lone window in the half building was partly obscured by paper Halloween cut-outs, and crudely lettered "SALE" and "2-4-Won" signs. The tall drink of water who ran the place was haggling with a would-be customer-seller (the place bought used clothing). He told the woman, "This isn't bad...no lariats or cactus on it, I hate patterned Western shirts. Take a buck?" Money changed hands, and the woman left, leaving Troy alone with the man in the store.

"Did you sell this cube?" The man (dirty thinning no-color hair fell down over dandruff-speckled glasses) took his sweet time looking over the cube, as if he never saw it before, despite his store's tag on the box. In a nasal, know-it-all voice he said, "Yeah, we used to carry this. Only sold a couple. Woman bought one, fat guy got the other. Sent the rest of 'em back." The man (an out-of-towner, Troy suspected, everyone and their second cousin knew *Toobie*) peeled something orange and scabrous off of his sweater, flicking off the matter like a scab. Finally, he realized that Troy still stood there, cube held in outstretched hand, and continued, "Company that went bust a year ago sent 'em along with a shipment of fly ice cubes and dribble glasses. Only sold two of eight. People'd pick 'em up, put 'em right back. Too heavy. Even if they gave 'em a second look, they'd put 'em back in the box. Said the colors were off."

"Where was this company based?"

"Indiana. I think. They didn't manufacture, they sent out stuff from elsewhere. Maybe my old lady remembers." The man headed for the back room, which was curtained off with a Mexican blanket. He emerged with a woman who was a good foot shorter than himself, with bleached blonde hair framing a hard-planed dark face....

Recognition flashed in Inez's sharp eyes as she squeaked, "I dunno where that shit come from. It ain't important." The man leaned over, whispered, "He wants to *know,* can't you try—" but she shook her bleached head (she had rubbed the blue off one eyelid, giving her face a lop-sided appearance), saying, "I ain't gonna look it up, neither." Sensing that even if he did find out where in Indiana the cubes were sent from, it wouldn't help him, the frustration of the past few days welled up inside Troy. He decided to give Inez a last shot. For Mom...and for Debi, his lost Debi of the flicking pom-poms....

Heading for the door, Troy said over his shoulder, "How *did* you break the sink off the wall in the jail in '70? Stu Sawyer never did figure out how you did it," then closed the door behind him. He faintly heard the man ask Inez what *that* was about, and heard her shrill back "None of your goddamned business!" With a slight smile, Troy got into the car, and revved the motor.

Debi rubbed her eyes—Troy thought of Inez's one bare eyelid and wondered when *she* blew into town again—then explained that she just couldn't sleep nights. Toobie's snoring kept her awake. "But you know how *he* is. If I roll him over he starts in worse." She winked at Troy, and he wanted to dry heave.

Realizing that this would be more difficult than he imagined it would be, he said, "Debi, I want to know something—it may sound silly, but remember how Toobie had—has extra cubes in his collection, duplicates?" He stood in the middle of the oval rug, holding the SUPER-DUPER CUBE in his arms like a baby, sweating inside his parka. It was still barefootin' warm in there. Debi wore footie socks with pink pom-poms on the heels.

She looked puzzled for a second, as if asked to answer the Riddle of the Sphinx while suffering from a hang-over. Then her lips pursed. "Oh...the *extras.* He tore them apart. Started in late September. Broke the handle on his yellow screwdriver...

set's incomplete now...." her voice trailed off, as she watched the silent, flickering TV.

"Did he take them all apart at once?"

A shake of her drooping curls, then, "He took his sweeeet time, started with the little—" (she made it sound like "liddle") "—gumball one. Popped it with a nailfile." She rubbed her red eyes and droned on, "Then he attacked the rest. Some took two nights. Bang. Bang. Bang, with the hammer. Had to get out of the house, escape the racket. *Bang.* Was working up to the big cube. Like this one—" she tapped the cube in Troy's arms with a hand that sported only two fake nails. Sweater fuzz clung to the adhesive patches on the other fingers. Unconsciously backing away, Troy asked, "Did—does Toobie still have the pieces?"

Debi nodded, and pointed a fuzzy fingertip at the hallway, crooked the finger to the left, toward the spare bedroom.

"Innare," she mumbled, "Unner the bed. Inna box." She looked ready to doze off on her feet. Troy guided her to the couch, and covered her with an afghan. Leaving the cube on the coffee table, Troy went into the room (it smelled of Bounce and mothballs) and knelt down next to the bed before lifting up the edge of the bedspread. "I *told you about putting* junk *under your bed, but did you* listen—"

The box was there, among the dust kitties; some of them clung to his sleeve when he pulled the box out. It was full of broken multi-colored plastic, a puzzle even Rubick couldn't solve. Only the two halves of the Boob Cube were recognizable. But all the parts were edged in black, or had black backs...no oxblood, no squares of off-colors.

Shoving the box back under the bed, Troy dusted himself off, then quietly walked back into the living room. Debi's mouth was open; her tongue shifted to one side of her lower jaw. The loose, fluttery noises were similar to those Toobie used to make, when he was a kid. (...*and* I'll *stay in bed while it* gets *him*).

Moving quietly, Troy went behind the bar and looked in the trash basket. The Walter's cans had a patina of mold along the tops, the peanut shells were soggy brown—and there was a scattering of oxblood plastic at the bottom. As Troy moved the basket out for a better look, he saw shards of glass, kicked under the bar. Part of a short bar glass. He lifted up Toobie's thongs, to look at the soles—tiny sparkling fragments winked at him in the ivory light. So, therefore—

Toobie tore his mega-cube apart, after days of trying. Finally, it gave, fell apart. Toobie found something of interest *inside* the cube (a mechanism? A battery? A *different* way of making the cube move?), and set it under or in a glass for safe-keeping, then called Troy, asked him to come by, see whatever it was. Next, the glass tipped over, or *something*. Toobie swept the remains on the floor, kicked it under the counter, took his feet out of his thongs...then, what?

What, indeed? Feeling sick, Troy wondered how a broken glass started a chain of events that culminated in Toobie winding up in a closet with a hole in the door, his throat clawed (*chewed*?) open, letting out a gusher of rich magenta blood....

Deciding that Debi wouldn't miss the wastebasket, Troy picked it up, took the cube off the table, and left the house, carefully locking the door behind him. Deciding that he'd have to get someone to go look in on her, Troy put his things in the car, and drove home.

IV. The Bad Thing

...it would come into *his closet,* in *there with him, and there would be no place to hide from the bad thing. No one to help him, no one to hear his cries and whimpers. The bad thing would get him,* eat *him, and no one would hear, they'd all have their fingers stuck in their ears, like...like...LIKE HE DID, when he created and sicced the bad thing on Toobie....*

Before Troy brought the basket or the cube into his house, Troy went in, scooped up Felix (he left a musky smelling indentation in the big throw pillow by the register), gave the fat grey tom a kiss on the head, and carried him next-door to Mrs. Armbruster, the old woman who owned Felix's litter mate. Troy told the elderly widow that he'd be leaving home for a couple of days, and wanted Felix someplace safe. She was delighted. "I'll take Felix anytime, Smokey enjoys seeing his brother, don't you Smokey-kitty?" (Smokey, who sat licking his paws, was non-committal.)

As he walked back to his house, Troy thought, *Just don't want him distracting me, that's all.* But when he saw the fuzzy Felix indentation on the pillow, his eyes watered. (*Only want you safe, boy...if the bad thing comes back, it won't mess with my Felix.*)

Not that he'd let any bad thing get past *him.*

Four torn fingernails (Troy didn't have much nail to tear) and three grazed knuckles later, he put down his screwdriver and sat staring at the unblemished SUPER-DUPER CUBE. It defied him with its wholeness under the pitiless glare of the white light bulb. (*Easy, Troy, must've taken Toobie days to figure it out... you could out-think him when you were ten years old.*)

After Troy fiddled for two hours with it, the rows were all mixed up, a muddy blend of alternately faded and too intense colors. Troy decided to take a look at the pieces Toobie had pried apart, to see if he could figure out how Toobie did it. Troy put aside the slimy beer cans, picked around the shells, feeling for plastic fragments. Soon, he had a pile of them on the coffee table. Pushing aside the whole cube, he tried to re-assemble the dissected parts.

But something was wrong with the scattering of pieces.

All the fronts of the individual squares were there; he made six neat piles of them on the table. Odd-shaped linking bits of plastic were there too, the parts which made the puzzle work... but something didn't add up. The individual segments *didn't weigh enough,* Troy checked; he slid a piece of the *Ewerton Herald* under them, and after twisting the paper into a hobo's sack, he set the parts-laden newsprint on the bathroom scale. A bit over two pounds. Heavy, but the plastic was dense, and there were many pieces.... The *whole* cube which he put on the scale weighed *four and a half pounds.*

Troy carried the complete and disassembled cubes into the living room, trying to reassure himself. *Maybe it's filled with a lubricant, inert materials...isn't* everything *composed of 90% inert material...plastic worms, fiberfill...blood?*

His hands shook when he picked up the big cube, but told himself that there was a *logical* reason why it was so heavy. Maybe (*oh please*) that's why Toobie called him. To tell Troy that the cube was filled with lots and lots of inert materials... something which disappeared by the time Troy showed up at Toobie's house. A liquid that sank into the carpet. or something sharp that was kicked under the bar with the broken glass. (*Sure...Toobie was so upset about breaking a glass he crawled in a closet and chewed his own throat open—like* fun....)

The broken puzzle, still in its wrapping of paper, mocked him, as if to say "here's the answer...*you* supply the question." Troy had questions, but he doubted they were the *right* ones. Obviously, trying to break the intact cube wasn't going to work, he had to—wait a second! Troy sat, cross-legged and dumbfounded, on the floor, replaying the scene in Toobie's living room. The quiet. The bar. The bare bar counter. If Toobie got into the cube, he must have used his bare hands. There were no tools lying about...and he doubted that Toobie had cleaned up just for his brother.

Troy picked up all of the pieces in turn, to study them under the white light. Aside from a few minor gouges, the pieces were unblemished. The parts he saw in the spare bedroom had the colored decals ripped off, some parts were sharply broken...but these pieces were smooth, soft, with no jagged edges. As if, given a century of time and a saint's patience, it could be reassembled. Troy tried...tried to pull a decal off one of the squares... and found that it was molded *into* the backing. Not inlaid, but a part of the square itself, with no bleeding of the color-edges.

But, holding the piece up near his eye (*the microscope was mine, the tag said so!*), a wave of repulsion rippled through him when he saw that the color itself, while appearing as smooth as a fake fingernail, had a faint *ridged* pattern, like real fingernails. Troy dropped the piece of plastic on his coffee table; it landed with the muted *thunk* of a finger tapping wood.

Shaking, Troy picked up the cube he once thought looked so *funny,* and turned rows at random. The sound changed subtly; the screeching wail grew deep, throaty, like someone trying to clear phlegm from his throat but not succeeding in swallowing the gunk down (*...and* squishy, *like that crud Mom cleans out of the drain…*).

With each turn of the cube, Troy tried to look between the moving rows; he saw nothing but solid oxblood softness. The cube sounded like a small animal caught in a trap; Troy was glad that Felix was with his brother Smokey next door. Poor Felix would go wild if he heard that.

Troy kept turning it, as if he did it enough, the cube might fall apart of its own volition. With each twist, he looked at all sides of the cube. The "pictures" Toobie had photographed came and went, as the room grew dark around the pool of light from the lamp.

While Troy aimlessly worked the cube, his eyes drifted over to the demolished cube. He wondered if something that could fit in there might fit in one of Toobie's bar glasses.

Suddenly, he felt a slight *nip,* a minute yet deep *pinch.* His left pinkie was bleeding...and a rice-sized bit of flesh was *gone.* Sucking his hurt finger, Troy dropped the cube—which revealed a scene on the bottom he had never seen before...one that was *worse* than the skull picture.

Three black squares in each corner framed cut-artery lips, glossy coral gums and *teeth* surrounding a black maw, *into* which a drop of fresh blood dribbled, then dribbled *out,* across the bottom line of teeth, over the gum line, and onto the lower lip, where it hung like a dewdrop.

In the strong light, Troy saw that the lips were *textured,* with thin vertical fissures, the way his own lips might chap in the cold…. Then he was on his feet, backing away from the thing on the floor. Part of him wanted to cover his eyes, turn his head, run from the room—but he watched the thing anyway, the *change*, the special thing Toobie *must* have wanted him to see that night.

It was a process which defied the narrow boundary between the beautiful and the grotesque. The cube gave a shudder, as if exposed to sudden biting cold. Some of the squares of muddy color went *in*, while others folded over or under each other; the cube was a soft, fluid thing, shuddering and contracting. The black maw sucked into darkness, lubricating from within by a substance that alternately repelled and gathered in the light. Troy pressed against the wall leading into the hallway, bleeding finger stuck in his mouth, thinking, *That's what couldn't wait. Toobie, you* ass, *you thought this was part of it. Something special that happened when you made the right picture appear on the cube...that's what you did before you called, you found its mouth, only were too dumb to know...or be* scared.

The cube gave a final shake, like the last shudder of the butterfly in the pupa before it freed itself from its tiny home. Then the cube was a cube no more, just a shucked pile of dead pieces.

Troy's thoughts were frantic, jumbled. *This is when he oh god no put the glass on, trapped it...oh no*, no, *get a glass, kill* it...slime, crud, *in a* drain...*oh no, please,* noooooa—

He ran away from the long *squishy* uncoiling thing that was once twisted and entwined between and through its protective shell...the covering which mimicked a cube, which it no longer needed. The carpet was soft enough for the tenderest of creatures.

Troy ran to the front door; in his panic he forgot about having to twist the small button set in the center of the knob, so the door wouldn't open. Panting, he whipped the throw off the couch and threw it on the bad thing, the formerly hidden thing, but that made it worse, made it *mad,* real mad at Troy. It used its teeth, needle thin in the yawning maw that should have been a face, but wasn't. When it worked free of the cover (*it* chews, *it ate*

Toobie, went right for the throat! It chews!), it slurphumped and slither-slid across the floor. Its thin gooey skin shone and didn't shine in the light.

Troy did a crazy darting and tripping dance on the carpet. *The bad thing.... I made it real...it waited and waited to get Toobie, it couldn't hide in the rocks, and it didn't fit in the spines of the books, and the baseball cards were too thin, but there was room in a cube, wasn't there? In the real big cube...the bad thing slithered around, looking for Toobie, and it picked the silliest place to hide, 'cause Toobie liked silly things, and no one suspected it and it hid real good after it got him.*

Troy darted around, dodging the slimy thing with the mouth-maw of sharp and *thin-pointy-hard* teeth, and the peed-his-pants boy inside Troy cried out, *Toobie, you big, stoooooopid lug you couldn't leave it alone, couldn't let it be, you had to rip it apart, open it up, make it real mad at you, like I was real mad so great big MAD at you, but I was only kiddin' 'bout the bad thing. I was only playin' a game in my head. I was so mad at you even if you couldn't help it you were so slow in the head, and I was mad at mom and dad but they were too big to get, not like you...oh, please, Toobie, don't let it eat me, don't let it get me too, I don't have nobody to help me, no mom, no dad, no Debi, nobody...like the lady on the TV with the little men, but the bad thing has teeth—it's not fair!*

No matter where Troy went, the bad thing, the thing Troy knew was *his* bad thing, the Toobie punishing and killing *bad thing* slumped after him, not satisfied with only a dribble of blood and a scrape of flesh (Troy saw his skin under it, under the goo—), smellsensing even more blood.

He tried to get into the bedroom, the bathroom, but it was too fast; it slip-slapped behind him, lapped at his heels....What *should* have been its eyes followed his every move. Troy bit down on the fingertip in his mouth, until his teeth drew blood mixed with thick spittle. He spit out the globby mess; the bad thing took off after it.

Troy slipped away from the thing, into a safe, dark place

where he could hide *real* good. Littletroy was pleased with the hiding place; it was cozy and tight, between the fuzzy cardboard box and the bowling ball. and there was a door to shut and wedge closed with his feet...as the bad thing outside slurped up its bloody tidbit before casting about for more....

...and it found Toobie at last, long after it was sent on its midnight mission on a shivery-cold Christmas eve. After years and years it found a way to find old dumb Toobie and get *him, oh get him so good, just like Littletroy wanted it to. It found a way to hide before and after it got him, but no one told it to* leave *after it got Toobie. It was* still *hungry.... Littletroy curled until the cramps came, until he was wedged as tightly in the closet as it had been coiled inside its camouflage, its Toobie-bait, waiting, enduring pain and friction, waiting for the one picture, the opening. Just as it did the second time, in the other cube after Toobie* croaked. *Toobie was only the start, 'cause it was still hungry. Just like Littletroy had been so mad on that dark, miserable December night, and Littletroy held his bleeding finger against his lips, 'cause only* sissies *cry. In darkness, the door shook and rattled. He saw the glistening curved needle teeth glint in the light from the hallway. Littletroy thought: rocks don't hurtcha, but you were so mean and so dumb I hated you* so much *I wanted to make you hurt like you hurt me, you always hurt* so bad, *Toobie, but the bad thing got you, yes it did, 'cause you* never stopped *being so* mean *and* dumb, *you made mom and dad hate me, I didn't put rocks unner my bed and I had a* nice girl, *but mom took her away 'cause you* needed *a nice girl—I hate you,* hate you, *I made the bad thing come so it could take you away...only its chasing me now, like them puffy men chased the lady in the cabin and... (...Littletroy remembered Palmer as he whispered that the little spacemen were* scared, *that's all; they just didn't* know, *that's all. They didn't expect the woman to be so big, they didn't mean to hurt her, just* scare *her a little...they were sent into big, dark space by someone else, and didn't* understand *how scary they'd look to*

the big woman. "*And people do the wrong thing, sometimes, when they're scared. Even if you know better, they do stupid things anyhow...see, Troy, the lady's OK., isn't she? The little guys were the ones who died. So don't cry for the big lady, 'kay, kiddo?*")

...and in the dark closet, Littletroy whispered, "I'm sorry, bad thing.... I didn't know you'd be so small and big Toobie would scare you, make you act funny...he used to scare *me*, too...I don't need you no more, bad thing, go way, 'kay? 'cause if you bite me, I'll *getcha*, like the little men in the round ship"—*Littletroy's hand reflexively sought out the bowling ball at his side, slipped through the unzipped mouth until his fingers slid into the twin orifices, lifted the heavy ball*—"I don't got no ax, but I got this so you better go way, *now...I* don't need you no more, bad thing, you were bad, but only 'cause I made you bad.... I was bad, so go 'way!"

Littletroy kicked the shaking door for emphasis, until the pounding of his feet was the only thing making the door move... and deep inside, in the place where Littletroy had lived, coiled inside of Bigtroy for so many years, Litlletroy pee-peed his pants and croaked *when the bad thing wormed its way inside and took him away with it....*

V. Troy

Avoiding his hurt finger, Troy picked up the pieces of the broken cubes, added them to the box of cubes, cube-books, Toobie-toys and unused memo pads. He dragged the overflowing box out to the curb, for garbage pick-up come morning.

He started to dial Mrs. Armbruster's number, to ask if he could drop over and pick up Felix, until he remembered the movie under the VCR stand. Gently putting down the receiver, Troy scooped up the boxed film and shoved it into his jacket pocket. He'd drive over to Lenny's place before it closed and drop off the film before he headed north.

To pick up Debi, and bring her home. She didn't need to

hear Toobie snore another night. Toobie had just caused his last sleepless night, for both of them.

The bad thing had taken Toobie away for good.

STREET COFFINS
with JOHN S. POSTOVIT

"I SAW YOUR KEY CHAIN's Daddy out by the Umbert house," Terri said with breathless nonchalance when she came back from her morning jog (very *early* morning jog, something Irene herself could manage only in a zombie-like lurch at that hour), and began peeling off her terry wrist bands and ragged Philadelphia Eagles grey sweatshirt.

At first, Irene thought that she'd been half-dreaming when she heard Terri's remark, but she was unable to drop her head back into the scrunched up pillow and try to catch another half hour or so of sleep (I *only* thought *she said that*—), not without hauling herself up on her elbow and asking through a mouthful of fuzzy teeth and stale saliva, "You saw my keychain's *what*?"

"Daddy." Terri had moved into the bathroom, a trail of discarded running togs following her like forlorn puppies. Irene flopped down onto her hide-a-bed, the iron bar digging into her back through the thin foam mattress and added foam pad. The bar was hard and unyielding, not unlike the casually uttered word her roommate half-shouted from the bathroom...and soon both the iron rod and the single word niggled Irene's peace of mind.

Shifting to a sitting position, her feet searching out her pink quilted flannel slippers (mukluks Terri called them, but Terri padded around barefoot, picking up hair, and dirt and who knew wha*t* on her soles) then got into her clean bed that way). Irene ran her fingers through her hair and rephrased her question.

"You said you saw my keychain's *what*? by the Umbert house—its Daddy?" As Irene sat down on her folding bed, her eyes wandered over to the portable TV, which she had been watching a scant four hours before (USA Network had run a great double bill during Fright Night—*Night of the Living Dead* and *I Was a Zombie for the FBI*, and work tomorrow or not, she hadn't been able to pass it up), and as the last of the sleep-slush cleared from her head, Irene thought, *Does she mean the Mr. Bones keychain? Good old puke-green Mr. Bones...as in a coffin?*

Terri flat-footed it back into the living room-cum-spare bedroom, toweling off her freshly washed, super-short hair, saying, "Am I speaking frigging Greek or what? I s*aid* 'Daddy,' like as in a big one that looks like the little one—"

Mukluk slippers forgotten, Irene was halfway across the room, reaching for her jeans, jabbering as she slid her bare legs into the limp Levis, "You saw a *coffin*? For real? What kind was it, wood or metal or—?"

"Metal, I think. I didn't like stand around and pay my respects. It was out there with some old mattresses and an old fridge—Clean Up Day, remember?"

"But what—why would the Umberts throw out a coffin?" Irene pulled Terri's discarded Philadelphia Eagles sweatshirt over her head, hoping its saggy shape would be enough to discourage any early-morning rapists wandering the streets. Even on the windy street, the smell alone would scare off Bigfoot, Irene decided.

Terri laughed, shaking her head of spiky wet hair, and said, "Only you would put it that way, Renie, 'why would the Umberts throw out a coffin?'—any *normal* human being would ask why they had it in the *first* place." Terri gave her roommate one of her patented 'Leave-it-to-a-horror-freak' snorts and rolled her green eyes before heading back to the bathroom.

Irene protested: "But I already know why they had one... remember how old man Umbert worked for that casket manu-facturer out on the county trunk? Before it shut down—"

"Oh, and so he helped himself to a floor sample, right? What'd they do, put throw pillows under it and put it under the window? Line the insides with a sleeping bag and use it as a centerpiece for slumber parties?"

While Terri went through the list of decorating possibilities, Irene rummaged through her purse for her key chain—two keys, house and car, on one of those round metal key rings, which was attached to a bright green plastic coffin. The little casket (no longer than Irene's middle finger) was hinged, and the lopsided hexagon top bore the *fleur-de-lis* accented inscription "Mr. Bones." A gentle push of the thumb would open the tiny bone box to reveal a partial diagram of a simplistic skeleton on the underside of the lid—a reminder of the days when the garish little key chain contained sour little bone-shaped candies. Irene had several other little plastic coffins, in red, white and brown, and used them to store everything from paper clips to gummed address labels. But the bile-green one was special, her good-luck token, and a constant reminder of her favorite kind of movie...the kind in which the coffin would be occupied by more than a skeleton diagram on the bottom.

Stuffing the bulky key chain into her jeans pocket, Irene asked once again, "Now there *is* a coffin out by Umbert's—you just aren't trying to turn me into a fitness freak, huh?"

"Not to worry...and you won't find any wheat germ in your Cap 'n Crunch, either. Now scram if you want to *see* that thing—it'll be light soon and I don't want to hear it around town that you've been mooning over some old coffin." Leaning out of the bathroom, Terri tried to swat Irene with a soggy towel, and Irene hurried out of the house (the front half of a house, actually—with apartments to the rear and above theirs, onto Myrtle Avenue, and walked in the rich blue-black semi-darkness to Crescent Street, where the Umberts lived. On either side of the avenue, the barely-leaved trees stood out in sharp, intricate Scherenschnitte relief against the gradually lightening sky, and the sickly greenish-purple glow of the street lamp at the corner did little to create a feeling of warmth and light as Irene passed under it. The lamp made a buzzing, insectile hiss—and the hollow *phck-phck* of Irene's sneakered feet on the cracked pavement failed to mask that irritating buzz above her. Only when she crossed the intersection (*just like in* Christine, *that fat kid getting plastered in the alley...and he had on a sweatshirt, too*) did she leave the persistent whine of the lamp behind her... but that meant that the coffin was nearer to her, too....

There was no reason to be scared...even if there were no cars about, no people, not even warm yellow rectangles of wakeful activity in the façades of the silent, dark houses. Even if the chirp and twitter of birds in the trees and bushes sounded *huge,* Hitchcockian. Irene assured herself that the Umberts had simply gotten *tired* of their coffin, that old Irv most likely picked it up as junk from the casket factory in the first place...most likely they'd stored it in their basement, while trying to think up a good use for it (*or they got tired of waiting for somebody in the family to kick off*), sure, that was why they had the coffin, why they'd put it out with the *rest* of their junk on Clean Up Day, Ewerton's annual spring rite. Sure, just a simple explanation....

As Irene walked in the brisk early spring darkness, hands jammed in the big front pocket of the sweatshirt, she found herself fingering the tiny coffin like a Black Mass rosary, a big prayer bead for the undead. The darkness turned the familiar brick-red siding of the Umbert house into an almost crawling patch of blackness looming two stories above her, and dimly, Irene could see an irregular mound of big junk—folded-over mattresses, one of those cone-surfaced bed toppers, a combination freezer-refrigerator with the doors propped open with pieces of two-by-four...and lying horizon-tally, its rust-patinaed surface sucking in the early morning light with nary a reflection, was the coffin. Irene fingered her Mr. Bones key chain until the plastic was greasy with palm sweat, and as she stood five feet away from the huge metal rectangle, her mind started going E.C. Comics.... *As the lovely young Irene reaches an unsteady hand toward the coffin,...touches it...the Slag Monster which she has eluded for so long emerges and turns her into* *a loathsome Slag-Monster duplicate of itself...*until Irene shook her head violently, as if to scatter and shake out the gory fantasy. Further down the street, a kitchen light winked on, and Terri's words ("...and I don't want to hear it around town that you've been mooning over some old coffin") came back, colorized the deep blushing red hue of embarrassment. Bad enough that Irene sat up until midnight, or later, watching late-night horror films while Terri got her healthful eight hours of snoring in her bedroom down the hall, and double bad that she actually liked what she saw, even the schlocky films like *Robot Monster* and *Plan 9 from Outer Space*. But even Irene herself wasn't up to everyone finding out her secret passion for horror flicks...not in whitebread Ewerton, city of women who followed soap operas even more avidly than they watched *The 700 Club*, who read skinny little white-covered romance novels during break time, and who talked endlessly about that dress Vanna wore last night on *Wheel of Fortune*. Hadn't Patti Halverson dumped over Irene's books in Freshman Biology because Irene had placed a copy of LeFrau's *Camilla* among her folders and, notebooks? Patti had told everyone in Bio Lab, "I think horror books are garbage—filthy junk." (The last Irene had heard of good old Patti, Miss Halverson had just had her third out-of-wedlock kidlet.)

The same shame mingled with defiant excitement ran through Irene once again as she looked at the tumbled heap of refuse out near the Umbert's woodpile (*I think horror books are...*), and after a moment of shivery indecision, Irene told herself, *Why, it looks sort of lonely*, in among the household crap, and without further thought—she strode up to the coffin and *touched* it, right near the place on the lid where it separated into two lids (one for raising and one for hiding the deceased's legs and feet).

Never before (despite all the funerals and visitations she'd gone to over at the Reish-Byrne Funeral Home) had Irene actually touched a casket. But the rust-dusted metal box before her was nothing like those shiny dark blue or rich green or mahogany tone caskets she'd seen surrounded by sprays of glads or mums or carnations—those resting places for loved ones had had such a high gloss that a single fingerprint might have stood out—as if to proclaim, "uh- huh, here it is, she done *did* it! Went and *touched the coffin* Ugh! Icky! Disgusting!"

But Irene could have touched this coffin all she wanted...laid her *whole hand* on it, raised the lid (a loathsome Slag-Monster duplicate), danced a jig on the damned thing, all without leaving the slightest impression of her morbid yet aching curiosity.

Yet...the one kitchen light down the street had turned into two lights, one in the living room now. And in the group home (where the city's mentally handicapped resided, along with Ewerton's best known Coo-Coo-Boo, The Happy Wanderer), some of the lights popped on in the upstairs rooms, and Irene told herself, *That's all you need—let the Wanderer see you jumping around on a coffin.* But the sky wasn't really bright yet—the high dome of the sky was still carbon-paper blue, adorned with an icy sliver of new moon...surely no one would *see*, or care, if she lifted up that rusty lid and took a peek *inside* the coffin.

Just to *see* if it was lined, that was all. To see if it was a finished coffin or just a shell, a former storage chest that got too rusty to keep around even the most cruddy of basement furnishings. But the halved lid was too heavy, too rusted shut to raise easily, and as Irene's fingers grew powdery with rust grit, she heard the tuneless tea kettle whistle of The Happy Wanderer, out for his predawn stroll. True, he didn't talk much, but he was a Reish, of the funeral home Reishes—and he'd know what a coffin was and what people shouldn't do to it or with it. Even if he saw her, got a good look at her face, Irene would die inside each time she'd *see* him shamble past...because she'd know that he knew. And how could she be sure that he wouldn't mention her early morning madness to his family? Or to the Umberts?

Making out like she'd only stooped down to tie her shoe laces, Irene averted her head from the Wanderer's imbecilic gaze, letting her long hair slide over her cheekbones. When the dusty shuffle-shuffle of the man's booted feet died down, Irene quickly got to her feet and cut across lawns until she'd made her way back to the front porch of the apartment and taken out Mr. Bones and her keys. Letting herself into the apartment, Irene made a break for the bathroom, but Terri still yelled after her, "Ah! I see that rust on your hands...was Dracula handsome?" Irene ran more water into the basin to drown out her room-mate's voice, but her cheeks still burned red...and not just from running.

The coffin wasn't far from Irene's thoughts that day as she stood in the assembly line at the sash and door, putting together window frames. The sheer unlikeliness of it, a coffin, resting on the curb on Crescent Street, niggled her, mingling in with flickering TV images of coffins whose lids rose from within, followed by the fluttering grope of a single white hand...she regretted not opening it, having a quick look inside, no matter how semi-scared the prospect of looking inside that rusted, silent coffin made her feel. As she worked, the bile-green Mr. Bones key chain pressed into her hip (she was smart enough not to leave her keys in her purse—more than one of Ewerton's more *colorful*—and crooked—citizens worked at the sash and door, and the lockers assigned to each worker were no more than glorified rubber-banded shoe-boxes), providing a constant reminder of her morning jog with darkness.

She *should* have opened it...after all, how often does the answer to a horror-lover's most secret prayer come *true*? Time after time she'd imagined herself offering up her white, curved neck to the glistening fangs, not wincing when pointed tooth broke tender skin...standing in the hot dryness of the factory, Irene hoped that none of her co-workers could read minds (as if such a feat *were* possible over the blare of Radio-WERT over the intercom)...but she couldn't keep a smile off *her* face. No doubt the cow-like matrons she worked with had similar fantasies, only set in the silken bed of a soap opera boudoir or the garish confines of the *Wheel of Fortune* set (Pat Sajak holding up the swooning contestant, copping an off-camera feel).... But the rub was they'd understand each other's drippy day dreams, and listen raptly to them over coffee...if Irene was to off-hand-edly say "Me? I was just wondering how a vampire bite would *feel*—" she'd no doubt be rewarded with a lap full of dumped Diet Pepsi and coffee and a horrified squeal or two.

As she worked assembling frames, making them ready for the glass, Irene remembered that Clean-Up Day in Ewerton was something of a misnomer; a designated day usually turned into a week, maybe two, and all the while the early morning and late evening would be a time of slowly roaming pickup trucks, the passengers leaning out the windows, looking for some likely garbage-cum-recyclable treasures. (Once she'd seen the occupants of two pickups all but slug it out over some pee-soaked mattresses and a rusted push-type lawn mower.) But she'd never seen anyone carting off a coffin in the flat bed of a pickup truck...not that a casket had *ever* been left out among the refuse specially set out for Clean-Up Day. *Still,* she told herself, while the bilious green Mr. Bones poked into the soft flesh near her hipbone, *I can't imagine anyone else wanting that coffin. At least not until I check it out tomorrow morning.*

Usually, Irene would be passing Crescent Street on her way home from work, but that afternoon an announcement came over WERT (thankfully interrupting a warbling country ditty that set Irene's fillings to throbbing), read by the Chief of Police himself; after a few false starts and some dead air after switching off his own mike, the man got down to business: "The Ewerton Police Department would appreciate any information on the possible identification of remains found at the Ewerton Dump... they are of a child, possibly five to seven years old—"

Why not say six and spare yourself the embarrassment of making an ass of yourself over the air, Irene thought sourly, immediately chastising herself for thinking such a thing when a child had died. The good if slightly inarticulate Chief explained that the remains were skeletal, and that "certain children's toys" were also in the recently ripped apart plastic sack which contained the remains. Both dentists in town drew a blank on dental records, and the Chief invited all "concerned citizens" to come and view the toys which shared space inside the body bag with the child, on the off-chance anyone recognized the toys as belonging to a child they knew.

While the Chief droned on, someone in the frame-assembly section yelled,"What happens if I recognize the toys and the kid's still alive that owns 'em?" "Then you kill that kid too," came the retort from the foreman, as Chief Stanley kept on yammering about all information being kept confidential, blah, blah, blah. Irene thought it both hideous and pointless; how did old Bib Stanley know that the kid was *from* Ewerton in the first place? Was there an added notice on the sign at the dump) "No Dumping of Out of State Children"? A part of her felt guilty over not feeling too bad about some poor dead kid stuffed in a Hefty bag—at least the kid was out of it now, above it all. Feeling almost wicked, she was tempted to add her voice to the clucks of concern and murmurs of dull amazement which filled the section of the sash and door in which she worked, "Well, I know where there's a coffin sitting in the street...maybe they can transfer the kid into that."

But she kept quiet (kept her horror-film tainted thoughts to herself) like a good little Ewerton drone. Blend in, fit in were the watchwords.

So Irene herself was rather shocked...when some of her co-workers asked her if she wanted to join them at the dump to view the toys. One of them, a guy named Steve Dickinson, joked, "Irene's always got her nose in one of those Stephen King books...maybe she'll get a kick out of this." Usually, Irene would have been miffed (actually, pissed off would have been more like it) by Steve's chaw-tobacco-scented jibe, but today she was in her element...true, the road to the dump was out of her way, but she could always swing past Crescent Street later on, to gaze lovingly at that big rust-encrusted metal people-box.

After their shift was over, Irene and most of her co-workers drove out to the dump, past Crescent Lake to the east of town. The bag and the body were gone (not that Irene had really wanted to see—or smell—them, but *still*...but the darkly sodden toys remained lined up along the ground like a police line-up in Toyland: an E. T, a badly discolored Smurf, some plastic dolls, a Miss Piggy with snarled filthy hair. Everyone stood down-wind of the tableau, even the officer on duty held his breath while standing over the toys. Steve Dickinson trotted off and puked up his lunch, and barely audible over the sound of retching, one of the women whispered to a friend, "At least you'd think they'd have hosed off everything...I mean we don't need the stink to know someone died, right?

No one present recognized the sorry combination of dolls and stuffed things, which made the officer sorry; he mumbled, "Wish someone'd made an ID...I don't wanna take this shit to the *Station*. Worse than a skunk...."

But aside from Steve up-chucking, no one was swooning or sick; Irene reflected that too many headless deer had been hung on trees on Ewerton lawns for too many years for people to get overly upset about an anonymous array of death-scented toys. Chalk it up to semi-rural living; dead bears strapped to the back of Scouts, splattered squirrels clinging to truck front tires and grilles. *But just mention vampires, and ghouls, and all hell breaks loose...maybe the real is easier for folks to take than the unknown, the imagined,* Irene assured herself as she drove home, forcing herself *not* to make a detour over by the Umbert house—she didn't want people to think she was morbid, for cryin' out loud. But tomorrow morning....

It was gone. At first, Irene told herself that it was a trick of the pre-dawn shadows, a fooling of her night-vision eye, but no, it was really gone, she realized as her footfalls rang hollowly on the cool air, as her elongated shadow (*long and black like a coffin*), a product of the sizzling arc light far behind her, spilled onto the Umbert's curb. The sodden foam mattress-topper was still there, tented and sagging, and the woodpile remained—but the fridge, mattresses and coffin were gone. She could imagine someone fighting over the mattresses, for a hunting shack or something, but the fridge was burned out, useless....and the coffin—

Terri clucked and shrugged over coffee, adding, "*I* saw the city truck around yesterday, before you came home. Picking up appliances, shit like that. Old siding too. They left the light stuff for the regular garbage men...hey, you figure out who that kid could be? Seems like so many people come and go, 'specially in the pre-fab development, you'd need a scorecard to keep 'em straight. Most everyone has kids, at least six dozen, and most of them in diapers—I'd go *see* the toys but—Terri pinched off the end of her nose with pink-nailed fingers. Irene shrugged (*my coffin, they took* my *coffin away and I didn't get to look inside, dammit*) and slurped her orange juice. "It's not too bad...just keep down-wind. And breathe through your mouth."

And all during work, while everyone else chattered about the kid, Irene's vision was clouded...by a rectangular, rather rusty shape only she could fully make out—or appreciate.

Whoever *took it...I hope they take good care of it, don't make it into a* planter *or something stupid.* She only hoped that if it was taken to the dump, it wouldn't be hidden under a bunch of rusted-out washing machines and electric ranges.

Now that would be undignified.

"It isn't there, Vampira." Terri added water to the Rice-a-Roni sizzling on the stove (Rice Pilaf, Irene's favorite), while Irene hid her red face behind the latest issue of the *Ewerton Herald.* ("Body Found In Dump, ID Sought" read the headline under the stylized Ewerton Ram logo on the front page....) Noting Irene's forced silence with glee, Terri put the lid on the frying pan and added, "I went out there to the dump, after work. Me and Sheri and Ann. We didn't recognize the toys, but before we left, I had a look-see. For your coffin. It isn't there. May be its occupant picked it up and carted it off on its back—"

"Says here that the kid was a girl," Irene drawled, peering at the remainder of page one's article, "And they cleaned her clothes, what was *left* of them. Says she had on a yellow nightie—"

"—if it was ever there at all I ran across little Ricky Umbert at work—"

"They found red hairs, too. And ribbons. It says they're going to send the skull *someplace* to get a clay face put on it—"

"—and actually *made* myself be nice to him so I could ask. Really, Renie, I don't think you appreciate what I go through for you! Know what he said? The Umberts never *put out any coffin.* Little Ricky, the fat creep, had no idea what I was talking about. Weird, huh?"

"—but I don't think that'll help. Terri, do you suppose...there's a connection between the girl and the coffin? I wonder—"

"No." Terri shook her head to dismiss the idea. "They don't bury little girls in huge coffins. Don't be so morbid, Irene! It had to be some kids on a practical joke."

"'I suppose. Do you think the clay face will help? They never identified some of those kids that fat slob Gacy killed in Chicago. I saw the clay faces on the late night news one time—"

"Late night news is all you ever watch," Terri said, getting up to stir the Rice-a-Roni, while Irene's newspaper hid a shy smile.

The next day, during coffee break (ten minutes, enough to drink a cuppa and piss it out before going back to the monkey work), Irene overheard Steve Dickinson tell the foreman, "Betcha can't guess what I saw out at Shipman's place." The foreman waited for Steve to tell him just what he *did* see, but Steve's limited attention was focused on his can of Classic Coke, and chugging it down fast so he could *see* if he'd won either a Hot Car or Cold Cash. The crumpled can rang and reverberated in the trashcan a few seconds after Steve let out a disgruntled "Shee-it."

"Well ?"

"Well what?" Steve let out a belch, looking quizzically at his on-floor boss. The foreman sighed and asked, "What-did-you-see-out-at-Ernie Shipman's-place?" (Ernie Shipman dealt in scrap metal, aluminum cans—like the one Steve had just tossed—and copper wire; he lived on the outskirts of the Woodlawn Development, across the river.)

"Coffin."

(Across the room, Irene's heart began a shuddering flutter, making her temples pound.)

"No shit?"

"Nah, swear to God an' hope to get run down by a train. A fuckin' coffin, out in his back yard." (Ernie Shipman's back yard was the size of a Wausau Home and ten times as messy.)

"Empty or full?"

"Empty, I think, but Ernie didden have the lid open, like an empty fridge. Big sucker, all rusted to hell—"

"Too big for the kid, huh?"

"Oh yeah, way too big. No handles, either. 'Less Ernie stripped them—"

"I dunno...lots of times they put kids into full-size coffins— oh, quit shittin' me, Steve—"

Her coffin. Steve was talking about her coffin. Irene kicked herself for not thinking of Ernie sooner; Ernie Shipman was a huge, roly-poly guy (before his brother Ed moved to nearby Lumbe, the two of them used to remind Irene of Tweedledum and Tweedledee when they'd stroll down Ewert Avenue early in the mornings), not too swift but people never brought that up on account of him being an in-law of Police Chief Bib Stanley.

That relationship enabled Ernie to run his metal yard business in a non-business zone, and it also enabled him to prowl the dump for discarded metal even when the City Council adopted a "no scavenging" policy then. And of course the two-junker limit on non-running cars didn't apply to Ernie, either. But folks thought he was a nice guy, usually good for a beer or two at the Rusty Hinge or Pearl 'n' Earl's.

Nice guy or dim-witted slob, Irene didn't much care...all she wanted was one more peek at her coffin.

Still, she waited a couple of days, not wanting to simply drive on out to Shipman's and take a peek at the coffin. Terri's words mingled with those uttered long ago by Patti Halverson the

Baby Machine, forming invisible chains which tethered Irene to her normal life, her mundane job of monkey work at the sash and door. But come night time, when the creature features came on Channel 13, or USA Network, she'd lie on her uncomfortable bed, thinking. And wishing, and WANTING...even though it was a *crazy* thing, really. Wanting to open up a most-likely empty coffin that Ernie Shipman no doubt cleaned out if it had been full in the first place. And the Umberts were too tight-fisted to toss out a *full* coffin. Be it full of old newspapers or decay sodden children's toys.

And while her co-workers still hashed over the finding of the child (Channels 13 and 18 from Eau Claire and Channel 7 from Wausau came into town to do the reports for the late evening news), all that Irene could think was, It's *there, waiting for me... just duck in some night and lift the lid...have to walk there, Ernie might hear the car.*

There was just enough moon out to silver the painted roofs of the junked cars which were parked willy-nilly behind Ernie Shipman's peeling white house, but not enough to clearly light Irene's way as she walked across the muddy, rutted ground toward the junkyard. She could feel the slithery-cold touch of mud on her bare ankles, like the rotted skin of a crawling child, a little girl slithering along the ground, leaving bits of her soggy, crumbling flesh behind her like some sort of huge shell-less snail (a yellow nightie, a yellow shell-nightie) leaving a trail of glistening slime, and when Irene forced herself to look down, half-expecting the muted gleam of bloodied bone, culminating in a tiny fingered claw (now quit *it, Irene*—), she instead saw something less formed but hideous nonetheless.. .an oily, faintly multi-hued sheen of swirling, iridescent liquid of some unidentifiable sort, lying in shallow puddles all around her. (Probably enough poison to give a person cancer or something.) As she squish-walked, eyes straining to make out one special shape among the dark hulks of cars and abandoned scrap metal, Irene's mind did its best to scare her: See those puddles? Know what happens to a body wrapped in plastic...Hummm? It rots, and liquefies, and lets out gases...oh all sorts of good gooey, drippy stuff...only in a tight plastic bag, there's no place for all the good gooshy stuff to go...so the bag swells up, and up, and then when something rips it open, it erupts—bam! And hold your nose—and all that's left is soup and bones...and a yellow nightie and some kid's toys—

The sound made her reflexively drop to her knees in a crouch, heart bam-bam-bamming against her ribs, mouth all ashes and limp rose petals, graveyard confetti. Only when the sound came again—the muffled report of a car backfiring off near the river—did Irene get to her feet, shamefully wiping off what mud and rainbow-swirled gunk she could from her jeans, to resume her search of the junkyard...a quick backward look told her that Ernie was asleep, his house dark and still. The moon grew slightly brighter, bigger in the starry sky, and gradually Irene made out the dark, rectangular oblong, resting in the farthest corner of Shipman's yard. Like a little child who has just discovered a new and exciting thing called *mud,* Irene smack-ran across the sodden ground, mind whirling with bits of vampire movies, the cool white shine of moonlight on rust-dotted car paint, the dead-earth smell.

The sound of birds chittering wildly all around her, all under-scored with the wanting, the need to stop being a silent observer of other people's horrific visions and fantasies. Irene almost skidded into the coffin before coming to a mud-splattered stop before its rusted, light-sucking surface. The key chain in her pocket dug hard into her panting body, a tiny reminder that up until this moment her fear-seeking had been carried out only on the smallest of scales, the safest of levels—

The rusty surface felt almost like skin, slightly tacky yet smooth too, like worn-out velvet, waiting for her touch, her fantasy-into-reality caress (*You girls can* keep *your Pat Sajak and soap-opera punks*—) and the hinges of the lid *screed* just loud enough to muffle the sound of mucky footsteps closing in behind her—

The last thing she felt was breath on her neck where her

braids left her skin uncovered, and just before the Blow came, she thought,Vampires aren't supposed to have hot breath—

The sound of the two-by-four hitting her head carried far and loud, but attracted little attention in this poor, almost always part of Ewerton. Ernie Shipman bent down to listen for her breath. "Damned thief, trying to swipe car parts from me! Now wait, start breathing, girl. Come on." Ernie looked at the piece of wood dangling from his hand and dropped it into the oily soil. He stomped it down some before returning his attention to the fallen woman again. *Damn. Don't even know my own strength*, he thought, grinning. Eyeing the girl, then the coffin, then the girl again, Ernie's slow mind made the connection, and with a couple of beer burps, he bent down and lifted the body, then kicked open the lid of the coffin, muttering in his jovial good-guy voice, "Shame to leave such a nice coffin empty," before dumping his burden and slamming down the lid of Irene's coffin.

"Sure wish I knew where the Umberts got th' damn thing."

TRICK OR TREAT

THE THICK CLOUDS SCUDDING across the full moon cast jagged shadows across Geoff and Jennifer's masked faces as they stood next to the boneyard gates, waiting.

Waiting for skies already inky to darken just a little more...for winds already bone-jangling to blow just a bit keener...and for the other hobgoblins already wandering the streets of Ewerton to return to haunts of their own.

"Heard any of them lately?" Jennifer tightened her grip on the battered paper handle of her "Trick or Treat" bag.

"Nope." The wind carried Geoff's reply like the forlorn hoot of an owl—*nooope*—into the neighborhood below them.

"You seen any cars, any kids?" Jennifer adjusted her Casper the Ghost mask for a final time, as Geoff shook his head in reply.

Together, they chanted, "Then it's *time!*" shook hands on it, and quietly made their way across wet leaves whose over-lapping golds, browns and reds shone in the icy-white moon-light like the scales of a coiled snake. Only the soft slither of small feet against. soggy leaves foretold their coming into the neighborhood.

Squish, slither across the leaf-strewn sidewalks; this porch light winking off, that set of drapes closing against the night.

Without a word passing between them, Jennifer and Geoff quickened their pace, knowing that they had to find the right house, *soon*. Before all the houses went dark, and silent, and snug.

In between the tall, darkened Victorian with the "For Sale" sign, and the weed blanketed vacant lot, the pair of hobgoblins stopped..

The house was small; brick and *cozy* looking, with a yellow bulb in the light fixture next to the front door. A greenish glow-in-the-dark skeleton hung in a darkened window.

"Must be the kinda person who sits in the dark, waiting for some kid to come to the door," Geoff whispered, *"Then* they open the door *real* slow, and let the hinges creak a little, so we get *real* scared!"—here Geoff's voice became a drawn-out croak. *"Then* they shine a flashlight on their faces so they look just like a—"

"Don't scare me like that, Geoff!"

"'Fraid?"

Jennifer looked at the tiny house, took in the bile-colored bony figure behind the window, then replied, *"We* can do better than *that."*

"Sure. You wanna knock?"

"I gotta hold this bag."

"Okay." The pair stepped up to the door, and Geoff pounded on it, twice.

Slowly, the shiny knob began to turn, just a little at first, then the lock clicked open. Fractions of an inch at a time, the door swung open, accompanied by the *scree* of unoiled hinges. The darkness within was suddenly punctuated by a lit-from-underneath face; all wavering inverted shadows and rheumy blue eyes.

"Whaaa-aaat dooo yooou waaant?" intoned the old man's phlegmy voice.

Holding out her sack, Jennifer pulled off her mask to reveal the naked white bones and gaping eye sockets beneath, while Geoff pulled his mask off with one hand, and jerked his head free of the rotted neck by grabbing his thatch of worm-riddled hair with the other.

"Trick or Treat!" they cried.

On their way home to the cemetery, Geoff and Jennifer

agreed that *next* year, they'd wait until *after* they got their candy before taking off their masks.

PART TWO
LIVE TO WORK, WORK TO LIVE

SCRAP WHEN EMPTY

JAKE-74 AND A TIC-TAC-TOE grid with an x in the lower left-hand corner on a cream-colored Soo line Color Mark boxcar. WATERBED LOU 7-80 on a rusty Canadian National boxcar. A smiling mouth with a tongue poking out over SQUIRREL IS NUTS on a dark brown tanker.

Sliding down further into the cracked and taped green vinyl seat of the car (so far down that if there had been a car right behind his, Paul's head would have disappeared from the other driver's view) Paul braced his knees against the dashboard, firmly under the palm-sweat stained steering wheel. Hands at the five and seven o' clock positions, fingernails picking at the peeling vinyl covering. Eyes wide open, scanning each car as it seemed to bow out toward him, then snap back into a gently curving line flowing to Paul's left along with the rest of the northeast-bound train. Long sucker; four engines up front (Paul had driven up to the crossing just as the bell began to clang, the red lights started flashing, and the white-red-black Soo engines *din-din-dinned* down the track from the west), at least fifty boxcars, flatbeds, gondolas, tankers, and more boxcars so far, and the line of approaching cars wound out of sight around the Red Owl down the way across the tracks. Stuck, Paul read a lot of words; some stenciled in the cars in white, yellow, blue, and black, words that belonged there, had meaning: NO RUNNING BOARD, 1½ COMP SHOES REQUIRED, WASH INTERIOR AFTER UNLOADING; and the other words, the ones scribbled in dense yellow chalk, quickly sprayed on, or scratched into flaking layers of rusting metal, words that had no meaning, or maybe forbidden, meanings: RAID IRAN, BOMB CARTER, IMP, KID '49ER-HOPPED FREIGHT IN 49 STATES; these words and numbers, and endless others. Paul preferred the latter, the impromptu bursts of humanity on hot metal and grimy painted surfaces. He tried to read every car, tried to spot the pale, human places on the rumbling, clanking metal boxes. If he had to get held up by the damned thing, he might as well enjoy it. It was either that or stare at the tattoo on his hand, watch the ink slowly shift under the skin. Both train and ink moved at a similar crawl.

JESUS SAVES! on an empty flatbed. Four clean, blank tankers. Another SQUIRREL, another smile on a Great Northern boxcar.... A newer JAKE, this one an '81, on an old Color Mark I.

If this mother doesn't pick up some speed, I might as well turn around and grab a burger at the A&W, Paul thought. He did that a lot, even if the buns on the Papa burgers were kind of hard. Better than lunch at home.... A lunch at home meant a luke-warm, drowned hot dog on a slice of week-old white (three for 99¢ at the IGA, and *dry,* might as well rip a tile off the ceiling, same effect), with that runny generic catsup, eaten in the front room with two preschoolers, Terri at her job—seven-to-three shift at the paper mill—so the babysitter would be there, all of them, watching "Return of the Archons" (Christ all Friday, weren't there any other *Star Trek*s in syndication?) on the tube, until he'd finally shout *"No,* I am not 'of the bod-eee!'" at the set, making the kids laugh and the babysitter edge away from him on the saggy couch. Terri didn't have the time to fix him a brown-bagger, and he was never good at stuffing a sandwich into one of those clingy, fragile little bags. So it was lunch at the A&W more and more often. He picked at the blue lines of his tattoo, traced the *SPA* encircled by one of those dinguses that stood for the word "at"—@. Lunch at the A&W, or the DQ—where he'd been headed a few minutes ago—meant that the kids saw even less of Daddy, but, well, they did have Mr. Spock.

Another SQUIRREL, another Soo boxcar. Delicate line drawing of a naked woman rear to him, long hair, slight smile on a sliver of visible face (don't I wish...) no caption on a Canadian National boxcar. Another WATER BED LOU on a Burlington boxcar.

There were a lot of cars in back of Paul now, every few boxcars or so they'd *beep-beep* their anger, cars bitching at other cars. Paul was used to hearing the gripes of his co-workers at the sash and door factory—"Why can't they switch at night?" "They should break the cars when they see there's a lotta cars," "Them big-bucks railroaders just like to see us stranded"— and he'd add his two cents worth, too. Better to join in than reveal the vague pleasure he felt when stopped by a train. Sure, it was inconvenient, and in the winter it was a bitch (the busted car heater didn't help), and if the cars were mostly new and clean it was boring, but to Paul, at times like this, the low *thrumthrumthrum* that shook the floorboards of *his* car, sending pleasant tremors into his legs and hands, and the dizzy way the passing cars seemed to leap right at him as they sped past seemed rather...inviting. And the crews, the way they'd wave to him in his car, or be talking to each other in the engine, or hanging on the handrails of the caboose, hair whipping in the wind....And off the train, they'd walk together uptown, eat at one table at the DQ or A& W, and bar-hop in a pack, sort of united by what they were, what they did. A railroader was a railroader, on or off the train. Not like him, bending over the window assemblies until his neck muscles were rubber bands aching to break. Doing "monkey work," as his educated asshole of a brother-in-law called it two summers ago when Mr. Brain tried to do the same thing. Bastard only lasted three months. Terri blamed Paul for baby brother getting canned, in between bitch sessions about how bad *her* neck ached when she came home. No, it wasn't "monkey work," but it didn't give him an identity, either; he and the guys at the factory didn't barhop or eat together, didn't even walk together after work. At home he was just at home. No, not like the railroaders at all.

JESUS LOVES YOU on a closed Chessie boxcar. Couple of blank tankers.

Paul pinched the skin of his hand, watched the blue letters distort under rough fingers. "Makes you look like a convict," Terri had said, once, a dozen times. He was a compulsive doodler; only once he'd had a big safety pin and a fountain pen in his pocket during a study hall.... At least he hadn't written FUCK SCHOOL or some other girl's name on his hand. *SPA*, for Samuel Paul Andersen, at least it was his *rightful* tattoo. Screw the convict bullcrap. He had a good job, didn't he? Didn't change how the windows turned out. Railroaders, now some of them had tattoos. Didn't make the trains crash.

Six empty, rusted-brown Soo flatbeds. My NAME IS S00 entwined on the logo of a Color Mark. *SPA* written in lower case script surrounded by a loop which began as the tail of the *A* and ended under the *A* on a corroded brown Soo boxcar. Three cream colored tankers..

Paul's mouth opened slowly, silently, save for the imperceptible smack of lip flesh parting. His hands dropped into his open lap like over-ripe fruit. He stopped seeing the other cars go past. Paul could still see those three letters surrounded by the loop so much like the thingie for "at." He had not seen them on a boxcar before. But he had seen them on high school book spines. On matchbook covers. On restroom walls. On the hand that lay in his lap.

A slight June breeze blew in and through the car, just enough to dry out the inside of his open mouth. Paul closed it reflexively, He could feel, not his heart, but his aorta pounding, thudding in the center of his trunk, but the rest of his body was still. He glanced right; he could see the caboose about a dozen cars down, a fist-sized black-and-white child's toy. Just starting to back his way back up the seat, Paul stopped—instead of rushing past him, the train began to slow down, moving so slowly that the wheels made a noise not unlike that of a tight drawer being pulled out of a dresser. The train stopped. Built-up momentum made the cars rock in place. As they rocked, Paul pressed damp fists into his patched jeans pockets, feeling the rough fabric pull at his knuckles. *Just an optical illusion,* he reasoned, *like the way the cars seem to jump out at me…. Just my eyes playing tricks on me. Besides,* he assured himself, *I've never touched any of those cars. Never.*

An air brake released with a hiss, the train shuddered. The cars did a push-me-pull-you dance to the right. *Just an illusion, just an….*

…Paul thought, looking into the rearview mirror. The car behind him was way too close, and his car was much too close to the tracks, and the street being too narrow, he couldn't drive away back to the factory and screw lunch. He could only wait, like a good little boy in some warped fairy tale, for something that just *had* to not be there. Or be something else. Or a joke. Or be some other guy's initials…*please, please be someone, else's—*

Two flatbeds bearing farm machinery. A rusting Soo gondola. Three tankers. A badly rusted, dirt-brown Soo boxcar, yellow identifying words peeling and flaking off, crookedly stenciled SCRAP WHEN EMPTY near a door held in place with a greying plank; banged-up old whore of a boxcar, hand-rails bent, the only clean and new thing on the whole car is the yellow chalk-marked set of initials—

The train stopped again when the boxcar was off to Paul's right. It was so rusted and corroded that it seemed to suck up the sunlight and devour it. Even the wheels failed to reflect the glare of the noon sun. The initials were about ten inches high. They were new; yesterday's thunderstorm surely would have weathered them if they had been drawn before today. Paul knew that if he touched them, the dust would cling to his fingers like dry pollen. But he wasn't about to do that. Doing that would make them real. Even though he could easily see them, and even though they did not go away when he rubbed his eyes or blinked hard, they were not there. If the train would just go away, just chug-a-chug past like the ones in his kid's Golden

Books, it would all be okay. He'd just go home, flop on the sofa, and tell the baby sitter to call work and tell them he was sick, had the pukes, the trots, whatever, but he remembered that the kids would be…bopping around, and squealing, and Terri would eventually come home and want to know why he was loafing while she had been—

Paul decided that when the train cleared the tracks he'd pop a Rolaids and go back to work. No appetite anyhow. But when the train moved left, Paul realized that work wasn't where he wanted to be. It didn't matter if he wasn't there, just put another monkey on the line and let him rip. He sat still while the train moved, sluggishly at first, then gained momentum—

A rusted boxcar bowed out to him, then pulled away. A tanker—not wanting to go anywhere but with the train, what else did he have to—a third tanker, a rusty Soo gondola, a flatbed with a John Deere—look forward to? Endless repeats of today, like reruns of—flatbed number three with a thresher—*Star Trek* the kids would unquestionably—a fourth flatbed, boxcar, boxcar, box—watch over and over, same thing daily, never getting—car, tanker, tanker, box—tired of it all, like Paul was *tired-of*—(bet *they* don't have to eat runny catsup)—car; box—this-whole-damned-life—sit-here-and-just-go-nowhere—he wants-to—car, ca….

Paul reaches out for the plastic steering wheel while the breeze which is stronger now because he is or rather the train is moving and blows hair into his eyes so that he has to brush it aside before he can grab hold of the flaking metal rail at the back of the ca—(go!)—boose.

The brakeman waves at the many cars which the train has held up for the past fifteen minutes. Some honk back. One hand waves back, middle finger raised. *Up yours too, buddy.* He notices that the first car in line on the southern side of the tracks, a rusted dirt-brown Subaru whose pale racing stripes are peeling and flaking away, is empty, and is gonna be the center of one hell of a pile-up once the other cars get moving. But it's no skin' off his nose. They all got it easy, sitting in their air-conditioned cars while he has to ride for hours at a time on a noisy (swear I'm going deaf), vibrating caboose all the way to Superior.

Paul would gladly change places with any of them.

DOES IT *PLOOP?*

ONCE IT WAS ALL OVER, I thought that I'd wiped up all the blood, but damn it, there's another spray of it. Across the ceiling, natch, above and a little left of the top of the china cabinet. Not that it was such a brilliant thing to do the actual killing in the dining room, but when a couple of hundred bucks is at stake, and time is short, I'm not inclined to be all that methodical.

Or neat, unfortunately, although I don't suppose hacking off a live head with a hatchet qualified for a single-paper-towel clean up. As it was I used up nearly a whole box of Spic and Span dissolved in one of those "one liquid gallon, one liquid quart" ice cream pails (it really pays to save them) and a jumbo roll of paper towels, and that didn't count the time I spent re-polishing the furniture after it dried off. Then there were the feathers, but I vacuum every day anyway—with two long-haired dogs it's a must—so I can't really bitch about *that,* but the damp carpet made the inside of my Hoover upright sticky, which meant having to take the blow drier to it, then scraping out the gummy residue of feathers, semi-moist Spic and Span, and residual blood with a putty knife, breaking two fingernails in the process.

(I swear, there is someone Up There looking down at me who has decreed, "Thou Shalt Not Have Ten Long Fingernails at the Same Time;" like it's a spare commandment with my name on it.)

Anyhow—there it is, a burst of stale brown splatters, something like the tail of a descending comet. I never imagined that a chicken could have so much blood in it. I mean, really, it's only a little bit bigger than a *football*, but I suppose the severed arteries did the trick. Of course, not being able to catch it right away added to the problem; if old Dead Fred from next door hadn't of picked *that moment* to start buzzing on the doorbell, just to ask if I'd mind if he trimmed the pine branches from my tree which hung over onto *his* lawn (the emphasis is eternally *his*), when he knew and I know that *99½%* of the time he lops the tips off those branches anytime he gets a yen to do so (as in often), whether I've given my permission or not.

I think he saw me carry in the chicken, and wanted to stick his two cents worth into the situation. Maybe he was hoping I'd let him kill it for me, just like the way he manages to materialize out of the ozone every time I start to do lawn work, plying me with wheedled questions and orders: *Sure you don't want to use my power mower? Do you really want to plant that there? You wouldn't have to cut your grass* so *often if you cut it short like mine. Can I trim your bush*? (And yes, he manages to make the last query *most* unbotanical.)

Not that I actually have to worry about Dead Fred Ferger jumping me while I'm bending down to pull a locust branch out of my hand-mower blades; he's so wheezy and bandy-shanked, besides being sixty-some, that a toddler in loaded Pampers could outrun him, let alone a woman my age, which is young enough to be his granddaughter. (And my paternal Gramps Winston, who grew up and schooled with Deadie Freddie, says that old D. F. wouldn't know "where to stick it even if he found it.")

It's just that I've never liked a guy, any guy, any age, whose eyes won't go up any higher than where I cross my heart when he talks to me. And besides that, old Fred thinks he's such a big shit in Ewerton, maybe even in the whole county of Dean, and no doubt the entire state of Wisconsin, just because he's been to Europe, Asia, and Down Under, since half the population thinks it's a big deal to bop on up to Canada for a weekend, and the rest of Ewerton thinks it's a bigger deal to drive three miles out of the city to the bowling alley-cum-pizzeria-cum-video arcade and video-tape rental place near the gravel pit.

And naturally, Dead Fred de-emphasized the fact that his junkets were courtesy of Uncle Sam and the U.S. Marine Corps, since he was stationed in those places during WWII and Korea. No, I don't know what war happened in Australia; maybe Sgt. Ferger versus the Kangaroos, or something equally earthshaking. But to hear them tell it—and *tell* it, on to infinity—be it outside the Red Owl, inside the IGA, around the corner from the Coast to Coast, in the driveway in front of his house, or. wherever he manages to trap some unsuspecting pair of ears; according to D. F. Ferger, War Hero, you just forget about John Wayne winning every war ever fought single-handedly (nobody could've fixed the Alamo), because, dear sir or madam, it was none other than Sgt. Frederic Ferger who made the world, the country, and the city of Ewerton safe for democracy, free speech, and the unalienable right to surreptitiously hack away at thy neighbor's pine tree, Amen.

The more I think about it, the more I am convinced that he did see the chicken. Because the pillowcase I was carrying it in started to rip as I was getting out of the car, and no doubt he was in his living room, taking his usual peeks at me through his blinds. Dead Fred believes that I can't see them move. Asshole. By the time I was on the porch, the bird's feet were out, so he had to have known.

Actually, I suppose it might have been easier to let him go ahead and do the actual beheading—did you realize that the eyes don't close right off? Not that I'm that fond of chickens, but...*ughhh*—since he's told me at least twenty times that he's dressed out everything from rabbits to a grizzly bear his father shot after it mauled some livestock back in the 1930s, I suppose killing a four-pound chicken would've been a cakewalk. No doubt he might have been neater than I was, but one thing would have been a given; he would keep blabbing so much that I never would of heard the *ploop*, which was the whole point of buying and killing the chicken in the first place. And asking him to kill the bird without talking during the act would definitely have aroused his curiosity (and Dead Fred is one being I don't want to arouse in any way, shape, or form), and the last thing I want him to know is that I'm a freelance writer. He would never be able to keep it under his baseball cap, and before long I'd be bugged with "Can you get me an autograph from Judith Krantz?" "Can you get me a discount on my *TV Guide* subscription?" (Not that I'd ever have a serious audience for what I write out here in semi-Bible Belt land, where horror and fantasy stuff gathers dust on the shelves until they send in the front covers for credit and throw the books in the dumpster behind the stores. And as for magazines, the hot sellers are *True Confessions*, check-out rags, and *Outdoor Life*. No magazine I've contributed to has ever turned up in the IGA or the drug store here.)

Frankly, I'm not into being conspicuous about my writing; I like my "bread-and-butter-and-Alpo" job at the office in the paper mill, which is dull enough to let me think up stories while I work. Sort of like overtime on regular hours. And for the actual time spent *writing*, my daydreaming makes me more money than my bookkeeping skills do. Imagine, getting anywhere from five to five hundred dollars a throw (depending on the market) for a few hours of typing, a handful of bond paper, and a little postage. And imagination, of course. Actually, a lot of imagination, except for times like last month, when I had to buy that chicken from the Mennonite farmer down country road QV, which led me to muck up my Hoover, and my nails.

My problem actually amounted to this: e.g. when I can't spell a word, I consult my dictionary, but when I don't know what chicken blood sounds like after the chicken's head is liberated from its shoulders, there isn't a single book on the shelf that can help me. Not that I had ever anticipated needing any help in the imagination department; when I decided to give free-lancing a try a couple of years ago, armed with my trusty Royal, Webster's, Roget's, Liquid Paper, and stack of bond paper bought during the "Back to School Daze" sale at Red Owl, and a little of the aforementioned imagination, I figured that I could rely on my mind to supply me with the answers to such pressing problems as, "What does a Mud Creature eat for breakfast?" or "Are vampires able to cast a reflection in a plexiglass window?"

Up to that point, I was "cooking with gas," as Gramps Winston used to put it, and after a scant dozen or so rejections, I was getting contributor's copies, checks, and contracts and even phone calls from the prozines, with the editors asking if this title change was okay, or if I could elaborate on this or that passage, or supply an alternate ending…little things that I could easily handle after a few hours of thought, maybe a night's sleep to supply a good, usable dream or two, nothing critical and certainly nothing I needed to actually act out—until I got the call from the East Coast office of *Bloodbath Quarterly*, which threw me for a loop. The editor had said:

"…really loved that story you sent in with the other proofs, but I'll pass it back to you, 'cause I'm not sure how the readers would respond to the part about the Forbidden Name of the Soulless One being spelled out in the—lemme find the page here, ah, got it—"gentle *ploops* of crimson blood flowing from the neck of the Golden Sacrificial Pheasant fell to the unholy ground below, slowly spelling out before the awed searchers the name of—" see, what I'm concerned about is that someone who knows a little bit about killing fowl like that might rip the story apart because of that passage. Being a city brat myself, I've never killed anything but a model airplane, so I…lemme take a different tack here, what I'm really wondering about is, the blood, as in does it *ploop* out or does it do something different? Maybe when you get the story back you can rethink the passage and then let me take another look at it, 'cause like I said, I *really*—"

Five minutes after I hung up the phone, I was in the car, headed for the farming part of town. I ran my story about having a boyfriend who really liked *fresh* chicken for dinner through a couple of times before reaching the farm, while visions of three-hundred-dollar checks danced in my head. To be honest, I felt kind of bad about planning to lie to a Mennonite, because all the ones I knew in town were really nice folks, and not pushy about their religion in public, but the farmer I spoke to, who was the uncle of a girl who worked with me in the office before she got married, didn't even ask me why I wanted a live chicken at 2:50 P.M. on a Friday, which really impressed me, so I added another dollar to the price of the bird, so he threw in an old pillowcase for free. The way I felt, if I didn't have to use the boyfriend excuse, I hadn't misled the fellow. (And even if I had used it, it wasn't a total lie, since my dogs Duke and Wolfie are boys, and they're just like friends, and they *love* chicken.)

So—there I was, on my way home with a flapping chicken in my car, which was soon carried into my usually clean house, and the boys were scratching at the inside of the bathroom door, whining to be let out, so after yelling at them to shaddup or no more Alpo, *ever*, I was holding the chicken by the feet, trying to open the door under the kitchen sink with my free hand, *only* the door sticks in warm weather, so I had to let go of the bird so I could rummage for the small hatchet I sometimes use to whack apart the big bones in the cheap cuts of meat I occasion-ally buy for Duke and Wolfie, which meant that the bird headed straight for the dining room, so I took advantage of the fact that the dogs had actually listened to me and shut up to grab the bird, put it on the table and—it comes to me at this point that most people who have lived either on a farm or near one know what happened next, so I need not go into detail here save for the fact that the imitation wood-grain formica top on my dining room table did not withstand the hatchet chop very well at all, but the tablecloth does cover it—at that point I discovered that the blood coming from the Golden Sacrificial Pheasant's neck *would not* go "*ploop.*" (When I rewrote the story, the Forbidden Name of the Soulless One was spelled out in the hot crimson calligraphy of spurting G.S.P.'s blood on the unholy walls of the Evil One's foul cave. That way the awed searchers didn't have to look down at the unholy and dirty floor.)

At that point in time, all I had to contend with was the Headless Chicken of Ewerton Hollow, which was doing its thing, much to my disgust, and to the delight of the boys, who smelled dinner, and began barking in anticipation—*and then the god-damned* doorbell *began to ring.* Since I happened to look like Sissy Spacek in *Carrie* after Nancy Allen and John Travolta did their thing up above the gym stage, I ended up wiping my face with wet paper towels from the kitchen before daring to open the door the slightest crack...which was enough to see good old Dead Fred's puffy baseball-capped bald head, full pink shiny lips working, endlessly working.... I yelled, "Go on, do what you want, Mr. Ferger, I'm busy now," and slammed the door in his pasty face. I had no idea what I'd said yes to until I saw him later on through my kitchen window, happily hacking away at my poor pine tree between sly peeks at my windows. By then I was plucking the bird, getting it ready for the pan, and the dogs' dinner that night, and I hated to stop what I was doing to go out there and chew him out, because if I did stop, I knew I wouldn't want to start up the job again. I hoped that Dead Fred would get his fingers caught in the blades of his clippers, the old fart. (By the way, I wasn't the one who started calling Dead Fred Dead Fred; folks around Ewerton started calling him that when he was a kid, on account of how he never tanned, no matter how long he stood around in the sun. Gramps said old D. F. always had the "ripe patina of an uncooked apple fritter.")

Long after Dead Fred packed the clippers in for the night, the boys ate roast chicken for dinner, and I started in cleaning, then typing into the night. Two weeks later, I received a check from *Bloodbath Quarterly* for three hundred and fifty dollars.

After I cashed the check, I thought that that was the last of the Great Fowl Murder, but it all came back when I saw that blood up on the ceiling. And me out of Spic and Span. But according to this flyer from the IGA which came in the mail today, they've got it on sale, so I might as well buy a couple of boxes. I think that I may have some coupons for it in the kitchen drawer.

I was planning to get it tomorrow, but I think I'll make a run uptown today, since I'm almost out of typing paper, too. The editor from *Bloodbath Quarterly* called a couple of hours ago, about the novella I sent in, "They Came from the Woodpile." A sure six or seven hundred dollars I'd been hoping for.

"….really fantastic stuff here, except for this problem I have with—well, maybe it's just me, I don't know how you could check up on this, but what the hell, I'll run my feelings about this past you—it actually all holds together except for this part from pages…lemme see here…forty-three to fifty-one, where the Bark Creatures have Aunt Ina tied to that cord of wood, and the bigger Bark Creature has picked up her ax with…uh… paws—"

Outside, I could see Dead Fred scooting around on his prat next to my property line, picking out the creeping charlie weed coming from my lawn onto his, using his bare hands to rip the plants out by the roots. He doesn't realize that I won't put weed killer on the stuff because I am fully aware that the creeping charlie drives him nuts. Sort of tit for tat for my poor lopsided pine tree.

"—and then after they hack at her a few times, just before they garrote her with their…um…tentacles, she gives this great impassioned speech about Mankind's right to use the fruits of the land, even the trees, and what I was wondering about was this…wouldn't all that hacking affect her ability to talk? Maybe it doesn't, but some med student might read it and—"

Dead Fred got up, dusted off his baggy chinos, and wandered over to the pine tree, near where the dogs were chained to the clothes pole, where he stood just out of their reach, barking at them. *Get 'um, boys*, I mouthed silently at the window.

"—and then fire off a letter about it to the 'Readers Rights' column, so I'll send this back so you can—"

Dead Fred can't understand how I manage the boys, tells me so at least ten times a week. "They must be bigger than you girlie; one of these days they'll break loose and raise hell in that nice house of yours, just pin you down and eat 'cha up, just gobble you down like a sheep," he prattles at me, no doubt wishing he could join them if they ever did that. He's worse than a dog; at least they shut up sometimes.

"—get a revision back to me soon, 'cause this issue will be closing next month, oh, and another thing, does a severed head really keep on living and trying to talk after it's been...uh, severed? Seems like I heard a line in a movie or read someplace that it does, but I'm way behind on the slush, so maybe you could look—"

Good old D. F. was watching me through the window. I gave him a little wave, and the shameless old pervert had the nerve to wave right back. He ambled over to the rose bush, probably dreaming of trimming it. Funny, he probably knows my house inside out, from when the old owners used to have him coffee klatch over every day—a fact he wistfully reminds me of several times a week. I know he'd give what teeth he has left to come *in*, would even settle for a cup of pee for the chance to cross over my welcome mat.

"—so, I'm looking forward to seeing what you can come up with, and until then—"

Gee. Dear neighbor Fred really has been such a help, what with all those offers of his mower, and the way he prunes my shrubbery for me. Bet he would just love a nice hot cuppa java, as he calls it. Jeeze, I've got to get that ceiling cleaned up before he comes. Wouldn't want any aroused curiosity, or anything else. If I'd been thinking that day, I would have spread around some of those big black trash bags that I keep under the sink. Wouldn't have had to use so much—maybe I'll pick up three boxes of Spic and Span. Never hurts to have some extra around.

I think I will leave the dogs *out* of the bathroom this time.

THE GERMAN LADY

FALL COLORS NEED skies of the clearest, purest blue in order to really look right...without that matting of procelain-hard azure, a person tends to miss the spider-veined intricacies of each saffron and sepia leaf silhouetted against the grey-black branches. Not to mention the scarlet maples, each leaf spread wide, like a stubby-fingered elfin hand, pressing hard to keep the shell of the sky safe above us....

I'd never thought of maple leaves being hand-like before I met the German Lady, nor had I worried about that inverted blue bowl above falling down, but didn't she say that bolts of summer lightening were really cracks in the dome of heaven, jagged fissures only the flat hands of the maples, their broad surfaces mottled red and orange and even jaundiced yellow from the effort of pushing, pushing upwards, could hold aloft until the sky could heal itself?

Was that really a German folk tale? No other German person I've worked for since then has even heard of such a story. Or was the German Lady aware of certain things concerning nature, and most especially trees and the places where trees can grow undisturbed that other people were simply ignorant of?

She'd told me she'd simply known about the jagged white-hot cracks in the summer skies, and how it was the obligation of the tallest maples to hold back the heavens, to keep the forests and the glades and the valleys safe until the winter frosts could help to seal over the almost-mended sky.

Just as she knew of so many other things no other man or woman had ever told me...including the way to trick me into killing her....

"You sure you won't mind adding Mrs. Rusalka to your schedule?"

Something in my boss's voice made me pause, as I started to hand her my time card across the desk in the front office of the personal care and light cleaning service where I'd been working the last five months since graduating from high school that late May. The name wasn't familiar (as were other surnames the rest of the workers at the service used to bandy about when talking about their problem clients, like the old woman who attacked her worker with ridged yellow nails and snapping dentures when the worker tried to throw out a moldy jar of applesauce from the elderly client's fridge, or the old guy who wasn't allowed to have matches or a lighter for his cigarettes, and threw a hissy fit if whoever was taking care of him refused to give him a match right then), but the way Nelda emphasized *"sure"* just didn't sound right—

"She doesn't conflict with my other clients, does she?" I asked warily, as Nelda plucked the time card from my fingers, and handed over my in-the-envelope paycheck. Nelda's glasses-shielded blue eyes were a bit too bright and wide-open as she said, "No, no...she's a lunch time client, needs someone to stay with her a couple of hours every weekday, from eleven to one. She's supposed to also get a bath, but so far she's refused that with every other—Not that she does much to get dirty," Nelda backtracked much too brightly, with one of those toothy smiles that runs out of steam before it can make the corners of her eyes crinkle.

"So...she's personal care, not just cleaning?" The former meant an extra $1.50 an hour, since either Medicare or the county was chipping in for the fee. And every extra $1.50 meant I was a small bit closer to paying for college next fall. But there was that abruptly cut-off "every other" part to think about.

Clients who refused to do certain things attracted the attention of social workers, and visiting nurses...and usually required the attentions of a succession of personal care workers, each more burned out and bummed out than the one before. So far, I hadn't had much opportunity to make use of that six-week course in personal care work which Nelda and her husband Win had paid for after I'd applied for a job with them. Most of my clients didn't require more than help getting in and out of the tub, or the occasional reminder to take their medicines (I wasn't allowed to actually dispense anything, just ask them to take the stuff). Plus cleaning their kitchens, bathrooms and sometimes vacuum their molting carpeting. Neither of my clients wanted me to do much more; usually they were too engrossed in their afternoon soap operas or *Lifetime* afternoon movies to even notice that I was around. But I had heard about how bad some of the other clients could be, from my fellow care-givers...how they'd have to listen to the same stories over and over again, sometimes within the same week, or day, or the way they'd have to admire whatever gee-gaw or whatsit the client's out of town relatives saw fit to send to dear ole Ma or Pop come the holidays, or, worst yet, how the old people would do strange things—like turn on all the burners on their electric stoves for heat, because they'd forgotten how to work the thermostat in their apartment, or hurry their workers out early, so they could take a secret nip from the brandy bottle hidden behind the SOS pads and furniture polish under their sinks.

"Well, sort of personal care...she's down for that, but you can't really force her—she's in her eighties. Y'know. You would have to remind her to take her pills, and be there to help her if she wants to bathe—"

Just as long as she doesn't go in her Depends, I told myself, as I said, "But there's cleaning, too?"

"Like I said, she's in her eighties...her house is really small, and she doesn't get out much, so there isn't too much mess—I could let you go talk to her today, just to see if.... She really *is* quite nice once you—anyhow, her worker is getting married soon, and won't be able to keep coming. It's only two hours a day," she wheedled, and even though I'd already had my daily fill of soap operas each afternoon, I also realized that it was an extra $1.50 an hour

Nelda had had to write down Mrs. Rusalka's address for me, since it was way out on the outskirts of town, close to the woods beyond the county fairgrounds, and the map in the phone book didn't show that particular road. Nor was there an address listed for her in the phone book itself—the old woman paid extra for having just her name and number printed in the book....Once I saw her house, though, I figured that whatever she had to pay to keep her address out of the book was money saved on cable TV bills...not only was the tiny bungalow-style place located at least a half-mile away from the nearest cable hook-up, but the mossy green-shingled roof was devoid of antennas or a satellite dish. Nor were there any of those bowl-shaped devices located anywhere near her front yard or out back, where the ground sloped down to meet the lowest branches of the pine trees which skirted the outer edges of the woods.

The no soap operas part was good, but I wondered if Mrs. Rusalka listened to that gawd-awful local WERT, with all those meandering, pointless talk shows before the equally hideous Polka Time from twelve to twelve fifteen? The name was Polish, even if Nelda had said something about the woman actually being German....

("Oh, I don't know if this'll come up, but sometimes the other gal used to buy Mrs. Rusalka some groceries, usually small stuff like bread and eggs if there wasn't much else on sale at the IGA—otherwise Mrs. Rusalka takes the bus there and back on Senior Citizens day—and one time she threw a fit when the woman bought the wrong bread. She'd bought caraway rye instead of pumpernickel rye...I suppose the seeds get caught in the old woman's dentures. Mrs. R. threw a real rumpus over *that*, though. Otherwise, she's just a sweetie...usually Germans *like* caraway seeds, I know my own Grandpa did, but"....)

I couldn't hear any radio thorough the opened windows, nor

could I see anyone moving inside—the way her windows were situated, I could see quite a bit of the rooms toward the front of the house, thanks to the opened curtains on the west side. The light-painted and papered walls inside helped, too; as I walked closer to the place, I could hear the hitching cadence of a loud clock *thucking* off the seconds within.

That was not so good. Praying that it wasn't one of those clocks which marked each hour with the songs of various birds, or high-pitched mewing kittens, I stepped carefully down the walkway, mindful of the irregular angles of each small square of concrete before me as they'd weathered the long, cold Wisconsin winters, heaving irregularily from the frost below, until I reached the narrow front porch. Like virtually all the front porches up this way, it had long ago been enclosed to make an extra small room back during the Depression—I wasn't sure if it was due to the rising costs of heating fuel and the need to eliminate a drafty entrance, or a more personal need to close up one's space, to shield one's self from the rest of the town, rather than sit out in the open each summer, enjoying the view and one's neighbors as they passed by on the street.

Virtually everyone did it, though. Yes my grandparents enclosed their porch back in the 1930s, as did most of their in-town neighbors...but I doubted that this house had ever rubbed siding with any other house along the road. There was nothing but oak and maple trees on either side of the bungalow, all grown far too tall and too gnarled to have been planted any earlier than the second world war.

I don't think the house had been painted since the 1940s, either. Most of it was deeply pitted dark brown brick, the color of burnt brownies actually, with about as much of a porous charcoal-like texture, but the window sashes had once been forest green, if the bits of pigment clinging to the whorls of the underlying wood's grain were any indication. The windows were glazed with glimmer glass, that peculiar vertically rippled glass common to very old houses out this way. They made the rick-rack trimmed cotton curtains ripple with wavy distortion, like heat shimmers on a late July road.

Although it was a relatively warm day for October, I noticed that those old windows had only been raised up an inch or two—just enough to let in a bit of breeze, and allow the sounds of that overly-loud clock to escape...along with the scent of something cooking. Not bread, but not anything remotely food-like, either. More like something...woody; a hint of pine, a touch of a raw vegetation odor, with an undercurrent of mossy aroma—

"Nelda send you?" The whispering, brittle sound of a heavily accented (German? Polish? Czech?) female voice startled me. I was standing on the first step of the porch, and a few feet away from me was the front door. A long oblong of beveled glass was set into the middle of the door, surrounded by egg-and-dart molding, but the rectangle of glass was covered from within by a long curtain...which suddenly shifted to one side, wrinkling in accordion folds behind one crooked yellow-nailed finger, as a narrow wedge of deeply wrinkled yet taut-skinned flesh surmounted by one hooded eye peered out at me through the door.

"Yes, Mrs. Rusalka...my name is Ashley Foster"—I held out my ID tag which hung around my neck toward the pulled-aside curtain—"I'm with the service. Nelda couldn't make it today, but she said to call the office if you had any quest—"

"I call office." The crooked finger and the slice of face were gone, as the curtain swung back into place behind the beveled glass. Apparently the phone was somewhere far from the door; while I waited for my new client to either tell me to go away, or to let me in, I leaned against one peeling porch column, arms crossed over the black folder all of Nelda's workers carried (with pouches for time cards, yellow personal-care time sheets, white sheets for cleaning-only jobs, and other assorted pamphlets and senior citizen newsletters supplied by the local nursing homes and adult day care centers in town), and stared up at the trees which surrounded the house. The slow-moving leaves were still flecked with thin veins of green amid the prevailing golds and dun-tan, but neither color seemed very bright against the wan, pale sky. One of those hazy, early fall skies flecked with thin wisps of ragged clouds, like shreds of cotton pulled from a medicine bottle with a too-small neck.

Looking past the warm-toned trees, to the looming woods beyond, I was reminded of the top of a picket fence—the finger-thin tips of the pines seemed to be all of the same height, forming a barrier between their outer-most ranks, and the rest of the forest beyond—

"I talk to office girl. You come in now."

Turning around, I saw that the door was open now; the sound of that clock was louder, and that earthy, verdant aroma was much stronger. But neither the steady *thuck-thuck* or the grassy odor disturbed me as much as the sight of Mrs. Rusalka.

That she was small and slight was an understatement. Barely five feet tall, she couldn't have weighed more than seventy-some pounds—virtually all of that had to have been bones and sinew. Her flesh was deeply fissured, like the thick ridges of an old, bark-covered tree, yet drum-tight, too, so that she lacked the usual dewlap of hanging flesh near her armpits, or under her chin, that other women her age had. She must have spent virtually all her time in the sunlight, for her skin was a deep tan, the color of strong coffee or tea spiked with a spoonful of milk or cream. Not that she looked as if she herself drank anything but black coffee or tea without cream or sugar—I wondered if she was one of those old-age anorexics I'd read about in the pamphlets Nelda left in my office mailbox each Monday. Some of the clients could be difficult that way; they'd say they'd eat "later" then throw away whatever margarine-tubs full of left-over food was sitting in their sparsely-filled fridges. There seemed no getting around the dichotomy: Either the old ladies fought to keep you from throwing away their mini-mold factories, or they tossed out perfectly edible food on the sly.

As I walked toward that opened door, I was soon close enough to my new client to look directly down at the top of her head—her remaining hair was spider-web fine, the strands sparse enough to let the slightly shiny scalp show through, especially near the part on the left side of her head. In contrast with her narrow-chested, stick-limbed body, her head seemed globular, like an annual bulb dug up come fall from the cooling earth.

And the clothes she wore only accentuated her elfin appearance—a clinging shell blouse, frayed Capri pants whose waistline was cinched in to form deep furrows in the dark fabric, and worn, narrow sneakers, with scuff-holes along the outer sides of the olive-drab fabric. But it wasn't until I was actually in her small living room, with its textured white walls and worn-bare oak plank floor, that I got a good look at her face. Once more I was reminded of an elf—no, not quite an elf, but not a gnome, either. A sprite, perhaps, a narrow-jawed, wide-foreheaded, small nosed pixie gone to seed. She certainly didn't look like any German woman I'd ever seen in this part of Wisconsin.

Realizing at last that I'd simply been staring down at her, I said much too quickly and probably too brightly, "Nelda said she's sorry not to have been able to introduce me to you—she had an ambulance run over to Lumbe today. But she gave me the duty sheet for you...I hope I'm in time for lunch. I'm not the world's best cook, but I'm sure I can whip up something you'll"....

"I cook lunch already. You wash dishes?"

"Oh yes, yes...that's on my sheet. Plus taking out your trash, sweeping and washing your floors, helping you with your bath if you want—"

"I don't need no bath now. And I throw the trash out back. I got a pile started for compost. The other stuff goes down in the pit. You do dishes now, OK?"

Nelda hadn't said I should actually start today, but as long as Mrs. Rusalka had already eaten, I figured I could "give" some of my time for free—just this once.

"Fine, that's no problem at all—"

"Kitchen's this way," motioning for me to follow her with quick bird-like motions of her crooked right arm.

I walked slowly behind her as she made her way past that

noisy clock (a large carved wooden thing covered with faux leaves, vines and dark round berries which hung on one knick-knack cluttered wall), and through a dark-framed doorway into an equally tiny room whose floor was covered with real lino-leum tiles, not those shiny plastic squares with the wood-grain texture virtually all the other old ladies I knew had in their small kitchenettes, and whose walls shone with a mellow patina of old grease. The stove was apartment-sized, with only two raised gas burners amid a clutter of ceramic spoon rests, chef salt and pepper shakers, and a blue plastic tea-pot shaped tea bag holder. There was a pot filled with the dregs of that pine-like substance I'd smelled brewing minutes earlier on the nearest burner.

The middle of the room was literally filled with a white-painted rectangular table with not four but five knobbed wooden legs (the fifth was right in the middle, straddling the seam where the two long halves of the table-top joined), and two matching wooden chairs. I could immediately tell which one she used; there were wear-marks in the flooring under the legs of the chair situated closest to the window which overlooked the wooded back yard.

Her fridge was also small, and old; I'd never seen a pink one before. Had to have been from the forties or the fifties, easy. But it fit snugly into an alcove in the wall, so it had to be original to whatever remodeling job had been done around that time. I did know from my grandparents that very old kitchens seldom had built-in cupboards, and this room did have them.

"My late husband, he bought me that icebox when I come here. Never needed no repairs, neither. Not like this modern junk. The other girl, she tell me, 'Go buy a new one, with ice maker in the door, frostless freezer'—I say, go take the frost from the freezer and put that in your drink. No waste that way."

I nodded, finally saying, "I didn't realize they made pink ones. I'll bet it does run good. They made stuff to last, back then." I didn't know if she'd noticed how the door handle was all rusted, or that the enamel finish was striated with grey stress marks. She had some magnets on that pink door; tiny braids of wheat, twisted into hearts and ovals, glued to small rectangles of black magnetic strips.

"I like your magnets," I ventured, then added, "And the wheat braids in the living room. They're really pretty—"

"I make. Used to sell, when my late husband still alive. When I go church with him. Once he die, I don't go no more. But made these for his church sales. I make braids corn, bark, soft twigs, too. Got them up on the walls, too. Used to make baskets, from twigs, bark...my fingers, they won't let me do that no more."

For the first time I looked down at her fingers; they were knobbed like old maple branches, the knuckles resembling those gall-things which sometimes created ball-like protrusions under the bark of some trees. But the nails were what really caught my attention—they were long, thick, and quite pointed, their surfaces ridged and yellow. I wondered if she'd polished them when she was younger....

Remembering something she'd said earlier, I asked, "When did you come to this country, Mrs. Rusalka?" Judging by her age, she had to have been a World War Two bride, so I wasn't surprised when she said, "I come here fall of 1945. My husband, Ellery, he had kin in Bohemia, so he stay for a while in Europe after the war over. On his way back from there he meet me in Germany. He like the forest, too, so we got along good. He go hunt in woods, when not on duty. Not with gun, but snares. The old way," she added with obvious approval." Me I spend time in woods...food hard to find after war," she added defensively, as if anticipating my disapproval.

Wondering if my predecessor had once offended her during a similar monologue, I merely nodded and smiled while she motioned for me to sit down in the kitchen chair opposite hers. Apparently it was forgotten that I was supposed to do her dishes (as it was, all I could see by way of used dishes in the room were the pot on the stove and a used teaspoon resting on the drainboard). Mrs. Rusalka pulled out her own chair with a dull scree of wood dragging on age-scuffed linoleum, and settled herself down, before placing both leathery arms on the bare wood tabletop and lacing her knob-and-stick fingers together, and going on in that odd syntax: "Ellery, he no know the woods so good when he go in, so he get lost come sundown. I been watching him, see, while he set the snares, and I figure, 'He's lost' when he tries to get back out of the woods by going in a different direction from what he come in. It get darker and the trees they get blacker, and soon sounds come from the thick parts of the woods, and I know, just from how he breathe, that he is scared. A man should no be scared, I think, so I come out of the trees, and tell him I can show him way out, as long as he share what he catch with me. Once he get over shock over me being there, in the woods at night, he says 'How 'bout I give you some of my rations? Government issue,' he calls them, before he add that he'd like fresh rabbit better, but if I want what he has, I'm welcome to it.

"I don't know what animal 'goverment issue' is, but it had to die of old age. I no blame him for wanting rabbit. But he give me food, so...I show him way out of forest—"

"Did your husband speak German?" Considering how poor her English was, I couldn't believe that she spoke the language back in the 1940s.

"His people, in Bohemia, they speak German. Lived close to Austrian border. So him and me, we understand each other. Spoke German in the house right up until he die. But I learn English, for his folks, for his church. So's I can fit in, that's what he tell me when he learn me English. But we no speak it all the time. But in Germany, he and I, we go hunt. I show him where most rabbits are. He take plenty, they make plenty more.

"But me and Ellery, we how you say, 'hit it off.' He spend all his free time in woods, with me. When it time for him to go, I no want to go, at first. Forest is my home—"

"So you were raised there?"

"Born there, raised there...my people, they live in forest. All time, live in forest. Even in war. I no like cities, too much noise, too much...*not* forest there. Always cutting down trees, planting houses instead of seeds. So...I gets to thinking, my forest is being cut down tree by tree while the city, it moves out and out. And Ellery, he says his home town is small, not like city. Lots of woods around, lots of trees among the houses. And I like name, 'Ewerton'—sounds like animals.

"But to leave forest...is hard. Almost kill me, to leave there. Away from forest is strange, but...I make do. Either go, and look for what forest in where I going, or stay and watch the forest turn to edge of city. On boat coming here, thought I would die... no trees, just water no can drink. No green, just grey-blue water, water...Ellery, he keep me going. Tell me about forest near his parents' house. This place—" she added, with a wave of her claw-nailed hand—"where we come to, after he bring me to US of A. His parents, they not know what to think of me. His momma, she say, 'She's so puny, can she lift up her own head?' only it's like she no expect me to understand. But Ellery, on ship, he learn me English. Not so good like he talks it, but I understand good. His pappa, he like to hunt, so come next fall, him and me and Ellery, we go hunt. Ellery, he buy me first pair of slacks, little lace-up boots, and this jacket—red and black plaid. His momma, she say like I no understand, 'She looks like she belongs next to Santa at the dime store come Christmas.' 'Course, I good-looking then...here, I show you"—and she was up and out of the room, tottering on those flat-soled sneakers of hers, while I continued to sit, increasingly intrigued, at her low kitchen table, with my knees bumping against that fifth leg set in the middle of the thing.

Glancing down at my watch, I noticed that over half an hour had gone by, but I wasn't due at my next client's house for over two hours, so I was actually happy to see her come back into the room carrying a worn black leatherette photo album. Placing it in the center of the table, with the pictures within turned my way, Mrs. Rusalka leaned partway over her half of the table as she flipped the thick, brittle black pages with her right hand, occasionally using the forefinger of the other hand to point out specific images to me as she spoke. The photos were crinkled-edged, black and white, and some were bisected, with two images per shiny rectangle of paper (I knew from my own grandparents' photo albums that this was a wartime effort to save paper), but, since they were black and white—and not fade-prone color—they were still crisp and well-defined, even after half a century. Seeing Mr. Rusalka, albeit a very young Ellery Rusalka, I realized that I'd seen him up until maybe five years earlier, shopping at the IGA and the Coast-to-Coast store, shuff-shuffing down the aisles on swollen, arthritic legs, a potbel-lied balding old man, who invariably wore a threadbare plaid hunting jacket, even in the summer. I did remember vaguely wondering where the old man had gone when I stopped seeing him in the stores, but hadn't known his name. His parents were wholly unfamiliar to me...as was the young Mrs. Rusalka. I was certain I'd have remembered her.

Her mother-in-law was right, if a bit snide. Ellery's young war bride did look like a department store elf in her new hunting jacket. Her hair was just as fine, but what with the permanent and all, at least it was fluffy. And the eyes which merely looked hooded and cloudy now had once shone with a dark, liquid glimmer—even in a two-by-two-inch image. Her skin was smooth and firm, the now-sharp bone structure merely hinted at back then. And as I surmised, her nails were just as long and sharp as they were today—and coated with a dark, shiny polish. While she wasn't beautiful, at least not in the Rita Hayworth/Betty Grable/Alice Faye way of movie-stars of that time, she was quite cute by today's standards. I could even imagine a man considering her to be sexy, albeit in a boyish sort of way. She never did have too much of a bust, even then, nor was she "hippy" in her new trousers. And her husband's mother was a typical European "motherly" type—pillow-busted, wide-hipped, and broad-faced under a loose bun of long hair. Much like the women in my own family album. Most of my people were Czech, too, and that barrel-body/thin arms and legs combo was to be seen in picture after picture in my grandparent's albums—on both sides of my family.

I wondered what my grandparents and great-grandparents

would've made of someone like Ellery's war bride. Twig-thin, tow-headed, and obviously not made for child-bearing. As if a Lost Boy had taken Tinkerbelle for his bride....

"Ellery's momma and poppa, they keep asking him when I make them grandparents, but all he do is nod his head over coffee in mornings, and tell them, 'We're workin' on it.' Thing was, we was and we wasn't. Ellery, he know I don't have babies, and it OK with him. His folks were old, and in a few years, no more asking questions. Then, no more talk of babies. Him and me, we got our forest, and small things come out onto the back lawn for us to fuss over. Ellery, he put out salt licks, we watch the deer, and the squirrels and rabbits. And the birds. Ellery, he hang up feeder, in back window. Was up there for years, until that storm in nineteen and ninety-eight. Don't know where it went."

Rising half-way up onto my chair, until I could sit on my bent calf, I leaned over the photo album until my head was almost touching the top of Mrs. Rusalka's; I don't know why I felt the need to whisper, but I said softly, "One of my clients lives in a government-subsidized apartment house...and word came down that nobody was supposed to have bird-feeders there— too messy on the lawns. Hers is just sitting in her apartment...if I can get it, would you be interested in it?"

"I pay—"

"No, no...the other woman's been planning to just throw it away. Garbage day is tomorrow...so, I could bring it to you the day after that. You'll neeed to buy some feed, but I'll hang it up for you..."

"I got some feed, in the fridge. From when I had the feeder. I go get—"

"No, no, I'll get it in a couple of days, OK?"

A pause, then, "Okay. You bring feeder, I'll help you put it up."

Glancing over at the height of her windows., I merely smiled and lied, "Yes, we'll put it up together, then...."

I never did do the dishes that day, before I finally had to get up to leave for my next job. And as I was going out the front door, I noticed several more photo albums sitting in a book case, and smiled to myself again....

It was when I was hanging up the bird feeder, while Mrs. Rusalka stood watching me, sharp-elbowed arms crossed over her flat chest, that she first told me about lightening cracks in the bowl of the sky, and the healing touch of the fall leaves. While I'd done a term paper on Norse mythology back in high school, I'd never heard that story, but Mrs. Rusalka was adamant: "It is old belief, older than gods. Only spoken of in the forest, among the wood-wives. Not something told to the city-people—"

"Wood-wives?" I bent over to pick up the still-cool bag of birdseed Mrs. Rusalka had had waiting for me on the kitchen table when I'd arrived earlier that morning, and as I untwisted the twistie which secured the cut-open end of the bag, the old woman explained, "Those who live in the woods...deep in the thickest parts. Fairies, some call them. They...help people, when they can. And when people help them, they reward them... wood-wife break her wheelbarrow, person fix it, the wood-wife leave person wood chips. Only come next day, wood chips are gold, wood-wife, she have power, in forest. But...forests they grow small, and wood-wives, they few. But they still believe old stories, and remember *why* what happen happens."

"Did your parents tell you about the wood-wives, when they were living in the woods?" The birdseed slid into the wood-grained plastic feed tray with a ball-bearings-spilling sound, the cool round grains and seeds flowing out to fill the four corners of the rectangular tray.

"Yah...I hear 'bout wood-wives there. I hear lots of things there. See lots...you been in forest?"

Retying the bag of seed, I asked, "Which forest do you mean? The Blue Hills over in Rusk county? Or the woods here—"

Pointing one curved finger, she said, "These here. My woods."

"No.... I've never been out this way before, actually. But they're beautiful woods...did your husband's family own this grove of trees?"

"Yah...they leave to Ellery, *he* leave to me. The gal who work here before you, her boyfriend string fencing around outside of my land, put up them signs you buy in the Coast-to-Coast store. So no one hunt on my land. That why I gots so many rabbit—" she added, nodding her spun-spider-webbed head toward a pair of running hares criss-crossing the yard before vanishing in the thick underbrush at the edge of the woods a few yards away.

I almost told *her* that deer, on occasion, could kill and eat rabbits, but I didn't know if that would upset her or not. Looking back on it now, I suspect she might well have had tales to tell me of such seemingly impossible things....

"The wood-wives, they not only fairy who live in deep woods. In some places, it is the men-folk who are of the woods...their skin, it rough like bark. But they seek human folk for company. All over my old homeland, Germany¹and around it, the forest people live in the trees, in the roots...all of them, they hate the city. While the city surround them, choke them off," here Mrs. Rusalka paused to wipe a droplet of moisture from the corner of one muddy-dark eye, as she leaned back in her protesting kitchen chair.

I'd been working for her for almost a month by then; outside the kitchen window, dark clouds scudded across the sun-deprived sky, while the wind blew the bird feeder against the many-paned window, where it hit the glimmer glass with a muffled *thonk-thonk*, forming a rhythmic counterpoint to the incessant *thuck-thuck* of that wind-up clock in the distant living room—on such a day, she and I didn't venture outside, and the old woman seemed diminished, smaller than usual.

It had gotten to the point where I prayed that our afternoons together would be sunny, or at least calm-winded. The German lady loved to walk around in her back yard, but she was so fragile and occasionally unsteady on her feet, Nelda had warned me not to let her go wandering about on her own outside. (Apparently the woman who'd worked before me hadn't liked being outdoors, so she'd simply let Mrs. Rusalka spend her days sitting in that radio and TV-less little house.)

And since I seldom *had* to do much of anything by way of cleaning (aside from the occasional pot-dish-spoon combo in the sink, or sweeping the broom over a dust-less floor), all that left me in the way of assigned duties was giving the woman a bath—which was another task she refused to allow me to perform. (Not that she seemed to need it; I never did see her sweat, nor did she smell bad—I never found out what sort of perfume she wore, but she invariably had an odor of cut grass and pine needles about her.)

Our time together assumed a pattern as simple as the outline of a fallen leaf water-seared on a sidewalk—we'd sit and talk at the table for a time, then go outside to fill the bird feeder, walk around the yard, perhaps venture a few feet into the woods themselves, then return to the yard, where the old German lady talked and talked of the woods back in Germany, and of the fairy folk and hunters there.

But on this afternoon, a few days before Halloween, there would be no going outside to take in the now color-saturated maples and oaks, no admiring the crisp silhouettes of the pine-tops as they seemed to graze the clear-clear blue of the autumn sky. I didn't want her to catch cold, nor did I feel comfortable holding onto her shoulders or waist to steady her as she walked. She wasn't the huggy-touchie kind of person my other clients were, and I respected that.

Yet, on that particular afternoon, I did find myself wishing that she was the type of old person you could reassure with a hug or a squeeze of the shoulders—she was feeling sorry for herself, and I really couldn't blame her in the least:

"When the forest is no more, the wood-wives have no place left. Oh, if they want, they can go to city, live unhappy...if they want. This not the way of the forest, but it is the way of staying alive. But...life away from the trees, the earth, it not life. Like I feel 'bout Ellery. Him here, life okay here near woods. Even with him parents, life still okay. Now...life just staying alive, you know? Before my body get old, stiff, I go walk in woods, sit under tree, feel the bark under my hand. Now…I sit in little house, listen to clock make too much noise. Shut the windows come Sunday, keep out those bells from town. That one good thing after Ellery's folks die. No more go to town to sit in church, listen to bells bang-clang. Made my head hurt. Only went for Ellery, to keep him folks happy. Once they gone, he no make me go into town. Once…he gone, I have to go in town. Ride on stupid bus. Rock back and forth when it stop-start. No way to live…*no* way."

In that regard, the way she felt lonely and useless and alienated, Mrs. Rusalka wasn't all that different from my other clients—sad old women living in too-small apartments filled with too much clutter from their former homes, watching soap operas they couldn't really understand, looking out windows officially devoid of bird-feeders, waiting for…whatever it is that happens when living turns into merely staying alive, then segues into…whatever happens once the living and the just being alive stop. But I also knew that a remedy to her personal case of the blues was only a few feet away, in those woods she so loved—

"Where are your rubbers?" I asked, smiling reflexively at the word even though the other, more current meaning was no doubt lost on the old woman. I had worn a water-proof jacket to work that day, one with a hood, which I knew would fit her—

"In my closet, I think. I not wear them for a while—"

"Wait here," I smiled, and hurried off for her bedroom, yet another tiny room filled with little more than two twin beds covered with frayed quilts, and a narrow dresser topped with an old-time oil lamp and some more of those little woven baskets she used to make. The rubbers—flopped over, dusty, but still relatively supple—were sitting on the closet floor, next to a couple of pairs of sneakers. The rain boots in hand, I scooped up my own jacket off the loveseat, and returned to the kitchen. All Mrs. Rusalka did was smile as I slid the rubber boots over her small shoes, and helped her on with the jacket. Holding onto her shoulders through my nylon-shelled jacket, I led her through the back door, and out into the yard. My hood was too big for her head, and kept sliding off, but she finally reached up with one yellow-nailed hand to hold it close to her face as we walked.

Around us, the low-dipping branches of the maples and oaks made furtive grabs for our heads as she and I made our way toward the woods to the north. Neither of us spoke—the wind would only have snatched away our words and made off with them, to jabber softly in the trees beyond. Under our feet, the lank grass was slippery, and I had to hold onto her shoulders with both hands just to make sure she kept her footing on the uneven lawn. From the way her shoulders were squared under my jacket, I realized that approaching her beloved woods, with their memories of Ellery—and the associated memory of her own childhood forest, back in Germany—was exactly the pick-me-up she'd needed.

And, as if sensing that one who loved them was once again in their midst, the very trees of those woods seemed to beckon to her, rippling and bowing, their branches dipping as if in reverence to her. As she walked along the edge of her small forest, the pines bent slightly as if bowing at the waist in respect. Glancing behind us, I saw the trees straighten once we passed....

Back in the kitchen, Mrs. Rusalka's weathered cheeks were flushed, and her dark eyes shone as she told me, "You come *here,* this Saturday...the man who deliver the heating oil, he tell me that Saturday supposed to he beautiful day. You come visit me, Saturday. No need tell Nelda or office. I pay—"

Remembering the rule about not accepting money, food or other gifts from our clients, I quickly demurred, but the old woman was insistent.

"No, you come. Saturday. We make trip into woods. Colors bright now, sky be blue Saturday, man who delivers oil, he say so. I show you how to weave them basket you like so much. Use bark from birches. Got some birches in the woods—"

"Are you sure? I thought there were only pines in there."

"Yah, yah, sure. I plant some, after I come here in 'forty-five. They grow, deep in woods. I pay you by show you how to make basket. That okay?"

Nelda had never said anything about learning skills from our clients; realizing that Mrs. Rusalka's skills at basket-making might be worth learning, maybe as fascinating as her stories of the wood-wives and the forest people, I found myself nodding, and making plans to meet her that Saturday, around ten or so in the morning....

That Friday night, I dreamed of twig-thin women flitting from tree to tree in a light-dappled mosaic of leaves, branches and fallen needles, only I couldn't quite make out their faces... but their laughter was the sound of needles rubbing against each other on the mossy forest floor, and the snicking rustle of bright leaf-hands clapping in the cool autumn winds....

The man who delivered the heating oil was right. That Saturday, the one before Halloween, was beautiful. The kind of a day when the air is so utterly colorless and crystal-pure, it makes the entire world sparkle like fresh-melted ice water. The sky was that *blue-beyond-blue* that only serves to make the colors of the leaves—all at their absolute peak of color and brightness—all the more brilliant, as if each leaf, each charcoal-dark branch, was freshly enameled onto a background of chiseled sapphire. Even the dead grass looked beautiful, the rough blades isolated and free-standing in the cool air.

The dark bricks of Mrs. Rusalka's bungalow were chocolate rich, deliciously warm against that bracingly cool blue sky. She was standing outside, dressed in a skimpy little cotton shift dress that looked like a pillow-case with arm and neck openings, and her knobby-kneed legs were bare down to her sneakers. While the temperature was in the upper forties, she wasn't shivering in the least, and politely refused my offered jacket. She did say something about her dress "still fitting" so I assumed it was the one she was wearing when she'd met her husband in that long-ago/afar forest in Germany, so many decades ago.

The crisp breeze ruffled her brittle froth of white hair, making it into a transparent nimbus on her large, round skull as she walked before me into the woods. Her steps were sure, though, so I didn't need to hold onto her shoulders as I followed her into the dense, sap-sweet pines. Once we'd lost sight of the yard and the house, it was as if we'd been transported to *her* woods, the ones where she'd grown up hearing those tales of wood-wives and sky-saving maple leaf-hands, and all the other strange, almost surreal stories she'd passed on to me—tales of housewives whose fork-pricked loaves of bread were spurned by the wood-wives who'd crept up to sweet-smelling kitchens, stories of hunters who found themselves pining away in the woods, trapped by the siren-song of rustling leaves and slippery needles underfoot. Her woods, the ones she'd inherited from her husband and her husband's parents, seemed wholly unlike the other groves of trees which surrounded Ewerton— they were nothing like the distant Blue Hills, either. Here, the branches seemed to reach for us, as if to caress our passing legs, or lightly touch our swinging hands. Underfoot, the ground was far softer, carpeted thickly with rounded mosses and interlaced fallen needles, and the partly hidden tree trunks bloomed with lichen blossoms amid the deep green stripes of moss reaching upward, toward the spreading wide-fingered branches.

While the birds had flown south, these woods still sang; the shift of needled branches produced a sing-song windy exhalation, and the distant rustle of sun-crisped leaves provided a rhythmic counterpoint. The sunlight was spotty, filtered, here shining bright like new quarters in the sun, there green-stained and watery. And still we pressed onward, as leaping rabbits and arcing squirrels kept pace with us, following us as Mrs. Rusalka occasionally said, "My birch, is coming up soon."

I hadn't quite believed that we'd find it, but suddenly, the floor of the forest grew flatter, with stubbly grass replacing the strewn needles, and there, within a ring of ground roughly twenty feet in diameter, was the birch tree the German lady had spoken of.

It had to be at least fifty years old, rising up tall, straight and orange-leafed in that eldritch space within the pines. The bark was creamy white, striated horizontally with dots and dashes of deepest charcoal. Behind me, as I stood looking up in awe at the almost perfect symmetry of its gracefully upward-sweeping branches, Mrs. Rusalka said proudly, "I grow, from small sapling. I put here, in special place in forest. The pines, they leave it be. Let it get sun to grow, the pines, they know not to crowd it. Here, I show you how make birch basket. Come, we peel off some bark...."

I felt a few qualms about peeling away that fleshy white thin bark, to reveal swaths of fleshy-beige below, but the tree did belong to my client, and somehow it didn't bother her to strip away the white coating of that beautiful tree, so, very reluctantly, I helped her peel off narrow strips of bark, until we had a large handful of the curling skin of that unspeakably gorgeous tree. Moving a few feet from the trunk, we sat down (I had to help her; her knees were stiff, and she had a hard time making it to the ground gracefully), and Mrs. Rusalka began to show me how to weave a birch-bark basket. Actually, it was more like a large mat, then pulled and tucked into shape—it looked nothing like the ones in her house, but I said nothing as she clumsily worked the strips of birch over and under each other, her knobby knuckles gleaming mottled pink-white in the bright sunlight. Once the "basket" was almost done (or so she claimed), Mrs. Rusalka looked at me and suddenly said, "Nelda at the office, she tell you my first name, no?"

I nodded; it was typed on the list of specific chores I was assigned to do for her: Sylwia, a name that sounded more Polish than German to me, but one I'd never chosen to call her by, or ask her about...until now.

"Yes...it's Sylwia. I hope that's how you pronounce it—"

"I guess it is. I dunno how it is suppose to be pronounce. My husband, he give me that name—"

"Gave you...you mean, he *named* you?" Surely, she had to mean that he'd given her her surname—

"Yah, he name me. 'Cause I don't got no name-name. No need, in woods. But once he meet me, decide to keep me, he say

I need name. So, he give me name. Say it mean 'from the woods' in Polish. Last name of one of his fellow soldiers—station in Germany. See, I had to have name, for him to take me out of Germany. He have another soldier make papers for me, black market. So's I can leave with him. Because my woods, they taken over by people from city. City move out, out, swallow up my forest. My Ellery, he ask me, 'You want stay in forest that just get smaller, or you want to try living like me, in town near own forest?' Others from my forest, they stay behind, go deeper into what left of woods...I want to live, I want...Ellery. So I make choice.

"I give up much, for life of little. But I thought was life, so...was good. I even wear red, the color of fear and blood and the city, to please Ellery. To be...folk. But I not keep radio of his folks, once they gone. *Too* much of their ways around me already. My way now, I 'spose. But part of me, still forest. Still know that the leaves turn red and yellow from stress of holding up the sky every fall. Still know how to make the skin of the birch into a thing of...folks. But the others...they stay. In German woods that are maybe not even woods no more. I not go back to see. I have my woods. You...understand?"

I wasn't sure if I wanted to, even as a part of me did. Looking down at the crude basket she'd woven, I wondered what it might have looked like if she had stayed in her old woods, the woods of her...younger days. I didn't know if she'd ever been a child—

"Is almost done," she suddenly said, with a whispering rustle of finality in her voice. "All need now is handle. You go to tree, pull off a long twig, with bark attach. Have to have twig and bark, for handle. To finish basket, no?"

Oh god, how I wanted to say "No, no finish basket" but she seemed so...serene, out here in this circle of brightness in her dark, deep forest that I couldn't refuse her. Getting up to my feet and dusting off my jeans, I took one look back at her before going over to the tree; she was sitting with her thin little legs stretched out before her, sneakers-encased toes pointing straight up, that floppy birch mat-basket on her shallow lap, her head wobbling slightly on her tiny, corded neck as she looked up at me. She was smiling as I turned my back on her, to reach up and feel for a long, protruding twig-like branch on that trunk.

My fingers found it before my eyes did. Working up a bit of bark under it, I began to pull on the twig, mindful to keep lifting up the long curl of bark beneath it, until I'd torn off an entire twig, plus about a foot of underlying chalky white bark. The freshly exposed trunk below was shiny and flesh-pink in the sunlight.

Turning around, twig-and-bark in hand, I started to say, "Is this O—" but before I could get out the "K—?" my mouth sagged open, in a soft gaping "O"....

She was gone. The errant breeze had already blown away her worn cotton shift, and gravity had pulled her empty sneakers soles-down on the ground. The birch-weaving rested on the ground, amid a jackstraws clutter of dried grey twigs which began to roll northward with the increasing wind.

I thought I saw a swift-flying sparkle of spider webbing, before it flew off into the surrounding pines. But I'm sure I heard the wind chortle heartily, a deep guttural laugh that sounded so much like Mrs. Rusalka's—like Sylwia's—heavily accented voice, that I felt moisture in the corners of my wind-teased eyes.

Wordlessly, I picked up the empty sneakers, and the birch-basket, and hurried out of those woods, the lower branches of the pines seemed to push against my back as I pressed onward, toward the waiting yard and abandoned bungalow. Once in the house, I dropped the empty little shoes in the closet, and hurried for the front door...but something made me stop, to pause silently in that white-walled, empty little house.

There were no clock-sounds. And the refrigerator was no longer humming in the kitchen. But I did notice something that had changed...the sunlight slanting in through the south window caught the braided wheat hearts and ovals on the walls, turning them into bright-shining gold—gold that came not from the once-living color of the wheat, but from finely spun and woven *metal*....

Remembering the German lady's tale of the golden wood chips, I didn't hesitate for a moment—Nelda's rule about taking things from clients had nothing to do with what had just happened out in those woods, nothing any human being could rightly understand—I took down every one of those golden braids, and gently set them in my purse.

I was sure it was what the wood-wife would have wanted me to do.... And as I walked out to my car, under the leaf-supported mending autumn sky, I am certain that I heard that wind-whisper, inflected so strongly with her unmistakable German accent, *Dank yooouuuu....*

REDEEM MY SOUL FROM THE POWER OF THE GRAVE

with JAMES B. JOHNSON

"But God will redeem my soul from the power of the grave, for He shall redeem me. Selah."
Psalms 49.15

"HEY. JOE."

Didn't see nobody, but the voice scared the hell out of me, me being half in and half out of the grave and all, and not half drunk yet—

"Mit-ter. you *sec-son.* please?"

A kid's voice. Behind me. Something to interrupt my lunch, gimme a break—

"Joe?"

I turned, stretched and looked. "Oh-oh." I scrambled up, careful not to drop my thermos, even though Paul Harvey says you can drop it from a ten story building.

"Uh-oh." The kid waved a shovel at me. I didn't know what the hell to think.

"Joe. you—" His shovel looked menacing.

I snatched up my own shovel for protection. He was grown but had a kid's face. Boss Sleasar would've called him a "Gook," but strictly speaking he was one of them Hmongs we got up here in Wisconsin.

He came toward me. I brandished my shovel like Robin Hood staving off Little John. "My name ain't *Joe*, it's Pendleton, and they call me 'Pinebox.'"

His face scrunched up. I remembered reading one of his kind had given his social worker a single bullet as a warning, when word around the state was that all them Hmongs' welfare might be reduced. On account of all of them thinking the promises Tricky Dick made to them after the war, about them being taken care of forever, were as binding as anything *else* Nixon ever promised. But he faltered now that he was up close and had to crane his neck to look up at me. I was tall even for an American, at close to six foot, and he was short for an Asian, less than five foot even. He waved his hand, pointing toward another section of the skull orchard—*cemetery*, rather. Sleasar don't like anything sounding inappropriate—to the public, that is.

"*You sec-son?*"

"Yeah. I'm the sexton, but I do damn near everything here and they still call me a gravedigger."

His shovel hand wilted. I didn't feel so threatened. I leaned on my own shovel and followed his gaze to the grave I'd just squared off. This boneyard has a backhoe I can make sing, but no machine—even if Boss Sleasar wasn't too cheap to buy it—can square off a fresh-dug grave so's the next-of-kin don't complain and one of them concrete vaults fit just right. You gotta do it the old fashioned way, from the bottom with a sharp shovel, scraping and edging. It's a talent like sculpting, but don't pay as good.

"You did that, Joe? Someone in there?" Southeast Asians must take a course in calling Americans "Joe." When I was in Thailand at the request of Uncle Sam, if they didn't know you, they used "Joe.*"

"Not yet unlessen the spirit's out here checking on its next place of residence."

He just gazed into the excavation.

Too bad they ban just horses and dogs out here. "Fella, I don't need no help—well I could use some. but Sleasar's too cheap to hire someone else."

The guy wasn't very big, but he was over thirty, easy, now that he stood up close, not so much like a high school kid. Them Hmong look like that sometimes—though I seen a couple taller'n me over there—especially the ones who tool around in nice new subcompacts or custom vans the church sponsors and welfare folks help 'em get. How the hell *do* they pass the driver's license test? Most can't speak American worth diddly, and this one wasn't all that articulate. But he dressed proper, no tank top and thongs and baggy shorts like most of 'em wear in summer. He wore chinos and a short sleeve shirt buttoned to the neck like a nerd. He sweated so hard his face looked like a beach ball just out of the pool, all flatly round and smooth and yellow-like under a tan. The natives I'd known in Asia were so white you'd think they couldn't color up. Hmongs I guess are different. Not to mention shorter.

He dropped his shovel and dug into his pocket pulling out a torn scrap of paper—not a bullet thank God. On the back were classified ads, so I knew it was an obit. "Death notice" sounds so bureaucratic. Boss Sleasar calls 'em "Stiffy Stats." The paper runs them back of the classifieds.

The Hmong cocked his head, hard brown eyes bright and unblinking, like them pheasants that trotted around the cemetery years ago, afore the Boss brought in foxes to kill them and run the rabbits and gophers and snakes off to keep 'em from messing up graves. Folks don't like to see a trail of rabbit rounds across Aunt Edna's final resting spot.

"You *sec-son,* I need dig up this lady." He waved the clipping at me.

"Oh, shit." The name on the obit was familiar, and the face more so.

"Weasel-Face," we called her, "Mrs. Sleasar" to her face. Ole Marie Sleasar, mother of Boss Andy. Me and damn near everybody else in town had had Old Weasel-Face for art class. "Chew gum and you'll wear it on your nose," was her favorite saying. You'd think some body with such a pinched ferret face would try acting different than she looked, but not her. Hair never even changed style from when it was frizzy thinning blonde, then gray. Maybe it was a wig. If she didn't like what art you done, she pouted like eggs in vinegar. I remembered her as a skinny old bat with pastel chalk in one hand and a drippy paint brush in the other, and *always* envisioned her with a T-square up her flat butt. She'd make red ink checks on pictures she didn't think "*artistic*" enough, *late goddamnya.*

Old Weasel-Face had retired a few years back just before the Hmong started settling here in Dean County. Wisconsin has the third largest Hmong population in the country; they like the smaller communities where nobody pushes their life and culture and all that radio talk show crap off on everybody else.

"Stop waving that in my face." I snatched the clipping from him. He acted like I'd insulted *his* mother: then I seen it. The guy was *hurting.* Weasel-Face's parting hadn't bothered me: I'd put red check marks all over the *inside* of her vault cover. One for every wad of gum I'd worn, and one for every check she gave *me.* But paybacks aren't always fun.

I shook my head. "Yeah, I'm the sexton. Who the hell are you?"

"Xiong. Neng Xiong." He tried to say it like an Oriental version of "Bond. *James* Bond" but his voice couldn't pull it off. The sorrow in him etched into the words. His surname was common here, the Hmong answer to Smith.

"Not only am I the sexton—" I liked that word, rolled it around in my mouth—"but I dig the graves, serve as custodian. Watch the place come night. Whatever Boss Sleasar decides I should do." I didn't care if he only caught one word in ten. Least he didn't nod and *nod* like many of 'em do.

"You sexxon, Joe?"

"Pinebox. And I said I was."

"Nevermind no permit from State Health Board, okay? I give you money." He stabbed two fingers at Weasel-Face's obit in my hand.

I shook my head violently. "Hold yer horses, Mr. Xiong. No

permission, no digging, no disinterment. Only the city—can do that in 'cordance with the State Board of Health. And a licensed embalmer's gotta supervise. Cemetery regs, pages eight and nine. I know my stuff."

The fella tried to say something but could only manage a fish-like gape. He pointed to the last part of the clipping.

I read it aloud: "'After her retirement, Mrs. Sleasar volunteered at Hunterstown Day Care. Buried with her was the last art project she and her students worked on, mosaic tile and popsicle stick picture frames, each featuring the photo of one of her day care students—'"

The guy could tell by my face I didn't understand the problem; when some old bat's son happens to be *Mr.* Hunterstown, as in owning, overseeing, or sticking his finger into every pie, his mother's stiffy stats include every last thing she'd done in eighty-some years. Xiong maybe hadn't read the newspaper long enough to realize *any* announcement about any Sleasar would be wordier than *Moby Dick* and five times as boring.

"Get sick, *die...only four*, Joe.... Pinebox you *gotsa* help."

I kicked sandy soil—best for digging. I hate the clay stuff. "Who's sick?"

He gave me one of them foreigner "Don't your kind know *anything*?" looks.

His mouth worked, then he calmed himself and took a deep breath. "You take picture someone, you take soul. In picture, samesame soul, samesame person. Picture with dead lady." He pointed at the freshly dug grave, then to the other section of the cemetery. "Samesame soul *with* dead lady. Soul go with dead lady, go land of dead, soul no more with live person of picture." He gulped. "Soul no more in body, body get sick, body die. Bad, bad thing in our religion. Dead lady steal soul—"

"Oh shit," I said intelligently. "Whose soul did Weasel-Face steal?"

"My son. *Can* you open grave? Save him soul?"

"Oh *shit*." I needed a drink.

His voice and looks told me he was at the end of his rope. Not to mention the shovel. He'd been through this song and dance for plenty of local petty bureaucrats. His being here shovel in hand told me this was his last chance.

I shook my head. "No can do, buddy." His face died.

"Lissen. You know what it'd take? Her body's been dead a while, though it's in a vault. It won't smell too good in there." Not necessarily true, but he didn't need to know that. "You'd have to dig up the grass in flats to replace it after. Then the backhoe and make sure you don't crack the vault. Then unseal the cement vault. *Then* unscrew or unsnap the coffin, I forget which she had right now."

He looked like he'd been gut-shot. "You got to get permission. Hell, I'd get fired first and maybe do some hard time. It'd be grave-robbing."

Some former Hmong tribesmen did animal sacrifices and weird stuff with eggs and incense, you read about it sometimes, along with getting caught killing deer out of season. They've strange ways, and a real different religion, but hell I don't hold it against them. If they really *believed* in soul-robbing or whatever they call it—

"This just your son? How about them other kids in the class?"

He looked up at me. "Maybe some 'Melican childs. I don't think? But other Hmong, nosir. His glue not enough yet dry, Mrs. Sleasar she say my son, Nkajo no take picture home."

"Dear sweet Jesus." Just because the belief wasn't mine didn't mean it wasn't a *belief*. But how many little kids dry up and die from losing their souls? I shook my head. "Friggin' ridiculous. I don't care what you say—"

"Mr. Sleasar, I talk to him." Xiong shuddered. "He laugh."

"Yeah. He swerves his Town car to run over puppies." He only done that two or three times, just to enhance his reputation. I'd call him a slum landlord but Hunterstown has none. He *does* own and milk some very low income housing, though.

Speaking of the devil, his big black Lincoln slowed to a stop on the nearby lane. The automatic window went down like a guillotine getting prepped. Sleasar stuck his greying head out.

"Pendleton. Meet me in the office. Now."

I could almost feel the air conditioning blast all the way over where I was. The window rose silently. The Town car started up, stopped, jerked into reverse, backed to its previous position. The window ran down again.

"You got help?" Boss Sleasar's wrinkled neck stretched out like an ostrich's. "I authorized no hiring." He seemed to see Xiong for the first time. "And I won't have any goddamn welfare-suckin', foodstamp cheatin', lily-livered, heathen *gooks* working for me. Tell him he's fired." The window zipped back up and the rear tires bit on the gravel and dug a parallel furrow I'd have to level out.

Xiong was open-mouthed. "He no remember me."

"You prob'y all look alike to him."

"It is his mother," Xiong spoke each word carefully, "who have picture."

"I doubt she knows it. Like mother, like son." To Marie Sleasar's credit, she did volunteer time and artistic "talent" to that day care center. One day I'll find one good thing to say about the Boss. "I need a drink." I retrieved my thermos, opened it, and drank straight. Grapefruit juice has a way of invigorating you. And vodka is a good eye-opener in the middle of a warm day. Or a cold day five feet down digging into tundra or whatever happens to the ground in winter hereabouts.

"He no remember *me*," Xiong repeated, with a hint of surprise—or hope.

"He doesn't remember nobody unimportant." I gulped again. Fortunately, vodka doesn't smell. "I got to go. I'll tell Sleasar you was lookin' for mushrooms or a lost dog—"

"Lost soul, Mr. Pinebox, Nkajo lost soul." He glared at me accusingly.

I didn't mean to insult him. "Lissen, Xiong. I don't got any other job prospects. Sleasar, he'll blackball me"

"No help?"

"I can't." This was terribly awkward. I had nothing against Cambodians or Laotians and their furrin' ways. I didn't even consider them heathens. If they was, I was.

His spade slipped from his hand and his shoulders fell like an avalanche.

"Lissen, I ain't updated my resume lately." My voice was lame. "I need the goddamn job, see?"

He just stared at me, resignation on his face. "Dollars?"

"Shoot, you don't got any more money than I do. And you don't look like an old geezer at the end of his string, either." Me over fifty, and not a damn thing to show for it.

"You not help?"

"I been saying that, see? You *don't* dig up the Boss' damn mother from her grave. Tends to ruin your seniority and employment future."

"My boy. He will die."

"I got a dead goddamn kid myself, understand? Dead, dead, goddamn *dead.* So I don't give a shit. I work here all goddamn day and all goddamn night and it pays enough to stay shitfaced half the goddamn day and all goddamn night. I ain't diggin' up no fuckin' dead art teachers illegally, not even Weasel-Face Sleasar. Look, go your way, okay? They'll hang your ass. Hell, they'll ship it back to Cambodia or Laos quicker'n a bunny."

I trudged across the graveyard taking a shortcut. Why couldn't Boss Sleasar just talk to me there? Or why couldn't he have given me a ride?

I remembered getting a ride from a Lao one time. A Lao or a Hmong; didn't make no nevermind to me then. Or now. for that matter. I'd took a train from upcountry to Hua Lampung, the giant railway station in Bangkok. Outside Hua Lampung, I was gonna hop a bus for Sukumvit Road when this albino-colored Lao offered me a ride in his old Volkswagen bus. "Hell. I don't care." I told him, "save me two and a half *baht* bus fare." I was half plastered on Singha beer from the long train ride.

The guy quizzed me a lot, asking about my job and all. Half the Laos were CIA. Maybe he was testing me. I didn't tell him nothing important. Hell. I was a staff sergeant at Takhli Air Force base upcountry. I worked in the motor pool, mostly on

Ford Econolines and pickups and Metro vans. But also at Takhli was a fenced-in area with an Air America station, which was a CIA air station supporting operations in Laos. I seen this Mel Gibson movie about Air America and all them Laos were talking Thai. I didn't understand that. Maybe then Laos talked Thai to Americans.

Anyway, this old boy, he gimme a ride to Soi si-sip-jet, soi 47, and I hopped out and went down the soi and never seen him again. My *tilok,* my pregnant almost-wife-girlfriend was there at her family's home to give birth to our son.

She did and she died. Then he died. I stayed drunk thereafter and Uncle Sam shipped me back to the land of the big PX and I didn't sober up and they gave me a medical discharge, like a lot of other vets. In Wisconsin, drunks aren't paid much never-mind, even vets.

Viciously, I kicked an old wooden cross. It didn't crack, just sorta fell apart. "Shit." Looking around quickly, I saw no one. I noted the location, pulled the rest of the cross up and took the remains with me. I dumped the wood in the maintenance shed and headed for the office, going in the back to avoid the show-room and salesmen—make that "funeral directors."

In Sleasar's office were the freshest of flowers—I mean "floral tributes"—delivered lately. It smelled sickeningly sweet. The receptionist, who was also Sleasar's secretary, smiled hollowly and pointed to the door. "He's waiting, Pine."

"What's he want, Coreen?"

She avoided my eyes. "God only knows."

She knew. When Sleasar complains, it's loud.

I knocked and went in. I know some about wood. He had it all. especially mahogany. Damn room looked like the inside of a giant coffin. Except he had plenty of pictures of himself all over the wall. Photos of him with congressmen, one senator, the last governor, and Wayne Newton, from his trip to Vegas.

He sat behind his desk, an overwhelming affair with enough curlicues to look like a miniature feudal castle.

I glanced at my hands. "Mrs. Stephen's cross fell down. I got to put another up."

He shrugged. "Have Coreen send them a bill."

"Yessir. You wanted to see me?"

He shot me a look under grey bushy brows that reminded me of his mother's hair. "In a minute. You payin' gooks to help you out. Pendleton?"

"Nossir."

He snorted. "Better not. Goddamn trouble's all they are. Get this, get that from welfare and the church folks, and they won't get their butts in a church to save their yellow hides. Complain about what they got, that they can do, but to behave like normal Christians...nothing but problems with their kind, Pendleton, nothing but trouble." The Boss gave a short snorting laugh. Xiong's words came back to me...and a little guilt.

The Boss *had* done that to Xiong's kid. On purpose. No way to better get even with someone, no matter how small the slight, than to dangle them by their own rope.

He added "You never spend your money, I figure you got tired of digging."

"Nossir."

He shrugged. "If you say so. Pendleton, I've been watching you lately. You're drinking on the job again, are you not?"

"Nossir." The bastard.

"We went through this before. I thought we had it all straight." *Double* bastard.

"Yessir."

"You promised me on pain of losing your job."

"Yessir." I stared at a photo of him off Florida with a giant tarpon. The dead fish was more attractive.

"And you claim you no longer drink alcohol during working hours?"

"Yessir."

"Yet...you still drink?"

"Upon occasion."

"You work days in upkeep and graves and nights as a watchman here, no?"

"Yessir."

"You never take time off?"

"I got nothing else to do."

"If you never take time off, when do you drink?"

"I—I—"

"You're always on duty."

I shrugged. No way would I come out ahead. He was in one of his moods. It happened a couple times a year, though not since his mother died over a month ago. I'd hoped for a change in him. I'd seen real tears in his eyes at the funeral.

Now that he'd put me in my place, he'd get down to what he really wanted. "I want Mother's marker cleaned, Pendleton, on a more frequent basis. And fresh flowers every day. The woman was a saint, and deserves them."

I knew he knew I knew where he wanted me to get the flowers: The best ones, too. "Yessir."

"All right get on with it." He wagged a finger at me. "And I caution you about drinking on the job—while you still have one."

"Yessir."

I left before he could think of anything else. Coreen gave me a not-so-reassuring smile. I went out the front not caring about exposing prospective customers to my "rough-hewn" appearance. You don't dig up earth for a living without gettin' some on your person. Funny how the Boss was worried about how I'd look to his customers: He only hired the burned-out vet to show what a goody-goody he was. I suspect the Boss was experiencing a sharp drop in his sense of civic vanity when it came to me.

Working for a man like the Boss almost made getting fired worth it.

In the maintenance building I unlocked the paint locker, dug out a bottle of vodka, upended it happily for a moment, screwed the cap back on and locked the doors.

I built Mrs. Stephen a new cross, painted it up nice and white, and went to install it. No need to bother her next-of-kin. Sleasar could afford my time and some lumber and paint. Mrs. Stephen had been elderly: it didn't bother me none to plant her in the skull orchard. It's the kids, you know? Vulnerable, innocent kids who hadn't yet growed into adults who understood life enough to face death. Maybe 'cause their future's snuffed. Us'n who got no future hurt worse when a kid's gone. There's something about mothers and fathers whose child dies as opposed to sons and daughters whose elderly parent dies. In Thailand they live to die. Manner of death and after-death are extremely important to them. Guys who served in Nam claim it was like that there, too. The good ole Mystic Far East. I hoped my kid and my *tilok* had wonderful afterlives.

I took the vodka and talked it out to Mrs. Stephen, but she wasn't much help.

I was putting the tools up in the maintenance building when everybody left for the day. Nothing was scheduled, services or what have you, so everyone was gone by five. Sleasar had left earlier, to check on his other businesses.

With a good buzz on, I had my old pickup deliver me to the spread of duplexes Sleasar had part interest in. Curiosity over-whelmed me. The Xiong clan was outside one peeling-paint 'plex, Neng and his woman and their older kids. Nkajo looked like somebody far away was slowly strangling a voodoo doll that looked like him. Poor little fucker believed what they told him about his soul. Did he even know he had a soul? Why try to convince a four year old he's gonna die because somebody took his soul to their grave?

I went away and got drunker.

I came back to see Nkajo again. Would my son have believed this shit? It was ten that night and I remembered little of the getting drunk part. But I remembered the vacant eyes of little Nkajo. And the resigned eyes of his mother and father. And the frightened eyes of the other Hmong kids. All of 'em just sitting on the concrete porch, not playing, not laughing, not like kids at all. Heathen. "gooks" or *whathaveyou*, that ain't right.

"Shit!" I told the whole kit and caboodle or passel or whatever groups Hmongs come in. "We'll need help. Can't run the backhoe at night, somebody'll notice."

Down deep. I didn't want to see Weasel-Face again, not alive, certainly not dead. Never mind what her son might do to me.

"Let us go 'fore I sober up and change my mind." I told Xiong.

It was nigh onto midnight and I was darn near sober and scared and I think the term is "illegal exhumation," aka "graverobbing."

There were four of us, me and Xiong and two others, maybe relatives, named Yang and Ying or some damn thing. Nobody saw them in the bed of my pickup truck.

Here we were, shovels and picks in hand the way we used to do it before backhoes and front-end loaders, four guys with hand tools, reminding me of being "closer my God to Thee." In those days, the stone orchard was a wilder place, with animals darting about even in the daytime. Xiong's buddies had brought a small cage with something inside. I didn't want to think about what it was—or what they were fixing to do with it. I'd read about their ceremonies.

The lantern hissed. I'd like to say the night was pitch black with storm clouds looming and shards of lightning, but the moon was three-quarters and high. A bit of wind, chilly for summer. The lantern still hissed, and a fox scurried, eyes big and glowing. The Hmong wanted to hop right to it.

"Hold," I said. "We gotta do this so nobody knows nothin' about it, unnerstand?"

They nodded in concert, indicating my enormous wisdom— or, more likely, just putting up with me to get the job done.

We could've cut the sod into flats two feet square, but Boss Sleasar would've noticed, so we cut and rolled the entire section and pushed it aside. It looked like a mammoth moldy mossy chocolate jelly roll.

To maintain what the regs call the visual integrity of the grave site, I laid out tarps and plastic ground sheets to hold the dirt. Then we dug.

Graves are thought of as six feet deep. Well sometimes. Suppose it's February and the wind is coming from the Arctic and Canada doesn't have the common courtesy to intercept it and the ground is hard as granite and the snow is deep—Well anyway, you figger, then you stick in a concrete vault that's big enough to hold a coffin—casket—and you put a concrete lid on the vault and presto, we only hadda dig down three or four feet.

We struggled to get the vault lid off and propped it on the side of the excavation. A crowbar broke the sealant and pried it up. Opening the coffin was tricky. Usually you've exhumed the damn thing legally and raised it out of the vault and set it on the ground outside. But Marie Sleasar's vault was the large economy size, big enough for two coffins. "Nothing's too good for Mother," Boss said.

I had a couple belts to jack up my courage and we slid the coffin aside to make more access to the locks on one side. In a New York minute I had the coffin ready to open...then just crouched there in the wavering light of the lantern.

"Pinebox. Do it!" Xiong dropped beside me.

I stared at the red check marks I'd painted on the underside of the vault lid.

I was having second and fifth thoughts. I'm not superstitious, but *I* know you don't screw around with the dead. Anyone who's been to the East knows it—it's different there. Some of that can't help but rub off on a man. Words like *Afa Qui* and all the chanting and incense and such. To them, it has *meaning*.

Xiong shoved me aside, stooped a bit, and lifted the top of the coffin. I held my breath. Three Hmong breathed out with relief. Finally, I exhaled.

The art teacher lay as she had at her funeral. There was a momentary sickening sweetness, 'fore the wind scooped it out of the grave and scattered it. The mortician removes all bodily fluids from several points and replaces them with formaldehyde or similar preservatives. Her face looked like fine spider webbing, or maybe millions of wrinkles overlapping. She remained as hard in death as she was in life, like a roadkilled ferret on the day of the first hard frost. Her dark Sunday dress looked like spilled ink in the coffin.

Ying or Yang shone a flashlight on her face. The beam traveled to her shoulder, then down her torso, and stopped.

"I'll be damned." I didn't whisper any longer.

There in her slightly clawed hand was Nkajo's picture.

"Get picture. Pinebox," Xiong hissed.

"Like hell. This is as far as I'm going."

One picture only. Thank God.

Xiong tentatively reached down and grasped a corner of the picture. He tugged but it didn't come. He tugged harder. I wondered if Weasel-Face's fingers or entire hand would come off, permanently attached to the tiled frame.

Xiong made an exclamation and pried her fingers off and the picture sorta leapt from Marie Sleasar to Neng Xiong. Xiong stepped back and caressed the object like it was Nkajo himself.

I scrambled out and grabbed another of what Made Milwaukee Famous, intent on getting my buzz back.

Xiong climbed out and joined Ying and Yang, covered cage in hand off to the side near some bushes, taking the lantern. It was a chill wind for mid-summer.

Ying and Yang produced some eggs and incense and began a ceremony I didn't want to know about. I popped another beer, the last one gone fast.

I looked at the unguarded grave. The wind was dead now. Something riveted my eyes, maybe my other senses. Something intangible...a wisp like a baby's breath on a cold winter morn, or the last spiraling drizzle from a stubbed-out Camel, *somegoddamnthing*, eked from the lip of the excavation. Wavered in place a second as if honing in on something, then snaked along after Xiong like the last gossamer vestiges of a jet's contrail at 35,000 feet. Only...no contrail sorta *skips*, like a kid who's playing and happy, not all sad and choked with invisible fingers on some duplex porch. The wisp wasn't big, but it wasn't small, just like Nkajo. Whatever it was, it dispersed when it reached the three squatting Hmong, wavering, then merging with the faint billows of incense.

Somebody walked over *my* grave. "Jesus" I tossed the empty alongside Weasel-Face's coffin. "Be right back." Ying, Yang and Xiong, chanting, did not hear me.

I hopped in my pickup and drove to the rear of the main building where they deliver the corpses—"dearly departed"—and the coffins. "Caskets." Using my master key, I went to Andy Sleasar's office and took it right off the wall, nail and all. He'd notice it was gone, but what explanation could he come up with? *Christians* didn't have the same worries "heathens" did. I insured I hadn't dropped any dirt along the corridor before locking up and returning to the gravesite.

The Hmong squatted and chanted, barely glancing at me. I took another beer down with me, feeling better all the time.

Weasel-Face hadn't moved. The nine by twelve professional photograph of Boss Sleasar and his tarpon glinted in the distant lantern light. I didn't want to touch her, but I curled her brittle fingers around the photo. Then I stood back and looked. Momma and her finest artistic expression. I drained my beer and dropped it next to the other empties. I almost put it in the coffin. Wondering about insubstantial wisps, I looked around uncomfortably. The fish was already dearly departed but maybe she'd take the spirit of dead fish smell with her. Maybe the road-kill puppies would find her and her sonny-boy.

I slammed the coffin lid closed, locked it, centered it in the vault, kicking beer cans aside, applied sealant to the top of the vault, tilted the vault lid back over it and let it drop. It took a few moments to align it, and paste more sealant around the edges.

For the first time that night, I breathed easy. Once the jelly-roll of earth and grass was back in place, and I mowed the grounds come morning, even Boss Sleasar wouldn't know what was what. Oh, there'd be plenty of bitching and hollering about the missing picture. Maybe he'd finally make good on his promise to fire me. Hell, the VA must be good for something 'sides sending me junk mail. I'd like to see the Boss get someone to do my job for what he don't pay me, let alone what he won't part with for a new guy. I climbed onto the vault and stepped out of the excavation and began shovelful by shovelful to hide Ol' Weasel-Face's final resting spot.

'Least she won't be so lonely down there no more.

Her loving son would never ask nobody, least of all the sexton, to dig up his Momma.

Not that I'd give permission, regs being regs….

THIS IS THE WAY WE WASH OUR CLOTHES, WASH OUR CLOTHES, WASH OUR CLOTHES

"—REALLY A *SWEET* OLD GAL, and you'd hardly have anything to do while you're there—"

Lynn started to protest, "I just don't think so—" but the woman from Job Service persisted, "—just do her laundry for her, some light housecleaning—she hardy makes a *mess*—and she's willing to pay above minimum."

"Let me think it over, 'kay? I already had a bad experience, y'know, with this type of thing. I mean, she *does* sound OK., but so did the last one—"

"Oh, not to worry, Lynn, *not to worry*."

Lynn bit skin off her lower lip as the Job Service represen-tative gushed in her ear. Something about the woman's forced jocularity didn't *feel* right.

"She's simply a *dear*, a little sparrow of a woman, very pleasant and even-tempered. Mrs. Todd can manage nearly everything on her own, except for the laundry and a little furni-ture moving—"

"Didn't you say it was just 'light' house keep—"

"Oh, not moving *beds*, or appliances, she just can't move her chairs and tables. To vacuum under them. *Really*, Mrs. Todd *needs* someone to look in on her—"

Lynn tuned out her caller's bright, frantic banter, as she

remembered her *last* caretaker job. Mrs. Perham had been close to helpless; she needed someone to help her on and off the commode, put on and take off her clothes, put the fat-handled eating utensils in her crooked fingers. Lynn hadn't minded *that* part of her job (Lynn prayed that when *she* reached her dotage, she wouldn't have to watch her body wither and twist, and trap her still-alert mind), no compassionate person *would* but Mrs. Perham's constant harping and needling had worn her down:

"Lynn, girl, you tied my shoelaces too tight."

"*Girlie*, the toilet paper is on the roller wrong."

"Fork in my *left* hand, child, *left hand*."

Lynn had felt guilty about leaving Mrs. Perham—it didn't help when the old woman died a few weeks afterwards, but at least the poor woman *was* free of her crippled body—and she did need the money now, but the memory of all the times she spent crying after a chewing-out from Mrs. Perham made Lynn hesitate.

"I dunno...I mean, I can *understand* that she needs help, but I don't think that I'm the person—"

"Nonsense, Lynn. I heard some very good things about you from Mrs. Perham's children. You have an excellent recommendation on file here—"

"Uh, how old is Mrs. Todd?"

"Her late eighties, I believe. Don't worry, she can walk. And feed herself, and you needn't help her in the bathroom—"

Lynn twisted the curly phone cord around her free hand while she thought it over. Surely, the old woman couldn't be that persnickety about a few simple household tasks; no black leather shoes to tie too tight, no pressing big-handled forks into stiff fingers....

"Uh, when does she want me to start?"

"I was so *thrilled* when Job Service called and said you'd be coming over," said Mrs. Todd in a delicate, whisper-clear voice as she pressed the arm-mounted control on her tweed easy chair. The seat began to rise, until the old woman was safely positioned on her feet. From where she sat across the small, crowded living room, Lynn let out a silent sigh of relief. She wouldn't have to worry about crushing the tiny woman's age-thinned ribs when helping her out of her chair.

Mrs. Todd's rubber-tipped cane *squeedge-squeedged* as the woman puttered around in her doll-house sized kitchen; Lynn wondered if she should get up and help her new boss in there, but she reminded herself, *Don't* push, *let her ask for your help... she has her own routine, it's her house. If she needs you, she'll ask.*

Over the metallic drizzle of water raining into a pot, Mrs. Todd chirped, "I almost didn't call Job Service again, the little that needs to be done shouldn't take up much time at all, Miss—Miss—sorry, I forgot—"

"Lynn is fine with me. Mrs. Todd?"

"*Yes?*"

"Job Service said you needed help with your laundry—I hate to pry, but is the machine down in the basement? I'd hate to think of you going up and down those stairs just to do your—"

"Oh no, no, *no.*" Mrs. Todd appeared at the doorway bearing a small tray of cookies and rose-patterned coffee cups in her free hand. Lynn rushed over to the old woman and took the tray; Lynn was about six inches taller than Mrs. Todd, and could easily see over the woman's humped shoulders and back, past her new boss and into the kitchen itself. Small pale pink refrigerator, apartment-sized gas range, and old-fashioned five-legged kitchen table, two metal folding chairs, sink—

There was a big cardboard sign, attached with common string, around the faucet; in wide, crooked letters it read: "Danger—Sink Hose Unsafe!!"

Before Lynn could ask about the hand-printed warning, Mrs. Todd continued, "I haven't been down there to do my clothes for a few months, not since I fell and sprained my hip. The girl who used to help me, she *quit*—" a trace of petulance crept into Mrs. Todd's tinkling whisper "—I don't know *why*, I paid her very well, but she just...she simply had a hard time *dealing* with my laundry. But you won't have her troubles, I can *tell*." Mrs. Todd gave Lynn's right biceps a squeeze after the younger woman rested the small tea tray on the coffee table.

Not quite knowing what to say, Lynn nodded and smiled, as the elderly lady went on, "You won't have a lick of trouble with my washing. That *other* girl, she was afraid to get her *hands* a little wet, that's all. No muscles for wringing—"

"Ringing? Sorry, I don't—"

Mrs. Todd's softly wrinkled pale face puckered into a *moue* before she asked, "Haven't you ever seen a wringer washer? That's what I have. Downstairs. Oh, I have one of those other uhm, never mind, there's no need to go into *that*," she concluded with a quaver in her voice, as she helped herself to a Lorna Doone.

Lynn sipped her instant coffee, while she thought, '*and you'd hardly have anything to do'—yeah, what else didn't Job Service want me to know? I wonder how they got my predecessor to work for the old gal? Offer her all the Lorna Doones she could eat?*

"—don't have much *to* wash, nothing hard to wring out like tablecloths or seat covers. Just my dresses, my dainties, a few other things. I don't have a dryer, that was when my troubles started. I was carrying the heavy wet things and I slipped. The clothes. They drip, and the steps are linoleum-covered—"

Lynn clucked sympathetically, and said, "My grandparents have the same problem. They had to put on these little ribbed runners, they go along the edge of each—"

"Exactly! Oh, I *knew* you'd work out, I just *knew,* dear. I have those little runners on the steps *now*, but my hip.... I can still go up and down, but *carrying* anything up...you understand, don't you?" Behind her trifocals, the old woman's large blue eyes were wavery, multifaceted. Lynn thought of rainbow-winged flying insects and immediately hated herself for thinking such things. Mrs. Todd *seemed* nice; she was a cheerful woman, and her neat clothes and neater house attested to her ability to do for herself. If she wanted to put cardboard signs on her sink, it was her business. For all Lynn knew, the woman might have grandchildren who liked to fool with the sink hose—

"Shall we go downstairs, Lynn? I've some dirties down there…."

Lynn was glad that the stairway was wide; she gently rested her hands on Mrs. Todd's bent shoulders as she guided her down the stairs.

The basement was nondescript, porous grey walls and a gradually sloping floor with a drain plate in the center. Old flower pots lined up against the north wall, rusted tools spilling out of a fuzzed-out cardboard soup carton. And two washing machines.

The wringer washer was like something out of a Ma and Pa Kettle movie; huge, rust-mottled and faintly smelling of bleach and strong soap. The roller bars were big enough to squeeze a small child through—Lynn suppressed a shudder when the image crossed her mind.

Unlike its antecedent, the automatic washer was new, a dust-filmed copper tone model whose instruction sticker pasted next to the top-loading door was still factory-slick. Lynn glanced up at the wall-mounted outlet box; the new machine *was* plugged in, apparently functional—

Mrs. Todd patted the old machine with a blue-roped hand. "Had this machine since my second anniversary. Mr. Todd bought it for me, hauled it down here himself. Oh, that was a sight!"

The old woman was babbling, her plump soft cheeks working furiously in time with her forced-out words. Lynn's teeth were set on edge; the woman at Job Service had affected the same lively, desperate tone.

Lynn glanced down at the floor; a pale green vinyl clothes basket filled with rumpled clothes rested near the base of the wringer washer. Nudging the basket with her toe, Lynn asked, "Would you like for me to start now? You'll have to show me how to do this—"

"Gracious, yes! Here, I'll start it up for you—"

From the way the old woman handled the machine, Lynn

realized that Mrs. Todd was *much* stronger than she appeared to be. Lynn watched in awe as Mrs. Todd forced the sopping clothes through the wringer, then twisted each garment with violent strangling motions before dropping it into the green basket.

Lynn carried the filled basket upstairs as she walked behind Mrs. Todd, who said as they left the downstairs and walked through the kitchen and into the fenced-in backyard, "You'd best let me hang the first few things, show you how it has—how I want it done. Clothespins are right on the line, no need to rummage for them thank you, Lynn."

The spring-type clothespins rode the clotheslines like roosting birds, dozens and dozens of pale tan pieces of wood—as Mrs. Todd took the wet dress from Lynn's hands, Lynn was struck by something strange. There were *seven* clotheslines strung between the two poles, instead of the usual three or four lines. Only about three inches space between the lines, and each dingy plastic-coated line was studded with clothespin after clothespin—*no* one had to hang out *that* many clothes at once.

Lynn shook her head, unable to figure out the weird arrangement of the clotheslines. Next to her, Mrs. Todd babbled on, "—don't *understand* about hanging up clothes. They let the *wind* blow through things, let them puff—see, Lynn, *this* is how I want the clothes hung up. Don't be stingy with the clothespins, plenty on the line—"

Impaled. The wet house dress was impaled with clothespins, trapped on the line like a small animal tangled in barbed wire. All the openings were shut with pins; four on each sleeve, and five to hold the neckline closed. Even the hem was weighted down with a dozen or so clothespins. The dress was attached to the lines by the shoulders, the waist, the edges of the hem. The breeze couldn't make the dress flutter, let alone fill the dripping fabric with air. Mrs. Todd looked up expectantly at Lynn, and an unspoken request passed between the two women: *Don't ask, just do please?*

A shaky smile hid Lynn's trepidation as she replied, "I should be able to handle this just fine, Mrs. Todd. You said it...*lots* of clothespins....

Lynn and Mrs. Todd settled into an easy routine; two days a week Lynn stopped by to vacuum, dust, and wash the clothes. Once, she asked about the automatic washer, a casual query about the age of the machine, but Mrs. Todd began to chuff, and fumble for her tiny bottle of heart pills, and Lynn didn't ask again. Nor did she try to find out why the hose attachment on the sink was *verboten*; she liked Mrs. Todd, and didn't want to upset her again. And it *was* her kitchen. Besides, Lynn wasn't able to experiment with the sink hose, to find out if it was defective or *what*, Mrs. Todd was always *there*, leaning on her cane just within Lynn's line of sight.

The elderly widow was always watching Lynn through the above-the-sink window as she hung out the clothes; occasionally she'd sweetly admonish, "Open hem, Lynn, I have lots of clothespins, no need to be stingy," or "Too much *puff*, don't let the wind in." Not carping, like poor Mrs. Perham, but with a gentle *urgency* that Lynn ultimately found disquieting. But the money was above minimum, and Lynn didn't come home and *cry* after work, so....

One afternoon, it began to drizzle soon after Lynn began washing the clothes, and Lynn had to hang them on hangers on the shower rod in the minuscule bathroom. As she worked, Mrs. Todd hung around the doorway, talking small talk, until:

"Lynn, have you ever noticed..." Mrs. Todd's voice trailed off, uncertainly, while she found the courage to go on, "...how the wind makes things...*puff*?"

From the way the woman said "*puff*," Lynn could easily tell that the seemingly innocuous word *terrified* her boss. Putting the empty, wet vinyl basket upside down in the tub to drain, Lynn dried her hands on her jeans as she replied, "Yes, I have... sometimes things really swell out in a big wind."

Lynn chose her words carefully; she didn't want to spook the woman any further. Mrs. Todd swallowed loudly, and her white -coifed head bobbed quickly, with shallow, jarring motions, before she went on, "Wind...it will *do* that. So big...things *puff* out so big and stiff—like water. You've seen water, in a ho—in a narrow place, how it makes it swell up, become stiff—"

Lynn didn't know what to think, what to say. Was her boss trying to tell her, in circumspect and veiled allusions, about something her late husband had done in *bed*? Or was the woman referring to the "unsafe" sink hose? Lynn sat down on the edge of the tub and listened patiently while the widow blathered on, "—it gets so big and *puffed* it's not like water or air at all, but something...different and strange—and you've seen how those things can make other things *move*—" Mrs. Todd's blue eyes goggled behind her thick glasses, and her pale tongue flirted with her thin lips before retreating behind her false teeth "—and when you add *machines* to the air and wind, you get all *sorts* of—of—but you've *seen* it, so you *do know*, don't you, Lynn? So I don't have to go into it *all*?" The widow's voice ended on a high, tremulous note; Lynn stood up and rested her hands on Mrs. Todd's shoulders.

"Yes, I understand *completely*," she lied, leading the old woman to the living room. As they walked, Mrs. Todd sighed, "I *knew* I could count on you, trust you. Not *everybody* understands about the *puff*, you know. Not everyone has seen—" and Lynn thought, *Smile, but don't laugh. You'll be old one day yourself.*

When Lynn arrived at Mrs. Todd's small brick house a couple of days later, she was surprised to see the widow dressed for shopping, in her good pants-suit and polyester blouse. Mrs. Todd had never left her alone, before, never trusted her to handle the washing and cleaning unsupervised.

"Now that I know that you *understand*, I can do my shopping while you're here, I worry so about leaving the house, even for an hour. The clothes are in the basement, and would you mind terribly if you did the dishes for me? That's sweet of you, Lynn. I won't be gone for more than two hours, if you get hungry, you know where the ice box is!" Lynn waited until her boss boarded the senior citizens minibus before heading downstairs.

Lynn ran her finger along the control panel of the automatic washer longingly; it had a "delicate" cycle, spin dry, the works. There were only a few pairs of support hose, a couple of dresses, a sweater and Mrs. Todd's go-to-church gloves in the basket, not *really* enough to warrant filling up the horrible old rust-bucket wringer washer.

The automatic started up with a merry rumble and gush of water. Lynn set the water level at "low" and was careful not to get the instruction sticker on the top of the machine wet when she took the clothes out of the machine, The wind was blowing outside, a stiff breeze that would dry the clothes in no time as long as Lynn let it blow unimpeded through the garments. Mrs. Todd would be gone for a couple of hours; everything would be dried and folded by the time she came home. She wouldn't need to see them puff out on the line, and she wouldn't get that wet, "glassy" look in her haunted eyes.

After Lynn brought the basket of nearly dry clothes upstairs, she paused by the sink and ran the water for a few seconds, until it was cold enough to drink. The water ran rusty; flecks of gritty red-brown coated the bottom of the sink. Not wanting the rust to settle, and dry on the sink, Lynn untangled the hose from the sign and the string, and rinsed out the sink. The hose worked just fine; Lynn left it pulled out as she rested it across the dividing wall between the two tanks of the sink.

Hanging the clothes took next to no time: just a pin here and there and everything was up, flapping crisply in the wind. Above the high wooden fence, Lynn saw the surrounding trees sway and toss in the breeze. Light on the leaves sparkled, and fluffy clouds scudded high above. A gorgeous day; Lynn loved afternoons like this. She almost hated to go inside, but the dusting awaited. Bending down to pick up the basket, she suddenly felt something tug the back of her flapping jacket—before the swift kick to her shoulder blades knocked her to her knees.

"What the—" she began, half-turning around to rub the sore spot. The wind-puffed stocking kicked her again, on the lower jaw. Lynn grunted; the foot of the stocking felt hard, as if filled with a foot of iron.

Puffed. The clothes were all puffed out in the strung wind, each garment fully shaped, tugging and jerking on the thin clotheslines. And the fingers of the gloves balled into fists, curled and uncurled, independent of the wind itself. Lynn scrambled on all fours, away from the clothes poles, but the wind was so strong it blew one of the gloves free of the line: the thin cotton hand landed in Lynn's hair. It clawed through her thick curls, the fingers digging until they found her neck.

She screamed, but the wind sucked the sound out of her mouth. Lynn reached behind her neck, tried to pry the glove out of her hair, but it was too strong, too *puffed*. A sob caught in her throat; she fell to her knees in pain, to crawl about on the grass. Her eyes squeezed shut in agony; the fingers pressed on her arteries, making her dizzy.

The filled stockings kicked her when she came too close to the clotheslines. When the nearest dress billowed near her, Lynn felt hard *knees* knock her chin, her forehead.

Puffed, *she was scared. Of them being puffed, so stiff, she said, and she thought I* understood.

With red-black hazed eyes, Lynn looked at the window, tried to focus on it as she staggered to the house. *Just stare at the window*, concentrate—she thought, before the nearest arm of the sweater hooked around her neck.

"No—oh, *nooo*," she gasped, both from the squeezing of the sweater arm, and because of what she saw, *in* the kitchen.

The sink hose was reared up, water dribbling out of its spout, as it watched Lynn through the window.

PART THREE

GOING AFAR WITHOUT LEAVING AT ALL

THE WI'CHING WELL

TRACI WAS ATTRACTED to *it* right from the start; made Rick *come* to this "Bates Motelish" off-the-highway place because of *it*, in fact: As it was, her seeing it in the first place was an accident—she had been looking through one of those, huge books which list motels, their rates, plus other important information for the would-be traveler (whether or not pets were welcome, handicapped access, etc.) and right under a listing for a Holiday Inn in northern Wisconsin—her honeymoon destination—she saw a listing for a small, Ma and Pa type of motel—the kind, she had thought went out of vogue in the 1940s or 1950s. The minuscule photo of the place showed a building which should have rightly been called a *hotel*...(a cracker-box oblong painted horizontally with two broad stripes of color, one dark, one pale, with rough stone facings on the front entrance, surrounded by scruffy tamaracks), but no, the sign on the front of the place, right above the nose-like enclosed entryway, said "Dean Motel."

Traci almost turned the page, thinking to herself, *didn't these people ever look up* "motel" *in a dictionary*? when she noticed it, snug against the left-hand (or was it the right-hand side, if you were exiting the place?) side of the building—almost hidden by the sweep of a tamarack branch. At first she thought it was a bit of good old northwoods schlock—white painted tractor tire planters, plaster lawn animals, plastic yellow daisy pinwheels and ceramic dwarves immediately popped in her mind—but a closer look, told her that what she could barely see in the grainy photograph wasn't just *another* redwood covered well.

Holding the heavy book close to her nose, and straining to get a better line of vision with her contacts (soft ones *were* more comfortable, but visual acuteness went right out the window), Traci saw that *this* covered well was seemingly made of stone (or was a good plaster fake) and that the roof-like covering bore a neatly lettered sign. Putting the book down on her desk, she dug around in her bottom side drawer for her magnifying glass. Feeling a bit like a female Sherlock Holmes (*only I've got Watson's figure*) she brought the small picture beneath the lens into sharp focus. There! She could *just* make out the larger line of printing on the white sign—another line was merely a thin line of squiggles and dots—and with a minimum of eyestrain she read:

"Ye Olde Wi'ching Well"

Putting away her magnifying glass, Traci thought that she had seen every "cutesie" spelling there was to be seen ("Olde Shoppe," "Littel League," and so on...to nose curling infinity) but the "Ye Olde Wi'ching Well" was a new twist. She remembered that a long time ago, in Ben Franklin's time, printers used to sometimes use a lower case "f" for an "s"—or was it the other way around?—but Traci couldn't *ever* recall seeing a "c" substituted for an "s." It also seemed to her that she had read a story in college, one by Poe called "Xing a Paragraph." But he had been referring to the fact that nineteenth-century typesetters sometimes ran out of letters and were forced to use x's, and then the Poe story *had* been a little bit of a put on—while something told Traci that *this* sign, on *this* well, wasn't a put-on at all....

As she stared at the picture, a thought came to her—*suppose the apostrophe used to be the top of a "t"*? Settling back in her desk chair (unpadded, although she was more than generously padded along the back herself), cradling the heavy book in her lap, Traci ran a finger all round the picture of the Dean Motel, and read that the rates were $30.20 per night for couples, that there was cable TV in each room, and that there was guest dialing, all the while wondering how she could convince Rick to drive thirty miles out of their planned way in order to allow her to visit this place. *Maybe. Just* maybe, she thought, *a wi'ching well would work better than a plain old wishing well...it can't fail any worse than all these stupid diets and slimming powders.*

She finally wore down Rick's resistance a week before the wedding. Her dress had finally arrived in the little bridal shop down in Eau Claire, and one look at it—a special order, 12-14 on the top, 14-16 on the bottom—made Traci willing to try *anything* (short of hacking off the flab with an electric carving knife) before she had to walk down the aisle in that gown. Not that she hadn't tried seemingly everything there *was* to try already. Fruit diets, doctor's diets, pasta diets, exercise, aerobics, plastic warm-up suits, velcro-lined skimming belts, the powders in the big cans, the liquid *stuff* in the little cans, the pills that weren't available in California that were supposed to allow her to sleep off the pounds, fasting, the diet pills, the diet candy that she pigged out on in one sitting, and even—horror of horrors—a week of balanced, square meals, one dessert a day, and no snackies....

She had been considering getting a tummy tuck (*"Just tuck everything, Doctor"*) but then the AIDS scare put that idea in the closet (*at least being plump won't get you in five years, like AIDS will,* she told herself ruefully), and her family doctor warned against the fat-sucking procedure as too painful... so there she was, with a half-and-half wedding gown (special order!), facing the nightmare of a lopsided-looking wedding picture in the paper (Rick could eat a silo of food and not gain one gram of weight).

It took her five days of wheedling and coaxing to get Rick interested in checking out the motel *before* the honeymoon, days of conversations which went....

"But what if we made reservations and got there and found out the place was a dump?"

"If we went to a Holiday Inn *like I wanted* we'd *know* the place wouldn't be a 'dump'."

"But a Holiday Inn is so...so *plastic*! Cookie cutter rooms, and bands across the toilet seats. We could stay in one of those *any* time. Honestly, Rick, *everyone* who stays in one of those places has no good stories to tell after. I mean, what's there to look forward to?"

Rick laid a hand on her ample left breast and gave her a leer. Swiping away his hand, she said, "Rick, we've been doing *that* for a couple of years now, so that shouldn't be the big surprise of the evening. Besides, don't you want something to tell the kids about twenty years from now? Funny stories about the creaky bed, or the funny-looking bathroom floor?" (*Or the* wi'ching well *in front of the building*? her mind taunted her at that point.) Rick must have read her mind, for he asked, "What's really bugging you, Trace? That dress? You know, if that's what's got you all jumpy, I don't give a damn *what* kind of dress you wear at the wedding. You can wear a bedsheet for all I—"

"Or maybe a *tent*?" she snapped back, before having to rub her eyes. Taking hold of her shoulders, Rick gave them gentle squeezes and said, "Aw, common, it was a *joke*. Besides, you're not fat, you're just big boned. Look at your Dad. He's a big guy, but he's not what you'd call fat in the least. Here—" he felt her waist "—I can feel your ribs easily, it's just that your rib cage is wide. Nothing you can *do* about it, kid...you don't exactly wiggle when you walk, so why worry? Lemme tell you, when someone stuffs themselves into clothes that are too small, *then* they look fat. Like Michelle does. The tight stuff she wears only accentuates the problem, makes her seem bigger—"

Traci smiled at that, adding, "She does look like...what was it Dolly Parton said when her dress popped at that awards show? 'Like ten pounds of mud in a five pound sack'? But Rick, she *is* blubbery fat, the kind she could maybe lose if she tried...not 'big boned' like you said I am."

Rick patted her on the head and said, "If your being big boned bothered me, would I have asked you to marry me? Huh? Do I care about your weight? Is your weight *you*? Now common, cheer up. Aw...will you perk up if we go to that damned motel of yours, to check it—"

The rest of his words were smothered in her bear hug.

During the drive up to the Dean Motel, Traci wondered if Rick had noticed the sign on the little wishing well (*wi'ching well!*) next to the entrance in the picture she showed him, but she didn't dare to ask him about it. If he suspected what she had in mind, he never would let her go there—*before* or *after* the wedding. (And at the worst, she was willing to even settle for an after the wedding trip to that well, although it wouldn't help the size of her gown or the picture in the paper which she *knew* would look awful.)

So afraid was she of spoiling everything with a careless slip of the tongue, Traci pretended to sleep most of the way up to the site of the Dean Motel (way up in Dean County), and thus missed most of the fall colors. However, there was always time to see them on the trip back. And if all went well, it would be Rick who'd miss seeing the fall colors on the way back... provided he could take his eyes off her in order to drive. *Maybe he likes me 'big boned'...but I'm sure even Rick wouldn't say 'no' to a* petite *me*, she thought as the sunlight burned red and warm through her closed eyelids.

She had fallen asleep for real shortly before they arrived at the motel, and Rick had to shake her awake. He had parked almost directly in front of the wi'ching well (*did he read my mind?*), and in the failing light she could finally read the sign— and the second and third lines of printing below the first..

> *Ye Olde Wi'ching Well*
> *wish not for desires*
> *but aske for trifles*

Something about that second, crudely lettered line made Traci shiver in her plaid wool coat, and for a second she wished that she had seen it *before* getting Rick to bring her here (*but what if you saw that on your wedding night, huh girl?*), then reason took over. *Of course any good wishing (wi'ching) well would have to make a claim like that—how would they keep the suckers coming back, coins in hand, if the sign proclaimed "Wishes Granted or Your Money Back!" or "Satisfaction Guaranteed Every Time!"*—so Traci shook off her feeling of foreboding, and helped Rick get their traveling bags out of the trunk of the car....

As they got out their things, the twin lights, set on either side of the doorway, came on with a yellow glow; some of the warm illumination spilled onto the small wishing well next to the protruding entryway, making the crooked, thick black words stand out in sharp definition. Rick took his bag, plus hers, into the building while Traci pretended to tie a bootlace which wasn't undone. As soon as he had disappeared into the dark and light green painted building, she hurried over to the well, a half-dollar in her pocket (*you gets what you pays for*). There *was* a window, a big one, in the lobby which looked out upon the wi'ching well, but luckily Rick had his back to her, and the old man checking him in was seemingly intent upon registering her fiancé.

Bathed in the golden glow of the artificial light, her breath a shimmering plume in the air before her, Traci stepped up to the well, coin in gloved hand. Reminded of the times when she wished the same wish (or variations of it) over birthday cake candles, wish bones, and first evening stars, Traci quietly mouthed the words "I want to be small boned for a change," before leaning over and tossing the coin in. When she looked into the mouth of the well (about the diameter of a large barrel) she suddenly felt dizzy and almost lost her balance. It must have been a light trick, she told herself, recovering, that thing couldn't be that deep, how would the owners scoop out the coins later on?

She refused to consider the fact that the coin didn't clink(!) when it touched bottom. If it did touch the bottom....

The old couple who ran this place (I'm Fred, and this is Famia, and none of that 'Mr. and Mrs. *North*' hoo-haa"). seemed glad to have business on what they called "a slow week, but just wait till hunting season, right, Famia?," and they seemed anxious to please their lone guests in the twenty-unit establishment; they offered extra blankets, more pillows, another set of towels, plus they hurried up to the room with spare bars of "baby" soap and book matches after Traci and Rick began to move in.

Once they—gently—got rid of the officious old people with their watery, eager eyes. Rick sat down and bounced on the bed, saying, "Passes the Creaky Test with flying colors. You want to check out the biffy floor or shall I?" Unable to hold it any longer (Rick had used the "last tree on the left" rest stops on the way up, for men it wasn't so bad, but how could a woman shake?), Traci said, "First dibs!," and raced to the small room and slammed the door shut behind her.

While she fumbled with her jeans and underpants, Traci noticed that her good old "love handles" were as big as ever, and wished that she had only thrown in a quarter, or a dime, into the (*where* was *the bottom*?) well, but maybe no one had thrown *anything* in there for a long time, and the old couple didn't seem so well fed now that she thought about it. But when Traci sat *down*, she felt as if she had sunk into the floor: *Just a smaller toilet*, she told herself, forcing herself to scan the cracked, faded linoleum beneath her jeans-swaddled feet, reminding herself that this *would* be a good place to stay during their honeymoon.

When she was through, and as she washed her hands, she almost lost her engagement ring. It slipped off with ridiculous ease from her soapy finger, and she had to quickly cover the drain hole with her palm before the ring slid down. *Funny*, she told herself, *your fingers don't look* any *thinner*, and she began to hold them up to the bright light of the bulb above the sink. What she saw—what she *thought* she saw—made her let out a barely stifled gasp, and Rick yelled though the door, "Whatsa matter? You fall in? Need help?" Traci shouted "No!" and tried holding her hands up to the light again, just to be *sure*.

As the second line of the sign came back with stunning force ("wish not for desires...") Traci looked with open-mouthed horror at the broad line of reddish illuminated flesh around each finger, and kept looking in vain for the places where the bone should be. Pressing her still-large but quite flabby feeling fingers to her face, she could *actually feel* her bones growing smaller, tightening under her finger tips. Unable to cry out, Traci thought, *the skin will tighten too, it* has *to pull in too*— until the door swung open behind her, and Rick—wearing *her* nightgown, and a bandanna on his head—came in, arm raised, soap in hand, saying, "Mother Bates says it's shower time!"

Sneaking a quick look in the mirror, and assured that she didn't look *too* different, Traci forced herself to start to undo her clothes, before Rick had a chance to do it for her. Maybe, if she was lucky, this all wouldn't take too long. She had another silver dollar in her purse, and if Rick fell asleep like he *usually* did after lovemaking, she could sneak down and make another wish....

If Rick had noticed, he hadn't said anything. A few times Traci had whispered to him (through jaws that meshed oddly) to be *quiet*, the old couple might be *listening*, and they hadn't even taken the time to dry off, but fell onto the bed in a wet heap, rubbing their moisture onto the pile of blankets and the bedspread. Burrowed into the bed and its many coverings, Traci lay under Rick, and although he didn't notice it, suddenly Traci felt as if she was being crushed, smothered, from *within*, and her eyes bulged wide open, pressed out, as she tried to reach the purse thrown so casually on the bed less than half an house before... and found that the bones in her fingers didn't extend to the tips of her fleshy fingertips.

Suddenly, Rick noticed it too, and pulled out of the vise-like pelvis with a squeal, but by then all Traci could do was point to the purse with a limp, fleshy finger, and her tiny teeth chattered out something that sounded like "Mall 'oned, mall 'oned" from the depths of her slack mouth, but Rick was too busy screaming to hear *what* the barely supported bag of flesh beneath him was saying.

As Rick was covered with a shower of blood and squeezed out matter, the couple sitting below him, in their apartment-office, listened in relief. *It*, out there, had been well pleased. *It* would be satisfied, and grant them a boon, perhaps a busy hunting season.

While they listened to the howls above them, they wondered what the woman had wished (Fred had seen her throw the coin in, and felt the *shift* of that *below* it when she gave it access to her deepest desire), what she had wanted so badly that she'd be willing to ignore, to *defy* the warning sign that Famia had so carefully painted. Good idea on her part—before the sign, all folks did was wish for silly things, piffles that hardly whet the appetite of what was below the old well. The sign worked like a "No Trespassing" sign, making people *want* to tempt fate.

The howls reached a crescendo while Fred leaned over the Scrabble game and whispered to Famia—although they whispered not to keep the young fellow *upstairs* from hearing—"I'll bet it was her weight. She looked like a big-boned girl to me."

Famia just nodded, and added on a double point word to the board.

BRINGING IT ALONG

OILY SWEAT POOLED IN the shallow cup of skin below Carey's larynx; indifferently she ran her right forefinger through the sweat, tracing invisible paths along the swell of each breast and up under her chin. Eyes shut tight against the writhing shadows smeared on the skin of the tent, Carey told herself that this time, she wouldn't give in to Gary, wouldn't *freak* again.

I'm in another part of the world, another place, another time, she tried to remind herself, while listening to the skabble and screech of the birds beyond the tent, the arrhythmic breathing of the tropical forest around her (odd-leaved trees and scrubby bushes rubbing against each other, snicking in the warm, moist trade winds)…but the maddening sense of sameness, of never leavinig home at all persisted anyhow.

Wisconsin was thousands of miles, and Carey didn't know how many time zones away, yet as she lay in the thin-skinned tent Gary had set up that morning, eyes crumpled in a wet-lashed line across her face, Carey couldn't help but think that the differences of time and location had been overcome, bridged with her fear.

Stiff and warm in her hiking clothes—save for the ankle-killing heavy boots Gary and bought for her—Carey tried holdinig her breath, ears straining for the sound of Gary's soft breathing, but the chitter of birds (*bats? The booklet in the travel bureau said they have* bats *here*) and the chitinous snapping of foliage in the distance masked any smaller noises around her.

Letting out breath in a shaky rush, Carey ever so slowly

ran her left hand along the bumpy air mattress, a half inch at a time, feeling for Gary. The brightly colored booklet in the London Square Mall travel-bureau stand down in Eau Claire had warned—in a breezy, reassuringly offhand manner—that centipedes and other crawlies flourished in the more primitive areas of the islands, but they could be avoided with proper care. Carey didn't know if they could squirm into the tent; slither up through paper-thin cracks, to scuttle along the velour surface of the air mattress, toward warm flesh…but turning on the flashlight near her right side would only make it worse. Better to quickly brush a hand against some recoiling, swiftly gone thing, rather than illuminate the tent and see dozens of slithering, slimy *things* adhering to the tent skin, ready to drop down on her when shaken loose by the vibrations of her screams.

Carey inched her arm out to its full extended length—no Gary. Placing her left arm over her stomach, she rubbed her tense, cramping abdomen, and told herself, *The tent is big, plenty big…leave it to Gary to go for the biggest damn tent in Honolulu. Just like that time in the Blue Hills last summer. Stupid tent was as big as a Wausau Home….* As she swallowed, Carey's throat made a little clicking noise, while she extended her blistered stocking feet forward, toes pointing sharply toward the far wall of the tent, until her right foot came in contact with something warm, rounded, and hairy.

Gotcha, she thought, gently feeling the smooth roundness with her sore-soled foot, almost saying aloud, "Gary?" before she heard the stead drone, a new yet comfortable sound within the tent.

Tweetie Pie. At first she'd balked at the thought of bringing along their cat on the long ride from the Eau Claire airport to their connecting flight, and beyond; the baggage handlers might lose his white plastic-and-metal cage, or let him freeze or die of thirst. But Tweetie was a hardy little stinker; he'd done fine up in the Blue Hills, hadn't he? Not so much as one picked-up tick, or a single hopping flea. At the airport he'd curled up into a gray-striped and white-pawed ball, broad, curved back exposed to the noise and confusion beyond his cage, nose tucked in close to his tail.

Just as he was curled up now, an incredibly hard little ball of cat; only his purr revealed that he was a living animal. Relaxing slightly, Carey gently caressed his back; his body was so sleekly fat that even the tiny knobs of his spine were coated, hidden. But her foot was so blistered and tender that Carey was surprised that she'd been able to feel Tweetie Pie in the first place. The pressure of Tweetie's flesh against her own was soon unbearable, so she shifted her foot so that the ridge of skin along the side of her foot (near the little toe) barely rested against the sleeping cat. Just enough contact to assure her that she wasn't all alone, helpless, under an alien sky, while resting on strange, hostile soil.

Dipping her fingertip in the cup of sweat over her neck, she drew tight circles along her collarbones, not unlike those she drew upon her flesh last August, in the cow-barn of a tent in the Blue Hills as she listened with gritted teeth to the song of the displaced killdeer near their tent. "Cow-wee, Cow-wee," the infernal thing called, mournful and shivery thin in the darkness. Beside her Gary had mocked, "'Caw-wee. Car-ree'... they're calling for you, Car-ree—"

She had rolled over, shielding Tweetie with her flopping breast, holding the cat tight against the chill inside her. Gary knew she hated the cry of the killdeer; hated that aching cry whitch hung like morning mist over the ponds and lakes of Ewerton, their hometown. For those birds seemed to be calling *her*, chanting her name in the eerie whistle-caw that sent shivers up and down her like someone tracing thin lines along her spine with long, sharply pointed fingernails—Freddy Kruger gone avian.

The cry of those thin-legged, skittering birds was better suited to shrill keening winds and sopping-wet cold marshland—not the gentle rustle of needles rubbing needles high above them.

To Carey, the killdeer was a thing of the water, of spongy ground and instability...and she hated it when they taunted her by name.

She had pressed Tweetie ever closer, bending her head down close to his purring warmth, trying to drown out that mournful cry—and in so doing, she missed hearing Gary slither out of the tent, to pad around outside and come around to her side....

The travel brochure promised mild temperatures in Hawaii—by Midwest dog-days standard—a mean temperature of only 74.9 blissful degrees, with an August high of a measly 78.3 tempered by northeast trade winds...but when they deplaned in Honolulu, it was a dizzying 99 degrees and the announcer for the early evening news show they caught in their motel room was at a loss to explain the heat wave.

Gary, toweling off after a quick shower—he'd left on his lei, a floppy purple thing that bounced on his bony chest—said matter-of-factly, "Talk about bringing it *along*," before padding back into the bathroom, leaving deeper-tan wet footprints on the light sand-colored carpeting. Carey stopped unpacking long enough to shout back, "What?' then continued to place newly bought J.C. Penney Hawaiian print shirts into the dresser drawers. The idiocy of the shirts hit her then; thousands of dollars spent to come to Paradise, plus whatever Gary'd spent to bribe the airport, taxi, and motel people into letting Tweetie bypass quarantine (oh, Gary claimed, there wasn't any quarantine for house pets, but Carey knew better—yet remained silent), and they'd brought along mainland Hawaiian shirts.

From the echoing bathroom, Gary shouted back, "Your fault, y'know," before turning on his blow-dryer. From the bathroom doorway, she watched Gary wave the dryer at his close-clipped coarse hair, until he noticed her and said, "The truth, y'know. No use running from the heat, it was bound to find us somewhere."

"You talk like an ass,'" she said flatly, bending down to pick up Tweetie and cuddle him close. A shield between herself and Gary. He'd never hit her while she held the cat in her arms.

Gary aimed the dryer at her for a second, a blast of hot dry air which dried the frown onto her face. "Just like you couldn't hide from them killdeers...re-mem-ber, Car-wee?"

She refused to satisfy him with tears or shudders of memory. Turning off the dryer, setting it on the edge of the sink, Gary leaned in toward the mirror, his lei swinging from his neck over the bowl of the sink. She wished the lei would have pulled the hair dryer into the sink...if it had still been filled with water.

As Gary checked over his hairdo, patting stray hairs into place (he used hair spray, even on his mustache, something Carey didn't like to think about too much), he continued. "Yeah, that killdeer musta been gunnin' for you...was a long way from where he was 'sposed to be, huh? Maybe he was sweet on Car-wee—"

Holding Tweetie like a baby, his head tucked under her chin, Carey had left the room, unwilling to hear Gary rehash the Blue Hills debacle yet another time...but within the week, Gary found a way to get even with her.

First, he grew tired of Honolulu, the *luau* at the motel was a bore, *poi* reminded him of instant oatmeal, leis were for jerks, and he couldn't find anything worth buying to send home to their friends in Ewerton. Likewise, Wahiawa, Waipahu, and Kaneoke were "nothing joints"; only fit for *Hawaii Five-O* cultists, in Gary's expert, world-traveler opinion. Gary, who had yet to set foot in Canada; Gary, who considered a jaunt down to the London Square Mall true adventure. So they'd crossed the Kaiwi Channel by private plane (Carey prayed their credit card would cover Gary's bored spell), but Molokai was likewise "*Magnum P.I.* country," and they finally found themselves back in their original motel, looking out the big window at the countless white-sided buildings below. By that time, their leis were long wilted, tossed away in neat motel garbage-basket liners.

Gradually Carey began to pack away the printed J.C. Penney shirts, decreasing the number of them resting in Gary's side of the dresser. Then came the morning, yesterday morning, when Gary came back to their room, arms loaded with bags from some sporting goods store a taxi driver had recommended.

From the size of the stash Gary brought back with him, the taxi driver had to be getting commissions for steering customers to the store. Carey had been half-glad to see Gary charged up over something, until he pulled out a pair of hiking boots for her.

Raindrops *plashed* against the tent; in her mind's eye Carey pictured the droplets darkening the nylon skin, sending tiny writhing shadows slithering down to the ground. Rubbing her aching foot against Tweetie's solid back, Carey decided that Gary had to be somewhere at the far end of the tent—Tweetie liked to sleep near their feet (in his good moods, Gary called the cat Tweetus-Feetus), and since *she* hadn't felt the cat until just a few minutes ago....

Knowing—or at least being *almost* sure—where Gary was comforted Carey, made her relax muscle by sore muscle. The heat might have been the same; the fierce, uncharacteristic humidity might have come with them, but *this* time, in *this* patch of wild flora, things were going to be different. Not at all like that time in the Blue Hills, when Gary goaded her into going to pieces, "pussy out," as he'd laughingly told all their friends later on that summer.

I have you beat this time, her mind shouted at him. *You can't pull the same stunt twice, buster.* For a moment, Carey felt galled by Gary's nerve; he'd gone through a lot of trouble (climbing around in brutal heat, plowing through strange plants, risking contact with dozens of scuttling bugs) just to bring her to a place in Hawaii that would remind her of that weekend in the Blue Hills All because she hadn't *appreciated* his joke the first time around....

Lying under the trees in the Hills, wishing that they'd never come to Rusk County, let alone the infernal Blue Hills, Carey had pillowed her head on Tweetie's flank, until the cat's soothing purr lulled her into an uneasy sleep...while Gary was circling the tent, seeking the best spot, waiting until he was certain she was deep in sleep—

"*Car-wee!*" The noise was monstrous. The mama killdeer of all killdeers crying just scant *inches* from her unprotected head. Tweetie jumped up in a scrabble of claws and bushy fur; her head and arms were clawed before she was fully awake. And she'd done some clawing of her own....By the time she was aware of what had really happened, she'd somehow ripped the tough shell of the domed tent, her nails broken and jagged— while all around her the Hills echoed with Gary's laughter. Face flushed red up to his hairline, he was barely able to wheeze, "*C-cu-car-weeeeee!*" before she came after him, talons out and ready to scratch that convulsing face to an oozing pulp.

Afterward, it was weeks before she talked to him, let alone let him touch her again.

The rain's drone softened, faded to a steady drip drip off the broad stiff leaves nearby. Through her eyelids, Carey could see the first red-black haze of predawn light. True, Gary had gone through a lot of trouble (down to making sure Tweetie was nearby, to shred her face again) to make the terror keen enough to disarm her, but Carey smiled a sweat-oiled grin in the darkness, telling herself that the fact that they were on some little bird-dropping of an island off the coast of Kahoolawe wasn't going to make a bit of difference. *Fool me one, shame on you, fool me twice, shame on me.* She'd heard that line on an old *Star Trek* rerun; it would've been more fitting coming from Jack Lord's lips, or maybe Magnum's pal Higgins, but no matter who said it first, the expression was apt.

And Gary had hired a helicopter to fly the three of them out to this godforsaken area of rock and scruffy vegetation, just to make sure that there would be no hopping in the car and driving back to Dean county, and home, and supportive friends coming when he pulled his little killdeer joke again. And they'd toted in enough food to last three days, until the chopper pilot came back to pick them up. Time enough to rub it in, laugh until his jaws ached over her "pussy" reaction....

As her eyelids let in more and more reddish light, Carey

tensed again; foot rubbing slightly against Tweetie's unmoving flank or back or whatever for luck, waiting for Gary's expertly mimicked, "'*Car-wee!*'"

Oh, she'd noticed that devil glint in his eyes as they'd tramped through bushes and low-branched trees to reach this clearing. And the way he'd swung poor Tweetie's cage, as if it were a railroad lantern back at his Soo Line job. *Jaunty prick, aren't we?* she'd thought, as she helped set up camp. And the way he'd stayed awake, so she couldn't hear his slight snore as he slept— very clever. But no joke could ever be as...*funny* the second time around. A thing which Gary couldn't realize—but she'd let him have the fun of setting up his little ha-ha, just to see his face fall when it didn't work.

More light, definitely. She felt a pang at missing what had to be a beautiful sunrise, and hated Gary for spoiling the moment for her. Sweat plastered her clothes to her body, a gummy shroud. Gently, she rubbed Tweetie's body, thinking, *Be calm, he'll probably* shout *it next to your ear, a blast of* "'*Car-weeeee!*'" *before the roar. At least Tweetie Pie won't claw me up this—*

—her right foot touched Tweetie Pie's back again.

Eyes wide open, breath coming in ragged puffs through her quivering lips, she sat up, trying to make out the semidark interior of the tent, trying to see just what her foot *was* touching—

What she saw sent her scrambling on hands and knees out of the tent, damn the centipedes and whatnot, she just had to get out of that tent, away from Gary's lifeless head jutting through the bottom of the tent. Tweetie wound around her legs as she finally stood at a distance, staring at Gary. He had left the tent all right, most likely with the coming of darkness. Then, just as he had done before, he scuttered around the tent, ready to stop on her side, to wait for the moment when she was completely asleep...only *this* time, he hadn't seen or expected the vine extending out of the bushes. The vine thick and strong enough for him to get a clumsily booted foot tangled in it. And when he fell down, his neck was impaled on one of the tent spikes.

And somehow his head popped through the bottom hem

of the tent, just the crown of short, coarse hair, so much like Tweetie Pie's *rough coat*—

They got the saying wrong, she told herself, even as she kept backing away from the rain-and-blood-splattered tableaux by the tent, *Fool me twice, death on you...oh Gary, you look so funny, what a crazy joke...and you didn't even get to say*—

From somewhere in the dense dripping foliage, dark foliage she didn't recognize and would never stop fearing, Carey heard that mournful, utterly displaced cry:

"Caw-wee? Caw-wee? Car-reeeeee?"

RIGENT—DOUBLE AGENT
AND THE SHOPPING
CART BUMP

IT: *"A strange magnetism which attracts both Sexes."*

—"Madame" Elinor Glyn

Tampons. Husbands, buying them for their wives, now that, that marked the beginning of the end when it came to me playing the Shopping Cart Bump with foxes, Grant Bakker told himself while debating whether or not to go for the bigger box of Peaches and Cream flavor Quaker Instant Oatmeal ("Two More Packets!") or pick up the smaller Flavor Variety box ("New—Strawberries and Cream!"). Man cannot live on Peaches and Cream indefinitely, so the Variety box went into the bottom of his cart, landing next to the bottle of Hot Ortega Taco Sauce and the poly bag of Kraft Shredded Mozzerella cheese.

Pushing his cart—the left rear wheel screeed with fillings-rattling abandon—over to the "Canned/Fresh Produce" hanging orange sign, Grant reminisced about the times he'd seen a sure She Cart rounding an aisle, loaded up with such feminine, tantalizing goodies as Clairol Herbal Essence Shampoo, Apri Facial Scrub, Slim Fast, Playtex Deodorant Tampons, Melba Rounds, and Summer's Eve, a cart worthy of an aerobics instructor, or maybe, (if Grant was verrry lucky) a female karate instructor; a cart just begging to be playfully bumped, which he would do with gleeful anticipation—and get his cart slammed into the Green Giant veggies display by some bruiser in a Dodgers sweatshirt and size 13EEEEE New Balances who'd growl "Back off, a-hole" before heading to the checkout, wife and/or girl-friend's shopping list held aloft in a massive paw. Once, Grant reminded himself as he tossed a small head of lettuce into the smaller top basket part of his cart, some guy had bumped his cart!

And as far as these new "meet Markets" went—forget it. Too many yo-yo brains dressed in skimpy tube tops and old geezers with slicked down hair and pencil elbows poking out of loud sport shirts. Grant had seen that picture printed nation-wide a couple of years back, the one with the old guy and young woman dancing in an aisle, holding aluminum pots over their heads (Maybe they were dancing the "Tin—man"), and the only time he had considered himself desperate enough to actually try and attend a singles night, one look through the glass windows of the store from the safety of his parked car in the lot told him "Loser City, guy...better stick to checking out the atmosphere during commercial shoots."

It was almost enough to drive him back to the laundermats, only his agent, Aaron "the Overpaid" Bromowoich, had warned him not to go doing that after the pilot—Grant's fifth in two years, and naturally the one he had decided had a snowball's chance of selling—got picked up by the network as a Friday night mid-season replacement. Even though *Rigent—Double Agent* had an option for only six shows, and five of those were already in the can, the damned thing hadn't been seen by anyone in the "viewing public" (a.k.a. the guys in the size 13EEEEE New Balances who bought tampons), yet Aaron warned Grant that letting himself become "overexposed" was akin to signing his own death warrant. When Grant told Aaron that that remark made him feel like a roll of past due Fugi Film in a "Half-Price" bin, Aaron wagged a manicured finger at him over lunch and warned, "Grant, Gr-aant, they see you behaving like one of them"—his tone suggested that hordes of slugs and centipedes were about to overtake Grant's Caesar salad—"then they might as well watch the guy next door through a chink in the Levelors. And Grant, think, if we get a food sponsor, like maybe the catsup guys who don't run through the sieve, how would it look if somebody sees you buying the kind that does run through the sieve like tap water? What if they take a picture—"

"Can't I bean 'em with a can of pumpkin pie filling?"

"No, smartass, no more stores, no McBurger places, no more laundermats and don't-give-me-that -smirk—aren't you even a teensie bit scared of AIDS, bubbie?—and no more picking up of the floozies!"

Grant had sighed over his salad and mineral water with a twist of lime; things hadn't been this bad when he only did commercials. Six of them, that's all it had taken for him to get noticed; first by the dips who wrote in to "TV Mailbox," "Glad You Asked That!," and "Walter Scott's Personality Parade" ("Please, some information about the hunk in the Egg-Drop Waffles commercials—I think I'm in love!." C.Y., Last Chance, USA), then by the industry.

Most schlimazels like Grant, plucked raw and barely trained from the commercial heap, got to make a couple of pilots before getting the kiss-off. But Grant Bakker had a quality which, had he been up and coming in the 1920s, would have been dubbed "IT." Not much talent, the basic drive of a hungry water leech, but lots of "IT," whatever "IT" was. (And this was long before Stephen King redefined the capitalized term, in the days when a would-be aristocrat named "Madame" Elinor Glyn held Hollywood under her passionate thumb.) At least "IT" got him a show, which the networks thought highly enough of to plug endlessly during breaks in the Superbowl this past Sunday. And "IT" paid the rent on the shamelessly overpriced high rise duplex Aaron moved him into last month, along with enough good food and good wine ("White, Grant, must watch those calories"—"Stuff it, Aaron") to last the month, which ended this morning. Where Aaron expected him to get more food, especially after solemnly warning Grant, "No delivery boys, they will sell their souls for a star's address and will start selling it on street corners to rubber necks in big tour busses as soon as they make change for you," was anybody's guess...except Grant's. After trying to reach Aaron for twenty stomach-rumbling minutes, Grant picked up an Egg McMuffin, then tooled down to the Mayfair. New show on the tube next week or not, soon-to-be Big Star Grant Bakker Esq. was hungry (for food and other... sundries) and the cash register didn't care how many shows he had in the can.

After finding a tomato that looked reasonably plump without seeming "gooshy," Grant was about to head over to the frozen dinners when he saw THE cart, slowly rounding to his left. It had to belong to one of the "sundries" that Grant hungered for (since the AIDS crap, not all starlets—or even atmosphere—put out); a huge sack of long grain brown rice, Ivory soap, alfalfa sprouts, low-cal Buttermilk dressing, a loofa, the current issue of *Cosmopolitan*, a L'eggs Egg, a single roll of Scott toilet tissue (pink), and a loaf of diet wheat bread. Had to be a She Cart. No feminine napkins or douche, but what self-respecting husband or boyfriend would buy a single roll of pink toilet paper? His lady would kill him, or worse, hog it all for herself.

The old tingly feeling started *in* his Fruit of the Looms and shot down to the soles of his 10D Nikes. Leer of anticipation forming on his flawless lips (commercial number four: Lip-Cote with Sunblock), Grant gave the He Cart a light push—just the slightest flex of the thumbs and wrist—which sent it gallantly sailing off toward heaven on four black wheels. Contact. A high-pitched "Oooh!" then an arm clad in a red satinette base-ball jacket snaked around to grab the handle of the She Cart— Grant got a quick glimpse of brilliant orange frosted polish on fairly short nails (good, she won't be a back-raker)—and yanked it around and back. Com'on and get me, Big Boy. Grant had thought that that ploy had gone the way of elastic feminine napkin belts and cyclamate sweetened soft drinks. If the force behind that cart was really playing the game, she'd be lingering in the next aisle, waiting for a bump from behind...on her behind.

Grant hadn't felt so goofy-giddy since the first time a girl let him French her (Angie Calder, at the now-defunct Ewerton Drive-In back in his home state of Wis-Con-Sin, in—could it be that long ago?—1960) and while he didn't know just What was waiting for him in Aisle 6 "Sugar/Flour/Cake Mixes" it sure as shit didn't wear size 13EEEEE running shoes!

In fact, she was wearing red high top sneakers, the kind with the big fat silver eyelets, fat patterned laces and thick gummy soles. Black panty hose, artfully snagged, electric blue pinstripe pedal pushers, a Hawaiian print shirt so loud and badly patterned that "Weird Al" Yankovich wouldn't touch it, and the red satinette jacket he'd seen before. With a clipped chenille applique of a bowling ball and two tipsy pins across the back. The hair wasn't bad; what he could see of it was caught up in a long wavy tail—no Mohawk!—and he didn't mind the color mauve. Her yellow baseball cap hid the rest of her hair.

Not quite the girl who married dear old Dad, but Hell, Grant was adaptable. Besides, he'd never had a punker type—she looks like a station identification spot for MTV—before. Take that, paparazzi! She was still walking ever so slooowly, perusing the unbleached flour. And could it be true...did Grant actually detect the slightest wiggle of flesh under those pin-stripes?

The cart was out of his hands before he realized it. After bumping her lightly in the buns, Newton's Law took over and rolled it home to Papa. Now. Don't blow it. He hurriedly slipped on his "Gee, I'm sorry Miss" face and lowered his puppy-dog eyes. (Commercial number two: close-up of his look of "oooh, aaah" as his on-screen wife brings out a box-mix cake.)

"Oh, Mister, I'm sorry I'm in the way, let me move over—"

All Grant could think was: What's her face...that singer with the wrestler friends—OhMiGod I've bumped a geriatric Cyndi Lauper Dress-Alike!

The bumpee's wrinkled face—more like wrinkles with a hint of a face underneath—lit up with a huge grin that showed sound teeth behind the green lipstick (which was beginning to bleed into the wrinkles surrounding her mouth, like shoots coming from a plant) before she shrilled "Ooooh! It's Grant Bakker! I cannot believe it!"

How thrilling, he thought, Gee whiz and golly gee, my first in-the-saggy-flesh fan...take'r easy, hot shot Double Agent Rigent, maybe grannies just want to have fun, too. Probably has a Nielsen box hooked up to her set. Maybe she'll get all her friends to watch~ or her kids—he noticed that her knobby, wrinkled fingers sported no rings—oh hell, she must have friends who will tune in....

"—never thought that I'd meet a Real Star in here of all places!" she was enthusing, making the words "Real Star" sound like they were in capital letters on a movie marquee. By now she'd turned her cart around to face his, and was babbling a mile a second in a very youthful sounding voice. Grant thanked God for that; when someone said "Old Lady" to him, he'd immediately think two things—quavery voices and saggy armpits under sleeveless cotton shifts. He smiled down at her (she was a good foot shorter than his six-one), noticing that under the harsh white glare of the store lighting, her green eyes sparkled, matching the twinkle of the rhinestones in the three earrings she wore. As she talked and gestured animatedly, Grant was overcome with a strange impulse; a part of him wanted to put his big hand under the hollow v of her jawbone and gently tilt her head up, and then he'd bend down, lips pursed...crazy, he thought, she's old enough to be my grandma. Clearing his head of the weird impulse, he saw that what bones were visible under the wrinkles and sag were good; maybe fifty, sixty years ago she would have been a fox.

"—used to be I'd see Real Stars all the time, but lately they all go around in-cog-nito like that Debra Winger girl, with no make-up, or nice clothes on, so's you can't recognize them, and their Fans just end up passing them right by, without a chance to even ask for an autograph—

(Take your "overexposure is a death warrant" song and dance and shove it, Aaron!)

"—should know about Real Stars, I've been out here from

the start, the very beginning, and if I don't know right from the first moment that I see a body that that person is indeed a Real Star, then he or she just isn't one!" Pausing for a second to chew a bit of green-coated skin from her lips, she then added, "Aren't I right?"

"Uhhh...yeah, I guess the star system isn't what it used to be—"

"Phooey, lots of these goomers traipsing around on the tube or up on the screen aren't Real Stars any more than—than... this here bag of flour! She dumped a five-pound bag of Robin Hood unbleached into her cart, where it sent up a fine white plume of dust motes. "Ain't got any Life in 'em, just a bunch of phoney-baloneys. Not worth watching out for. Now when I was young, that's when the Stars were for Real. On screen or off, no mistaking them for common people." Tossing a packet of Robin Hood Applesauce Muffin Mix in next to the flour, she moved her cart down the aisle, continuing her harangue. Grant dutifully followed, bemused by her intensity. And those really... green eyes. His fingers, as they held onto the handle of the cart, longed to feel the thin bones under her jaw....

Despite the fanzie-groupie mentality, she had a certain gauche charm, not unlike that Granny Pot poster he had hanging on his dorm wall back at UCLA (where Grant was working on his degree in Biology—was that really fifteen years ago? he idly wondered), making her seem both hip and out of it at the same time. Clara Peller goes punk, that sort of thing.

He threw a packet of corn muffin mix into his cart as he followed; not that his coming along or staying behind would have had an effect on the loud burble of words which issued from that leafygreen mouth, effectively drowning out the spirit-less grocery Muzak which surrounded them. (Now I know the source of Milady's appeal...her tender green lips have tapped the starving root of my forgotten biologist's heart—aw, bullshit.)

"Like I was saying, if anyone should know about Real Stars, it is me. When I was young, I worked for some of the best of them, or those who should have been the best, all of the Real

Stars right down to their—"

"You worked for some of them? Now that's really something...care to drop any names—I mean, if you don't want—" Grant had a sudden vision of alienating his only Big Fan, maybe his lone Nielsen viewer....

"Mind? Oh, no, I'm proud of what I did...for those beautiful people. Ah me. God bless their dear souls. Mr Bakker—Grant, then—put down that ground beef! No good for you. No, no! Ground turkey's much better—that's a good boy! As I was saying, I worked for some of the fastest rising Stars in old Hollywood, back when the place was called by its rightful name, Hollywoodland."

"No kidding? I never knew it was called that. And it was all written out in white letters up on the hill—"

"All thirteen letters of it. 'Course, after some starlets took the big dive off the final "O" they eventually tore down the last four letters. No use invitin' more bad luck. But anyhow, back at the birth of it all, I was a cleaning girl for none other than Miss Gladys Smith, also known as—" she fanned the sides of her wizened face with wide open hands in a "Ta-Da!" gesture "—Mary Pickford! I didn't stay on for too long there, what with her baby brother Jack getting hitched to that beautiful Miss Olive Thomas.... Lordy, what a pretty woman, and such a talent, too. Not only Mr. Ziegfeld's Follies when she was no more than a girl, but later those movies—*The Tomboy*, and, naturally, *The Ziegfeld Girl*. Anyhow, since they were kids themselves, just twenty or so, they wanted someone their own age to work for them, and Miss Pickford let me go. A great thrill, let me tell you, being a heartbeat away from the big screen like that. Later that year I got to go to Europe; Paris, France, in fact, with her. That was 1920, September of the year—"

"Must have been exciting—" (She must be old, Grant Baby.)

Waving her orange-tipped fingers around her head in a rather flapperesque gesture, she trilled, "Lordy, yes! And me from a dinky mining town up in northern California. Pity, though. I didn't get to see much of the city before I came home alone."

Changing the subject with a toss of her purplish ponytail, she wagged a finger at Grant, "Those taco shells aren't the good kind, see, these here are made from stone ground corn, not the processed goop." She removed the offending box from his cart and exchanged it for the brand she recommended.

Too enthralled by her history lesson, Hollywoodland style, Grant forgave her pushiness (poor thing is used to doing for people) as he asked, "Not to be nosy, but what happened that you got sent home alone? Did she fire—"

"Oh no no no! It wasn't anything that I did!" She placed a bony hand on his tanned forearm, leaning close. "Miss Olive couldn't send me home. She died, you see," her voice lowered to a clear, firm whisper. "Killed herself, as a matter of fact. Swallowed toxic bichloride of mercury granules—nasty stuff— right in the best room of the Hotel Crillion. Spread out her new sable cape and laid down mother naked to die. When I saw her after I woke up the next morning, with the bottle still in her hand, I packed my bags and bolted before any of the hotel staff saw her. Chicken poop thing to do, in retrospect, but I was just a scared mining town girl in Froggie-land, and me not knowing the lingo, I figured I'd better amscray!" Up close, her breath smelled of Juicy Fruit gum; such a pungent, youthful odor made her story of long-ago death (if Miss Olive had lived, would she look like her?) seem all the more unreal. Yet, now that he thought about it, Grant did seem to remember reading or hearing about Olive Thomas, perhaps a Sunday paper magazine article, or a rehash in a check-out counter rag. It seemed to him that she had had dark hair. Long, wavy, touchable dark hair.

"I was just lucky that I found my round-trip ticket in my panic!" she continued in a normal sounding voice. "But that wasn't the end of the sorry affair. Later on, agents of the U. S. Government cracked a drug ring, and in the notebook of a dope pusher, guess whose name was listed...as a steady customer? A lot of people believed it, that poor Miss Olive was doing dope, but I am not one of them. Olive was a common name then, as was Thomas. Nor did I believe that Mr. Jack was hooked on that horrible junk, but once a rumor's allowed to run away, there's no use shutting the barn door to keep it in! It almost made me leave Hollywoodland for good, it did!"

"But you didn't," Grant prompted nonchalantly, placing a jumbo roll of Mardi Gras red tablecloth check paper towels into his cart. She placed the matching paper napkins in her cart before replying.

"For a couple of years I stuck to cleaning house for minor people in the business—camera men, editors, and such-like. No life to 'em, a real bunch of dead beats. Even did a little extra work in pictures I can't remember the names to. Got two bucks a pop and a box lunch for each one I did. Sort of hand to mouth for awhile. Didn't meet any rising Real Stars, either. But within a couple of years my dry spell was over, and I was back on top, working the Westlake district, here and there, but mostly at a director's house on Alvarado Street. That was until he passed on, and I took my services elsewhere—"

"Who was this director...I mean, I was wondering if I'd ever heard of him—I mean, was he big in the business?"

Her green eyes sparkled with a gleefulness that seemed inappropriate, under the circumstances. "I should say that William Desmond Taylor was a big man...he stood over six feet tall! Sorry to pull your leg, Mr.—Grant, but yes, he was very important. A bigwig with Famous Players Lansky, had all the girlies crawling over him like flies on a candy apple. In fact—" now breathing her Juicy Fruit breath as close to his ear as her tippy-toes stance would allow "—Mr. Taylor was in the habit of keeping little souvenirs, if you know what I mean. Lacy things women didn't show in public—not like these girls letting their bra-straps hang out—things you didn't show except to your Mister. He was a real Romeo, but had a face like a mule's backside, if you want my opinion. Real live wire, though. Man was rippling with life. When they found that prissy Mary Miles Minter's little pink nightie in his stash after his shooting, it blew her star right out of the heavens. Didn't do Mabel Normand or Mrs. Shelby much good either when he—"

Minter and Normand were familiar enough to Grant, but who the hell was Mrs. Shelby?

"She was Miss Minter's monma. All three of them gals were having affairs with the fellow, right under each other's noses. Very sticky, all them comings and goings...a neighbor lady thought he was shot by a woman...the likely scenario, if you ask me. Somebody probably trying to get her bloomers back, mark my words."

Fighting off the urge to cup that little chin in his big hand, Grant knew the answer to the question he was about to ask, but the need to know for sure made him ask it anyway. "But you went back to work for the Hollywood crowd, didn't you? Even after your two bosses died—"

Nonplussed by the darkness of his tone, she replied, "Why yes! I loved the business, even if I wasn't in films—extra work don't count, actually. Now don't go thinking that all my bosses went and died on me the minute I set foot in the door. They didn't at all. Take Mrs. Reid for an example. Just because her Wallace was hooked on the smack, "dope fiend" the trades were calling him, and passed on in the looney hatch back in '23, doesn't mean that I had anything to do with that. Wally was a goner from the dope no matter what I did or didn't do. Once that pusher was at the studio, that "Count" fella, as he called himself, or he was called, I forget which—and you'd die if I told you who he really was, a man you'd never suspect—anyhow, once the "Count" fixed someone up with dope, they were as good as dead. Some sooner, some later, but all as good as dead in the end. You don't do drugs, do you Grant? Good. Because, know what? You remind me a little bit of poor Wallace...especially around the nose. Anyhow, Florence—Mrs. Reid, or maybe you've heard of her as Dorothy Davenport, her old screen name—she didn't die until her natural time came, and since Wally died away from home, while he was 'put away,' I never thought of him in the same way I did Miss Olive or Mr. Taylor. Wally was a live wire, though...."

"But Miss La Marr...poor dear, live-a-lifetime-in-a-day

Barbara, after she passed on I did feel awfully jinxed. Barbie passed on in '26. Nice girl, bit flighty, but OK., had umpteen husbands. Never got enough sleep, why two hours a night isn't enough for a mutt's flea! Claimed she had 'better things' to do, like get hitched over and over...and shoot smack. The junk was the cause of her death—just sucked the life right out of her—but good food, natural things, and lots of sleep can yank the biggest monkey off a—"

Grant paused in the middle of two rows of cleaning supplies, the sharp odor fighting for his attention (commercial number three: "Honey, is that floor really dry? With a shine like that?"), while he hung back as she progressed to the next aisle. "The Girl Who Was Too Beautiful," he said softly to himself. And she had been, if the pictures he'd seen didn't lie. Her, he remembered. Douglas Fairbanks, Sr. discovered her, if he remembered correctly. He wondered if his Technicolor shopping partner (and you scoffed at Meet Markets) had given Miss La Marr a reference from Fairbanks' former brother-in-law, Jack Pickford, widower of Miss Olive...now don't be a prick, Grant, he scolded himself, suppose someone poked fun at all those unsold pilots of yours, old bat can't help it if she's unlucky. Typhoid Mary of Hollywoodland, with the thirteen letters.

"There you are!" Grant's rear end was bumped by the metal cage-work of her cart, oddly cold through his worn Klein jeans. Pushing her cart abreast of his, she went on with her recitation, oblivious to the squall of the toddler behind them which rose high and shrill above the Muzak: "Hurt me, lady hurt me...got my han' Momma, mean lady hurt me!" and the exhausted drone of his mother "Shawn, the nice old lady didn't hurt you...now shut up!"

"—and everyone just knew that old Louis B. had something to do with what came out of those speakers during His Glorious Night, why poor Mr. Gilbert sounded positively neutered, and it's a fact that he had a very nice voice; I should know since I heard it every day when I worked for him and that snooty Ina—"

(Behind them, the toddler sucked on his swiftly purpling hand and screamed between sucks, "Lady hurt me!" as his mother mumbled to him to shush up already....)

"...such a horrid shame, since other people who didn't know him face to face believed that John Gilbert really did sound that bad, no wonder poor Jack went straight to the bottle, especially after that bitch—excuse my French—that bitch of a wife Ina Claire left him, so it was no surprise, at least not to me, when he finally drowned in it in '36. Lemme see, that was the...fifth year I'd worked for him, but let me reiterate, the man had a very lovely voice." She placed a small bottle of Ivory dishwashing detergent next to her paper napkins before turning to Grant and asking, "Did your grandparents ever tell you about Dish Nights at the movie theatres? The local Bijous would do anything to get folks to spend a dime at the films; Two Fers, Marcel Night coupons—I went to get quite a few of those myself until I discovered purple henna, which looked quite natural with my black hair—where was I? Oh yes, just all sorts of promotions to bring in a warm body. I enjoyed the movies so much, best way to spot new Real Stars, that I had to take on a weekend job while I was still working at the Gilberts."

"You were able to get two jobs? At once? So soon after the Depression? You must have had some damned impressive references." Grant recalled the stories his Grampa Baker—one "k" in those days for Grant, too—told him about his hometown Ewerton during the Depression; how the movie theatre closed down, not to be replaced until the '50s with the now closed drive-in; how Old Man Ferger at the Founder's Bank tried to shoot himself and only succeeded in blowing a new doorway between his office and the one next door; how the Town Council had to put up a "Jobless Men—Keep Walking!" sign next to the "Welcome to Ewerton" sign...yet, somehow, this woman had managed to find two jobs while times were hard. Granted, the job situation in Hollywood was somewhat better than in rural Wisconsin, but could it have been that much better?

"Oh, I did, I did. The industry takes care of its own, no matter how low on the totem pole you are...you should know that. Got me a dishwashing job, two nights weekly at a little place tucked away in the Palisades...and I know you'll recognize the lady's name, the one who ran the joint," she taunted coyly. Fighting to keep his hands from cupping that small jaw (weird, Grant, weird—), he took the bait. "Try me."

"How 'bout 'Thelma Todd's Roadside West'? Have the bells started ringing?" Without waiting for an answer, she scurried off toward the Cards section. Grant covered the distance, cart wheels screeeing, in two easy strides. "Hey, who doesn't remember that dish? The 'Ice Cream Blonde' in all those Marx Brothers com—"

"And it's a pity they never did find out who killed her, either."

An image that Grant hadn't wanted to recall came back to him; a tousled blonde, bleeding onto a fur coat, spilling out of a car like some sort of gory Cracker Jack prize falling out of box. She had had such a lively smile—oh shit, now I'm thinking like her, 'lively' this and 'live wire' that...."

"Pretty girl, vivacious as all get out, but I really didn't get the chance to know her all that well. She looked real good in her coffin. Yellow flowers. They had a blanket of yellow roses over her." She began to search through the Sympathy/Get Well selection of cards on the long rack. Grant saw her orange-tipped fingers linger over cards meant for families who have lost a male relative, and something deep, something protective of himself at a primitive level that even surpassed his strange longings just to kiss those green smeared lips once, made Grant attempt a fast, but polite break for the checkout line, and freedom. Toes crossed in his Nikes in hopes that she'd refuse, Grant said, "I'm afraid that I'm done with my shopping. Would you like me to carry your bags? Or do you have some more shopping to do—" Plucking a card out of the Sympathy assortment before her, she gave him a big smile, then tore a shred of skin off her lip with a hungry, almost mindless motion, bringing a thin line of blood to the surface. Flicking the bit of greenish white skin aside, she said, "No need to wait, I'm all done, too. And I wouldn't want to miss out on the chance to take a walk to the parking lot with a Real Star. They are so rare these days!"

Ignoring the slow writhe in his guts, and the rebukes of his subconscious, Grant dutifully followed her to the nearest checkout lane. As his hands fanned the smooth surface of the cart handle in preparation before the inevitable grasping of her fragile chin (will her hat fall off when her head tilts back?) Grant vaguely recalled Aaron, and his warnings, but dimly, a siren blowing under miles of swirling water. Maybe, when he got home, he'd call Aaron, let him in on Grant Bakker's first weird, but cute (when she was young, she must have been a—) fan...preferably while sipping—no, make that gulping—a double Scotch on the rocks. And screw the calories. Her eyes... soulfully, flawlessly green. Maybe, after getting done with her, he'd need a triple Scotch, forget the rocks.

As he followed her out the automatic doors, his hands unconsciously spanned the bag he was holding, spreading just wide enough to support that tender jawline.

From three blocks away, Lt. Wynter couldn't tell who was in trouble in the Mayfair parking lot, the old lady bending over the prone man on the ground, or the man himself. From her vantage point on the motorcycle, the police officer couldn't quite tell if the man was trying to fix a nearby car or simply lying there... putting on speed, the officer soon saw that the woman (middle aged, definitely—sun must have been shining in my eyes) was trying to do something to the man, who was quite still on the ground, it did and didn't look like CPR; the woman (wait a minute, Wynter, that's no woman, looks like a co-ed, college kid, probably...only wasn't her hair lighter before? Must've been the sun, the things these kids spray on their hair—) was doing the mouth to mouth part all right, but no heart massage. As Lt. Wynter came within ten yards of the scene, she noticed that the girl (college girl hell, that's a kid, barely a teen-ager, poor thing, not knowing what to do in an emergency) wasn't coming up for air herself, but grinding her mouth down hard on the man's unmoving face, and for a second the officer wondered if she had stumbled onto a street girl and her trick, but when the girl heard the motorcycle coming close, she looked up; tears in her eyes, and motioned for the policewoman to come closer. Clumsily getting to her feet (looks like she ripped her pantihose, helping the guy...it's what a good Samaritan can expect nowadays) the girl stammered in a choking voice, "He fell down! I was heading for home and I saw him fall down, grasping his chest! I didn't know what to do! And I wanted to ask him for his autograph, too! I did the mouth to mouth thing, but it didn't work! Is he dead?" As she checked the man's pulse (White male, mid-forties or older, six-one or two, maybe 150-60, and what the hell did she say about an autograph?) Lt. Wynter was taken aback by the girl's remarks. Looking up into the girl's face (most of her green lipstick had smeared off onto the man's slack face), squinting her own eyes against the sun's glare, Lt. Wynter asked, "You know who this man is?"

Brightening considerably, considering that she had just been rubbing noses with a dead man, the girl chirped, "Oh yes! He's—he was—Grant Bakker, the commercial guy...he was gonna be in that show they advertised on the Superbowl, that *Rigent-Double Agent* one." Then, as if noting the officer's disapproving stare, the girl adjusted her yellow baseball cap and spoke in a slightly more appropriate tone of voice, as if it had just dawned on her that she was standing a sneaker's length from a dead man.

"He was really good...I could tell, just from watching the commercials, that he was gonna be a Real Star"—her voice added the caps—"and when I saw him here, just before he began to clutch at his chest, I thought 'There aren't too many Real Stars like that anymore—'" Despite the fact that the girl was an obvious movie mag junkie (or worse) the officer found herself liking the child, for some odd reason. True, she botched the mouth to mouth and apparently didn't even attempt any sort of CPR, no matter how crude (as if the TV hadn't shown how to do it often enough...she could have at least pounded on his chest a few times, that's been known to work) but yet...Lt. Wynter couldn't stay angry with the little thing.

Standing there, looking down at the officer, forlorn yet somehow in command in her shiny red jacket and pathetic looking flowered shirt, not to mention those ripped up hose (the officer had a fleeting, painful memory of her own mother beating her with a wire coathanger for wearing her miniskirt too short on a school day.... Christine Crawford, you ain't alone), the girl fumbled in her jacket pocket for something, all the while giving the woman hunkered down next to the dead man a look of longing, of sadness that could be so easily remedied...as Lt. Wynter double-checked the man's wrist for a pulse, her hand ached to touch the creamy skin under the girl's tiny chin, to cup the delicate bones in her hand, tilt that head of glossy purplish-dark hair, and—

Totally straight all her life, the policewoman shuddered upon realizing what her mind was asking her to do, and she told herself, This kid isn't a whore.... I'll stake my badge on it, but I don't know what she is. Poor thing, she's had a bad experience—wait a second, Wynter, don't go soft on this one....

The girl put on a pair of sunglasses; red plastic heart-shaped frames. The perspiration on her small nose made them slide down half-way, and Lt. Wynter realized that the girl reminded her of someone...as the girl bent down to pick up the two Mayfair shopping bags (a roll of red-checked paper towels topped one, and a roll of pink t.p. and a rolled up issue of *Cosmopolitan* topped the other) the officer knew who the girl looked like. Sue Lyons and the poster for *Lolita*. While still crouching down, the girl said to the officer, in a gum-redolent whisper, "Do I have to go to the station? I'm supposed to be home by now, I'm bringing the food for a party, and if my parents find out about this" she cocked her head toward the dead would-be TV star "they'll kill me!"

Years on the LAPD made Lt. Wynter well aware that the girl was lying about something, and that she should get a full statement from the girl, at the station, but the ache in her fingers to just cup that chin once, and bring her lips close to those which had recently tasted death made her—urged her—to tell the girl, "This is pretty much an open and shut case, I don't think I'll need a statement after all. Why don't you just go on home." She noticed that the bag with the paper towels held a package of rapidly thawing ground meat "—before your meat thaws out." Get away from me, please kid, please.

Hefting the two full bags, the girl got to her feet, and smiled a thank-you at the officer, then began to furiously chew her gum. The smell was odd, for some reason; familiar, yet not the wild sort of scent the police woman associated with young kids. The girl slowly began to walk away, and once again, the officer's urges got the better of her.

"If you decide to make a statement, just come to the head-quarters in this neighborhood. Ask for Lt. Wynter. Lt. Carrie Wynter," while her mind raged *Don't tell her your name, my God*—

Without breaking stride, the girl looked over her shoulder and said, "I don't think I'll be able to make it, but I'll keep that in mind," in a tone of voice that said she wouldn't, that she would forget all about the police woman, in her quest for Real Stars. With capitals.

Sighing, Lt. Wynter couldn't help feel both sad and relieved.

DEAR D.B.

AT FIRST, I ONLY thought that good old Super-super goofed, *again*. After all, the man's command of the "Engleesh as she is spoken" isn't the best to begin with (but you would think that living in the City for umpteen years would make a difference—sometimes I'm sure that English is doomed to become the United States' second language), but even *he* should know the difference between *gringa* and *gringo* (at least that's how I think the "Spanish she is spoken"—I never did take that course back in Ewerton High)—but at the time I decided that it would *not* do to gripe about it. He does allow me to keep Wolfie and Duke (neither of whom will *ever* be mistaken for lap dogs) up here in the apartment, which is not the most common practice here in New York City. (And if I'm not a good girl, he'll confiscate his Roach Motels!)

Anyhow, Roach Motels and the boys aside, when Mr. Hernandez said what he did to me, I had just gotten back my proofs for "The Mouth That Would Not Die" from *Bloodbath Quarterly*. The editor scribbled that the "...That Wouldn't Die" sounded a bit "flip." *As in Wilson,* I was tempted to scribble back in the margins, but you learn to keep such thoughts to yourself, especially when there's a five foot high slush pile generated by writers just dying to get a shot at *BQ*. (Instead, I told myself I'd change it back when the anthology of my work came out.) As usual, the galleys came back with the standard note, "Running late, get back ASAP," and so on. I had only found three typos, all minor, when Mr. Hernandez knocked, asking for the rent, and for once he *didn't* make some crack about (pick one or more): my halter top, my shorts, my body, and/or my single female status. (Thank goodness for two mammoth *male* doggies at a time. Like that! And I used to think good ole Dead Fred Ferger back home in Wisconsin was bad! Spare me from the Latin lover type!)

Instead of his usual "How's de preety seenyorita?" line, Mr. H. kept it short, but right before he left, he bent down to itch Wolfie's head and said something about, "You boys protect the young *gringo,* okay?" but I didn't really *think* about it until after I took a second look at the proof sheets (noticing the initials of the guy who typeset my story in the upper left hand corner of the first page—he was the one that the editor at *Gore Magazine* wrote to me about; she said that he really liked "that D.B. Winston's stuff,' if I remembered her letter correctly), and even then, I figured that Mr. H. made a simple mistake...but after I went to the drugstore, what Mr. Hernandez said began to niggle at the back of my mind.

Not that the trip to the drugstore and back was eventful— but, in a way, that *was* the problem. All I had picked up was a box of tampons, some cheap typing paper (is there any other kind?) and a few stamps from one of those mini mail-box shaped dispensers (the kind that gobbles your quarters and usually forgets to stick out a tongue of stamps), and even though a few of the toughs from the neighborhood were lounging around the counter and by the door for once they didn't give me a hard time. Once, one of them offered to help me "put in" a feminine product (shades of Dead Fred and his "can I trim your bush?" remarks), but this time they just stood around gassing, playing with the dials on their boom boxes (which I swear grow out of their shoulder blades) and scaring the bejesus out of out-of-towners who happen to find themselves in this part of the city *(not* your highlight tourist attraction here!). And I actually made it *back* to the apartment house unaccosted...and I didn't have the boys along for moral support, either. (When I walk the dogs, *no one* approaches me—if the *boys* don't scare them off, there's always the option of beaning someone over the head with the pooper scooper!).

But *that* day, I only figured I'd lucked out. It wasn't until I called the super to come and take a look at my leaking faucet (the roaches were taking sides for swimming teams in my sink) a week later that I realized something was *wrong,* really off-kilter. For one thing, Mr. H.—who usually broke both legs' running to come spend time with the *gringa*—made some excuse about not being able to make it until after supper. I figured that perhaps he didn't realize it was *me,* the "Preety *señorita,*" so I said who was calling, taking pains to pronounce my name *very* plainly, and after I did, there was this *pause* on his end of the line, and I could hear this Spanish-language radio or TV station in the background (like something out of *The Possession of Joel Delaney*; the part when Shirley MacLaine goes slumming in search of help for her brother) and only after I'd shouted *"Hello?"* into the speaker a few times he came back on the line, muttering that he'd be up right away, but before I hung up I heard him grumble something about the *"loco gringo:"* At the time, I thought to myself, *Maybe you should write* "I *Am Woman" across the front of your tee,* since it *did* seem funny... then. As it was, Mr. H's visit was uneventful; he growled that he had his food waiting on the hotplate, and hurriedly fixed the faucet, but as he was leaving (and Mr. "Do Not Disturb—Night Job Sleeping" Door Sign—as if a "Night Job" was an entity that needed sleep!—was just leaving *his* apartment across the hall), Hernandez happened to say to himself, "Goddamn *loco gringo* sonsabitch," which prompted Mr. "Night Job Sleeping" to chortle "Goo'night, fellah" at me. I almost sicced Wolfie and Duke on him, but figured, why waste the effort? They might have gotten food poisoning from the jerk. I decided to get them to bark at his door some *day...*his sign didn't say "No *Barking*"!

However, I didn't get a chance to mull over the day's events, since the *BQ* editor called; would I consider some last-minute editing on 'The Mouth That..."? Nothing major, just a few changes near the end? After scrambling around for a copy of the

MS (not much of a scramble, considering the size of my Roach Motel room) I dictated the changes over the phone, and at that point things *really* began to get weird, for between lines, he kept asking "Got a cold, D.B.?" "Can you speak up?" "Bad connection" and I wouldn't have paid any undue attention to that if I'd still been living in Ewerton, where bad connections were the norm—but he was calling from an office only a couple of miles away at the most! After he hung up I told myself I'd have to get Super-super to come and look at it (since Ma Bell was slaughtered, calling the phone people is a fool's errand)—when he got himself some glasses, or after I made up my "I Am Woman" shirt. And that was when things were still fairly *normal.*

Two weeks later I got my check for "The Mouth That…," and went to the bank to try and cash it, I hadn't been in for about a month—but that isn't an *eternity*—yet the teller, a woman who I *thought* would recognize me (I'd been to her a few times before, during other visits) acted like I'd caught the first ship from Mars and landed on the roof of the building five minutes before, and jumped down to the lobby through the ceiling. Now I'm not a naive person, even though I was born and raised in a small town. I'm aware of the fact that New Yorkers simply don't have the *time* to be slavishly polite to every Tom, Dick, and Henrietta who walks through the door (unless they work at Bloomies and are busy trying to get you to submit to a cosmetic makeover—then they act like they'll sell you the city for a string of beads and some feathers!) but I was expecting a teller at *my* bank to treat me like a *human being.*

The woman gave me a strange look when I submitted my check and passbook (for deposit of part of the check; I'm not crazy enough to spend the whole thing at a pop), looking from the book to me and back again, like something wasn't computing for her. She began to act as if I'd just handed her a scribbled note topped with the words "This is a Stickup!" and stammered something about needing some "recent identification" and I reached over, took my things, and said for her to forget it, and left, while she stared at me as if I was Al Pacino carrying a long flower box under one arm. While I walked to the subway station, I began to think about the past few days and decided that the Big Apple (as the folks back home love to call it when I phone them—in the background I can hear Mom yell "Arlin, c'mere, it's our girl calling from the Big Apple!") had gone wormy for me. I mean, Ewerton was *bad*—it was deeply entrenched in that old system of "Oh, you're Arlin Winston's girl," or "Her? She's old Palmer Winston's grandchild," or worse, "Devorah? That's old man Winston's son's little girlie." When I got my driver's license, I had almost expected it to say "Devorah Bambi Winston, daughter of Arlin, son of Palmer, grandson of Porter," or something semi-Biblical like that. It was so *frustrating*; if I had stayed back home, I wouldn't have ever had a chance to be *me*, but I would have either been dubbed "*So and So's child*," or "*the such-and-such girl*," or—if I had married one of the local-yokel Ewerton males, eventually I would have become "Joe Blow's *wife*," or "the mother of Dick and Jane," and so on to infinity. Part of the reason why I cleared out of there was the fact that I had had no hope of carving out an identity for myself; in a small town a person is never a *person,* period, but either the offspring of someone or the parent of another...at least in New York, I figured that a person would be known only as his or her *self,* without a centipede-like trail of relatives hanging behind them. All I wanted to be was *me*, D.B. Winston, writer, but after all this *gringo* and "better identification" stuff, I was beginning to wonder if I should go and have my gender and vital statistics tattooed across my forehead!

Crawling out of my pool of self-pity long enough to look up for my station number, I noticed that I was sitting in a subway car full of boom-box babes, all big, all poorly dressed...and *all leaving me alone*. And there wasn't a Guardian Angel in sight.

When I reached my stop, I hurried off, hoping to leave before my traveling companions came to their senses. During the walk home, I toyed with the idea of working this all into a story. It had worked for me in the past...as evidenced by my still uncashed check.

After a bit of arm-twisting I got the super to cash my check for me (I used an automatic teller to make my deposit later on), and settled down with a new stock of groceries (and seeming *tons* of Alpo!), trying to catch up on my writing. Just for the hell of it, I began a story called "The Metamanphosis," While I was busy writing that, the *BQ* editor sent me a black and white photo mockup of the cover for the next issue—a real stunner. I'd had my name on the cover of more than a few issues, but this time was the first time that a cover illo had been based on *my* story. I liked the way J. K. Potter put the reflection (distorted, of course) of the killer on the old-man's spittle-moist teeth, inside the cavern of that drooling, vacant mouth. And next to that: A HAIR-RAISING TALE OF NEIGHBORLY REVENGE: *THE MOUTH THAT WOULD NOT DIE!* BY D. B. WINSTON. As I looked it over, I realized why the editor had opted for the title change; this way it was a bit more on the Lovecraftian side. If only my Grandpa Winston (the former English lit teacher) could have seen that! (I wondered if *Gramps* would have had trouble with my gender, too....) But the story beckoned, a sure five hundred dollars if I could get it done and accepted at a prozine, so I put the cover mock-up aside and got down to business, thinking that the heroine/hero of the story was the only with big problems....

By the seventh of June, I realized that I *had* it with crazy New Yorkers. Never mind the *gringo* bit of the month before, or Mr. "Night Job Sleeping"'s jibes (I'd *give* him something to go banging his walls—and bellowing—about), or even the snafu at the bank—just who would have thought that the sort of thing would happen at *Bloomies*? (Saks, *maybe*, but good old *Bloomies*? My God, they let Paul Mazursky make that *movie* there! If Robin Williams could *defecate* there, I thought they'd be good sports about almost *anything*!)....

Hold on, try to calm down. I must try to figure out what went on, where it all went wrong...(Put it down, good old black and white.) But thinking about it, even after everything *else* which has happened, still makes me shake...it didn't *seem* like the end of the world, not *then*. But it was *close*.

Anyhow—I went there to buy myself a new half-slip, some panties, and maybe a nightgown if the pennies stretched far enough. So. Once through the door, I made my way past the endless cosmetic counters, mildly surprised that the floor-walkers didn't rush up to me, begging me to let them spritz me with some much-too-expensive perfume, hoping I'd find it irresistible and buy five gallons of the slop, or just spray me and ask *later* for permission. Usually, by the time I'd made it to the second floor I'd end up smelling like a cheap streetwalker on Friday night, but that day I lucked out and escaped the scented hordes. It really seemed like my day, no Lorelei-like calls from the cosmetic clerks, begging me to wander over for a make-over, and I rode the crowded escalators until I found the intimate apparel. I was happily looking over the unmentionables, no stuffing things into my jeans pockets, no hiding panties in a false-bottom bag, simply minding my own biz-niz, when the saleslady came up, hovering like a poly-cotton hummingbird. With too much eyeshadow. She began to pester me, asking if I was looking for "something for a special someone?" Not under-standing why she couldn't go bother one of the dozens of other shoppers milling around us, I said, "No thanks, just browsing until I find something I like." I held a pair of panties up to the light, trying to see how sheer they were, when she tried another line of questioning.

"Did you happen to have someone special in mind? Maybe that would aid in your selection—" Thinking *read my* lips, *honey*, I tossed over my shoulder, "Just looking for something for myself, if you don't mind. Thanks for asking." She didn't leave. I could smell her, and feel her breathing down my neck. Turning around, I saw her give me a *look*, like I had feathers growing out of my ears, or a less appropriate part of my anatomy, then exit Ms. Too Much Eyeshadow. Followed shortly by *my* exit. I figured that she'd have to take a coffee break sometime; I'd check out the undies then. Walking away, I remembered that the World Fantasy Con would be coming up soon, and decided to check out the junior dresses....

Bad move. And no warning signs this time; the salesclerk initially left me alone, in peace, while I looked over the racks of new fall arrivals and she didn't even flinch when I picked out two reasonably priced street-length dresses (one with a side slit, the other a sweater-dress) and approached the counter. Then—

Her: "Will that be cash, charge, or—"

Me: "Oh, no, not yet...could I please try them on? I have two items here—"

Her: (look of utter "slap-me-silly" shock on her face) "Uhhh—"

Me: (getting *mucho* disturbed) "Okay, I'll leave one here and take them in one at a time, if that's the prob—"

Her: "I'm sorry, sir, but you don't understand, this isn't *that* kind of store—"

Me: (completely disturbed now) "*Sir*? Are you *blind*, ma'am? All I want to do is try on these dresses—"

Her: "I-I-I'm afraid that *you* can't *do* that, at least not *here*—"

Me: (something *beyond* disturbed) "Miss, is there a *problem*? Is there a limit on the number of dresses I can take in there? Are you afraid I'll shoplift these? You are welcome to come in the dressing room *with* me if that's what's got you worried—"

Her: (barely stifled scream, by now we have an *audience*) "Please-leave-this-store-immediately! *Be-fore* I have to call the manager!" All of the above with a plastered-on *smile*, for cryin' out loud! Thinking that I would have caused less of a disturbance if I'd put my head under her skirt like Robin Williams did to Maria Conchita Alonso in that damned *film*, I threw the dresses on the floor—by now people were openly staring, then shoved their noses in Fabric Care tags when I stomped past—and started doing a number on my Bloomies Charge card with my nail clippers while riding the escalators to the ground floor. I hope all the little pieces jammed up the mechanism, too.

During my ride home—my unmolested, unpinched ride

home—I wondered if New York was going through a gender-blindness epidemic of some sort.

Not long after the Bloomies fiasco, my contributor's copies arrived, along with a little note from the *BQ* editor, which was to let me know that in this year's *BQ* Reader's Poll I'd placed as the fifth most requested author, up six places from last year, et cetera, et cetera. There was more, but at the time I wasn't in the mood to read on. I mean, I figured he didn't *know* what was happening to me. And I wasn't about to call him up and announce, "Hey, by the way, the *funniest* thing happened at Bloomies last week, even better than that scene in *Moscow on the Hudson* where Robin Williams puts his head under the sales clerk's skirt. Only they wouldn't even let me try *on* a skirt, let alone—"

He probably would have attributed it to my fertile mind, my writer's flair for the dramatic...but even Larry Olivier couldn't top *this* situation's dramatics. And no one could be *this* imaginative.

The dogs, my *boys,* my trusty Wolfie and Duke, began looking at me strangely. And they sniffed me more, the wary type of snuffle with no wagging tail they used to reserve for good ole Dead Fred the helpful back home neighbor (bless his nosey soul!) and now for Mr. H. when he comes down for the rent. It couldn't *be,* not *really* but the dogs were acting as if *I* smelled like an old *man.*

By the next day, I realized that something was *bad* wrong. When I picked up the phone on the second ring, the *BQ* editor asked *me* if *I* was home! I didn't know if he bought my line about a bad connection, but I kept crinkling the wrapper from the boys' Gaines Burgers (even Lorne Green would gag on Alpo day after day) next to the receiver, so I think that maybe I fooled him—and doing something like that to him made me feel like week-old fishbowl scum. The call was about the novella he'd bought some time ago—would I mind if he split it into three parts, and ran it in three issues? I was so rattled by then I almost made the suggestion that I'd be happy if he ran it a line at a time until kingdom come, but then reason shut my mouth for me, warning, *why blame this mess on your* editor? So far he hadn't called me "Sir" or *gringo*! However, once he hung up, I dug out my old cassette recorder from under the bed and taped my voice, then played it back. It sounded fine—and feminine— to me, but it made the boys howl...and the sound of Mr. "Night Job Sleeping" banging on the wall was sweet music to me, but by the following day *nothing* could have made me smile.

That day, what went on went beyond *wrong*, *bypassed strange*, and entered *bizarre* at full tilt.... And all I did was go down the hall to the *bathroom*, something I've done hundreds of times since moving to the city, to this apartment-cum-tenement. And while I wasn't actually *friends* (or even very friendly) with the people on my floor, things were non-hostile enough to allow for a bit of overlapping when it came to using bathroom stalls; after all, total strangers use the same restroom at the same time in all sorts of public places with no hassle. At least I knew the other tenants by sight and occasionally by name (from matching bodies with name plates on mail slots), and they likewise "knew" me. Or so l had assumed. And I thought that Mrs. Pendleton (Miss? Ms? All I knew was that she always took the Social Security checks out *of* the box labeled "Pendleton, S") was one of the friendlier souls on my floor, at least she'd grunt "Lo" as she passed by a person in the hallway, hunched over her walker. Even the boom-box babes on the corner didn't bother her. But that day you could have heard her clear into the Bronx, the way she carried on when she lurched out of the stall and found me at the sink washing my hands. Goggling at me from behind her trifocals, chins quivering, papery white lips working in indignation, and then yelling, "Ain't you got no decency? Getcha kicks outta *listening*? *Pre-vert*! Raised in a *baarn*? No sense of *shame*, young man? Terrible, just *terrible*! Listenin' in on old ladies! Pig!" And she trod on my instep with her walker as she passed me for good measure. (And it hurt like nobody's business! She came on like some sort of Hell's Grandma!)

I thought I could hear Mr. "Night Job Sleeping" laughing at me, all the way from the bathroom to my room. When I got in, locked the door and sank on to a kitchen chair, the boys wouldn't even lick my hands.

No doubt they thought I was a "*pre-vert*" too.

Venturing out only when nature's call couldn't be ignored, I worked in isolation on the rest of "The Metamanphosis," and on a whim I decided to try sending it in to that holy-of-literary-holies, *Skin Magazine*. The one the 7-Elevens wouldn't touch with two flag poles soldered together. I figured it wouldn't hurt; one of the assistant editors there knew my work from previous tries, and once I got a handwritten note scribbled on the bottom of a rejection slip, telling me to please try again, that the editor of the magazine knew my work from *Bloodbath* and liked it. They got my name wrong on the note, calling me "Dear Mr. Winston," The note *was* a nice touch, and since I'd be appearing in the next three issues of *BQ* anyhow, I decided to give *Skin* a shot at "The Metamanphosis."

If I had any hopes of pulling stakes out of this dump (the nerve of that old biddy!) I had to start pulling in contracts from the top markets...a lot of them.

In retrospect, sending in that story to *Skin Magazine* was the best thing I ever did—considering the circumstances I had fallen into—but at the time, when I finally got it through my thick skull what was going on, I didn't *want* to believe it....

After a month of slinking to the bathroom, avoiding Mr. Hernandez and his mumbled *gringo* remarks by sliding the rent under his door before it was due and telling myself that it was *normal* for a woman *not* to hear lewd comments from men on the street (despite the fact that I still wore skimpy summer garb), I got a call—not from *Bloodbath,* but from *Skin Magazine*...and not just from someone in the fiction department. I was speaking to Mr. Father-of-Skin-himself, the Man Mr.-Meese-Would-Love-to-Bring-to-*His-Knees*, the *editor*. *Him*, his *Skinness*, talking to *me*. The clods back in Ewerton would have done number two in their sanctimonious overalls while tsk-tsking in horror (the few stores in Ewerton which reluctantly stock *Bloodbath Quarterly* only do so for a week before ripping off the covers and tossing the pages in the dumpsters, ever since that braless she-demon graced the Fall cover a couple of years back—welcome to the Bible Belt, folks!) while the hometown girl passed the time of day with Mr. Pornography, Esq. Actually, the guy seemed very nice, not sexist at all.

Very politely, he asked for "Denton Blair" (my pen name—if my mom's egg had got it on with a Y sperm instead of an X way back *when*, it would have been my real name), then corrected himself when he noticed my real name—D. B. Winston—typed at the top of the page, next to the "Member, SFWA." (I suppose days spent ogling bare, tanned flesh can mess up a guy's eyesight.) Either way, he wasn't surprised that I was a woman (while we chatted, I thought *how* nice, *a man who prints beaver shots who isn't a macho, "where's your husband, little woman?" boor...*), then he got to the point; he wanted to run "The Metamanphosis" in the January issue, and my heart almost pounded right through my chest and popped out of my t-shirt (John Hurt with his Alien-in-the-chest would have had nothing on *me*), and I had to keep reminding myself, *don't grovel, woman! Don't drool on the receiver and electrocute yourself! Suppose he wants some revisions!*

As I mentally congratulated myself for making a sale to *Skin* without an agent (*mine*; mine, *the money will be all* miiiine!) I had to do a double-take when the editor said, "You had me going there, D.B., the part in the story where the protagonist is still a woman is *fantastic*—I do know my women, and *I* almost believed for a minute there that you *are* a woman! Believe me, man, that is no mean feat, fooling an old *letch* like me! By the way, I've been following your *Bloodbath* work, and I wish we'd have grabbed some of your stuff sooner—you're right up there, fellah. Not a King or Barker yet, but someday, right? One more thing, do you still want to run this under the Denton Blair name or—okay, I'll change it right now. Well, nice talking to you,

D.B., and thanks for thinking of us..." and so on, and when he finally got off the line I threw down the receiver and began to paw through my files (some system—an old cardboard box from Keebler cookies I keep under my bed....I don't think Stephen King ever did it *this* way), looking for all my correspondence, rejection slips, contracts, and whatnot....

After culling what I wanted, I spread the mass of papers out on the floor (the dogs were stretched out against the walls, rumbling at me, heads on paws, eyes half-lidded), and began looking them over carefully, pausing only to swat away an occasional roach...looking at the pages *fearfully*, too....

It was all there, in unwavering black on white. My name, "D. B. Winston," on my submissions (upper right-hand corner, except for the occasional wise-guy editors who wanted it on the *left*-hand side, like it *mattered*), no "Devorah," no "Ms." or "Miss," or any indication of my sex, no inkling given that "D. B. Winston" *was* a woman. Oh, *occasionally* my checks from *Bloodbath*—including the one which caused me so much grief at the bank—came addressed to "Devorah Winston," since the editor there wormed the name out of me while I was still living back in Ewerton, but those checks were the exception, not the rule...according to my contracts, my few magazine subscriptions, and my bills, I was "D. B. Winston, Neuter"...except now, even *that* was subject to debate....

Likewise, those 'zines which sent me either handwritten or personalized form rejections were all part of the pattern—either "Dear D. B," or "Dear D. B. W," or "Dear D. B. Winston," *or*, much worse, "Dear Mr. Winston"...something which had— ohmigod!—amused me before! While the people who knew me, who saw me daily, still thought I was a woman. What did the opinion of someone I'd never seen matter? *I* knew that I was a woman, and everyone else *seemed* to know it when they saw me...then the loss of my literary femininity didn't seem very threatening. In fact, I figured it was *helping* me! Apparently others thought the same thing; one of the letters I got from the editor over at *Gore Magazine* (who did realize that

I was a woman) put it best: "It's fun when I get the occasional comment about '*D. B.*' Winston: that guy's work is really good: Tee-hee. Ah, the prejudices of the genre. Did you know that V. C. Andrews didn't know about her publisher substituting her initials until her first book came out?"

I only hoped that V. C. Andrews didn't have to go through *this* happy horseshit! Maybe that's why she gave interviews, telling people about the change...but I think that people at least *guessed* that she *was* a she. But most of my stories take a male point of view (or woodpile creature point of view, and so on), so the readers and editors had no way of *knowing*—unless I actually told them that I was a woman. I picked up a rejection slip from that new small press 'zine, *Prophetic!*, and read with blurring eyes, "All this time, my husband and I thought D. B. Winston was a man! What a surprise to see you sign your name 'Ms.'" That cover letter, the one I signed with a "Ms" (a rarity for *moi*, it must have been Susan B. Anthony's birthday, or some other such pro-feminist occasion) was a pure exception on my part, and I hadn't signed one like that to a new magazine I'd submitted to in months. Even my personal correspondence was genderless, and generated male-oriented responses ("Dear Mr. Winston, We are sorry you were dissatisfied with new Doggie Dinners..."), all of which seemed so *funny* at the time. With a growing sense of dis-ease, I scanned the contributor's copies of the 'zines which had run my material, and was confronted with table of contents after table of contents crediting my stories to "D. B. Winston" or "Denton Blair" (and remembered that all the junk mail in my kitchenette garbage bag was addressed to "*Mr.* D. B., et cetera"—once I realized that the Great Computer Network Hook-Ups had my gender wrong, I was sure that I was *doomed*!) and on top of it, few of the magazines I had things published in bothered with author's pages (even if they did, how many people actually *read* those things?).

As the editor at *Gore* had pointed out, most of the writers in my field *are* men; readers *expect* them to be men, for who knows *what* reason. It was that automatic assignment of gender on the part of readers that led me to use my initials instead of my name on my work, and played a part on my choice of a male *nom de plume.* Years ago, I had read an article about breaking into the publishing market that suggested that men have an edge when it comes to certain genres, and since I never liked my name *anyway* (to me, Devorah Bambi Winston had that good old cheerleader Pom-Pom-Girl-Prom-Queen-Sorority-Sister ring to it, and plain old Devorah Winston had a small-town paper-mill-office-clerk-playing with-her-typewriter feel to it... which is what I *was* at first, when I started submitting things), so using my initials had seemed so appealing, so natural, so crisply efficient...and, unbeknownst to me, so very *masculine*, not merely androgynous, as I had hoped.

Crazy as it all sounded, it did make sense; wasn't that editor astonished to find out that I was really a woman? Which, in turn, meant that the impression that she and her husband had gotten that I was a man a strong one? And those readers writing to the *Gore* editor, about liking that "guy's work." After all, didn't Peter Pan, or some other fairy-tale kidlet, say that "wishing makes it so"?

(I know he said "Clap your hands for Tinkerbelle," and all *that*!) So, if that's the case, wouldn't "Thinking makes it so" also apply? A wish *begins* as a thought...suddenly I remembered the note that the *BQ* editor put in with my contributor's copies, the one with the reader's survey results. That meant that a lot of readers—a lot of very *imaginative* horror and fantasy loving (*and* believing? I wondered)—readers had asked for my stories, many of them no doubt thinking (*believing*) that I was a man. I found the note, and if I had had doubts before "... fifth most requested author, behind Bloch and Williamson and Koontz, and you'd be surprised to see who else you topped on the list. Some of the readers can't help but scribble comments in the margins about their favorites, and about you they wrote, 'He's my favorite,' and 'That Winston dude scares me' I guess the readers really got into those macho-hero adventures about pagan sacrifices and bird blood worship you wrote while you were living in Ewerton...."

—*That* was the capper. If only he had written one "Tee hee," or "I set *them* straight," or...I could only come to one conclusion. Even though he used to know that I am a woman, somehow, he had forgotten or his mind had told him something else...or maybe, because so many people now believe that I am a man, he's doing so as a matter of course. Even the people I had just met, all of them were treating me as if I were *actually a man.*

It was funny, but after I finally figured it out (more or less), figured out what happened to me, *I couldn't do anything about it*! Bellevue may be overcrowded, but it was within the city limits and convenient. A good place to hide the "pre-verts" who *pretend* to be women....

What made me hurt—above and beyond the embarrassment, the shouting, the bruised instep where old Mrs. Pendleton tromped on it—was the fact that even *telling* people that I was a woman didn't seem to help anymore.

Then, while I sat on the floor, hardly noticing the tickle of roach legs on *my* legs, I *thought* of something. And got to work.

By the time I was through, my hands and fingers were a hurtin', my eyes were blurred from staring at endless black letters (sort of slate grey towards the end) marching across illuminated white paper, my tongue was coated with that slimy, gummy residue from licking too many stamps and envelope flaps (why wouldn't those damned dogs lick something besides their paws and fannies?)...but, finally, I was done. And I thought that it might work. *Had* to work. Please, pretty please with sugar on top work...and sugar on the bottom, if that might help.

From the afternoon when I sat on the floor, bemoaning my bizarre fate, to the day when I finally called it quits, a month later, I had written eight short stories, three poems, and a criticism of faceless/personalityless/mindless killers in 1980s deadteenager mad slasher flicks ("Down with 'Jasonism' or Norman Bates Won't *You* Please Phone Your Mother?"). Plus cover letters for each submission with my full name, as in "Ms." and

"Miss" added to the bottom sign-off—the works. I had to wait until dark to send them off (in a weird way I *missed* the sexist comments from strange guys); to both magazines which knew my work but not my sex, as well as newer 'zines I'd never tried before. Even though I left late, someone yelled "Drag Queen" at me from across the street...and I was only wearing a sundress! (It was too hot even for shorts, and besides, I thought that maybe I had to do a little *believing* on my own, to speed up the process....)

Only a week later, I couldn't help but think of that kiddie book, about The Little Engine That Could, who said "I think I can, I think I *can*, only in my case it was more like "I think I am, I think I am a WOMAN!" It happened! A cabbie, one I'd never seen before, who brought me home from a movie I took in one night (only fools and vampires ride the subways come night, whether people think they are men or not!) actually said "Thanks, lady," when I told him to keep the change. I could have kissed the slob, three days' stubble or not! And better yet, I soon got back replies on most of the things I sent out; all with either rejection slips or contracts (!) addressed to "Miss" or "Ms." Winston!

I figured that it *had* to be working; Mrs. Pendleton didn't snort and toss her hair-netted head when she saw me coming down the hall, and Mr. Hernandez had finally stopped calling me a *"loco gringo."* All this put me in such a good mood I even considered springing for a long-distance call home. You know, "reach out and *touch* someone"—sung in *soprano*, for a change! The dogs were even licking my hands again, no more rumbling and tail-thumpless greetings. I decided to brave Bloomies again, too....

My wonderful mood continued when I got my contributor's copies of *Bloodbath*; the J. K. Potter cover was even better in color. Seeing it reminded me that I had to contact the editor about changing my name on future issues, but I figured that I had plenty of time for that. That night I tried calling home, no answer. They probably were at the bowling alley-cum-arcade, renting video tapes or something stimulating like that. I decided to try a daytime call, what the hell, surprise the folks, make 'em happy. Share the feeling.

More joy the next day; my check—my *great* big *check came* from *Skin Magazine* for "The Metamanphosis," made out to "D. B. Winston." Looking it over, I decided to write The Editor and let him know that I wanted the by-line of the story changed. *Shouldn't be a biggie,* I told myself, kicking myself for actually forgetting something like a sale to *Skin*! Maybe I had *wanted* to forget it, make it not so by forgetting that something in my life had *prompted* such a tale…besides, I was sure that Mr. *Skin* Editor would get a kick out of the "Bambi" part of my name. I couldn't wait to tell my folks about the big check, but there was no answer in either the morning, afternoon, or evening. Slightly saddened, I tacked the check in a place of honor above my bed and resolved to call again the following morning...but something kept me from making that morning call.

The mailman had a hard time getting my contributor's copies from *Skin* into my box; the envelope covering them was badly torn. When I saw them, I ran down the street to the nearest kiosk, and found that the latest issue of *Skin Magazine,* with "D. B. Winston's 'The Metamanphosis'—a Study of the Ultimate Identity Crisis!" advertised on the front cover, just to the left of the model's barely covered nipple, was out for sale.

I zombie-walked back to my apartment ("the Ultimate Identity Crisis!") and after I locked the door behind me, I sat down on the bed to read the "Under the *Skin*" author's section. A brief mention of me was in there, a few lines about my publishing history, capped by the line "he is one of the best up-and-coming horror writers in America."

He, as in *me.* I looked in the tattered envelope which had held my contributor's copies. There was a note in there, written on *Skin*-logo paper, From the Editor. Said how much he liked, no *loved* the story; how he bumped an *Updike* from this issue to make room for my tale, so that his readers could enjoy it *now.* Said again how the first part had *almost* fooled him. Said he enjoyed talking to me in July. Said I should subscribe, special rate, to *Skin,* so he could use my name and likeness ("send a pic, should've asked in July, but the story just blew my mind and I forgot to ask") in those advertisements he runs in the front of *Skin* "Denton Blair Winston—a *Skin* Reader and proud of it:" Said I should think it over and call, collect. Said there'd be money in it for me. Said I should come to the mansion, meet the "gang." Said his readers were bound to go wild over the story. Said I seemed to be a great guy.

He's right. *Now.* The man isn't only *rich.* He's *influential.* As I finished the letter, Mom and Dad called *me;* they'd seen the new *Skin* on the back stands at the Ewerton Pharmacy, and wanted to let me know how happy they were. Dad said he's proud of his son. Mom said she hoped the gold-diggers wouldn't be after me once I made the "big bucks."

I *am* an only child.

And I didn't *think* my name is Denton. But I guess it beats Devorah.

Mrs. Pendleton spit at me in the hall; I ducked just in time. I wonder if I can find a *suit* at Bloomies for the World Con?

What *do* men who read *Skin Magazine* get for advertising the fact?

I think the boys and I may need to move out of this place.

Thanks to Peggy Nadramia, editor of Grue, *and Debo-rah Rasmussen, editor of* Portents, *for their kind permission to use quotations from their letters to me.*

A . R. Morlan, 1987

HUNGER

WHEN DAVID FARLEY came to New York City, he was a hungry man. In all ways. The job he landed proof-reading junk mail quelled one form of hunger; David was a small man, anyway, and rice, beans and pasta dishes were his forté since college. And being a careful man, conservative in his tastes and habits, he thrived in his poverty, living cheaply, but proudly. One room, hot plate, bath down the hall.

With autumn came the chance to apply for a job at a real magazine; sf fiction, major news stand distribution, subscription base, and paid lunch hours. Proof-reader, and part-part-time assistant to a senior editor. David applied, and another pang of hunger was silenced. But old hunger was stirred: David's scant income was cut by a third. He was demoted from hunger to near-starvation. YMCA, roach motels extra.

Months later, come September, on an afternoon when fall still seemed months, years away, David was hurrying back to work, crossing West 49th at Ninth Avenue, his mind on the miserable toothache throbbing along his left lower jaw, and the fact that he had had to leave the dentist's office with only an appointment he could never afford to keep, when he almost ran into...her.

Her stench hit him first; fulsome, squishy-moist, like toes trapped in too-tight sneakers. Yet, there was a vague feminine odor about her, a sour yeasty tang that made David's mouth fill with bitter saliva. She was coming from the direction of the Port Authority Bus Terminal, but David doubted, instantly, with certainty, that she was one of the homeless who camped out around there, hoping to bum money off tourists in exchange for carrying a suitcase from the inside of the terminal to the sidewalk beyond, or sitting huddled in ratty blankets, like fraying cocoons, in the hard plastic seats within.

The woman—middle aged, old, eternal? David couldn't tell and didn't want to know with any certainty—was too flyblown, too far beyond normal pity or revulsion, for anyone to come near enough to slip her a quarter or let a dollar bill flutter into her cupped palms.

She might have risen from the streets, pulled from the spit and wrapper and ripped movie-ticket encrusted sidewalks like a heat shimmy, to waver and sway in the sun, all but invisible for her natural camoflage, save for her sick redolence, and save for her fluttering nostrils, her liquid hooded eyes.

Slowly, she moved in a curious sliding shuffle, a wind-driven pile of sweat-ribboned scraps and debris, clinging slap-dash to her undefinable body. Oblivious to David as an empty Styrofoam cup rolling down the broad ribbon of sidewalk, she inched forward, head twitching and bobbing, heavy under the layers of folded and twisted sweaters encircling her filth-encrusted dreadlocks.

That she was black seemed an afterthought, a mere chance of pigmentation under her patina of grime and dried mucus clinging to the furrows near her nose, her mouth, her heavy-lidded eyes.

Her clawed hands, the fingers twisting in configurations which spoke to David of alien hieroglyphics, shapes whose meaning was unknowable, unclean, framed palms of chalky white-grey: a sick, bloodless color which was scored with broken lines of embedded dirt, a map of the unknown lands from which she had shambled forth into the late summer sun.

Appalled, yet stirred by a numbing hunger to see just a little more, to look fully before looking away, David stood close to the curb, watching the progress of the street person as she oozed across the street (no cars whizzed past her; instead they eased far away from her, as if fearing what contact with her might do to their glossy paint jobs, their glittering radio antennas), her reek a live thing in his nostrils, stinging the tender flesh there, and clawing into his brain, touching soft, dark, shuttered places....

Only, David stood there a second too long. She turned her massive swathed head, only a degree or so to the left, but enough. Eyes like oily marbles, cloudy with only the memory of dark color locked on his rounded blue ones, and in that second of contact without touch, David *saw* her; the tatter of pilled lace adorning one side of the Peter Pan collar on one of the layered blouses she wore, the fresh scab clinging to her bitten lower lip, an orange plastic child's bracelet encircling one greasy wrist, the toes-gone greying sneakers with the tongues lolling across her high-boned insteps.

And, in that second of seeing, came the *feeling* of a hunger deeper than the soul, deeper than eye-pupil-blackness, of hips -knees-shins-toes-souls numb from moving, moving from nowhere to anywhere for ever, of looking for something for so long that remembrance would be of no help when and if the thing arrived in sight...of *wanting.*

The woman's hand made contact with David's bare forearm before he could jerk away, step back onto the safety of the curb, and run down the crack-veined sidewalk. And in the second in which David did slide his arm out from under her twisted hand, David sensed (*knew*) that if he hadn't moved, the woman would have been all over him, pressing her raggy body against his thin, sport-shirt-and-droopy-tie-covered chest, cradling her massive woggling head in the hollow between his head and collarbones, *feeding* off of him.

For the hunger was there, in her gelid eyes and cracked, working lips, and David found himself spinning around so quickly he almost caught his foot on the curb and splayed forward into the sidewalk; almost, but not quite. From the slight elevated safety of the street itself, David stared down at the woman for a second, before walking a block down West 49th until he could lose the woman in the steadily thickening traffic.

David hurried back to work, almost running now, his tooth-ache all but forgotten as bitter saliva swirled in his mouth, like acidic fire he couldn't spit out into the gutter, lest the woman be drawn to the expectoration....

Yet, as he walked briskly, jacket draped over his free arm (his clean arm), he kept scrubbing his forearm, the one she'd touched, against his hip, scrubbing the flesh until fresh sweat made the skin sting, until he could no longer feel the lingering heat of her fingers there, pressing down on his skin.

It was his own fault, for waiting, for gawking...but had she any right to linger by him, when he had no offering of money in his hand, and no lure of fancy clothing or assumed wealth?

Neither of them had had any right in looking, in lingering, yet...the fact that they both had done so niggled at David, as did the persisting sense of want, of need, of *hunger*, he'd felt rising off the woman like steam from something warm, hidden, suddenly exposed to pitiless cold.

And with the persistent memory of her, of her smell, of her unwelcome touch, David felt the reluctant opening of something deep and scarred within him, the flying open of shutters, the splintered wood banging against moldy walls of bitter remembrance....

Before David came to New York, before he finished college, to be exact, his grandmother had gone crazy over the course of one spring and summer. Just what happened to her already-slow mind was hard to say; when people dropped by to try and talk some sense into her, she'd burrow further into her saggy and worn lavender sweater, pull her hairless, shiny, skinny legs close to the legs of her rocker, and let her frazzled mane of stringy brown and grey hair fall over her greasy face before barking, "Mindyerownbusiness!" in that phlegm-clotted voice of hers. Soon, people learned not to stop by and urge her to see a doctor. Soon people quit coming to the house altogether.

And then David's grandmother retreated to her bedroom, off the living room, leaving her door open only wide enough to watch a sharply slanted image of the television set in the oppo-site corner of the living room. David's family sometimes heard her cough, or sneeze, or snore loudly and moistly, a sloppy fluttering buzz that all but drowned out the television. (Turn up the volume, though, and she'd mumble sing-songed accu-sations: "Inconsiderate bastards" "Need some *manners* around this *house*" so David's family just began to edge closer to the set, like guilty moths.)

And she *did* things: Broke David's sister's little glass carousel, the one she'd received after appearing in the chorus of the college summer musical of the same name; broke the base of the fragile spun glass bauble, then tried to re-arrange the shattered fragments next to the base, but Susan *knew* what had happened, and bawled out loud before saying in a few choice words when she saw the damage. *That* only brought the old lady out of her room with a shuff-shuff of her frowzy blue slippers and shaking of her plush red bathrobe (and this was in July, hot, sticky, muggy *July*), and with every step the old woman's mouth was working, working, making the turkey wattle under her chin sway and shiver like the last glob of misshapen gelatin in the bowl.

And as this thing that had once been David's grandmother called Susan and the rest of them vipers, bastards, liars and fuckers, David breathed through his mouth; after weeks cooped up in her bedroom (emerging only to sneak food from the kitchen which lay beyond the bathroom which was connected to her room, or to occupy the sole bathroom long enough to cause extreme discomfort for the rest of the family), the old woman *stank*. The smell was worse than the lingering odor she left behind after she finally flushed prior to vacating the bathroom, more cloying than excrement, yet sweeter, too. Like chicken gone slimy, or old perfume soured by sweat.

The old woman had been spending less and less time bathing over the past year or so—self-righteously she claimed that since she never sweated, she couldn't smell bad, even though David's mother had to wash the old woman's clothes separately from those of the rest of the family, because of the greasy-sweet bacon reek her garments gave off—so David should have been used to the smell, but he wasn't.

David's grandmother's hair hung down from under her bandanna in greasy, limp strings, too clotted with dirt to move in the rush of air from the fan in the corner. Idly David wondered what had happened to the woman who'd gone religiously for her permanent every spring and fall when he was a boy. *That* woman was his Gramma. Not this...creature which bellowed in a throaty croak, shaking a yellow-nailed finger at his sobbing sister. Reflexively backing away, David wondered how anyone could have loved the woman in the red robe long enough to help her conceive David's own mother. By the fall of that year, David and his sister were back in school, but his parents moved out of the house which his mother and grandmother co-owned. There the old woman puttered about and half-starved herself, even though their town had Meals on Wheels and Kinship for the elderly.

The old lady alienated every able-bodied man in town who cut lawns, shoveled snow or did any sort of handiwork, until she reached the point where the house was slowly going to rot and David's folks *had* to stop by to bring her food and to arrange for the house to be fixed up. And still the old woman used every opportunity to cut down, criticize, and out-and-out insult everyone with whom she came into contact.

David wouldn't go to visit her—what Susie did was her own fool business—but a few times he grudgingly spoke on the phone with her. Upon hearing that saccharine warble "Goooodbye!" he'd slam down the receiver with one hand, and whip her an unseen bird with the other. Sometimes he'd mumble "Bitch" for his own benefit. But still...he couldn't help but feel funny when he opened the card Mom relayed to him from the old lady for his twenty-first birthday. The unsigned card more suitable for a young boy than an adult, with the note written in a shaky, huge hand which was folded around a $100.00 bill:

"Dear David;

May you have the 'Happiest of Birthdays' every day of the year. To me you have been the joy of my life always.

Love,
your Gramma"

The note made David mad and sad and a little bit exasperated. He couldn't forgive the old lady for the way she'd been, even *before* she went out-and-out crazy, but...*yet*...something inside him told David that *he'd* been the rotten one, no matter what names she'd called him when he was a teenager, no matter what she'd done to his graduation pictures (sneaking into his room, into his desk, to grub around in his papers for the pictures of her posed with honors-graduate David—so that she could draw huge blue ball-point-pen goggle eyes over her own shut-against-the-flash-glare thin-lashed eyes), no matter that she'd bemoaned the fact that his parents bought Susie a carnation and rosebud corsage when she graduated high school, saying to whomever was within earshot, "We could have bought a loaf of bread for what that flower cost."

For she was his grandmother, even if she stank, even if she was a balding, wattled, greasy bloated *whathaveyou* by the time she finally died of ovarian cancer. He'd had to take the word of his family about her bullet-hard bloated belly under the greasy robe, and the other physical changes. He'd refused to come to the funeral, knowing that he'd smell the lingering odor of her flesh over any flowers in the church....

Just as he knew that buying the bouquet of flowers from the vendor near the Museum of Modem Art (he had no appetite for the wares of the hot dog and cold pop vendor also camped out near the broad front steps of the museum) was his way of trying to tell himself it was all right that he'd stopped to gawk at the street person, that he deserved a little something beautiful and sweet smelling and fragile-alive to comfort himself, something to stop the hunger he felt within himself for human contact, for time spent without the need for money to exchange hands— even as the lingering memory of the foul woman's touch burned his skin from within, and a nagging hungry voice whispered within him, *What she was offering you wasn't wrapped around a $100.00 bill....*

David Farley's hunger diminished when he was offered a promotion at his sf magazine after a year of diligent, uncomplaining work. Assistant Editor, a permanent desk, and no more missed appointments at the dentist. Good-bye YMCA, and left-behind roach motels. One room plus kitchenette, and half bath on the lower west side. He no longer walked anywhere near the Port Authority Bus Terminal.

A scant five months later, a second promotion; editorship of a sister publication of his sf magazine, an experimental soft sf/fantasy venture David didn't expect to last six issues, but the money meant good cooked meals at home. Recipes which didn't call for rice, beans, or anything but the fanciest Italian pasta.

The (temporary, he assumed) editor's chair meant that David had suddenly, magically, reached what he considered the inner circle. During the annual party thrown by the parent publishing firm, he was sought out by toadying would-be writers, and treated with some measure of respect by established figures in the genre. Other editors called *him*, and sometimes agents would take him to lunch, sometimes buy him drinks. Nothing cheaper than white wine, nothing consisting mainly of beans.

When an agent for a well-known but recently luckless sf writer (the supposed best-seller wasn't, no matter how well it had amassed votes in the Nebulas) offered to take David to lunch in order to sell David on the un-best selling writer's latest novella, for serialization, David (who had already half-made up his mind to buy the novella anyhow) feigned indecision and accepted the invitation. Anything to escape the ever-growing mound of subs piled on and next to his desk.

The bar near Broadway and Fifth wasn't crowded as David and the agent waited for their drinks, but the man in the cheap tie with the stripes going the wrong way insisted on standing right *next* to David. While the agent was present, playing up his client, the wrong-tie man was easy to ignore, but the agent was wearing one of those clip-on beepers; when a call came through from the agency, the agent downed his Manhattan, bid David a hasty, temporary fare-well and trotted off in search of the nearest pay phone. David smiled slightly over his Tom Collins; the lapels on the agent's plaid jacket didn't line up right. That secret nubbin of superiority David had gained over the agent was sure to mean that he'd get the novella for what he was offering, not what he was being asked to pay.

David was still bent over his drink, waiting for the agent, nursing the last few sips of liquor, when the backwards-tie man spoke up. Shimmering circles of ghosts of the glasses already downed ringed the man's folded hands resting on the bar. In a far corner of the wall, the brackets-mounted TV was tuned to CNN Headline NEWS (stock market listings scrolled across the bottom of the screen, a busy ribbon of blue); the volume was too low to hear, but some report about the on-going shuttle problems at NASA was on. File footage of the *Challenger* appeared; as it mushroomed into white mist and oblivion, then did it again in slow motion, Mr. Wrong-tie said slowly, solemnly, "Know what I was thinking...when it happened? Not *now,* but the first time?" David sipped his drink, not letting on that he could hear anything, least of all the man beside him.

"Was sitting in the living room, watching, and all of a sudden Bill Murray's in my head. In *Stripes*, the scene with the fancy drill work—" Wrong-tie was pantomiming a shouldered rifle, that much David could see out of the comer of his left eye "—an' when they ask Bill where his commander is, Bill, he shouts, '*All blowed up, Sirrrah.*' And Bill, he was in my *head*, all that day, day it blowed up. Just Bill going, '*All blowed up*'—"

David quickly thumbed some bills out of his pocket, left them by the tall sweating glass and vacated the bar (the agent would just have to haul mis-matched lapels over and look for him), Wrong-tie's shouted "Sirrrah!" booming over-loud in his ears.

Outside, Fifth Avenue was almost devoid of pedestrians, so there was really no reason why David should have bumped into anyone, or stepped on any living thing, until....

....the cat wound itself through and around his legs, forcing David to come to an off-balance stop in mid-stride. When he looked down, the cat was still there, a dark smudge against the already darkening sidewalk.

It was just standing there, off to his right, looking up at him with pus-covered green eyes. It was a male; the spreadout face and almost flat nose were unmistakable. Unneutered. And either old or starved enough for it to have a splatter of stiff white hairs in among the flat black fur. The ears were the shape and texture of rotted morrels, almost without points. In fact, the cat's ears were so cauliflowered that there was almost no openings left in them.

The left hind paw was missing from the hock on down. The tail was short, fading away to pencil-thinness. Stiff, broken whiskers jutted out from either side of the mouth, and from the lips hung pendulous rodent ulcers. One fang was broken off close to the gum line, the top of the tooth encrusted with shining, mottled black and brown tartar, like mold gone unchecked on the skin of Brie cheese.

A three-legged cat...wandering around in New York City. David looked around, assuming he'd see a street person nearby, waiting for him to take pity on the animal and offer money to its "owner." Yet another scam, like the black youths and not-so-young men who hung near intersections, waiting for a red light and the chance to swish a filthy rag or squirt fluid from a pump bottle on the windshield of some car, and who wouldn't wipe off the scummy water until they were paid. Fivers or better. Not that David didn't pity those who called cardboard boxes or sheets of newspaper spread over a grate home. He'd lived the borderline life himself, or as close as dammit to borderline. And the hungry animals hauled around by street people may have been company, family, even...but David felt sorrier for the ones who hauled their kids around from shelter to abandoned car to park bench.

But the cat was alone. Ungracefully it sat on rat-furred haunches, staring at David with pigment-spotted green eyes. No one passed either of them for a few seconds. The wind picked up, a cool pressing hand urging him to get back in the bar, or go to his office, or get back *home*, but something about the cat (the very smelly cat—its odor wafted up to him, redolent of old ear wax, dried excrement and whatever else the animal had rubbed against) made David hover over it, numbed mentally and physically.

Perhaps David hovered too long, for without so much as the characteristic wiggle of the rump, the cat sprang up into his arms. Up close, its smell was a living creature in his nostrils, clawing up into his brain, pawing open a forgotten nest of memories. The cat flexed rough-padded paws on his jacket, worn yellowed nails pressing his skin through the double layer of fabric. The thing's mouth was foul; the setting sun glinted off drool-slimed rough lips. And yet, his eyes were so trusting, so utterly, unequivocally *trusting* that David was sure the cat would willingly snuggle into his jacket, hiding silently and gratefully during the subway ride home. David could even feel/hear the thing's stomach rumbling, through his jacket and shirt. But the moment came when David had to either support the furry body with his arms, or let the cat drop.

When the cat hit the pavement, it paused to stare at him— not with reproach, but with that same blind trust and affection. Before David could make up his mind whether to follow it or to briskly walk away, the cat lifted its pathetic rat tail and scooted off, moving surprisingly fast on three feet.

The odor of its paws remained on his jacket, a sharp tangy reek of old pee, cement and vegetation. Park grass, perhaps, or straggler weeds growing up between slabs of broken pavement. Brushing off his jacket, flicking away flecks of something dried and brown and unpleasant, David felt his tongue curl, finally flattening against the roof of his mouth in distaste and something else, something like guilt....

Before David and his sister and Dad and Mom and her mom (not yet crazy, but boy was she getting there) moved from the crappy house on the far outskirts of town, the *dump* with no insulation, no running water, and no sidewalk, that had been all they could afford many lean years ago when they first moved to Ewerton, Wisconsin from downstate Illinois, to the much better house close by downtown, the big white cement-block house with the high ceilings and hardwood floors in most of the rooms, David's family had to get rid of the cats. Not the *indoor* cats, not Diablo and Blackie and Arthur, but Missy (Arthur's mother), and Bandito and Terri, his litter mates. Females, all unspayed ("Not enough, not enough *money*") had already mated with both sisters, producing sickly litters (Terri's kittens had all died), so Grandma's decree went down—the girls were to be banished to the chicken coop in the back yard. They were in heat constantly, some sort of hormonal screw-up (or maybe cancer, David realized years later, after Diablo—also unspayed, but relegated to the back porch of the old house—lived for another eighteen months with mammary cancer, finally dying in his parents' new house, after the hegira from the big white house), and half-wild to boot. So Dad, hoping that they could eventually have the three pretty females fixed, always in that hoped-for *later*, fenced them in, put them in the chicken coop where they lived for a year, maybe more. Living on scraps of food and oatmeal, by Grandma's decree.

David hated thinking about it all, about how brutal life in the country had made them. Like starved creatures themselves, all of them. The hungriest time in his life which David sought to bury deep, deep in his subconscious—a time he almost *did* manage to forget...except for what happened to the cats.

The three cats weren't too bad off in the coop; they were fed, their poop was shoveled out for them, and the snow covered their pee come winter. The walls of the coop were thick and sturdy. (His mom *had* put her foot down when it came to Diablo, the cat he and his sister found out by the sash and door factory two summers before their move. Diablo was delicate, a refined and good cat, and she lived in the house, or out in the back porch when in heat. Grandma bitched, but Mom was getting fed up herself by then.) But when the money Mom and Dad had saved for the new house was finally loosed from Grandma's account, she laid down a last ultimatum, a final jab in her fury about being ousted from the ugly house in the country she'd grown to love. The three indoor cats could stay in the new house. There was a basement for the males. But the "crazy cats," the females who spent their days pumping, endlessly pumping their hind-quarters when not eating, Missy, Bandito and Terri (named for the black patch of fur around one eye, like the people in those old Terryington cigarette advertisements) had to *go.* As in...as in on the day after they'd moved into the new house (the day the old lady kicked Diablo just because she was pissed about moving away from "her" home), David and his dad drove out to the old house, bearing a last breakfast of hot oatmeal and milk in a big plaid thermos (it was late February, not *cold-cold* out, but still—) for the girl cats. David watched them slurp up their final treat, until he had to walk away to stand behind the ugly grey house and wait with eyes shut while Dad fired his rifle. Four times. Four times, for three cats.

And in the pick-up on the way to school, the high school set out in the boonies on the other side of town, David half-listened to his Dad say how the cats didn't run away, but waited their turn, trustingly. David didn't ask which one got shot twice, or why she'd been shot twice, as the last warmth of the slain cats seeped into David's feet. Dad had placed the bodies in a plastic sack in David's foot well, prior to driving their bodies out to the dump. Cats there or not, David wasn't about to swing his feet over by Dad.

Years later, when Diablo died, his folks said to hell with the city ordinance against burying pets in the city and laid her to rest outside the living room double window. And planted a rose bush over her that grew middling tall, high enough to reach out and snag you when you least expected it to do so. And no matter how many cats his folks and his sister got later on, David could still hear those four shots. For three cats. But Dad said they didn't run away....

After figuring *Screw the agent, screw the meal*, David trotted to the nearest subway entrance, but he kept seeing the last image of the black tom cat, the last look he'd gotten before hurrying away from the bar. The cat had only scurried so far, just close to the mouth of a narrow gap between two buildings. Then it stopped, sat down, and *waited* for him. Even after he'd let it drop to the ground. Even after he'd scooted off, bumping into people going the other way. It had looked at him without rancor, waiting patiently for him to return for it. And David didn't stop shaking inside, tongue still protectively jammed against his upper palate, until he was jerking along with the moving subway deep under the ground where the cat was still no doubt standing, waiting for him in pure trust and faithfulness....

When David's magazine folded, not after six but fifteen issues, David went back to doing what he had done before. Assistant Editor at the sf magazine. He was used to the work, and the money was still good. David even managed to move to better digs, three rooms plus bath, not too far from Central Park. He ate at better restaurants, ones which never featured beans or rice in their entrees. He gradually gained some of the weight he'd lost in his physically hungry years, but still got enough exercise to keep himself looking reasonably fit, reasonably hungry, and held onto his savings. The YMCA still had rooms to let.

Then, after some of the stories and novelettes from the last issue of his now-defunct magazine went on to gain berths in the Nebula, Hugo, and World Fantasy ballots, and a story actually won a Hugo (and was rumored to have come in very high in the Nebulas), David's ship came in. A cargo ship, at that. He was offered the editorship of a rival sf magazine, the one whose pages supplied most of the *rest* of the writing award ballots.

At one and a half times his old salary. Taxi time. His days of walking past stinking street people *(she* touched *me, with those claw hands—)* and mangy gimpy cats were all but over; when no taxis were available, he knew which routes were free of hooded watery eyes and trusting felines, or nearly so. When necessary, he lowered his eyelids, washing unpleasant scenes in a veil of wavering rainbows and eyelashes. He began to take vacations, far out of the city, where the street people did not dwell and the animal shelters had the time to round up limping strays.

Then, not long after his Christmas vacation in Pennsylvania, David was forced, due to traffic, to drive back into the city through Harlem. The Lincoln Tunnel was jammed with inching cars, and unfortunately the George Washington bridge wasn't too jammed, so David reluctantly drove through Harlem as quickly as traffic and the slippery streets would allow, all the while feeling a nameless dread, a calling of poor to formerly poor that pulled at him like the irresistible force of gravity upon a body falling from a great height to the hard coldness of the pavement below. The rented car was his awning, his shield against the brutal pull of gravity upon his body, his memory, his heart, upon the deep hungering void within him.

David tried to keep his eyes on the ice-encrusted center line, tried not to notice the dull splotches of the people's faces outside the car—the street sitters (more than a few with dogs and scabrous cats in tow, still more with vacant-eyed youngsters), the wanderers, the crazies lashing out at the icy air, the wall-slouchers. He tried not to see the broken windows, the badges of wood and chain-link and tin the buildings wore, their shining surfaces failing to shine much in the white-cold late afternoon light. Newspapers yellowed to the color of dying, jaundiced skin, fluttered a few inches above the ground, too bedraggled to take full, free flight.

David tried to keep *moving*—until the yellow light turned to red too late for him to spurt past the yellow line, and David found himself caught. The heater puffed warm air at him, air that gradually took on a different, worsening smell as the light stubbornly stayed red. David tried to breathe through his mouth, but that only made his mouth taste terrible, like yeasty old underwear and sweaty rags and rancid bacon and ear wax and dried dung and old sour tom-cat-pee and pungent vegetation. With an undercurrent of freshly cooked oatmeal....And still the red light shone, misting slightly in the cold, stretching seconds of agony into minutes of agony. Thinking that a watched light never turned green, David cast his eyes off to his left, looking up, up, *up*—and then, he saw the window.

At least twelve stories up in a fourteen story building. A grey-tan structure, most windows jagged teeth surrounding maws of black within, save for the window near the right hand side of the building's front façade. The one almost near the flat roof, the one with the old air conditioner jammed into the glassless space.

Rags, mostly red plaid against dingy white, were stuffed around the gold-tan air conditioner. A few raw tatters flapped listlessly in the wind, overhanging the window sill outside. What space there was above the air conditioner was filled with some jagged glass, taped in place. And then David saw the swipe of black against the top of the window, a glancing shadow with only the mere suggestion of a form. *But the black shape was cat-sized.*

And only as the light finally flickered back to green did David's mind admit to him, *Someone* lives *up there. In the emptiness, the filth, the cold...*and it could, it just *might* now, have only three legs. And its owner could be layered with Peter Pan collared blouses and rags, and crowned with a turban of old sweaters. For perhaps want had found trust and formed a *home*, not just a dwelling, a squatter's nest, but a *home*.

David found a parking space between a rusted-out Saab and a muffler-less Ford of uncertain make or year. His mind a dizzying rush (*paw gone below the hock eyes like oily marbles Dadfiredfour times wonder who got blasted twice rancid bacon smell on* her *on her clothes "joy of my life always" it waited for me in the alley*), David did remember to lock the rented car—the hub caps were on their own—before hurrying up to the boarded-up front door of the building. Tin under the wood, and a thick chain. With a padlock. No go.

Thankful that the biting cold made the gangs of kids and roaming adults sluggish, huddled near warm steam gratings, David hurried around to the back of the building, squeezing through a bricked alley. The very bricks smelled bad, as if something reeking and maybe even oozing had rubbed against them frequently. And the stubbled, broken cement between the narrow, hovering walls was dotted with mounds of pale, runny cat excrement...and one pile still steamed, pure fragile white steam.

There was no opening to the back of the building, but there was a long fire escape, rusted herringbone stitches against the crumbling fabric of the structure. As he uncertainly ascended the metal ladder, feeling like a dizzy kid climbing his first big slide in the park, David wondered if the street woman had had enough of the bus terminal. Either that, or her stink and her strangeness had long ago become too much for even her fellow cocoon-sitters to tolerate. As the rusty railing left chalky, gritty stains on his soft-gloved hands, David figured that the cat (*it can't be* that *cat, not* all *the way over* here) wouldn't mind a little stink for company, not with its sewer breath and crap-encrusted paws.

The fire escape slats were surprisingly sturdy, the flat rungs clean from frequent use, no doubt. That odor (that horribly familiar odor) clung to the very metal, lingering in the cool air, enough to make his eyes water...but he did remember not to go opening his mouth again. As it was, he'd had to spit a few times over his shoulder to rid his tongue and teeth of the fulsome after-taste of the car's forced air heat. And as he climbed, pausing at each landing, he ticked off the floor numbers on his cold-stiffened fingers. Starting again on his left hand after the tenth finger was ticked off, his steps grew slow, faltering. Suppose he walked into a crack house? Suppose someone *killed* him? But the worst "suppose" of all stopped him in between the eleventh and twelfth floors, where he stood vulnerable and unshielded on the open metal steps. Suppose the woman and the cat really *were* there...waiting?

Just what he'd do under such a circumstance was something he'd only know by finding out—and then just doing it, period.

When he reached the twelfth floor, the window nearest the fire escape was broken out, all shards of glass carefully removed, no doubt to facilitate easy entrances and exits by someone perhaps swaddled in layer upon layer of filth-stiffened clothes.

As David climbed into the building through the window, his nostrils quivered when his face brushed too close to the wood frame, for her smell had rubbed into the very wood, in the places where the paint was only a colorless memory. But the smell did keep his mind off the fact that he was doing gyrations up over a hundred feet in the air, in Harlem, with only a metal staircase between him and the filth littered alley below. At least no one was in the alley; David could only imagine how idiotic he looked, breaking into a building while *wearing* a Yuppie uniform of L. L. Bean slacks and down-filled jacket.

In the hallway of the twelfth floor, David had to think hard, trying to remember which windows, and how far in it was, for all the doors in the twilight-dark building (as seen from the street), and it wasn't at the end or the middle but somewhere in between—and as if in answer to his mental question, the third door from the end on his left opened slowly, casting an elongated triangle of light into the hallway. Pale light, weak and wavery as if coming from a flashlight with bad batteries. And the pervasive smell grew stronger, more nose-stinging... yet comforting, too, in the way the odor of food soothed hunger pangs when he was a little boy. It was the street person from 49th and Ninth, not a crack dealer or a pimp with a messed-up brain and a sharp knife—

—at least that was what David hoped, as he walked forward slowly, cautiously. The yellow light was further marred by a strange shape, also elongated, but with a thin upright tail. The appearance of the dark shape was followed with a yowl, not of anger but of feline recognition. Soon the thing was rubbing on his legs, leaving rank hairs on his corduroy slacks, but oddly, David didn't care any more, just didn't give a tinker's damn about getting fur on his pants or cat-paw stink on his jacket. He scooped up the lumpy animal into his arms, hoisted the purring beast on his shoulder (its broken whiskers tickled his ear) and then tentatively knocked on the inside of the open door before entering the street woman's lair.

The bad smell was compounded by expelled human gas, fresh cat pee and some sort of found food that was going bad. Weak dirty light came through the mended top part of the window, and the grill of the air conditioner was a snaggle-toothed dead mouth, jutting into the room where she had made herself a nest: old crumbling newspaper, shed rags, limp vegetable things of uncertain variety, old sneakers, rusty bike parts and green-fuzzed cans.... And she sat in the middle of that nest turbaned and dreadlocked head even bigger than he remembered it, the furrows near her mouth even deeper and blacker than he remembered them to be.

But her eyes...even without the feeble rays of the battered flashlight stuck in one clawed hand, they would have been *beautiful*. Still oily, still hooded, but...wondrous to David nonetheless. For sheer *wanting*, sheer hungering *need* had to be nothing less than beautiful, transcendent, even.

The cat draped itself on David's shoulder, purring, kneading his flesh through the padded fabric. And although its eyes were flecked with clumps of brownish pigment, half-blinding it, still the trust and love shone through, spreading sun-like warmth across David's cheek. His skin felt almost warm, so dazzling was the trust in the cat's green eyes. It blinked kitty-kisses at him, just like the cats used to do back home. The trust it held in him was that complete...as the woman raised her hands toward David, beckoning him with her hooded oily eyes.

And without thought, hesitation or trepidation, David moved closer to her, the street person whose odor all but caused the air to shimmer and David's nostrils to collapse in on themselves. When he was less than eight inches from her, close enough to feel her body heat, David knelt down, let those hungering talon -like hands with the horny black rimmed nails rake lovingly against his jacket sleeve, down, down to his gloved hand, and exposed wrist. He did not flinch when she rested her flesh against his, basking in whatever it was she was leeching from him, his being...but he did speak. Softly, so as not to shatter the radiance of this room, this place, this moment. David whispered:

"Grandma, I am so sorry...and girls, Missy, Bandito, Terri, *I am* so *sorry*...but what could I *do*? It was so hard to love—but the hardness didn't make it not so, do you see what I mean? But it wasn't hard for you all to love and trust, even when the craziness made it hard to know what was within you even when I wasn't worth the effort. Even when it was hard for me I ran and ran from where I was, from what I was, but it didn't stop me from hungering, from needing what I couldn't take or ask for... but look. Here I am. I know sorry doesn't make it right, can't change what was wrong...but...well the feeling was *there*, somewhere, in me. *There*, y'know?"

And then the smells and the sorry sights blurred away from him, runny and watery as rain, as strange fluid squirted on a windshield. And later, he remembered the touch, on his sleeve, his face, the back of his neck, but the fingers and paws were all wrong—yet right, too. The fingers were too much like those he'd remembered from the time before his Gramma went crazy-mean. And the small paws were too soft, too numerous by far.... But not wanting to shatter the precious thing given to him after long years of needing, of hurting, of hungering for forgiveness, he kept his eyes shut as he backed out of that stinking place, only opening them when he reached the hallway.

Then he ran, not daring to look back, to *confirm*, until he reached the window exit and barreled down the ringing metal steps, his breath a faint hazy plume behind him. When he reached the dark alley, he paused for a ragged breath; then, when his breathing was normal, he made his way back to the street where he saw in the frosty glare of the streetlight that his hub-caps, antenna and windshield wipers were gone, but the sight of his denuded car only made David smile. He hoped that whatever money whoever took the parts had gotten would go a little way toward stopping whatever hunger had driven the person to thievery in the first place. It didn't matter to him which altar the person prayed before, seeking release from their private hunger and want.

It didn't matter to David at all, as he climbed behind the wheel, and headed for his apartment, not even stopping on the way home for something to eat. He was quite full, for the first and final time.

Author's note: Inspired by the non-fiction of Alan Rodgers, this work is nonetheless 90% autobiographical. In the memory of Missy, Bandito, Terri, Blackie, Diablo, Arthur, and Rocky I. And Spooky and Thelma, too.

PART FOUR
(UN)REALITY, AS WE KNOW IT

FROM THE
FAR AWAY NEARBY

WISCONSIN ISN'T ANYTHING like New Mexico, but as I stood there in the Painter-Lady's private gallery, looking at her painting of the wonderful, yet childishly simple thing that Bill and Will once made for her, I realized that not only people, but places, are more or less universal after all. Especially when it comes to how those things Bill and Will spoke of, the mundane magic of matters like entropy and what they called the "tourist economy," can change what is wondrous into that which is merely *wondered-about....*

Gwen and I didn't know about the aliens who lived down the street from us until the day they built us that air-conditioner, but then again, we almost didn't even know about the air-conditioner until it was just about finished because we were fighting so much about what we were going to watch on cable that steamy, the-air-just-sort-of-sits-in-your-lungs July afternoon that I don't think we would've heard Godziila stomping on the roof until maybe the ceiling fell on the TV. Even then, I doubt we would've stopped arguing....

"Not fair," Gwen pouted, throwing another Cheeze Puff at me from the half-filled bowl of them in front of her. (She always dumped the store-brand cheese puffs Mom bought into a bowl and thew away the crinkly wrapper, just so she could pretend that she was eating the fancy-brand cheese puffs, the kind with the animated cheetah spokescat.)

'Course, Mom was the same way; she'd hide the box from the IGA macaroni and cheese and tell us it was the expensive kind, the *cheese* and macaroni brand, but Gwen and I knew the difference. The IGA stuff was yellower.

"But they'll be showing the same old videos in another couple of hours...I'll bet. They show Duran-Duran videos all the time...."

"But not right now—and now's when I wanna watch—"

"Yeah, but right *now* I wanna see the sports, and that won't be on in another hour."

"So...you could tape yours, and we could watch mine," Gwen protested around a mouth of cheese puffs. Her whole face was dusted with blaze-orange gritty cheese powder, like she was some bee who'd been snorting pollen.

"No we can't!" I could've dumped the whole bowl of cheesies on her head and mashed them in her sweaty hair, I was so mad. "You know our VCR don't record off the UHF!"

Which was true. Our VCR was an old Betamax, twice as big as the proverbial breadbox and almost as useless, one of the early ones from like about 1980 and it only recorded channels two through thirteen, period, and her MTV was on channel twenty-one, and my sports show was on WTBS, which was way down the dial at number twenty-seven, and so neither of us could tape our show while watching the other one.

Gwen and I had been having this same argument ever since the local cable company finally got in some of the *good* channels, and some of the stuff Mom liked, like CNN, but they put them all on the UHF band, so we couldn't tape them on the Beta VCR Dad left behind when he and Mom split up a couple of years back. (Mom used to look at it and tell us, "That's your child support, kids" only then I didn't know what she meant. I was only ten and a half years old back in 1983.)

At first Mom tried to stop us from arguing, but once summer kicked in and she got busier at the fancy restaurant across town where she worked the buffet counter, and tables when they were really busy, she said she was glad she had to go to work, just so she wouldn't hear us screaming at each other.

But it wasn't just cable-TV that drove us nuts that summer; our little house was *really* hot, on account of us not being able to afford air-conditioning, and also because none of the windows were aligned to allow the wind to blow through-and-through the house. There were blind alleys and pockets of dead, hot air everywhere. Especially in the living room, which was real long and kinda narrow, with the TV and VCR at one end, and a pair of double-paned crank-handled big windows at the other end, only the one window's handle was busted (the little notches on the crank were worn smooth), and the other window had this crack in one of the double panes, so that it was all cloudy and foggy-looking in between the glass. Mom said it drove her buggy to look at it, which was why we kept a pair of thin curtains made from beige bedsheets pulled across it. Only trouble with the curtains was, once they were pulled over the windows, it was hard to remember if the glass part had been cranked open.

On that afternoon, when Gwen was tossing those curls of orange coated corn at me, and I was flicking them back at her, the window wasn't open. We were both so sweaty we glimmered in the reflection of the show flickering on the TV tube, but it was so hot, so sun-burning hot outside we figured it was one of those six of one, half a dozen of the other situations and just stayed inside.

So we didn't notice what was going on outside the house, on the other side of those big crank-out windows, until I heard the hollow sort of pounding, like someone was thumping an empty aluminum soda can on the top of a cardboard box.

"What's that noise?"

"Your brain cell playing solitaire," Gwen said, lohbing another puff my way. For an eight-year-old, she could be one royal snot.

I reached over and turned down the volume on the TV, to hear the noise better. Thock, thock...coming from the direction of the sheer curtained windows behind us. Now I have to tell you here, we had this big old black walnut tree growing about ten feet outside the double windows, and we were used to the shadows it cast on the curtains—huge wavering—gnarled shapes that looked like one thing one minute and something else the next. But there were some different shadows on that window now—a gigantic, near-black shadow of something stuck on the exposed window glass to our right. And there were a couple of moving shadows flanking the big dark one....

I don't know who was out the door first, me or Gwen. But we ran across the rectangular concrete-floored porch, down the cement steps with the wobbly iron railing, and around the side of the house as one.

And I don't know which one of us saw it first, but Gwen was the one who said, "Hey, watcha doing?"

In their matching mesh-backed baseball caps, overalls and sweat ringed tee shirts—not to mention those identical black-framed sunglasses—the two guys pounding on our window looked sorta like the Blues Brothers and little bit like those baby twins on the "You Been Farming Long?" poster at the feed mill, the boys in the Oshkosh b'Gosh bibbies.

One guy was somewhat taller and thinner, while the other was kinda stocky. More like Jake and EIwood. Only they were both awfully pale, especially considering that they'd been working out in the sun at least an hour or more—judging from the looks of that...*that* now attached to the old window like a sack of spider eggs, they must've been busy for quite a while before I noticed them. As for what they'd been working on, it looked like a cross between a chrome-plated cheese puff (the baked kind, though), and a jumble of vacuum cleaner attachments. And how, I don't know, but it was stuck tight on the glass, and sorta jutted out and down from there. Plus there were flat black rectangles stuck all over it which kinda looked like bike reflectors—they had that flat pattern embossed on their surfaces. I didn't know what it was, but I was sure Mom was gonna hate it.

"My Mom's not gonna be happy about this," I said, after the two guys ignored Gwen's question, and, since Mom always said, "Ted, you're the man of the family now," I stepped up to the nearest, skinnier one, and tapped him on the shoulder, saying, "I *said* my Mom is *not* gonna like this—"

"Nooope, you *said* she's not gonna be happy 'bout this," the taller guy drawled, sorta sounding like Sheriff Andy on *The Andy Griffith Show* reruns on TBS. The bigger guy just kept doing what he'd been doing before, softly tapping on the end of the curly silver thing where it was attached to the glass, using some hollow thingie that looked like a flattened piece of muffler pipe.

"Well, whatever he said, *you* knock it off!" I hated it when Gwen spoke tougher than I did, and cuffed her one on the shoulder before telling both of them, "You guys take that...thing off my mom's window—now!"

"But it's awfully hot," the heavier guy said, in a southern-yet not-really-southern drawling voice, just sort a slow and easy-going, "And you folks got no air-conditioning. So me and my brother here, we figgered we'd help out. Wasn't doing anything else no-how, right?"

"Uh-huh" the taller one replied. I almost thought they were going to announce that they were on a mission from God or something, just like Dan Ackroyd did in the movie that one of Mom's boyfriends rented for us one time from the video store over in Ewerton (our video store in Lumbe only carried VHS tapes). But the tall guy didn't say much more, just went back to doing whatever it was he'd been doing with the silver coiled blob before we'd come outside to tell him to get lost.

"How'd you guys know we don't have an air conditioner?" I finally asked, not expecting an answer, but the taller guy said in that practically Sheriff Andy voice, "Didn't see no box on the ground or sticking from the windows, and since you have some of your windows open, we figgered you didn't have one."

The guy was right. And I felt ashamed, like all the neighborhood (which was mostly a lot of retired people, or the cruds who moved in and out of the rental houses at least three times a year per house) knew by looking that Mom and Gwen and I were just scraping by. Like it was written on the side of the house in barn red latex or something.

I was about to say something defensive, something offensive, too, when Gwen came running out the door again (I hadn't realized she'd gone in), letting it swack! shut behind her. She was all smiling, and out of breath—but she wasn't sweaty-looking anymore, either.

"Ted, you gotta come feel," she said, grabbing my hands and pulling me up the steps and into the house...where everything was frosty and—beautiful inside, like when we'd go to our friends' houses or inside the IGA and feel the prickly chill on our skins. Even with some of the other windows open (or had-been-open; I saw through the doorway to the tiny dining room that Gwen had shut the other windows), it was wonderful inside our house, not all sticky-ucky like usual for almost half the year. Wisconsin summers can be the pits.

And the cold was coming from the one window; no air blew in, but the window was icy to the touch even through the thin curtain.

"Mom's gonna be mad, right...Teddy?" Gwen taunted. I would've dumped the cheesies on her head for real, except that she was already out the door and running to the strange guys, yelling, "Hey! Do you guys know how to make our Betamax get cable—and play VHS tapes?"

I was out the door and down the concrete steps before the shorter one answered Gwen; tossing his muffler-pipe tool down onto the dandelion-crowded grass, he half-turned to Gwen and said, "A Betamax that don't get cable...and won't play VHS tapes. Bill, there anything in the pile of stuff behind the trailer we can use to rig up their machine?"

So the taller guy was Bill. Bill gave the big silvery cheese puff on the window a tapping pat before scratching the place where his sort of no-color darkish hair met his forehead under the bill of his cap, then said, "There's a whole lotta junk in the pile. Must be something I can use. Lemme go see," and he took off for that old dark green-painted trailer with the attached garage that stood at the end of the street on the side opposite where our house was. There weren't supposed to be trailers in Lumbe proper, but this one had been grandfathered in before the ordinance, and since the garage was attached permanently to it, it wasn't likely any of the renters would haul it up and truck it off any time soon. Not that everyone on the street didn't wish someone would go do just that. It was an ugly place; the paint was pulled *away* from the wide siding in ridged flaps which showed peaks of the old yellowish paint underneath. And the windowsills were flaked grey-white. Usually welfare families rented the place; the last bunch had four kids, plus the mom, the dad, and a grey-and-white cat. In what couldn't have been more than a one-bedroom trailer. But that family had fenced in the back yard on account of their kids wandering off (once the little girls showed up in a neighbor's back yard, naked and using their swing set), and later on when the neighbors complained about the husband's junk car collection, he'd pried off the best bits from the rotting hulks and tossed the pieces in the fenced-in yard.

Which is where Bill was headed. Behind him, his companion was noodling around with the little black rectangles on the silver coil, while Gwen was watching, so...since the bigger guy didn't look like a weirdo or a pervert (like those fat-ass Shipman brothers in Ewerton), I left Gwen to watch him, and followed Bill to the green trailer. Bill was unlatching the gate when I caught up with him. Beyond was an expanse of muddy-dried ground with only a few straggles of grass poking up through the sun-baked brown clods, ringed with a rusted silvery-gold assortment of metallic junk—besides the car parts, there were old house radiators, the sides of burned-out burn barrels, old toasters, loosely coiled rusted wire, used batteries, tubeless TV sets, and lots more junk too rusted and weather-beaten to identify.

But Bill strode up to one heap of crap and began rooting in it like he knew what was buried there. I leaned over the open gate and swung back and forth on it while he dug around, butt up, and when he finally stood up and turned around and saw me, he did act startled, his pale face going slack under the shadow of his cap-bill.

"Whatcha doin', kid?"

"Watching you...Bill. What you got there?" I motioned my head at the handfuls of shining metal and the avocado-colored four-slice toaster carcass he held against the belly of his overalls.

"Oh...buncha stuff. Parts...for your VCR. 'Cuse me, I gotta go inside for the rest. Here, you take this over to Will."

"Will? Your folks named *both* of you guys William?"

Bill walked toward me, covering the distance between us in three scissoring strides, then, as he dumped the load of "stuff" into my waiting arms, he said, "I'm William. He's Wilford. We fix up stuff. I'll be right back."

The armful of scrap metal and the toaster were still relatively cool, as if they'd been resting well hidden in the pile. Through the window nearest the garage, I could see Bill's capped head bobbing around in the trailer. He seemed to be rooting around in a box of something down low by the floor, before standing up again, and heading for the front door. When he rejoined me by the gate, I could see lots of colored wires with twisted copper raw ends jutting out of his bibbie top pocket, the one over his chest, and more coiled wire, a plastic-handled screwdriver, and some rubber-gripped pliers stuck in his side pockets over his hips.

"C'mon, kid, let's go fix up your VCR," he said over his shoulder as he started walking back to my Mom's small white house down the street. I ran after him, mindful not to drop any of the things he'd given me, and panted, "Hey, Bill, I don't think we can afford to pay you, least not what we probably owe you. Air condition—it cost a lot—"

"But what we used didn't cost us nothing. Just stuff from the pile out back. Was all going to rust or rot anyhow. Might as well get some use outta it," Bill explained in that careful Sheriff Andy voice of his, before adding, "'Course, it don't come with a warranty, either. Once it breaks, it's broken. So...we don't take no pay, OK?"

That seemed logical, but still, I wasn't too young to know about things like labor costs on a repair bill, either. "What about your time? The guy who fixes our furnace always adds extra for that—"

"That's 'cause he needs money to live. We...barter for stuff. Like ducks with the tourists. We do things, people feed us and whatnot. You folks got food?"

I was still wondering how the ducks fit into all this air conditioning and VCR conversion stuff. "Yeah, we got food...but what about the ducks?"

Bill stopped one house away from ours, right in the middle of the street, and turned around to face me. "You know how ducks migrate? How they stay here in summer, when the tourists and the locals go fishing and sunning themselves by the river, or by the lakes? Well, the ducks make folks happy, so the people feed 'em stuff. It's a form of tourist economy for them. The ducks do what comes naturally to ducks, and people reward 'em for *being* ducks. Like...me and Will do what just comes to us, and people feed us, keep us *going* for as long as we're here, which is how we rented the trailer. We done some stuff for the guy who owns it—"

The guy who owned the ratty green trailer and attached garage was named Sleasar—"Boss Sleasar" to just about everyone in Lumbe, Ewerton and Hunterstown in Dean County—who *also* happened to own the cemetery, two laundromats, a couple of car washes (one self-serve, the other automated), a whole bunch of low-rent wrecks like the trailer on our street, and even an apartment house in Ewerton packed with a lot of Hmong families the Lutheran church brought over back in 1980 or so.

"—fixed up the triple loader in his one laundromat so that it only spins out half as much as it should, so's people need to spend more to get all the water outta their stuff. And we made him some water heaters for his apartment house that don't use the electric or the gas to heat water. He hooked 'em up to the garbage compactor in the basement, so's the heaters all run on trash. For now, at least. Old Andy" (which was Boss Sleasar's given name) "—he was real impressed with the triple loader while we were in there washing our stuff that day, so after we done his water heaters, he let us stay here. Until we go, but before that, there's stuff to do."

As Bill and I walked across the patch of loose gravel which served as our driveway (the house had no garage), toward Will and Gwen, my sister turned to me and said, her voice all light and airy with awe, "Will here says that come winter, this'll add 'radiant heat' to the house, so's we don't need to have the furnace up so high! Think Mom'll hate that too?"

I was going to tell her to stuff it, but I didn't know how Bill and Will might take that. Then again, if they rigged that triple loader to not spin out right, I didn't think there was too much they would disapprove of that we might do....

"Your VCR in there?" Bill pointed one callused thumb in the direction of the front door. Like we'd have it sitting in the basement or something. "Yeah," Gwen gushed, as she led Bill and Will into the living room, which I sure hoped they wouldn't be able to see all that clearly due to wearing sunglasses and going from a bright-lit outside to a darker inside. What with Mom working so much, the place was a mess. And smelled like sweat and cheap cheese curls.

But Will and Bill were sweaty, too, so I don't think they noticed. The bowl of cheese puffs didn't stay full of puffs for long, though. Gwen had to go to the kitchen and dig out the extra bag Mom said was only for the weekend (and it was just Wednesday), for the two guys to eat while they worked. Pretty soon the living room was messier than before.

Parts of the VCR, the broken toaster, and all those colored wires Bill had brought over were spread out across the matted-down brown-white-black semi-shag carpeting, and both the guys were sitting in the middle of the mess, the bowl of replenished puffs rapidly dwindling between them. They didn't talk as they worked, not even to ask what the other was doing. One would pick up something unasked-for and hand it to the other, then the other one would tighten something the first one had just shoved into something *else*...and as Gwen and I watched from the doorway to the dining room, she turned to me and whispered, "How we gonna pay them?"

"They don't take money. Just food."

"I can see that...but a bag of cheese puffs doesn't equal an air condition and a—"

"We're gonna have to eat supper, aren't we?"

"Mom is gonna hate this...."

"Not when she's always bi—complaining about being hot," I shot back.

Gwen crossed her arms just like Mom would do when she was pissed about something, and said, "Hot's one thing. You know how she don't like company after she's been working. And you know her, she'll wanna pay 'em—"

I wondered if Gwen had heard some of those...sounds coming from the bedroom on some weekend nights after Mom brought home this guy or that guy who'd done her some favor at work (even something like leaving a big tip with his bill), *but* I told myself that eight was still too young to figure out what I'd just been able to figure out myself.

"—and her tip jar's not too full after *you* broke the windshield wiper on her car—"

I was so relieved to realize that *that* was what Gwen meant by "pay" that I didn't even mind it when Bill cut in, "Windshield wiper? I can fix that, too," then went back to what he'd been doing.

"It's already fixed, but thanks," I said quickly, then pulled Gwen into the dining room, then into the kitchen which was so tiny there was no room for even an eating counter and stools, so's we had to eat in the dining room, even though Mom thought it was a bit "pretentious"—once we were in there, I said, "Listen, those guys don't need to know anything more about us, OK? It's bad 'nough we'll have to explain all this to Mom, without *you* sayin' stuff about company and whatnot, *OK*?"

Gwen stood silent for a second, listening to the muffled

metallic sounds coming from the living room, then whispered back, "I didn't mean *pay 'em*...like after supper, in her *room* pay'em. I mean like the repair-guy pay 'em.

So, she had heard the sounds from the bedroom. Well, there wasn't anything I could do or say to make her not know or understand all that, but still...I hated to think that she did know. About the sounds.

Suddenly I was really glad about the air-conditioning...if the house hadn't of been so cool right then, I know I'd have been sick right there on the yellow-white mottled vinyl flooring. Gwen didn't seem to be bothered about it at all, which just made it worse.

"Kids, I'm home—uh, who the hell are you guys?"

Mom. I'd forgotten that the restaurant in Ewerton closed early every third Wednesday of the month for their local Kiwanis Club meeting.

"I'm Bill, and this is *my* brother, Will," Bill was sayinq as Gwen and I ran into the living room, where Mom was standing with the screen door and the inner door wide open, so that there was a patch of wavering heat around her as she stood sweating and drippy-haired in her uniform dress and snap-on apron.

"It's okay Mom, they're doing some stuff for us. All they want is a meal in return, isn't that right Bill?" I said in a rush of words, even as Mom's eyes darkened and narrowed behind her glasses.

"That is right, Ma'am. My brother and I do odd jobs for a living, and we find that dealing in food and other sundries is just...easier. We've been enjoying these—" he held up the nearly empty bowl of cheesies "—and we'd be happy with anything you care to serve us. We're staying in Mr. Sleasar's trailer, down the street—"

"Ohhh...Andy's place. Ohhhkaaay, I see," Mom said, as she looked down at her arms, which were starting to goose pimple on the forearms below her uniform cuffs. She'd driven up to the house on the part of the street which was opposite the air conditioner, so I stepped through the maze of parts littering the floor and said, "C'mon Mom, *you* gotta see this," and steered her back outside and down to the side of the house.

Once we were standing next to the big coiled silvery thing, she grabbed the top of my arm and hissed, "What the hell is going on? Why are those two guys sitting in the living room tearing apart the Betamax?" She didn't seem too impressed with the silvery cheese thingie on the window, for some reason. Maybe because the Betamax was our "child support" and all.

"Gwen asked them to convert it to VHS...and make it UHF compatible. After she saw this—"

"Can they do that?" her frown eased a bit, and the vertical worrylines disappeared from between her eyes, as she dug around in her apron pocket and pulled out a slightly bent cigarette and her lighter.

"I...suppose," I said, "they have those 8-track to cassette converters," and when she blew out a billow of hazy blue-grey, she said in a more even tone, "I suppose I better buy some more food...those guys look big. They say how much they want in exchange for this?" She flicked dying ash in the direction of the black-studded silver coil which was stuck like a snail to the glass. The thing was already covered with a sheen of moisture, which dripped down onto the weed infested grass under the window.

"No...just a meal, I guess," I mumbled, hoping I wouldn't hear any noise from her bedroom that night.

"They eat tuna-mac?"

"Probably," I shrugged, "Boss Sleasar gave 'em the trailer, but then they did do all the water heaters for him and the triple loader at the—"

"Well, tuna-mac'll have to do. Tips were shitty today," Mom said, before walking back to her car and saying just before she shut the door, "Tell Gwen to put a big pot of water on the stove in about fifteen minutes, OK?" then reversed the car and headed down the street back into town.

Bill and Will had the Betamax reassembled and...augmented before it was time for Gwen to set the water on the burner. The

VCR itself looked pretty much the same, but instead of the top which rose up when you pressed a button down, there was the toaster positioned on its side, with the four openings enlarged to just two, both of which now had flap-like covers on them made from what looked like panels from metal blinds. And there were now ten buttons—six original, and four made from old manual typewriter keys with "6" "+" "/" and "G" on them—to press. The latter four were, as Bill informed us, "Dual picture, VHS record, VHS-playback, and Beta-VHS switch-over. The first one's for playing one picture in the corner while you're watching something else."

The VCR looked like it might do a lot more than play two different channels on it when you pressed down a key marked "G"...like maybe take off for outer space and keep on going—

Gwen and I must've been thinking the same thing, but as was her wont lately, she blurted it out first. "Were you guys the ones who taught E.T. to make his phone to call home? Or did he teach *you*?"

Bill and Will just stood there with their hands in their bibbie pockets, half smiles on their faces. Even out of the sunlight, both of them looked awfully pale. And neither of them had much in the way of beard stubble, either, now that I could see them closer. Finally, Will spoke:

"Aw, that was just a movie...nobody used nothing to go callin' home. Trouble is, what with how space and time work, by the time that little feller called home-home, like where his planet was, it would've been far into his own future over there, soo? More than just space between stars and all. Should've said, 'Phone Mother-Ship'—"

Funny thing was, here we were, Gwen and I, standing in the living room talking with aliens, and it was...just like standing in the living room talking with the guy who repaired our furnace, only he wore a blue uniform with a name patch on it, and a cap that read "Lennox" on the sew-on patch. Only Bill and Will wouldn't be sending Mom an invoice. I don't even think they'd started up mail service—but it wasn't like you'd *think* talking to aliens would be like. They sweated like us, sounded like people we'd seen on TV, and just wanted something to eat...like we did.

"Oh no, the water!" Gwen sputtered, when she looked at the clock on the VCR (which Will and Bill had left pretty much alone, aside from somehow changing the light-up colors from red to a sort of dark red-orange), and ran into the kitchen to start running some water into Mom's mac-and-cheese cooking pot.

Once she was gone, I said to both the men, "So...when the ducks leave the lakes and rivers up here, they go south. But where...do you go when it's...off-season?"

(Even now, some twenty years later, I'm a little proud of how well I managed to put such a delicate question.)

"Oh, all over. Depends on what needs to be done where," Bill replied.

"Oh." They weren't much more forthcoming than real ducks would be. I decided to go back to Gwen's original topic. "So...if you guys could 'phone home' where would 'home' be?"

Bill took his hands out of his pockets and reached up to take off his cap. Under it, his longish hair was all sweaty and mussed. Combing it down with the fingers of his free hand, he said, "The name of it wouldn't mean much to you. You'd probably forget it as soon as I said it. But Will and I, we used to do some work for a woman down in the Southwest, the Painter-Lady, and she used to have this saying, used it for letters and such. 'From the Far Away Nearby.' Let's just say that that's where me and Will hail from. It's...close enough."

I was about to protest that he could tell me where he and Will came from, that my people weren't about to go invading his home planet or anything like that, but I heard Mom's car in the driveway, and just said, "Oh...OK. Like the next solar system, right?"

Will smiled, and took off his cap. "That's—right. Or near as dammit."

Then Mom came to the door, and for the time being we spoke no more of solar systems or calling home...where ever "home" was for Will and Bill....

Mom went all out for supper. She'd bought the special kind of mac and cheese (cheese and mac, actually) with shells instead of that skinny elbow mac, and a packet of sauce in a silvery pouch, the kind Gwen had to knead first before Mom stirred it into the hot macaroni. Then she added not one small can but two of tuna, the kind with the little mermaid on the label, not the IGA kind. And she put it in to a separate bowl instead of just leaving it in the pot and putting that on the table. Plus she had salad on the side, and opened a fresh bottle of French dressing to go with it. That was store brand, but Will and Bill complimented Mom on its wonderful taste and aroma. Smells apparently were important to their kind.

Eating seemed to be, too. They weren't as bad as those aliens on *Saturday Night Live* who crammed everything into their pointy heads, but each of them ate two helpings of tuna mac plus a salad. And drank a lot of coffee afterwards.

"Are you gentlemen from the south? I detect an accent—" Mom was fishing for compliments, what with her fancy diction and all, She used to talk that way around guys she thought might make good step-dads. I half-expected them to say "We're from France" but all Will said was, "Originally...we move around a lot, though, as it is, we'll be heading south of here soon, Illinois, most likely."

Mom wrinkled her nose before she thought better of it. People in Wisconsin tended not to like Illinois folk. (Or Minnesotans, either. Michigan folk were OK as long as they were from the Upper Peninsula.)

"Not too soon, I hope," she recovered, offering them another cup of coffee to go with the plate of cookies she'd bought— again, I'd never seen cookies on a *plate* unless it was Christmas.

"Yeah, actually, quite soon," Bill said. "We've pretty much done all we can do around here, for now, with what we have on hand. At the trailer."

"Oh, but Lumbe has a lot of places that need fixing, I'm sure you could find more odd jobs…."

"Wouldn't want to take jobs away from the locals," Will

replied, "We just did a few things which needed doing, is all. Time to move on."

While the adults were speaking, I was thinking. About the big silver do-hinkey jutting from our window. And the rewired VCR still sitting on the living room floor. Plus those garbage fueled water heaters in Boss Sleasar's apartment house. Stuff that needed doing, but also stuff that gets noticed...in a way that might, so to speak, make people want to keep those migrating ducks trapped by freezing lakes or rivers. It was a wonder old man Sleasar hadn't alerted the newspapers about what they'd done for him, but that would've meant explaining things to the power company...this way, he could just make out like he'd shut off the heaters—Or that the triple loader was just running slow....

But even as I half-shivered in the delicious coolness of the house, I knew that soon people would be hanging around the house, poking and prodding the silvery coils. Asking questions, walking over to that green trailer....

"Ma'am, this was a truly fine meal, but it's getting late and my brother and I need to start packing for our trip," Bill said gently, as he got up and half-bowed at Mom. His brother nodded his thanks and rose from his seat. Before they left, they did put the VCR back in its stand, and showed Mom how to operate it, then they headed down the street for the narrow, peeling green trailer with the attached garage.

Once they were gone, Mom said "Damn" to no one in particular, and walked heavily back to the kitchen to do the dishes. Gwen and I played with the VCR for a while, taping stuff off the UHF band, but after a while, as the sound of dishes clinking against the steel sink rang softly from the kitchen, Gwen and I looked at each other and wordlessly turned the volume up higher, then softly shut the door behind us as we quitted the house....

The shades in the green trailer were drawn, but very bright light spilled out along the vertical spots where the shades didn't meet the windows. Too much light for just a lamp or two or a TV. And there were muffled noises, overlapping voices and snippets of music, coming from inside that closed-doors-and-windows trailer. Too much noise for a TV or even a TV and a radio going at once....

"You wanna knock?" Gwen didn't wait for a reply before hitting the warped veneer of the front door with her knuckles. Within, the overlapping sounds grew dimmer, and a man's strange voice yelled, "Game."

That voice wasn't southern. It didn't quite sound like a man. As in human....

Gwen gave the dull brass-tone knob a tentative twist. The door opened smoothly, silently—not all screeing and rusty like when the welfare couple lived here. And as the door opened, there was a slice of bright, bright light against the darkening outside—

Every bit of wall-space and floor space in the long living room/ kitchen/dining room was filled with TV sets, stereos, VCR's and snaking coils of wire which plugged not into outlets, but into a thing made from what looked like a blender merged with a toaster oven gerry-rigged to a car battery which sat in the middle of the floor.

Will and Bill were also sitting on the floor, remotes in hand, flicking them randomly at this TV and that VCR and this stereo—the screens all flickered with dozens of images: fishing shows from the Eau Claire station, *The Blues Brothers* off a grainy videotape, commercial news shows, one screen filled with static alone, and too many more to clearly remember. I do recall that Jake Blues was doing cartwheels in a church.

Bill and Will were slack faced, still wearing the sunglasses neither of them had removed during dinner, but their voices were different: They had this echoing, tinny ring to them, not harsh but not soothing, either. Then, gradually, with each turn of the head toward a different screen, their voices took on new accents, new inflections. Bill sounded a little like Elwood, while Will's voice was a bit Jake Blues, and a lot more like that short guy who played the dispatcher on that TV show *Taxi*. Sort of gruff, but nice, too.

"So...you kids came over to say good-bye?" Bill said, while cueing up a record on one stereo, some old black man singing a bluesy ballad. I just nodded, but Gwen blurted out, "Why won't you stay? Are you afraid someone will find you out? 'Cause of all the stuff you made?"

"Not really, kiddo," Will said, switching from a fishing show to a cable channel showing a doctor operating on someone's foot. "The stuff's not the problem. Entropy will cover our tracks—"

"'Entro—?" I began, until Will took over. "*Entropy.* Your lingo for eventually-breaks-down. Like, what goes up, comes down someday. The opposite of if it ain't broke, don't fix it. With our stuff, it can't be fixed, so who's to know how it ran in the first place, eh?"

"But while it's here, enjoy. We know how things go, but as long as no one else does...who's the wiser? It's like those ducks. While they're here, they're fun, but once they fly south, people get to thinking of other stuff. So...once we go, and our things stop working, who's to believe they ever did work? It's all just a lot of stuff and junk."

The noise-upon-noise around me was making me queasy. But I still felt a pure surge of impending loss as I looked at Will and Bill sitting there on that matted down, dirty green carpet. Sure, we'd enjoy the air-conditioning, and the improved VCR, but once they were gone, what then?

"Chances are, by the time your new stuff breaks down, your Mom will have bought new stuff to replace it—everything is made to die. People, too, kiddo...it's the curse of free radicals. That's what happens when your body cells use up oxygen and... use the men's room afterwards. Something we don't have to worry about, but sometimes entropy isn't the worst thing that can happen," Bill said, and I didn't want to know if he could or couldn't read minds, too.

"Yeah, Teddy, even entropy has its place in the universe... not a bad thing when you consider the alternative," Will added, fishing around in one overall pocket for something, which he handed to me. Pressing the object into my hand, he said, "For you to remember us by after we go to the next far away nearby. And it won't break down, either...too elemental for that."

The object he placed in my hand was ovoid, warm to the touch, and strangely soft-pliant. I just glanced at it long enough to see it was golden orange colored and had something stuck inside. If I'd have looked at it longer, I would've started crying.

Next to me, Gwen said, "You two been here a long time. Is it just you two?"

Bill nodded from his place on the floor. "Too long. Like I said, sometimes entropy isn't the worst thing to fear."

"No," I found myself saying, "you said entropy isn't the worst thing that can *happen*—"

Both the aliens smiled at that. Only Will replied, "'Happen'— 'fear'...for us, it's like you people say...'same difference.'"

"Will we...entropy?" Gwen had a hard time pronouncing the word.

"Eventually...eventually. But sometimes it takes a long time— that Painter-Lady, down in New Mexico, she's still hanging in there, and she's old now," Bill said, then leaned over to take Gwen's hand in his. "You're sharp like she is. I...suspect you'll give entropy a run for its money, kiddo."

There was a lot more I wanted to ask the aliens, but somehow I sensed that they needed their time with their TVs and their music to prepare for their next stop in their migratory pattern. Taking Gwen's hand in mine, I walked her out of their trailer, and shut the door behind us. There was an almost full moon out, and as she and I walked home, I looked at the object in my palm. It was a blob of amber, with an insect the likes of which I'd never before seen embedded in it...along with a transistor chip, delicate, intricate, obviously man-made circuits upon which the insect had alighted before being slowly covered with the resinous amber. The chip inside might've been subject to that thing called entropy that Will spoke of, but the coating was far too primitive to succumb to something as destructive as entropy.

I wondered, briefly, if Will had watched the amber flow down, then harden around that long-extinct insect, then dismissed the thought—I couldn't handle the prospect that so much time had passed for Will or Bill....

It wasn't until years went by, years during which first the VCR then the air conditioner broke down and had to be relegated to the same scrap heap behind the long-abandoned trailer down our street, years when first Mom, then Gwen married, and moved away to parts both far away and nearby (Viroqua and Ewerton, respectively), that I learned who Will and Bill's Painter-Lady was, and where her work could be found. New Mexico, as I said, is quite different from Wisconsin, but entropy works its insidious wonders there same as it does here. Will and Bill never said what they'd built for their aging Painter-Lady (who eventually did die, but not all that soon for a human), but as I stood in her own one-woman museum, in the white-walled starkness of those angular viewing rooms, before an equally stark and somewhat enigmatic painting of a sky, a moon, and a ladder suspended midway between the flat ground and the moon, free of any ostensible support, I think I know—I think I can at least guess—what sort of "job" Will and Bill (or whatever they were calling themselves at the time they lived near Ghost Ranch) had done for their Painter-Lady.

And while the ladder they'd rigged for Georgia O'Keeffe may've fallen down long ago, I don't think the forces of entropy will affect her painting of it any time soon. Paint may not be as sturdy as amber, but it is almost as elemental....

THE CAT WITH
THE TULIP FACE

*For Sassy, with love,
And for Little Guy (1983-1988), in remembrance*

Author's Note: This novelette is a prequel to my novel
THE AMULET, *and takes place in late 1986, a year
before the events in the novel.*

MEAOW.

"Kitty-kitty?" Arlene asked the humid early morning air, as she glanced up and down Wisconsin Street. Darkness welled in recessed shop doorways, and gave an inky sheen to the large display windows. The greenish-white street lamps were too far away to cast much of a glow where she stood, midway between the tacky novelty shop and the building which used to be the Ewerton Savings and Loan but was now a lawyer's office *(after the Century 21 Realty office came and went)*.

A fine mist settled on Arlene's exposed face and forearms; she rolled down the plastic backed canvas sleeves on her outsized slicker and tried calling again. "C'mon, Kitty-kitty. It's okay, I won't hurt you." She could hear the cat (kitten? It sounded young) crying, but the humidity in the sluggish July air made it difficult to pinpoint just where its cries originated.

Meeeaow!

Closer, and louder now. Arlene walked forward slowly, heading toward the tiny diner that used-to-be-a-clothing-boutique to the north of her. In the distance she heard a truck's many wide tires snick-splash along one of the side streets behind her. At this hour of the morning—just before four—the only things moving on the streets of Ewerton were out of state truckers, the last stragglers coming home after an all night party held in one of those walk-up apartments nestled above the department stores, the occasional stray animal—and Arlene.

Plastic mesh shopping bags in hand, Arlene had Ewerton all to herself in the mornings. She was the Queen of Ewert Avenue, the Owner of Wisconsin Street. *And the Duchess of the Dumpsters*, she often joked with herself as she leaned into the back-of-the-store dumpsters, her fingers sensitive to the feel of aluminum cans, the odd piece of discarded merchandise, or even the past-its-due-date box or carton of food.

And stray animals. Often, she'd unintentionally scare a wild cat or something smaller and quicker that she wasn't about to try to scrutinize in order to determine its species. And some mornings, she had footsore canine company for the length of a few blocks, until a slobbery tongue touched her hand in farewell and the empty streets rang with the sound of dog nails doing a chitinous tap-dance on the concrete.

But these had been animals hungry, tired, or just plain lonely enough to allow Arlene to pick them up and scavenge them like an aluminum can, or an old box of breakfast cereal. Not that she thought of her pets as refuse, or cast-offs, though. Arlene treated all of her "finds" with respect, be they inanimate or animate. The aluminum cans were washed, then carefully crushed flat, prior to their storage in black plastic bags in the basement (and their subsequent return to the recycling truck come Thursday). The rust-dotted kitchen tools, chipped dishes, and one-left cards of kitchen magnets or corn-on-the-cob servers were diligently scrubbed, mended or matched with other odd-lot items waiting in Arlene's already cluttered kitchen drawers.

As for the animals...Arlene was a couple years short of being able to collect her own Social Security, but what with her late husband's SS checks, and the modest sum he'd left in the bank for her, she had just enough to pay her utility bills plus her considerable veterinarian bills. If a cat or dog needed food, she bought it name brands plus those expensive treats in the fancy little cans or boxes, while she ate weeks-old spareribs from the IGA dumpster. Should the animal need flea shampoo, she used only a half a tablet of denture cleaner in her chopper-hopper each day. When she wrote out the checks for her animals' shots each year, she *didn't* write out a check to cover the cost of her Ben-Gay and non-aspirin.

If you take it in, you take care of it. That thought alone was enough to banish any temptation to pamper herself. She had lived over sixty good years, years of plenty. *And I still have plenty*, she stubbornly told herself many a morning. *Only difference* is, *I don't have to pay for all of it.* That some of her finds— the four-legged ones—ended up costing her money she really couldn't afford to spend so freely never fazed Arlene, living alone as she did, with no children or grandchildren—or even many friends, for that matter—Arlene considered the love of her "babies" payment in full, thank you. While she knew that she'd have to make the little she had last until her own SS kicked in, Arlene had long ago decided that a life lived without *giving*, to *someone*, wasn't a life.

Her years with Don had proved that to be a fact.

So there she was, an old woman with ridiculously thin ankles which vanished in a pair of velcro-strapped running shoes, walking briskly down the street, her good ear cocked and waiting for the next *Meaow.* She walked faster, both out of need and urgency. With the gradual lightening of the sky, it was urgent that she get home before the delivery trucks began to arrive at the stores, and the graveyard shifts at the sash and door and paper mill were let out. And she knew that that cat (kitten?) *needed* her.

Six years of combing the pre-dawn streets had taught Arlene that for a little animal, alone and scared, dawn is too late. With the coming of light come cars with drivers who speed up when they see something small and frantic trying to cross the street.

Arlene had toed many a pulp-headed animal to the curb during her "normal" shopping hours.

But if she could find this cat before the coming of the light—*Meeeaow*!

That was why it was hard to get a fix on its cries—they came from *above* Arlene. Looking up, she saw the kitten sitting on the high window ledge of the dentist's office close to the intersection of Wisconsin Street and Fourth Avenue East. That window set in the gray stone facade was a good five feet off the ground, a small window with a deep ledge, recessed enough for a tiny kitten to hunker down close to the glass.

"Aw, c'mon, kitty, you can come closer, I won't hurt you," Arlene coaxed, as she stood on tiptoes and reached for the kitten. At five foot four, she was just tall enough to brush the animal's silky coat with the tips of her blunt fingers. The kitten was warm, exceptionally so for an animal which had most likely been sitting on that ledge all night. Its fur was as fine-textured as washed silk; as the kitten breathed its fur undulated like wind-whipped draperies, a most peculiar sensation.

The kitten stopped crying, and edged closer to Arlene; two huge black ears surmounted a mottled white and black wedge of a face. It looked to be about three months old. In the spill of the street-lamp, Arlene noticed that the kitten's eyes were tiny, baby-like. They glittered against the surrounding white fur like pebbles in the bottom of a fish tank, all watery and rounded.

Then, as if it had sized Arlene up and found her satisfactory, the kitten jumped off the ledge into her waiting arms. Upon impact, it began to purr, a loud rumble that radiated from its chest outward, making the ribs and skin vibrate. Arlene undid the top snap on her slicker and tucked the kitten inside; as she did so, her fingers brushed against the base of the kitten's tail. Gonads the size of large peas filled the scrotum.

As she positioned her left arm under the kitten, Arlene thought, *Awfully big down there for such a tiny baby boy...must be older than I thought.* Arlene's bag of cans clunked against her leg as she walked, but soon the kitten's purr drowned out even that noise.

By the time she was halfway to her home on Polk Avenue, the kitten was kneading her stomach.

Not only was the kitten older than Arlene had first guessed, he was...*uglier* than she'd realized. When she first brought him home, she hurried past the cats and dogs winding around her legs and shoved the wiggling kitten into the bathroom; she dreaded having to give all ten of her animals flea baths just in case the new arrival was crawling with the little brown varmints. After dumping some food into a saucer (also scavenged, a little white bowl with a childish picture of a spaceman on the moon in the bottom), she opened the bathroom door long enough to shove the food inside and slammed it before the kitten ran out. (There were litter pans positioned all over the house, including the bathroom, so she wasn't worried about any accidents after the kitten ate.) But she didn't get a good look at her newest find until after she'd fed her other friends, then brewed a cup of Earl Gray for herself.

While the other animals whined, scratched, hissed, and panted outside, Arlene quickly opened the door and slipped into the bathroom. The kitten was sitting on the toilet tank, in a Sphinx pose. Sitting sideways on the toilet seat, her back to the bathtub, Arlene said as she stroked the kitten's seal-sleek fur, "Gracious, you are the most *awful* looking kitty I've seen yet." The kitten blinked a kitty-kiss at her and began purring, as if she'd just said he was the most beautiful animal in the universe.

The kitten's capacity for affection wasn't in keeping with his appearance; not only were his ears *way* too big, so huge they almost met in the center of his upper head, but his face was all... wrong.

The too-small green eyes were only the beginning. The kitten's forehead and nose were all of one line, unbroken by dips, bumps, or anything. Just a straight slope from the too-close ears down to the nose leather. Arlene's cats, while not purebreds, were similar to each other in that their noses all dipped down parallel to their eyes in a pleasing sloping "S" curve. Years ago, Arlene had a cat named Louie who closely resembled an Oriental Shorthair, and even *his* nose had had a slight dip to it.

But the kitten's nose resembled something drawn with a straight-edge. Head-on he looked even worse, for his white face was marred in the middle by an irregular blotch which completely obscured his nose, leather and all. When Arlene glanced at him fast, it, almost seemed that he had no nose at all. And his tiny, slightly bulging eyes didn't add to his beauty, either.

Gently pulling back the kitten's gums, she said, "Just want to check your teeth...*good* boy." Wiping off cat spittle onto her smock top, Arlene frowned to herself. This kitten had his canines. Top and bottom, almost fully grown in. Which made him..."Hum, lemme *see*—I found Guy-Pie when he was about five months old, and he had *his* canines" (not to mention over a hundred fleas which Arlene had drowned in a jelly-jar glass) "so you're pretty close to that age, aren't you?"

The kitten purred in agreement. Arlene patted his sides; the ribs stood out like the tines of a serving fork held an inch above a table. Pitiful. The skin was sucked in close to his rump and guts, and his stifle bones felt like marbles under Arlene's hard fingertips. And his all-black tail resembled a licorice whip.

Outside, from where they waited in the hallway, the other cats rattled the door by sticking their paws under the jamb, while the dog nails made staccato scrabblings on the linoleum floor. The kitten ignored them, intent only on Arlene, who had owned, loved, and buried enough cats to know what that look meant.

Like it or not, Arlene had a baby on her hands, a baby who had found himself a new Momma.

Suddenly, the kitten sighed, reached for her hand with one huge-toed white paw, and rested his head against the worn blue toilet tank cover. A smile worked its way onto Arlene's wrinkled face, and stayed there. Patting the kitten's flanks, she whispered, "Why do I get the feeling that there's going to be a lot of jealous animals around the house, hm?"

The kitten blinked his minuscule eyes in reply, and purred louder than ever.

Arlene knew from experience never to take an animal in to the vet's office on a Monday; not that she had much *else* to fill her days, but she still hated to waste her time sitting in a noisy office full of yippy-yappy hunting dogs and *poodles* whose nails needed clipping.

She did call the veterinarian office ("Not *another* one," the receptionist had half-joked) to make an appointment for the next day; stool test, full shots, the works. And in between making sure that her other pets were given extra hugs and soft chewy treats, she spent time in the bathroom with the kitten (who had the most indelicate habit of crawling into her lap while she was seated on the toilet; she had to hold him so he wouldn't fall through to the water in the bowl).

The more she looked at him, the *less* offensive his face became to her; by evening he was almost *cute*. The black parts of his fur glistened with delicate rainbow colors, like the wings of a cowbird or blackbird, or the surface of certain black-red petaled flowers. And the *shape* of his face reminded her of something…by that night, when his cries pulled her from her bed, and she had to try to show him—again—how to use a litter pan (her efforts were wasted though, since he let his bladder go on the toilet tank cover, and did the other thing after jumping into the sink), Arlene finally realized what the kitten reminded her of….a tulip. One of those bi-color ones, with the sharp points on the top of the petals, and a narrow base where the flower joined the stem.

After he finally did his duty, and Arlene scooped the b.m. into an old yogurt cup for tomorrow's test, she came back into the bathroom and held the kitten for a few minutes before going back to bed herself.

"Thass all right," she crooned, hugging the scrawny kitten, "Thass all right, you're a good boy." The kitten kneaded her shoulder; there was something odd about the way he did that, but Arlene was too tired to figure it out. She'd have to ask the vet about it tomorrow.

Morning was only a few hours away, and there was scavenging to do.

"You know, you ought to set yourself up as an official shelter," the veterinarian joked as she looked in the kitten's huge ears, checking for ear mites. "That one passes inspection, let's see the other one." The vet's dark-rimmed fingers poked in the cavernous depths of the kitten's left ear. Arlene shuddered; she knew that both the vets had to tend to area cows, and horses, which meant that no matter how often they washed their hands their nails were still stained, but dark nails always gave her pause.

"I don't think I could stand working in a shelter. I'd want to keep all the animals," she finally replied, as the young vet began to palpitate the kitten's abdomen. As her fingers worked their way over the fine white and black fur, Dr. Hraber said, "I thought you did that already, Mrs. Campbell."

"Only the ones I find. I don't think I could cope with ones brought in from all over." Talk about abandoned animals made Arlene uneasy, bringing back memories of all the cats and dogs she'd either picked up or had wandered on her porch. Like Guy-Pie, with his rough pads and way of grabbing whole chunks out of the food bowl and running halfway across the room with them before he'd eat. Big gentle Rowdy, her leather collar stripped of its tags and attached name-tag, just an old yellow hunting dog no one wanted on the hunt anymore. Bubba, huddled shivering next to the Coke machine at the Red Owl, chunks of cow manure stuck in his white fur, his ear tips chewed by God knew what, too beat and broken to even let out a *meaow.*

And those were only the animals *she* had found. Arlene had never answered one of those "Free Kittens" or "Puppies to Give Away" ads in the *Ewerton Herald*; for her, looking at them all was wanting to take them all home. True, she worried about people from labs or pit bull breeders coming to take the little animals, but as long as she didn't *see* them, she wouldn't let it pain her overmuch. She had her "children" to look after; if God saw fit to put one within her hearing or seeing, that was the animal she would take in. Just as she picked up cans or went rooting for week-old bread in back of the IGA. There was only so much she could do. Some things, unfortunately, were simply out of her hands.

"—think of a name for him yet?" The vet's question startled her. Arlene pressed her hands against the kitten's pathetic hips, and said, "Haven't given it much thought...nothing much suggests itself, does it?"

Across the white examining table, Dr. Hraber suggested, "Duke? He looks like a Duke's mixture—"

"No, my Don liked John Wayne. The name would make me think of him too much." (Arlene let the doctor assume that she didn't want to think of Don because the memory was painful— as it was, she missed the Duke more than she ever missed Don.)

"Hummm...well, we have to put a name on the vaccination certificate—"

"Silky? His fur is so soft—"

"Sounds good to me. That good with you, huh, Mister?" The vet opened Silky's mouth, and ran a dark-rimmed finger along his gum line. Silky endured the intruding digit patiently. As Arlene watched, she remembered that she had meant to ask the doctor something *else* about the kitten, but couldn't remember it now. Instead, she asked, "What kind of cat do you suppose he is? He's different-looking—"

"What kind?" The doctor waited a beat, then, as she cupped her fingers under Silky's chin, said, "*Ugly.* No, seriously, it looks like there's either Siamese or Oriental Shorthair in there, but I've never seen a cat like him before. I guess something bred with something different and it looked like this. I wish I could've seen his parents. Sometimes different breeds don't cross very well, do they, Silky?"

Silky looked gravely at Dr. Hraber, as if to say, *Please don't make fun of me.* Arlene wasn't the only one to notice that expression, for Dr. Hraber dropped her bantering manner and said, "The stool test should be done in an hour or so. Do you care to wait around or call later?"

Tucking Silky's wedge of a head under her chin, Arlene walked out of the examining room and into the waiting room, saying over her shoulder, "I'd rather call later, if you don't mind."

Outside, after she had paid for the shots, Arlene nuzzled Silky's head and murmured into the cat's sweet-smelling short fur, "Nasty lady said my little boy's ugly...we just won't listen to her, will we? We won't pay the least bit of attention, none at all."

But all the way home, Dr. Hraber's remark niggled at Arlene.

The *Cat Breeds of the World* book was written on a junior high level (which is where the book had come from, a discard from the middle school library), but the pictures in it were excellent, so Arlene suffered through the namby-pamby text:

...the Oriental Shorthair is a very long, lean cat, with strong muscles. The body is shaped a little like a tube, with extra long hind legs. Some people think its legs look a little bit like a race horse's legs.

The Oriental Shorthair's fur can be many different colors, as well as colored in points like its relative the Siamese (see page 59). The fur of this Oriental breed is very short, and fine-textured, like silk.

(Arlene looked down at the cat curled in her lap and said, "At least your name fits, baby.")

Oriental Shorthairs have big green eyes, and even bigger ears. Their faces are triangular and....

Arlene looked at the picture on the facing page, but there was only a slight similarity between the dark gray cat pictured and the purring kitten on her lap. The Shorthair's whiskers were too long (Silky's were an inch and a half and less), and there was at least an inch or more of space between the ears themselves. Silky's ears all but met in the middle of his head; there wasn't room enough on top for Arlene's little finger to rest. A little over a quarter of an inch at the most. And the Oriental's eyes were huge, luminous and take-your-breath-away green. Her kitten's eyes were a little bigger than the fingernails on her forefingers, ovals of less than half an inch at the widest point. *Much* less.

The bodies of the two cats were closer, but there were still differences. Silky's hind legs, while longer than the front ones, weren't racehorse-high. And now that she looked at his front paws, Arlene realized what was wrong with them, what had hovered at the back of her mind since the night before. Silky had no claws. He had mottled pink and black pads, and the little fleshy dew-pad on the sides, but no claws.

Sick at heart, thinking that some clod had had Silky declawed then dumped him to fend for himself, Arlene gently flexed one of his paws and turned it around, looking for the telltale sunken incision lines of a declawed cat. Her Beanie, many years ago, had been declawed when her neighbors gave the cat to Arlene before they moved to the Cities. That calico's feet had felt limp around the tips of the toes, where the first joint had been removed along with the nail. And there had been those sunken ugly scars...but Silky's feet were almost perfect. There were the right number of metacarpals under the skin, with no empty places under the skin and fur. He just didn't have front claws. His hind ones were there, needing trimming in fact, but the front paws were free of crescent-shaped nails. Holding the cat's paws dose to her bifocals, Arlene saw that there weren't even any holes where the claws *could* come out.

Letting go of Silky's feet, Arlene said, "Don't worry, your secret's safe *with* me. I won't let that mean old doctor make fun of you, call you a freak. She'd probably call you a mutant, or worse."

But as she sat on the lowered lid in the bathroom, listening to her other pets mill around in the hallway beyond the closed bathroom door, Arlene hugged Silky close as she wondered,

What else might be wrong with him...inside?

Once Silky was free of the roundworms the doctor found in his stool sample, and Arlene was satisfied that he carried no fleas, she let him have the run of her small home. Initially there was a lot of hissing, barking, pissing, and scratching, but within a week Silky had settled in beautifully. Within two weeks the older cats were fighting over whose turn it was to wash his cavernous ears, while the dogs took turns chasing an old wiffle ball around the floor with him.

Silky learned to wait with the others for breakfast, while Arlene combed the streets and alleys, looking for cans and whatever else was there waiting to be found, taken home, and utilized. Once she even found a rubber jingle ball (along with a couple of almost perfect Ekco pizza pans). And July turned into August, which turned into September (which felt like October; Arlene blamed all those space shuttles NASA sent up to foul up the jet stream and ozone layer), and Silky was now one of the family...albeit a slightly lonely member of the family.

The dogs were all over seven years old, and tired quickly, while the next-youngest cat was Guy-Pie, at five years old. At first he had been Silky's "best buddy," but then Arlene noticed how Guy-Pie had trouble swallowing, and even more trouble breathing. *Respiratory infection,* she told herself, and tried to take his temperature, but the tortoise-shell cat bucked and kicked like a bronco horse when she tried to do *that*, so she gave him amoxicillin drops that looked like watered-down Pepto-Bismal and smelled like cherries. (She always kept a bottle of dry amoxicillin powder on hand.)

Guy-Pie took the amoxi without complaint, but he didn't get any better. Putting her ear to his ribcage, Arlene heard a strange hooting and whistling, and said to herself, *Pneumonia...or perhaps pyothorax. They're always fighting over some little thing, nipping ears and tails...maybe someone bit Guy-Pie in the chest and I didn't notice. Guy-Pie has never been a complainer....*

It wasn't pneumonia, and it wasn't pyothorax. The cat's temperature was normal, but his X-ray wasn't. The other veterinarian, Dr. Mertz, was as gentle with Arlene as if the old woman was his own mother.

"It's a tumor in his upper chest. It's pressing against his heart and thorax. I don't think he's in pain, but I can give him cortisone pills for the duration. Now there's a *slight*, and I do mean very slight chance that it might be an abscess, although I can't find any healed scars on his chest wall. I have this medication, clindamycin hydrochloride—"

Guy-Pie fought this clear, bitter-smelling new medicine, but he didn't cry or complain after Arlene squirted it down his throat twice a day. Once, he did jerk his head, and a drop of the liquid touched Arlene's lips. It was vile, the way paint thinner or ammonia probably tasted. Making herself lick her bitter lips clean, Arlene cried, "Oh, Guy-Pie, I'm so *sorry*...but I have to give it the old college try, don't I? Don't we?" and hugged the trim dark cat with the little upturned nose and big frightened green eyes close to her flannel shirt. And as she cried into Guy-Pie's smooth tan stippled black coat, Silky watched her from where he sat on the counter, small eyes solemn.

And for a month, then two, Guy-Pie ate, still lost weight, kept on taking his pale orange pills, yet never complained, while Arlene forsook her daily dumpster dives, telling herself that the recycling truck only came every other week anyhow, and that she didn't need to gather as many cans.

The older cats and dogs took turns sleeping next to Guy-Pie; washing his head and ears, purring for him when he could no longer purr for himself. The tumor grew; his chest swelled in either direction. Silky tried to wash his friend into activity, until he realized what was up (or so Arlene let herself believe) and merely slept next to his cobby-bodied friend, waiting.

And when Guy-Pie ate no longer, even after Arlene rubbed the soft smelly food on his ever-paler gums, she wrapped him in a blanket which she held against one shoulder, while she carried the old black gym bag she'd found near the middle school in her free hand.

She couldn't bear to let people see her carrying a dead cat through town on the way home.

November wind, sharp and silvery pure as a freshly honed blade, whistled through the little gaps where Arlene's scarf and thin gray hair met. She was walking along the curved spur of tracks near the depot, past the place where Dean Avenue curved out in the opposite direction to the west, scanning the rusted tracks for the right stones. Guy-Pie was a good cat, a beautiful cat. He deserved the finest stones to cover the flattened round of disturbed earth in the backyard. Her pea-coat pockets were heavy and hung low with the rocks she'd already found. Grays, pink-grays, and jagged bits studded with shimmers of mica. (The shine of those stones reminded Arlene of the liquid green light in the back of Guy-Pie's eyes, just before the injection—)

Not worried that a train would run over her (the Soo Line had been sold years before, and the buying company cut out the Ewerton runs), Arlene followed the gentle curve to the west, walking stiff-legged down the middle of the boards, her feet moving in a strange gait as her feet sought out each nearest plank. *Tracks aren't made for walking*, a calm part of her mind thought, as an old image came back to her. Guy-Pie as a kitten, dignified even in his hunger and footsore condition, as he stood on her front porch. Such a pretty kitten, not long and scrawny like most adolescent cats, but perfectly formed and solemn. And how the other kitties had taken to him, with none of that nose-out-of-joint tomfoolery.

("—he's had five good years, Mrs. Campbell, that's the most anyone could've done for him. And remember, he had a recessed testicle when you found him, and if that had remained inside him, he would've been dead in a year from cancer. You gave him years he wouldn't have had. And he was good to your other cats, and that new kitten of yours too—")

And he'd even sat quiet while she plucked off all the fleas that survived his shampoo. Guy-Pie was the best kitty she'd ever had, until Silky came along, at least. And while Silky wasn't like Guy-Pie, not in a lot of ways, he was good in *his* own way.

It had almost done her in when she brought Guy-Pie home, and placed him on the floor, then dragged the other animals over to see him. She had read once that that was important, making sure that the other animals in a household knew that one of their friends was gone. The dogs howled and took off after seeing him, and most of the cats did likewise, except for Silky. He had reached out one white paw to touch Guy-Pie's flank, and when his friend didn't respond, Silky let his head hang down but didn't leave Guy-Pie's side.

Pausing to dry her leaking eyes (*it's the wind, cuts like a razor it does*), Arlene realized that she'd walked well past Dean Avenue, all the way up to the depot. The old rust and cream painted building was abandoned now, with the warped boards showing through fine-grained and silvery in the pale sunlight. On the side facing her were all the old wrought-iron benches bolted to the concrete platform, and above the benches was a multicolored flutter of paper; all sizes, shapes, and shades, attached with thumbtacks, tape, and staples.

After the Soo buyout, people began to treat the old depot like the world's largest message board, putting up layer after layer of paper which grew rust-runneled after a good rain. Shoving her chapped hands into her already full pockets, Arlene stepped across the rusted rail and made her way toward the gravel and stone studded dead grass which lay between the rails and the depot.

Some of the posters were weeks, months old, and wind-worn, while others (written on lined notebook paper, or on patterned recipe cards) were obviously, painfully new:

"Cloths made to order. Any size, any fabick.
You suply the pattern.
Call 555-8743 P.M."

"4-Sail: One (1) used trailor top, like new.
Also almost-new RV, and new child-size RV...."

"To Give to GOOD Home; two Persian kitties,
litter-traned and gentile—"

Arlene had to laugh at the part about the kittens being Christian, even as she mourned the ignorance of the person who wrote the message. There was an address as well as a phone number on the piece of lilac notebook paper, on 7th Avenue East, less than a two—block walk from the depot. For a few seconds, Arlene wavered, torn by her inner misgivings.

On one hand, she had vowed not to take in cats that someone else might want, yet on the other hand, Silky was lonely, and needed a young cat—or cats—to run with....

Thinking that no one would mind, Arlene tore the piece of paper off the depot wall, and stuffed it in her pockets along with Guy-Pie's rocks.

"*I said* will you shut them kids up already?" The young man pushed his long limp blond hair out of his colorless eyes (and past a whey-colored expanse of forehead) as he yelled at his wife in the other room. The shapeless young woman in the thin cotton maternity top only shrugged in reply and shut the door connecting the living room to the sunken back bedroom. The din of the six (seven? surely the young woman had to have been babysitting some of them) children was muffled by the door as the sweatshirted young man went on, "That sign's been on the depot for two weeks now. I was almost set to...*you* know...the kittens." The pale man made a two-handed gesture indicative of something being drowned, forcibly. Arlene nodded dully.

"I told my wife that she's gotta be careful who Mr. Clean mates with, but my wife lets her out into the yard any old time—"

"I take it Mr. Clean is a queen?"

"Huh?"

"A *female* cat," Arlene said succinctly, thinking, *And he claims he's* breeding *cats?* while the young man bent at the waist to scoop Mr. Clean up as the plush red cat sauntered by.

"The kids named her 'fore we sexed her. Name stuck. But she's pure, I got papers somewhere," the man lied glibly, not knowing that no cat is ever issued papers unless it has been sexed. Arlene let his *faux pas* go. She couldn't wait to pick up the kittens, be they pure Persian or not, and get out of this tiny house that smelled like old French fries and stale beer.

Rocking in place on the littered carpet, Arlene asked, "Are the kittens in the house? All my cats live indoors, period."

Nonplussed by her pointed remark, the man pushed a stingy lock of hair behind his ear and said, "They're in the garage. Play in among the old engines and stuff. Course we got rid of the good ones, sold the last of 'em this week. These two aren't for breeding. They're objectionable, y'know. If that makes a difference, I mean."

It was Arlene's turn to be confused. "'Objectionable'? As in—"

The young man led her through the sunken kitchen, out a back door which connected directly to the garage, saying, "Their coloring. It's red, but not the right red. They got tiger stripes on their heads, but no *tiger* markings on their body. Their Ma, she's pure red. Most of the kittens were, 'cept *these* guys." The man scooped up two wiggling balls of fluff crawling near an engine on blocks, and handed them to Arlene.

She let out a soft "Ooooh," and cuddled the kittens under her chin. They were gorgeous, pure Persian as far as she could tell (although one little tail did look a tad too long), with orange eyes and pale orange pug noses. Not quite Peke-faced, but with adorable dips in their noses, and wide flexible white whiskers. They reminded her of those little Troll dolls popular in the 1960s, those pug-ugly dolls with the long manes of odd-colored hair and flat round eyes, only Troll dolls were never this adorable.

"What do I owe you?" she asked as a formality, remembering that she had left her wallet at home. Luckily for her, the man shrugged and said, "Aw, let it go. Saves me the trouble of having to kill 'em. You will have 'em fixed, won't you?"

"Certainly. I believe in prevention," she added, realizing that the jibe would go over his head, but feeling the better for having said it.

After fitting the kittens into her pea coat (her breasts had shrunken from age and disuse), Arlene hurried away from the sorry prefab on 7th Avenue, toward her home to the south. The rocks in her pockets beat against her hips with every step, but it was a good ache.

As she expected, Silky and the new kittens (both males, whom she dubbed Puff and Fluff) got along famously—after a few "I-was-here-*first*" hisses on Silky's part. And as she patted the stones into a rough heart shape over Guy-Pie's grave, she reflected that maybe things just worked out for the best, no matter how painful they seemed initially. One cat died, she went to look for stones for him, and she saved two kittens from death. A minus, but followed by two pluses. She still hurt, but she would heal.

And Silky began to act like a kitten again.

Come December, Arlene guessed that Silky had to be going on ten months old, but he just wasn't *growing.* True, his body had no more hollow spots, and sleek muscle had covered the painful bone, but he just wasn't any bigger. Even Puff and Fluff grew; they were close to his size after a month in her house. And it was too cold out to go lugging him to the vet just to have her tell Arlene that she had to expect mutant cats to be different. (Dr. Hraber already called Silky "Bug-Eyes" in honor of his still-bulging eyes.)

Arlene had already held off getting Silky neutered; occasionally he sprayed near his pan, and attacked at least one of the dogs each day, hugging with his big-toed funny paws as he chewed on a big floppy ear, but Arlene kept hoping that he'd get a late growth spurt and fill out properly. Even as she knew in her heart of hearts that he was done growing. He hadn't gained weight since November, and nothing about him had changed since October. (On Halloween some children who came Trick or Treating spied him looking through the window and asked—albeit innocently, "Is that a Spuds Mackenzie cat?")

Once she'd gotten over her fussing and fuming, she had to admit that Silky *did* resemble the tiny-eyed dog in the beer commercials. But she never loved a cat more than Silky, not even beautiful, patient Guy-Pie, Lord rest his soul. Silky was always there, showing up in the oddest places; at her elbow while she rolled pie dough, on her lap when she went to the bathroom, dropping down onto her shoulders from on top the high bookcases flanking the front door, purring all the while.

Puff and Fluff took up some of Silky's time, but not all of it; every night, he curled around her head on the pillow, strange soft paws gently kneading her thinning hair. No other cat was allowed on the pillow—on the bed, yes, the pillow never—but Silky rested there as if he *belonged* in such a high up, exalted spot. He reached inside her and filled the hollow spot left after Guy-Pie's passing, filled it and then some. Long after he'd chosen her for his Mama, she chose him to be her Best Boy. She still loved the other cats and dogs, in her own way, person to animal. Silky was...different. Not only in looks; she'd long ago gotten used to his looks. In spirit, in *soul,* he was different.

But it wasn't until that January that she learned just how utterly different Silky was from other cats.

Arlene was making hamburgers in the kitchen, from meat she'd found and oatmeal, onions and spices she'd bought. Knuckle deep in the gooey reddish mixture, Arlene heard the cats doing *something* in the living room—something noisy enough to hear, but soft enough not to be easily identified—and yelled out, "Cats, you be good, hear? Or no supper tonight!" (She never made good on the threat, but it nonetheless usually worked.)

The noise continued, a puzzling muted wooden *thump* (like

someone pounding on a board with a wool-wrapped hammer), then a long silence, then a sound of contact followed by all of the cats running around. Quickly mashing the meat and seasonings together, then placing the bowl of unshaped hamburger in the oven—she knew better than to leave *anything* edible on the counters—Arlene ran her hands under the tap, and flicked off the water from her fingers as she stomped into the living room: She was about to say something, yell something, when she noticed the odd way the cats were sitting around the front door in a wide semi-circle; all facing the two bookcases flanking the door. All the cats...except Silky. Out of the corner of her eye, she caught a blur of white and black; Silky bounding from the floor to the chair by the window to the top of the bookcase between window and door.

The other cats (as well as a couple of the smaller dogs) were watching Silky intently, as if they knew what was to come next. Arlene watched too, as Silky positioned himself on the bookcase, back legs tensed as if he intended to jump onto something higher than the bookcase then wiggled his whipcord body, tensed all over, and leaped into the air—

—and didn't come down on the other bookcase, but kept going *up* in a graceful-beyond-imagining arc, his funny clawless feet spread until the skin was stretched taut between his metacarpals, and his huge, delicate, wind-cupping ears grew large, swelling out like a windbreaker sometimes does in a strong wind, *billowing* out above his tiny wedge of a head like miniature sails—and he was suspended there, in the air, for what had to have been seconds, until he turned his head and changed course to a point between the two bookcases, and still he didn't come rushing down, but *floated,* as easy and gentle and beautiful, oh *God* so beautiful, as a dandelion seed freed by the wind to drift on the invisible currents of the air.

Arlene stood numb, watching as Silky settled gently to the ground on all four feet, making only the slightest amount of noise. Just enough to have been puzzling when heard from afar. Afterward, he and the other cats ran around the room, in sheer excitement over Silky's incredible feat. And Arlene wished that her knees weren't knobby with arthritis; she wished she was small enough to run around in circles with her furry children, and had the right voice to bay out loud and purr and—and—she didn't *know* what.

It was a sight to howl over, to screech and *meaow* and cluck over. No human sound, no human word, could express what she was feeling now. It was joy. It was awe. It was more than her heart could keep inside without exploding like a firecracker suspended in a hot July sky.

She bent down and grabbed Silky; painful knees or not, she and the cat danced around the living room, bouncing with giggles and purrs off the walls, the furniture. It was a *miracle*, as only new, as in brand-new life can be a miracle.

Silky wasn't a mutant, something to be ridiculed, even if he was a *mutation*. He was what the Cat had been striving for through the centuries; a creature of the air, a creature dappled by the sun sliding over its warm fur as it glided with the wind. One with the land, one with the air. Matching the startled birds in their flight. Escaping the ground-bound dog effortlessly. In the back of her mind, Arlene had always wondered who could've been so cruel as to put Silky in that high window...but he was lighter then, with the same huge ears. Suppose he jumped up, hit an air current, and *floated* there?

Holding him away from her body, Arlene now understood Silky's form, its *purpose*. Webbed feet, to buffer the wind. Sail ears, for the obvious reason. Strong legs, for take-off. Super-flat, super-silky fur, for low wind resistance. Few whiskers, so as not to interfere with the airflow. Small eyes, to keep flying dust out.

Just like the birds, she thought, *or the flying squirrels.* Her sudden comparison between cats and squirrels reminded her of another species-to-species comparison someone else had already made.

The Cornish Rex cat, named after the Rex rabbit. She'd seen the picture in her *Cat Breeds* book....

When Arlene pulled out the worn book and sat down to read it, the animals and Silky quieted down too. Silky was in her lap as she paged through the book, until she came to the picture of the thin curly-haired brown cat. She scanned the next page, picking out the important facts: "discovered in 1950 by a Cornish rabbit breeder," "Kallibunker was 'backbred' with his own mother, which means that instead of trying to mate him with another bloodline they—" "ten years later another curly-haired cat was found near an abandoned tin mine in Devon, England."

Arlene frowned and backtracked to the part about the "back bred" situation. She didn't like *that*, not at all. When Arlene was a girl, her old cat Mammajamma mated with one of her sons. Papa had had to kill the kittens, during school so little Arlene wouldn't see it. *I wonder how many times they tried this "back-breeding" business?* she asked herself, as Silky gently kneaded her thigh. Arlene paged to the back of the book, to the index, where she found the heading "Spontaneous Genetic Mutations." One of the breeds listed there was the Scottish Fold. According to the text, a kitten named Susie was born in 1961 in Perthshire, central Scotland, at the William and Mary Ross farm. Twenty-one days after Susie and the rest of her litter were born, little Susie's soft ears did a 180 degree flop forward and stayed that way. And a new breed was born.

The Rosses realized what they had in Susie (*did you dance around the barn, making swirls in the straw?*), and began to breed her, even though the British Governing Council of the Cat Fancy refused to acknowledge or license the cat on the grounds that the cat couldn't *possibly* hear, let alone have its ears cleaned properly. The new breed was banned in Britain as a show breed. Nine years later, the United States recognized the Scottish Fold. By that time, standards of perfection ("*Objectionable?' As in*—?") had been established: small, tightly formed ears. Round head with firm chin and jaw. Short nose and neck. Broad nose, large eyes. Short rounded body. Medium legs and tail. Short coat. Coats of all colors, eyes of blue, gold, or green.

Then came a passage which made Arlene hug Silky closer to

her pap-like breasts, and bite her lower lip:

...breeding the Scottish Fold is very hard to do. Two fold-eared cats should not be bred together. When they are, the kittens can have tails that are too short, or stiff legs.

Another part of Scottish Fold breeding which can be tricky is knowing how long to wait until a true Scottish Fold's ears develop the characteristic 180 degree fold. The breeder has to wait a full three weeks before the....

Closing the heavy book with a muted *chuff*, Arlene asked aloud, "And after the three weeks are up? What then...the bucket of water in the back yard, or a shoebox full of babies left for the vet to kill?" A part of her mind told her that she was being melodramatic; *Silly, where do you think they get the straight-ear cats for them to breed with?* But still, what of the kittens who weren't *right*? The ones with the less than round heads, or the long tails and hind legs? What of those objectionable kittens? Surely, the breeders simply couldn't afford to keep the mistakes around, no matter how adorable they might be.

A crinkly ripping sound made Arlene pause in her thoughts, and look down at her feet. Fluff was undoing her running shoe straps, pulling on the long strip of Velcro with his teeth. Fluff was the kitten with the longer tail, the sassy, aggressive one. Arlene wiggled her toes, and both Persians jumped on her feet, hanging on with their short legs. *Cute as the Dickens...but objectionable. It's a rotten, rotten world, isn't it, fellows?*

As if intuiting her thoughts, Silky reached with his left paw to gently caress her chin. The pad was softer than apple blossom petals, and surrounded with a tickly fringe of short fur. Arlene enclosed his paw with her larger hand, giving the paw a light squeeze. Silky blinked his ludicrously, sensibly tiny eyes and rested his wedge head on her chest.

Stroking his velvety ears with her free hand, Arlene said softly, "What's it to be, Silky-love? I can take you to people who know cats, who really breed them. They'd know, they'd understand. Study you, breed you. Give you a fancy name. 'Wisconsin Squirrel Cat;' or 'Ewerton Flyer.' You'd be in all the cat books, next to a picture of one of your great-great grandkittens." Silky reached with his other paw to touch her face; Arlene pressed it against her cheek, bending her head low to his. Clear drops of moisture fell on his fur, to roll down slowly.

"But it isn't fair to all the objectionable kittens, is it? And there would be objectionables, Silky, even from a kitty as perfect as you. Happens all the time...and there aren't enough suckers like me running around to take them in. And I do hate waste, I hate to see things go unused, *unappreciated.*" Silky butted his head against hers, as if he understood and agreed. *Maybe he does realize*, Arlene thought, *Maybe, just maybe, he really does....*

When Silky let go of her face and curled up on her legs, Arlene sat stroking his incredible fur for a few seconds, before lifting him off her lap and placing him on Dan's old ottoman. She then walked over to the phone and dialed a number she knew by heart.

Arlene timed it just right; she only had to wait outside the vet's office for a few minutes, which she did while standing with her back to the fitful wind. And Silky—wiggling because he was hungry—was wrapped in enough blankets to keep him in-the-womb warm.

When the veterinarian's assistant opened the door at eight o'clock, Arlene shifted the squirming kitten to her other arm as she walked into the half-lit waiting room. Behind her, as the assistant finished turning on the rest of the lights, the woman asked Arlene, "Did you finally decide that Silky had grown enough?"

Arlene uncovered Silky's head; he yawned and blinked kitty kisses at her. "Yes, he hasn't gotten any bigger since October...I guess he's ten months old by now, don't you think?"

The assistant pushed a strand of her black hair out of her eyes, and paused to rub Silky's ears as she made her way behind the reception desk. "He sure doesn't look it, but maybe his momma and father were small cats. Or he might be a—"

Not wanting to hear about the other option, Arlene said, "Poor Silky thinks I'm punishing him...no food or drink since midnight. Had to put him in the bathroom overnight, just to keep him from the other animals' dishes. We didn't like that, did we?" She leaned over to nuzzle Silky's fur with her slightly bulging nose.

"Well, he'll be happier once he's healed. It's hard on an un-neutered male if he doesn't mate—but I shouldn't have to tell you that. You've had a parade of kitties in here over the years—"

Like Guy-Pie. And Bubba. And Puff and Fluff in a few months. But it's different with you, isn't it, Silky? Not just an end to a couple of gonads, is it, boy? But I just won't be around to take in all those objectionables…. God forgive me, but I won't be.

The assistant reached over the desk to take Silky from Arlene, saying, "C'mon, big boy, let's put you in a nice cage until the doctor comes. Oh, what a good *boy,* "she crooned as Silky butted his head under her chin. After Arlene scratched Silky's ears and bent down to kiss one of his extended paws, the assistant headed for the back of the veterinary clinic, saying over her shoulder, "Y'know, Silky's really one in a million. Usually they're either stiff as boards or clawing the walls at this point."

And softly, so softly that the assistant never heard her, Arlene replied, "He really is at that, isn't he?" before she left the office and walked face first into the cutting December wind.

Also in memory of Sassy, Puff and Pumpkin. Rest in peace, sweet boys….
A. R. Morlan, 2010

OKSA'S CHILDREN

"Not again," Martha hissed through gritted teeth, as the shimmering fingers of ice crashed on the cement front step, sending shards of brittle icicle fragments into her boots, her tote bag, even her partly open purse.

This was the second time in a week that the icicles had formed on the tiny jut of plywood, two-by-fours and shingles which overhung Martha's front door, and the second time the swinging storm door had sheered off the icicles, pelting Martha with bullets of frozen water.

"Damn," she muttered, running her fingers through her bangs, only to feel bits of ice adhering to her hair. Stepping carefully over the scattered ice chips, mindful of how slippery the tiny rolls of icicles could be (and still nursing a bruised hip from the fall she took earlier in the week while walking over the pencil-sized shards), Martha waited until she reached the sidewalk to pause and take a look at her house. Her almost new house, bought only two months ago this upcoming Friday, back when the weather was still daytime-balmy, and the nights only frost-gritted and *pleasantly* cool.

In October, there had been no icicles gripping the eaves, no translucent milky fangs gnawing her front stoop overhang; only drifts of fluffy gold-yellow maple leaves blanketing the shaggy lawn, the kind of leaves Martha used to like to jump on and burrow into when she was a small girl. The sort of leaves she still couldn't resist shuffling through to this day, kicking them up in scrabbling sprays of clawed color during her daily walk to work.

Staring up at the house, shielding her eyes against the rising sun (which transformed the icicles on the rest of the roof into painfully brilliant daggers of light and blazing color), Martha kicked herself for not installing heat coils on the roof back in November, before the weather became too cold for any workman to do the job, or even *want* to do had she thought to ask someone to come out.

"Too late now," she mused out loud, her breath surging out white and nebulous in the sub-zero Wisconsin air, before she shouldered her purse and picked up her tote bag.

But Martha hadn't gone more than a block down the street before she found herself turning around to stare at her house, half-knowing and half-fearing what she saw there.

Even though the sun wasn't yet high enough to warm the air, there was a good six inches of new icicles fringing her porch overhang....

"Is this the latest in food preservation?" Carol tapped Martha's purse with a press-on nailed finger, the impossibly smooth curved nail making a brittle clicking noise as it hit the wide-opened zipper running the length of Martha's Stone Mountain bag.

"Huh?" Martha stirred her cup of yogurt, swirling the fruity syrup at the bottom through the white gloppy mass on top, as her eyes followed the tip of Carol's pointing finger...then stopped stirring when she noticed what rested within her purse.

Gleaming in the banks of overhead office lights like polished glass beads, the pellets of ice rested lightly on Martha's folded tissues, leather billfold, and foil-wrapped packet of Pamprin, still intact after four hours spent resting in a half-closed purse in a well-heated office. Still unmelted.

Carol delicately picked up one of the icy orbs, rolling it in her brightly-tipped fingers until the whorled pads were slick with moisture. Martha filled her mouth with fruited yogurt, until she knew she couldn't speak easily.

"Ye gods, this thing's cold," Carol yelped, dropping the pellet to the nubby carpeting between their desks. The bead of ice rolled away, past their work station and off toward the lobby of the insurance office. Swallowing reflexively, Martha finally said, "I walked to work...must've chilled the bag," before scraping her spoon along the surface of the yogurt, avoiding the blobs of strawberry dotting the creamy snack.

"What did you do, walk from Siberia?" Carol said around the remains of her granola bar, before gulping it down with a throat-shuddering gulp. Martha had worked with Carol since they'd graduated from Ewerton High School six years before, sharing their lunches together daily, but she had never stopped wondering why Carol's throat jerked so much when she swallowed, nor had she ever grown quite used to it. Martha waited until her stomach unknotted before answering,

"No, just the usual ten blocks."

"Oh, yeah, I forgot, you moved to this dump of a town, didn't you?" Martha didn't bother to reply; Carol had helped her pack when Martha was moving out of her above-the-bakery apartment in Ewerton before Martha's move to the house in neighboring Lumbe. Martha had spent twelve years in school with Carol; the latter's forgetfulness no longer phased her. The jerking throat at lunch, yes, the lack of functioning brain cells, no.

As Carol picked up scattered granola crumbs with the moistened pad of her right forefinger, Martha scooped up her saved cache of strawberries and slid them into her mouth; after swallowing them unchewed (like she used to do with her breakfast cereal fruit when she was small), Martha said, "You should've seen it, the icicles were hanging down like those whatchamacallit's you see in caves, all across the overhang. By the time I was halfway down the street they were back—"

"Not in *this* weather," Carol mumbled around a granola-coated finger, before licking it clean and wiping it off on her jeans skirt.

"Carol this *is* Wisonsin, remember? Ever seen anything

behave in a predictable manner?"

Taking her time to digest the multisyllable words, Carol finally protested, "But the ice has to melt a little to form an icicle...either that, or you have heat leaks somewhere. Your house got a new roof or something? Maybe wasn't put on right?"

Martha flicked on her computer terminal, her eyes focused on the humming gold and black monitor screen, as she tried to picture her house. The roof was of indeterminate age, not in obvious decay, but there were rust runnels staining the back of the house. But she didn't recall seeing any tell-tale heat shimmers rising up over the house, either.

"....don't think it's the roof," she said with finality, indicating the subject was no longer open to discussion, as she booted the filing program and resumed her work. Next to her, Carol just shrugged and said, "You'll find out when the next heating bill comes, I guess."

Martha barely heard her; as she tapped the almond-beige keys, her mind was fixed on ribbed tapering columns of ice, coruscating in the pure white winter sunlight, a thick wetly glistening fringe wrapped around her roof, hanging down, down, midway down each window, like see-through prison bars.

And the icicles had started forming early, much too early, really; they had already been thumb-thick in late November, wrist-thick soon afterward, and no matter how often she had taken the business end of a broom to them, knocking them off to fall into the snow surrounding the house (they broke into segments as they fell, leaving nothing but dark depressions in the snow, occasionally capped with flat severed base sections), by the time four or five hours had passed, they would be back, sending bands of prismatic pastels across her white walls as the setting sun passed on through their icy surfaces.

Martha used to check the progress of her icicles against those of her neighbors, mentally comparing thickness, length and speed of formation, until the morning when she had pulled aside her kitchen curtains—and saw only icicle upon tightly spaced icicle blocking her view, a rippled curtain of frigid water.

After that day, Martha realized that comparisons no longer mattered—or counted. Her life took on a pattern, one she had not counted on when she spent her afternoons lazily raking up her leaves into plastic garbage bags (to be nestled against the sides of the house for insulation), followed by feet-up-on-the-coffee-table reading and TV sessions; hurry home, attack the icicles with her broom, rake the snow off the roof, hack at the ice base with the snow rake pole, then hurry in to eat, catch a little CNN on the tube, then start on the icicles again, beating down the foot-long projectiles until it was almost time to get ready for bed. And come morning, they would be anywhere from a foot to a yard long, almost mocking her past swipes with the broom....

And then came that first morning when they had blocked the storm door; the day she had slipped and fallen. Her hip still ached where her nubby-covered office chair touched her flesh.

"—I should drive you home?"

"Pardon?" Martha glanced at her watch before looking at Carol—4:57 P.M. Carol even had her coat on, that horrid belted plaid thing she had worn her last couple of years in high school. Oddly, the coat bothered Martha, although she knew not why.

"I *asked* if you want I should drive you *home*," Carol repeated as she flicked each of her plastic-tipped fingers against her thumb in turn; it sounded like icicles *pinging* as the broom lopped them off the eaves. Martha shut down her computer, reached for her purse, barely suppressing a shudder as her fingertips brushed a moist, cold orb within.

"Y'know, I don't even know for sure where you live...."

"Ten blocks north...."

"North, south, *smouth*, you'll have to show me."

For a second, Martha felt the queasy whirl of *deja vu*; Carol's sash-belted coat, the old "north, south, *smouth*" rhyme of hers.

Pulling on her coat, Martha assured Carol that she'd show her where the house was, until her voice cracked as the piece of ice adhering to her collar touched her bare neck....

"Oh Martha, you *didn*—!" Carol gave Martha one of those

"You *devil*, you" winks as Martha asked, confusion edging her voice, "'didn't' what?"

Taking her gloved hands off the steering wheel (somehow obscene in its lambskin cover), Carol wagged a forefinger in the old "naughty, naughty" gesture before adding, "Whadja, wanna do, relive that night we killed the children?"

"*Children*?" Martha had her hand on the door handle—Carol's stupidity was one thing, but talking about killing *children* as if it were *funny* was another.

"Oh, you remember…old man *Oksa*'s children":

Martha released the door handle, and folded her hands on her lap. She hadn't thought of Mr. Oksa in a good five years. Old Man Oksa from Typing 102, the basic course everyone at Ewerton High took their sophomore year. Not really *old*, but a combination of diabetes and God knew what other ills had aged the short, dapper man; given him the mottled skin and wrinkled fingers of a much older man. But he wasn't old-looking in a decrepit way, not like Mrs. Winston in the history department, or her husband Palmer Winston in English (the old letch); Mr. Oksa's suits were always complete and neat, down to his silky striped and paisley ties, and button-collar shirts. With the little chain-like dohingie which held the collar together under his tie.

And his pale blue eyes (cloudy with cataracts, but still alert enough to spot goof-offs ten rows away) twinkled behind his glasses every time he'd write something in shorthand in the student's yearbooks—and Martha was always wary about getting one of the secretarial students to translate what he'd written, just in case it was something fresh, or dirty. Mr. Oksa may not have openly peered down girls' blouses, like Old Man Winston (or stared at the cute boys in each class, like old Una-Pruna Winston did), but he enjoyed teasing all the girls in a gentle, semi-raunchy sort of way. Not going far enough to get himself in hot water, but amusing himself all the same—even if all the girls didn't share his pleasure.

And Martha and Carol and the rest of their clique, Scooter Anderson, Larry Kominski, Larry's girl Maureen, and a couple of other kids whose names had fuzzed out in Martha's memory, they'd all found Mr. Oksa to be just *too* uncool. Too frigging much to take on a three-times-a-week basis. It wasn't that he was silly (which Ewerton teacher wasn't an a-hole was the question), or a bad teacher (hadn't he promised Martha and Carol passing grades of "C" as long as they promised *not* to take his Beginning Shorthand class come second semester?), but he was just so gung-ho about the weirdest things….

Like when he insisted on putting that picture of old Quinton Kelly's mongrel into the yearbook, the one where the old mutt was sitting on one of the Homecoming floats after Dusty Parks and Bobby Grey hoisted him onto the Pep Club's entry in the early October parade. The annual editor Craig Reish (of the stiff-pickler Reish family) had fought with Mr. Oksa about including the picture, but Mr. Oksa, being the annual advisor, was the one who sent off the paste-up pages, and he had final say-so on what went in….

Or like when Mr. Oksa put in candid hallway shots of some of the students nobody liked in among the filler pages, the Cliqueless-Wonders everyone avoided because it was the thing to do in those petty high school days….

Or especially like when he was all puffed up with pride after the editor of *The Ewerton Herald* went out to Mr. Oksa's house in neighboring Lumbe to snap some pictures of his "children" during the end of the first semester of Martha's sophomore year…the resulting front-page photograph was on every bulletin board in the school, and within a week all but the picture on the board outside Vice Principal Inglass's office (nobody wanted to mess with Crazy Wally) was either torn down, or fancifully embellished with graffiti and/or crudely drawn dangling balls over the long penis-like icicles.

Oksa's "children" were nothing more than what Martha's crowd dubbed "bitching ice," frozen H20—and they got front-page coverage, something which both baffled and irritated his students, especially when Crazy Wally Inglass had photocopies of the *Herald* picture made up to pass out during the home basketball games, and actually hauled Mr. Oksa down onto the gym floor come halftime, just so everyone could get a look at the father of the ice children. (Bad enough that Inglass' brain cell had fallen asleep during its umpteenth game of solitaire, but the way Mr. Oksa lapped up the bored applause was *just too much.*)

And it had been during the rest of the last home game in December that Martha and Carol and Larry and Maureen and Scooter and his girlfriend from Hunterstown, Sarah Cooper, and those other kids in the clique whose names and faces were a blur to Martha all snuck out of the gym and piled into Scooter's old Chevy wagon, the one with no back window and the eight track player that wouldn't go to program three, and headed for Lumbe, where Mr. Oksa lived.

Martha shook her head, trying to dislodge the memory of that night, of Oksa's house surrounded by children, and flatly said, "This isn't the house. Oksa's house was stucco covered. And there was a porch—"

"You've never heard of a thing called siding? Or remodeling?"

"No way...I read over the deed when I bought this place. Oksa's name wasn't on it. Every other Tom, Dick and Harry, but not Oksa...your cousin from Lumbe, Mr. Welfare, was the owner before the last couple lost their FHA loan on this place," she began, but Carol cut in, "You remember what a cheap putz Oksa was. His wife used to have to sew his suits for him, 'cause he was too cheap to buy 'em new...do you think he'd lay out bucks for a house, when he could *rent*?"

"But that's dumb—you have nothing to show for it—"

"Do you suppose he intended to *stay* there after his kids graduated? Remember, Tim was a senior when Oksa kicked off? Once he was gone, do you think they'd hang onto a barn like *this*?" Carol asked, indicating Martha's house with a leatherette-covered hand.

My house, not Oksa's, Martha stubbornly thought, as she watched the last rays of the sun bathe the house in a pale reddish cast, icy strands of glowing towhead hair surrounding a head of creamy paneling. This house isn't anything like Oksa's, not at all.

"I don't see how you'd remember anyhow. The picture in the paper was grainy, and when we went out to the place it was dark, and we were all half-smashed," Martha argued, as the icicles barring the front door seemed to inch toward the cement stoop.

Carol turned on her engine, a not so-subtle reminder that Martha should get out of the car, before giving Martha a smirking smile as she said, "A person doesn't forget something like that, Martha."

Martha snuggled deeper into her snug-sack, plastic mug of hot cocoa warming her cold red hands, her eyes only half-focused on the TV screen, her ears immune to the sounds within the house, as she remembered the night they killed Oksa's children. If the "children" had been flesh and blood, not already the icy stiff, surely they'd all be found guilty of premeditated homicide at the least...and first degree murder at the worst....

Scooter's Beach Boys eight-track seemed to be stuck on *Barbara Ann* all during the ride from the EHS gym to Larry's garage (where they picked up the weapons for that night's slaughter) to Lumbe itself, eight miles away, and as they passed around the cans of Leinenkugels' beer and the bottle of strawberry wine Sarah Cooper had smuggled into the basketball game under her parka, the guys were all singing with the band—"the Bitch Boys," as one of the nameless-faceless kids called them and the closer to Oksa's house they came, the more the lyrics slurred and blurred, until *Bob-bob-bobber-Ann* became *Bopp-bopp-bopper-Ann* and finally just plain *Baba-ba-baba-Ann*, and Maureen got sick in the back seat, only it was okay because Larry aimed her head out the window that wasn't there anymore, and after 'Reenie got the upchucks, everyone cranked down their windows, and the wind scraped Martha's cheeks like those plastic ice jobbies they sold at the Coast-to-Coast store, sheering off the sweat from her cheeks, leaving them expectantly raw and tender, and all the while the wagon jumped and skidded over the patches of glare ice on the road, especially when Scooter gunned the car to ninety mph through the partially fenced off sports field at Lumbe Junior Hi-School, missing the fence at the opposite side of the field by scant inches.

Ba-ba-ba-babba Ann, went the guys, and Larry was waving his broom out the window, *swackking* the stop sign poles at the intersections.

Martha and Carol and Sarah and Marueen and that other girl who was nebulous in Martha's memory gathered up the brooms and shovels and garden hoes after Scooter snugged the wagon up against the snow-mounded curb near Oksa's house, the two-storied stucco house surrounded by the biggest, thickest icicles any of Martha's clique had ever seen—the biggest icicles *anyone* had ever seen in all of Dean county, actually.

And the icicles were so big, so huge, so…so there, period, that for a moment everyone stopped *Ba-ba-ba-baba-Anning* for a change and just stood there, brooms and hoes and shovels in hand, looking.

Bigger around than a man's waist at the top, and tapering down to forearm size, Oksa's children ringed the old teacher's stucco house, their bodies rippled and lumpy, covered with dewlaps of wetly rounded crystal skin; parting only before the front door, they shielded the windows, and hugged the shutters, protecting the house of their father. The rim of ice along the roof was massive, a smooth lip of onyx which branched down in crooked fangs. And when Scooter played his flashlight across them, the children flickered with dull gleams of yellowish-cream, a glow which seemed to radiate from *within* each ponderous icicle, an inner flame which rippled and shuddered within columns of ice.

"Bitchin'," someone whispered, and then, as if each of them was presented with a choice—to either adore or destroy, with no middle course allowed—they fell upon the children, weaponed arms upraised, mouths open in a primal yowl of animal pleasure. Martha had a shovel, that much she remembered; she'd gone for one of the melted-candle-shaped children positioned near the front of the enclosed porch doorway, hacking at it with the side of the shovel pan, until a spray of crushed slush flew out into the distant street-lamp-illuminated darkness beyond, the pieces of flayed ice glinting with a rainbow scintillation of muted reds, fiery green, and twinkling blue.

They didn't stop hacking and slicing and bashing until all the children were dead, until the bigger sections *gave* way with a creak and a groan and muffled-by-snow sigh, and Oksa's children were nothing more than misshapen ice cubes spilled from a gigantic cooler.

And then they piled back in the wagon and *Ba-ba-ba-baba-Anned* all the way back to the Ewerton gym, where the crowd was coming out of the gym and heading for the parking lot, and they all stayed in the wagon until everyone else started pulling out of the parking lot, just so Crazy Inglass wouldn't notice that they had only been in the lot for a short time. And Scooter dropped them all off at their houses; Martha and Carol used to live next door to each other, so they hung on each other and giggled all the way to Carol's front door, only all the while she had ridden back to Ewerton, Martha couldn't get the glare of the chopped ice out of her eyes—a hovering blueish afterimage that colored her line of sight, like getting caught with a flashcube's glare.

Martha saw that glare again Monday morning, when Wally Inglass announced over the intercom that Mr. Oksa had died over the weekend…right after he'd come home from the basketball game. Heart attack. The school would be let out early the next day, so kids could attend the funeral. But Crazy Wally never mentioned the dead children; Martha's clique never mentioned them either, because (as Martha figured) good old Wally was probably waiting for someone to start bragging about what they'd done to the ice-children, and then Wally could pounce, with suspensions, expulsions, and criminal charges, followed by a big lecture to the student body in the gym, like the People-Have-Been-Skipping-Pep-Rallies-Again one Wally gave back in September. Martha listened to Inglass' oily voice go on and on about how much everyone would miss Willy Oksa, yes-sirree-bob, while all she could see was the pale blue gleam of shattered ice…the same blue as her dead teacher's twinkling eyes.

And Mrs. Oksa and Tim moved to Ewerton by January, and still no one in Martha's clique mentioned Mr. Oksa or his ruined children…not until Carol insisted that Martha had actually bought Oksa's old house.

Carol was wearing her belted plaid coat that night, and she kept on yammering that "north, south, smouth" bit…she had a broom, and 'Reenie got a hoe, and the air smelled like puke and strawberries and that herbal perfume cream that came in a little compact, the kind all the "in" girls wore…. "You've never heard of a thing called siding?" she asked, but this *can't* be the house, no way.

Martha spilled the remains of her cocoa onto her snug-sack when first one icicle, then another and another, let go of the eaves with a grinding crunch and a muted thump as they pounded the snowy ground; curling into her easy chair, she covered her head with the sack and kept repeating, "Can't be… can't be the house," until she fell into an uneasy, icicle-lullaby induced slumber, and before she lost her grasp on consciousness, she told herself, Must be warming out there….

An icy blast hit Martha in the face when she opened the inner front door; only with difficulty did she open the screen-storm door, pushing against the restraining ice beyond the weight of her right shoulder and arm. The crash of broken ice was deafening, thunderous, lingering in her ears as she made her way down to the sidewalk. Martha glanced at her neighbor's homes, at their nearly snow- and ice-less roofs, and then looked at her own ice-shrouded dwelling…not a window remained visible, not a single horizontal line of siding could be seen. Dizzy, Martha began panting, her mind going the proverbial two-forty: *The heat, I didn't turn up the heat…house got cold, that's all…not*

Oksa's house...not his children, oh please, don't blame me, it was Scooter's idea.... "Go give old Oksa something to be shit-faced-grinning about all right," and Larry said he could get the stuff to knock 'em down with...but this isn't the house, where's the porch, where's the stucco...it's just Carol being dumb, not knowing where she was or what she saw...just the same town, and okay, maybe even the same street, but this can't be the Oksa house...oh please, not anymore....

As if in answer to her inner plea, Martha noticed that the ice was a bit thinner near the front door frame, just transparent enough for her to make out a couple of strips of siding...siding that could be pulled away from a wall that really wasn't stucco, no matter what Carol insisted, but it wouldn't hurt to look.

The ice felt hot under Martha's fingertips as she pounded and scratched and gouged the exposed section of siding, until her bleeding fingers, the nails torn deep into the fleshy pink base, pried loose one strip of siding, the board cracking and splintering as she pulled it away from the pale blue stucco surface beneath—and as she turned around to run, the arms of Oksa's children reached down in a thunderous embrace...a caress which felt like the repeated blows of a shovel before Martha once more saw the brilliant glint of blue, before the children pressed their hands over their eyes, shutting out all light and deafening her ears with the sound of their second, final passing to the home of their father.

SOFT

THE CAR WAS STILL THERE. Be it abandoned or merely forgotten, Farris couldn't quite tell. He had first noticed it, parked in the northernmost quarter of the car wash parking lot, close to the Dumpster and the second vacuum machine, at least four, maybe five days earlier. Just a parked car, weathered dark blue paint job fringed with an ombre layering of rust-pocked paint, blue-flecked rust, and finally a ragged lacy fringe of pure, brittle rust along the bottom. A typical northern Wisconsin car. Probably a second-hand vehicle.

Since it wasn't quite in the way of the waste management truck which came by early each Tuesday morning, it hadn't given Farris much cause for real concern. As long as it wasn't blocking any of the wash bays, he doubted his boss would care all that much about its presence.

Not that Farris didn't care. That first day (Monday, Tuesday?), he had wondered why someone would park their car in such a place. By doing so, the owner had to walk at least three blocks in order to find another place which had a change machine. If, indeed, change was what the driver was seeking.

The coin machine at the car wash had been broken over the weekend and into the early part of that week. But considering how fragile the automobile's lower surface was, Farris somehow doubted that the owner even meant to wash it in the first place. And it was parked three feet short of the vacuum nozzle's business end. Farris had checked that out himself, on the second day the car remained on the lot.

He knew he should call his boss about it, have him make the call to the towing company, but the standard policy all over town was simple—Vehicles Towed At Owner's Expense. If you can locate the owner. And then make him or her pay the fee. Otherwise, for all Farris knew, he himself might be liable for the tow charge. On his salary.

And that sucks, Farris told himself as he walked over to the car. He hunkered down and peered through the driver's side window. The entire car was dirty. All of the windows needed cleaning, but he could still see the unmistakable silvery dangle of keys stuck in the ignition. So...if the keys were left there, then the door should open....

The hinges gave out a whispery scree as Farris pulled the driver's-side door open. He peered inside, taking in the lingering odor of fast food wrappers, a dying Little Tree (faded dark blue New Car Scent), old caked mud in the foot wells, and something else which was just beyond his olfactory grasp, yet nonetheless was undeniably familiar in its commonness.

"Dump job," he whispered to himself. "Insurance probably ran out. Or he's gonna make the repo man work for this one."

The car was an old model Toyota, and gradually Farris realized that if this thing hadn't been paid off at least a decade ago, the repo man should have been looking for it before now. Nobody wanted this junker.

Easing himself into the car, feeling the unpleasantly worn hard spots on the driver's seat where the person's butt had reshaped the formerly pliant cushioning, Farris peered over the frayed contour of the headrest to see if there might be anything worth grabbing in the back seat. Balled up fast food joint bags, sun-faded cellophane wrappers from extra large, red-hot burritos, stomped-flat big slurp drink cups, assorted crinkly wrappers from hard candies. And just beyond his range of sight, the corner of a burger place bag, not crumpled, but perhaps still filled with...something. Maybe uneaten food or, better yet, aluminum cans. Some people did that—went to a fast food place but didn't order their overpriced, over-iced sodas, instead opting for their own favorite brand. And aluminum cans were up to forty cents a pound.

Backing out of the car, Farris clonked his head against the door frame, then crab-scuttled, still squatting, over to the back driver's side door. The bag was full, that much was apparent when he finally got the rust-hinged door open. But the open end of the bag was tucked under the front seat, so he had to lean in and pick it up to see what was inside.

In the hazy April early morning light, which was at best a wan shade of phlegm, the contents of the bag looked to be the aluminum can Farris coveted. But when he reached in and his cold fingertips made contact with the object within, the first thing he thought was, Mold? Why would something like this be all slimy soft?

Aluminum doesn't mold. Pulling his fingers out, he reflexively began rubbing them on his jacket, but there was nothing there to rub off...no slimy residue, no clinging foul-smelling ichor deep in his nailbeds.

Farris had worked at the car wash long enough to be familiar with the sort of trash people routinely dumped out of their cars into the paired trash receptacles close to the wash bays. He had emptied enough bags (after first searching their cigarette-ash dusted contents for aluminum cans) to be familiar with just about every bad smell and disgusting surface imaginable. What he'd just felt in that bag wasn't one of them.

It was then that he noticed the bag was far too heavy to hold a lone soda or beer can, even though the paper masked contents— what he could feel through the logo embellished sides and flat bottom—seemed to be a single object. Something cylindrical, long and flat-bottomed, like a can, but yet, somehow, it felt totally wrong.

Tilting the bag in his hands, Farris listened for the fluid slosh of an unopened beverage can. But all he heard was a muffled whap!, as if something flat, wet, and heavy had slapped up against an enclosed area.

"Damn!" he muttered, setting the bag on the hood of the car.

Taking both hands off the bag, he leaned over to peer inside. He noticed then the bag was printed with a long past promotion based on a movie which could now be purchased on DVD over at the Dollar General, Ewerton's newest store. He also noticed that for an old burger bag it was in almost new condition.

Over his shoulder, the sun's rays changed from thick phlegm to pure spit in hue. And he was able to make out the contents of the bag with ease. It looked like a can...an unadorned, silvery-grey can, with no pull-tab or any other means of getting at whatever it was inside. It was a bit bigger around than a soda can and as tall as an energy drink. And when the watery rays of the sun filtered over Farris' shoulder and hit the can, the thing did not shine. The direct sunlight, as weak as it was, seemed to make the thing ripple, its surface taking in the sunlight without reflecting it. As if it were....

"Soft," Farris whispered, as he rested a trembling forefinger on the top of the thing. Even as his eyes kept telling him metal, his fingertips insisted, no, fleecy, but...pliant, not quite malleable, but still slightly...*squashy.*

When he lifted it out of the bag, his eyes persisted, hard metal can, while his fingers caressed and deftly explored every smooth yet downy part of the thing, all the while crooning to his confused senses, *so close to spongy, so soothing, so supple.* For their part, his eyes weren't quite lying: it was metallic-looking, and its rigid geometric symmetry did imply hardness, but yet....

It was still soft. A low-napped surface, rather like velveteen, more textured than suede without being either velveteen or suede. Where raised ridges along the top or bottom should have been, the place where a can opener would dig in and bite through the sealed edges, there were instead deliciously pliant, raised nubs which he gently waggled back and forth under his thumb. There was weight to it, and some sort of internal arrangement which lent itself to being shifted when the object was moved. But no visible means to getting at whatever was inside.

Behind him, Farris heard a car's tires scrunch onto the cold asphalt of the car wash parking lot. Without thinking, he scooped up the old fast food bag, placed the soft thing inside, and placed the bag inside his jacket. After slamming the car doors shut, he hurried over to his booth next to the touchless automatic wash bay, his work station for the next six hours.

Despite its seductively tender surface, Farris kept the thing in the bag while he sat in his booth, half listening to the oldies rock radio station playing on his almost new portable radio ("almost new, as in he'd found it in one of the garbage bins between the wash bays, the antenna bent, and in need of batteries). Now and again, he would look at the bag itself, the way it just barely obscured the contents nestled inside. How old could that bag be? At least one of the stars in that movie had died last year—of natural causes. So aside from the whole DVD-for-a-buck thing, this bag had been deliberately saved, kept free of the dirt which permeated the remainder of the car.

Even the upper edges were only very slightly frayed, as if whoever had saved the bag and used it to shield the object from the light had only looked inside the bag on special occasions. It might not have been stored in the passenger-side foot well. The thing might have been sitting on one of the seats and merely slipped off when the owner parked the car. Maybe he or she hadn't belted it in properly.

Remembering how his father used to put tinfoil knobs on the ends of the television antenna ears when he was a kid, Farris gently eased the object, still in its bag, against the antenna side of his small radio. Usually, almost anything metal would amplify the output of the thin telescoped metal wand, but even with the thin paper shielding, the thing that looked like a can did nothing to improve the radio's reception. Which confirmed that his eyes were lying to him. But that didn't necessarily mean his fingers knew the truth either. He would have to look at it.

Rubbing the booth's small countertop clean with his jacket sleeve, he placed his right hand into the bag. He kept his fingers and palm clear of the slightly frayed upper edges of the paper least the oils from his skin might somehow soil it. He kept moving his hand downward until his fingertips met with that hidden softness. His fingers dug into the surface slightly as he grabbed it and lifted the thing out of the bag. When he set it on the counter, it seemed to almost imperceptibly settle before it regained its former state of quiescence.

Whatever it was made of, it was solid, seamless, and curiously non-reflective. Farris couldn't even see the upside-down, spoon-like reflection of himself he might have expected of such an object.

If it was fabric, surely there would have been a seam somewhere, an overlap of whatever it was constructed from.

Had it been extruded, egg-like, from within something? Nothing Farris had ever seen on Discovery or The Learning Channel even hinted at such a thing, be it live or fabricated, that could simply pop out an object such as this. It didn't look organic nor did it seem to be fabricated—even hot dogs had those distinctive little wrinkled twists at the ends. But neither the top nor the bottom (or bottom or top—both were uniform in their lack of indentations or finger-sized means of entry) indicated any sort of machined cut or any indication that the thing had originated from anything at all.

It simply was. A tall-ish, wide-ish, sort of shiny in a clean skin rather than polished metal way sort of thing. A "sort-of-like-something-like" thing like that French painter Farris once saw on television—that guy who painted normal-but-weird things like a train coming out of a fireplace, or people with apples or some sort of fruit for a head. Whack job stuff that people paid lots of money for in art galleries.

For a heady moment, Farris imagined taking the thing to an art gallery, maybe the Walker over in the Twin Cities (for that was the only art gallery in the immediate area he actually knew how to get to). He imagined presenting this *thing* to the curator or whatever they were called, the guys who bought the art for the gallery. Farris would put it in a better bag, of course, maybe one from that little gift shop in the mini-mall downtown, the one that sold candles you could get for a buck at the Dollar General for six or seven bucks a pop and gave you a fancy bag with dream catchers printed on a creamy-white background and rope handles. Anyhow, once it was in a nice bag, he would ceremoniously place it on the reception desk at the gallery (or whatever the curator used for a desk), then lift it slowly from the bag, watching the eyes of all around him slowly widen and begin to glitter with anticipation as everyone waited to hear his asking price for this wonderful, incredible object.

Then he remembered yet another show he'd seen on TV, one of those true crime things on Court TV or A&E or one of those channels that kept him company when he couldn't sleep. Some guy was trying to sell fake art—copies of stuff, plus other artwork made to look more or less like the things real artists had already painted, only the real artist never painted that particular piece. Anyhow, the fake-art-selling guy had to create something called a provenace for these paintings, which boiled down to some sort of proof of past ownership, as well as reviews and whatnot from previous gallery showings of this fake art…all to create a history of this fake, so's it would seem like a real, old, painting.

And all Farris had was the ancient burger joint, movie-tie-in bag. Which was really old, but definitely not any sort of proof of past ownership for what was inside it. There wasn't even a receipt in the bag for the original burger meal, let alone the… thing itself.

Continuing to bask in the remains of the fantasy for a couple of wistful seconds more, Farris found himself staring at the object, even as he kept his hands in his lap. Perhaps touching it too much might mar the finish somehow. He was already disoriented from the lack of reflection in its fleecy-bright surface, as if he and the object weren't quite sharing he same space, even though it was obviously sitting on the countertop and casting a dim shadow on the glitter-flecked Formica surface beneath it.

When he saw a car pulling into the bay nearest his booth, Farris quickly lifted the thing up (trying not to notice how it shifted within his thumb-and-two-finger grasp) and put it back in the bag. He didn't want anyone asking for change to see the thing, perhaps wonder what it was, ask about it, or even go so far as to possibly link his find with the abandoned car out by the Dumpster. By the time the man from the car came over to the booth, dollar bills in hand, the object was safely on the floor, tucked between Farris' feet, like a baby penguin.

On the way home, in his car, Farris placed the bagged thing in the passenger side foot well, close to the center console. Where he could see it but anyone looking in would see only a fast food bag. As he turned each corner, he thought he could hear it subtly shift within the bag, the contents smacking against the side nearest the rubber-matted floor. For a moment, he had a vision of the thing's interior bubbling up, like a shaken beer can, ready to explode with the slightest jarring motion. After that, he made each turn more slowly, more carefully.

When he got home, he tucked the bag into the crook of his left arm, cradling it gently against his side, least he press it too hard and somehow distort its shape. As he walked, the bag made tiny, whisper-crinkling sounds, in harmony with the muffled semi-liquid slosh of whatever was inside it.

Inside his apartment, he first swept off his coffee table all the old magazines and copies of the local newspaper he always dug out of the car wash trash bins. Then he set the bag down in the exact center of the *faux* walnut finish of the table's surface. He didn't open the bag—he already knew that it wouldn't reflect any of his mangy belongings, nor would it glow subtly in the reflected shifting light from the TV. But it was important to him that it be near him as he sat and watched the television and ate his microwaved meal.

He briefly entertained a horrible fantasy, one of putting the bag, contents and all, into the microwave just to see once and for all if it was metal or not. But the sickening cruelty of his thought made him shiver, as if he'd been sprayed with icy beer from a dropped can. Not to mention the image he ever so briefly allowed into his mind of what the object might do if it was trapped in that garage-sale microwave.

After his dinner was heated, he ended up placing it on his knees rather than on the coffee table, lest the heat of the tray cause an unwanted form of condensation on the surface of the object in the bag. As he ate his food, Farris wondered if he should remove the object from the bag, let it fully share his space, but he decided against it. It seemed fitting that it stay in the bag, as if that were its natural environment. Although he had no animal which might knock the thing off the table, perhaps play with it, or worse, chew on it, it just seemed to Farris that whatever it was, it was better off in the bag. It wasn't like he didn't know what it looked like, and he didn't need to keep looking at it in order to continue to puzzle over the thing.

That night, his TV programs were only half-watched and barely comprehended. His eyes kept flitting back to the bag and his thoughts centered on the thing within the bag. It didn't seem right, it being left alone in that rat-trap car, tucked under the driver's seat with only its hind end sticking out like a rabbit trying to hide, not realizing that its white-daubed tail was fully, vulnerably visible.

He wondered if whoever owned the car even knew the thing was in there, among all the debris piled in the back foot well. On one hand, if they unknowingly left it there, without having opened the bag, and felt what was inside, he was stunned by their lack of curiosity, of their blindness to a strange reality. But if they were aware of it, if they had perhaps put it in that bag, either for protection or to simply hide it...what of that?

How could they be so heartless? To take the time, the effort (minimal as it admittedly was) to shield the thing from the elements, from the overly-curious, from prying eyes, then to turn around and just leave it, along with the pedestrian, completely worthless car, seemed hopelessly contradictory to Farris.

It was worse than dumping a dead animal in a Dumpster. Like that stillborn puppy he'd found in one of the municipal green garbage cans that sprouted each spring along the public parking lot a block west of downtown. He'd been looking for aluminum cans and there it had been, still encased in the birth sac. Still, it had just seemed wrong to Farris as he looked down at that pup.

He decided that sad applied to the soft thing in the bag on his coffee table, too. Not dead sad like the tossed-out puppy, but abandoned sad. Forlorn. He wondered if perhaps he should put it up on the TV so he could look at it as he watched the set. But again, the possibility of heat and whatever invisible rays the TV might give off affecting the thing in the bag stopped that train of thought.

Farris then considered holding the object in his lap, of stroking it or just brushing his fingertips against it during commercials. But he didn't know if he could stand having it sitting in his lap, not with the way whatever was inside had of shifting. And there was that memory of how it seemed to settle down on the countertop at the car wash. He didn't want to know what it might feel like, settling down in his lap.

So he spent the night alternately watching the TV screen and the bag, noting how the shifting wash of colors on the screen cast flickering images on the slightly crinkled side of the bag. The fact that he could not clearly see the thing inside made it all the more watchable—it was like watching an eclipse through one of those pinhole-in-a-paper-plate thingies...you had the experience without the danger.

Not that he actually feared the soft thing resting in the bag— but there was just enough that was not right, not normal, not... expected about it that he was just as loath to touch it as he was unable to stop thinking about the thing. Reluctantly leaving it on the table when he went off to bed, he found himself tossing and turning in his narrow three-quarter-size bed for hours before telling himself he was just getting up to take a pee—that's all— even though he made a detour into the living room afterwards and picked up the bag by the sides. He placed it on the fruit-crate bedside table he'd rigged up and, after positioning himself on the side facing the bag, he finally drifted off into an uneasy sleep.

Farris wasn't one who remembered his dreams come morning, but as he carried the thing in the bag out to his car with him, prior to heading off to the burger place for a bacon-muffin sandwich, he half-remembered something to do with what was inside the thing in the bag, and how it wasn't really very pleasant, but things did seem to get better once they'd gone back into the can-shaped thing...on their own.

He was only mildly surprised to see that the car was still there, in its spot, near the Dumpster. The town cops never came to the car wash because the inmates at the county jail washed the cop cars, so it wasn't likely they'd ticket the thing, and if his boss didn't know about it...well, Farris wasn't going to say anything either.

Once he'd settled into his booth and placed the thing in the bag near his radio, he kept glancing out at the car, wondering if it was a local or not. He knew he could look at the tags, see if the sticker was from this county or not. He'd already noticed the old red-letters-and-numbers Wisconsin plate from several years back, but he kept telling himself it didn't matter. Whoever had left it...whoever had left the soft thing hidden in the back foot well...wasn't coming back. Something told him they had left the car as a way of leaving the thing. Hidden, protected, but out of their lives. He wondered if they had brought it into their house each night and slept with it—close to their side as he did. He doubted they touched it all that much.

He himself hadn't touched it—not since yesterday. But that didn't prevent him from noticing how slightly warm to the touch the bag was when he lifted it out of the car. Like the way a person's butt gets when they sit for too long on a warm car seat. When he left for home that afternoon, he deliberately wore his gloves when he carried the bag out to his car, just so he wouldn't know if it was cool from the counter or still at body temperature.

He found himself eating in the kitchen, looking out his

second-story window over the sink, rather that at his usual place in front of the television—rather than in the living room with the thing. He hadn't been able to bring it into the kitchen, didn't want it on his countertops where he kept his food.

It seemed clean, close to shiny, but he still didn't want to take any chances.

When he sat down to watch TV, he sat sideways on the couch, feet on the far armrest, left shoulder facing the bag on the table. He'd seen most of the shows several times already, but he watched them again, just because they were something known, something understandable. Not something intangible, even as it took up space in his apartment—something seen, felt, and weighing a little too much for its size and shape, but still utterly incomprehensible on all levels.

Yet, too—well, too special to merely toss aside, to drop into an open Dumpster or to (yet another beyond horrible errant thought) add to the bag of aluminum cans sitting just inside his front door.

The brief image of the object passing through the crusher on the rubbery conveyor belt was unbearable. Yet, it was tempting in its sheer doableness. There was nothing to stop him from it, which made the prospect all the more painfully irresistible.

Farris hurried to bed that night, leaving the pliant, silvery-grey thing inside its bag, but he must have gotten up to pee while he was half asleep, for when he got up in the morning and shuffled into the living room, the first thing he saw was the thing, sitting next to the paper bag, simultaneously luminous and opaque, and the worst of it was, he was sure that if he'd touched it, even in his sleep, he would have been able to remember such a pleasant-repugnant sensation—at least he had hoped such an experience would jolt him into wakefulness.

The bag couldn't have tipped over nor could the thing have rolled out. Neither was the thing on its side and there was no way it could have righted itself, let alone stand the bag back up.

Farris skipped the trip to the burger place. Getting to work early, bag resting on the back seat of his car, buckled tight against the back of the seat, Farris parked his car close to the abandoned car by the Dumpster. The keys to the abandoned car were still inside and it wasn't difficult to pop the trunk open.

The interior of the trunk was even messier than the back seat and foot wells of the car itself. Old flannel shirts, mismatched socks, a decayed bumpy foam mattress topper, more burger and taco place bags, plastic lids from soda cups (all punched in for diet drinks), and several straws with teeth-flattened ends. Farris made a secure nest in the middle of the discarded trash and old clothes, one just large enough for the bag still strapped inside his own car.

As he was about to put the bag with the soft, shifting thing inside into the trunk, he felt a pang of guilt, followed by that intense, blood-pumping rush—the kind he used to get when he'd swipe something small and easily palmed or shoved up a sleeve from the convenience stores or the old IGA (before security cameras became the rage). He felt like he had when he got away undetected—an undeserved freedom. But was there any sense of sweeter relief than not getting caught? Even if that sweetness was tempered by a slight aftertaste of bile?

It wasn't like he was going to just toss it...as long as the keys were in the ignition; chances were that someone, someday, was going to take the car away from the car wash lot. And once they did, all that was in the car would be theirs. Their responsibility, their guilt if they did something to the soft thing. If they were capable of feeling guilt.

Once again, that fantasy about presenting the thing to the people at the Walker came to Farris, only with a variation—this time he merely said he bought it, sight unseen, in a box of stuff at some sale. That was it, an estate sale, where you bid on a whole box of stuff. That way, if they wanted it, they could have it. It was his, and then it was theirs. If they wanted it.

It would take at least a tank full of gas to get to the Twin Cities, but Farris told himself that he could try to save up for the gas, and put the bag back in his car. He wasn't up to putting it in the booth with him. He didn't think it would mind staying in the car for the day. And if he belted it in tight enough, he didn't think it could work itself free of the bag.

A tank of gas. A full tank, not just a top-off, he kept telling himself as he sat in his booth, alternately watching the car by the Dumpster and his own car parked close enough to let the thing in the bag know it could very easily end up back in the first car, down in the cluttered foot well, if it didn't stay in its bag.

And as the sun rose in the sky, Farris kept one eye on his car, watching for stray muted glints of diffused light on silvery-gray, all the while muttering, "If they want it...it will be theirs, if they want it...."

RIVER OF GLASS,
MIRROR OF WATER

TINA HEARD THE MIRROR break before she even realized that it had fallen off of her dressing table—a sharply staccato tinkling, like frozen rain pelting a storm-window, only less rhythmic, more ominous.

And in the half second before she reluctantly turned her head in the direction of the sound, that old, old wives' tale flitted across her mind—Break a mirror—seven years bad luck. So it was with a distinct *moue* of displeasure forming on her half-lipsticked lips that Tina let out a low, keening whistle of disappointment as she peereddown at the shattered remains of the hand-mirror sparkling on the hardwood floor and realized—too late—that the sleeve of her robe had snagged the mirror's slightly-tarnished handle...and when she'd moved her arm up to begin applying the lipstick, the mirror had been knocked off the dressing table.

From behind her in the hallway, Tina could hear the steady, heavy footsteps of the cleaning lady (the woman who came in twice a month to vacuum, dust the walls and ceilings and whatnot, all the bothersome things Tina and her husband didn't have time to do between their respective jobs) coming down the narrow length of crosswise plank flooring which separated the many smallish bedrooms on either side of the upstairs hall. And every other step, the woman's mop handle thunked hollowly against the plaster walls, creating a strangely arhythmic counterpoint to her footfalls.

"Everything okay in here, Miz Brooke?" The woman's voice echoed weirdly, mingling with the remembered sound of that breaking mirror as Tina quickly replied, "Oh, I suppose...just broke the darned mirror, that's all. Guess I'll have to get used to seven years of bad luck—"

"Why so?" This time, the woman's voice was clear, bright and over-loud as she stood in the doorway, arms akimbo, her mop handle jutting out from her right side like a third, withered limb.

Wishing she'd never brought the subject up at all, Tina pushed her vanity bench away from the table with her upper thighs as she began to kneel down next to the fragmented, still-reflective shards of silvered glass, and muttered, "You know...seven years bad luck for breaking a mirror, that old superstition—"

"I know a better superstition," the cleaning lady interjected before striding purposefully into the small bedroom, her footsteps ringing like cannon shots before she, too, knelt down next to the fragmented mosaic of reflective and non-reflective chunks and slivers of glass; from somewhere (just *where*, Tina couldn't begin to imagine) on her person, the woman produced a small dustpan, the old fashioned enameled metal kind with the half-cover on top to better hold in the swept-up dust, and began to deftly pick up the bigger fragments with her thumb and forefinger before depositing them into the dustpan.

"No wait. You'll cut yourself," Tina began, but the older woman just smiled and said, "No time for a broom...but we do have to get up every last piece right away. You'll be wasting time enough just running down to the river—"

Tina cocked her head to one side and stared at the cleaning lady through narrowed eyes as she slowly said, "'Running down to the river—' Is this part of your superstition?" even as a part of her feared that the woman had taken leave of her senses— while armed with jagged, sharp bits of broken glass.

Using the meaty side on one callused hand, the woman swept the last of the fragments into the dustpan. Then, as she held out the pan with the handle toward Tina, she solemnly ordered her boss, "No time to talk about it right now—you got to carry this down to running water and throw it all in. *Now*—"

The cleaning woman's tone of voice was so dark, so...*sure*, Tina didn't wait to question her further but instead grabbed the enameled metal handle and hurried out of the bedroom and down the stairs with her untied robe flap-flapping behind her like a great pair of blue terry-clothed wings until she reached the back door in the kitchen and hurried out without bothering to close it behind her, then ran down the flagstone-lined path leading through her husband's flower garden, took a sharp right where the garden merged with the short, scrubby trees and vines growing on the gently sloping hillside above the river and kept going, even as the sharp stones beneath her slippered feet dug deep into the flimsy soles...and only when she reached the moist, waterpolished stretch of sand-embedded stones along the shallowest edges of the river did she pause to catch her breath. Beyond her, the waters of the Dean River lapped at the sandy, rock-strewn shoreline, their ripples tinged rusty-dark in the early morning sunlight while, further out, the dark waters wore an undulating, silvery skin of coin-dappled sunlight.

It was into the sun-mottled, wind-rippled river that Tina tossed the contents of the dust-pan; as the pieces flew in the air, some of them caught the earliest rays of the sun in blinding flashes of light that burned a cool, spreading green on Tina's eyelids after she momentarily closed her eyes against that white-hot glare.

Even after she opened her eyes, she could still see the after-image of that reflected light, like a fuzzy, spreading haze, a third eyelid of greasy distortion obscuring her vision. But the distortion wasn't so great that she couldn't see the people across the river, the ones from Minnesota who'd moved in this past summer, staring at her as they ate breakfast on their decks... and it was only then that she realized that her robe was hanging open, and she was still wearing her nightgown underneath, plus her mop-fluffy slippers.

While carrying a dust-pan....

Hoping that they could see her mouth. Tina smiled bravely, if a bit foolishly, at the watching couple, waved the dust-pan in their direction, then scrambled back up the slope, grabbing low tree branches and winding vines for purchase as she headed for her still-open kitchen door....

It wasn't until after she'd hurried back upstairs and dressed herself, then slowly and calmly walked downstairs for breakfast, that Tina casually asked the cleaning woman, "Why *did* I have to throw the pieces of that mirror into the river?"

The woman stopped dusting the living room ceiling before turning around to look at Tina, replying, "For luck...the running water is supposed to wash away the bad luck, take away those seven years of it. Least, that's what my grandma used to say...." She turned away from Tina and began jabbing the old-tee-shirt covered broom into one corner, as if the matter were closed for discussion.

Wondering if perchance the woman merely came up with this old wives' tale simply to humiliate her, make her look the fool in front of the neighbors (*especially when those Minnesotans already look down on Wisconinites*), Tina took another sip of coffee, swallowed a bit too loudly, then went on, "Strange, how I never heard of *that* one...usually, all people ever have to say about mirrors is to be sure and never break one—"

"Perhaps them that had no rivers or streams handy just forgot about the rest of the legend," the woman offered nonchalantly, as if *she* with her imperfect grammar and arcane wives' tales, somehow was in possession of a wisdom greater than that of a legal secretary like Tina.

Trying to top her employee, at least for her own sense of dignity, Tina said, "Perhaps the people who kept throwing things into their rivers ran out of room in there, and the pieces of mirror weren't swept away anymore," before picking up her purse and heading for the door. But, as she was just about to close and lock the door, she thought she heard the cleaning lady's voice reply: "That which ain't swept away, comes back to haunt another day."

Tina didn't realize that she'd forgotten to bring along her lunch until a few minutes before her scheduled lunch hour; luckily, the only pressing matter on her calendar that day was typing up a will, and that wouldn't take her more than an hour or so, so she was able to drive home for lunch...but as Tina drove over the stretch of Riverview Road which ran parallel to the river, something caught her eye as her car glided along the pavement.

Something bright—much too bright to be mere sunlight on moving water.

Slowing down the car by five miles per hour, she craned her neck in the direction of the river and noticed that some of the large, hump-like rocks which jutted out of the river like the backs of semi-submerged turtles were covered with sparkling flecks, like bits of embedded mica or pyrite.

But those rocks are just...rocks. Dull when the sun bakes them and shiny dark when they're wet. They don't *sparkle*!

But even with her rate of speed slowed down to twenty miles per hour, the oddly twinkling rocks were soon past her; thankful that no one was on the road, Tina backed up until her car was just above and parallel to the partly submerged rocks. She had to roll down the slightly tinted windows to get a better look at the huge, boulder-like stones, but once she did, there was no mistaking the source of that unnatural sparkle.

The irregular segments of her hand mirror had somehow washed up onto the rock, as if they'd merely skimmed the surface once they'd been tossed onto the river instead of sinking as they should have.

While her eyes darted frantically, Tina noticed that the edges of the water were more scummy and sudsy than usual (*the paper mill must've dumped out another load of by-products again*), reminding her of her childhood tub filled with bubble-bath and the buoyant tub-toys she used to purposely sink before they'd magically pop up again.

"That which ain't swept away—"

"No. That's just uneducated foolishness," Tina mumbled as she rolled up her window and gunned the motor...but as her cleaning lady drove past her, going into town, she found herself too scared *not* to dutifully smile and wave at the albeit ignorant woman, who in reply smiled broadly and motioned toward the river with one sturdy, large hand....

Once she'd eaten, in a kitchen whose blinds were drawn tight against the possible prying stares of those people from Minnesota who seemed to all but *live* on that deck of theirs, Tina debated whether or not she should call in sick for the rest of the afternoon, leaving the will for tomorrow, but remembered that tomorrow would bring still more work in addition to that which she hadn't finished today...so after deciding that she could take a different route into town, one which would take her far from Riverview Road and the river she could view from the road, Tina slung her purse over her shoulder and quitted the darkened house—only to feel the cold *plash* of rain on her face and hands as soon as she'd shut and locked the door behind her.

But there was something strange, despite the normal coldness of the pelting drops...it wasn't until she glanced down at her sleeve that she noticed that the moisture wasn't spreading in a bloom of one-shade-darker moist color on her blouse, but was instead beading on top of the fabric in crystalline, tear-like pearls of clearest transparency....

Hail...but yet, *not* hail. Hail was icy-translucent, like baby snowballs or misshapen, small marbles like the milky ones she used to play with as a child. Not perfectly clear, like tiny glass balls used by fortune-telling fair-folk. Yet, as they began to cluster in her crooked right arm, along the bend of her elbow, Tina realized that the rain-balls (for lack of a better word to call them) weren't totally transparent after all.

For each tiny sphere reflected her pinched, puzzled face in miniscule, rounded perfection.

Moving her arm quickly away from her trunk, Tina winced as the pearl-like mirrored balls fell noisily to the cement driveway below, mingling with the other now-shattered orbs which covered the grass and the street beyond. Making a deep, animal-scared noise in her throat that stopped short of being a real scream, she hurried back into the house, not stopping until she'd found and exited the kitchen door, and then ran through the garden and the scrub vegetation beyond until she reached the rocky-sandy shore of the river...which now stood in stiff, icing-like peaks and frozen curls between the twin shores, reflecting the cloud-scudded sky above with a rippling parody of normalcy, like a carnival fun-house mirror flipped onto its back.

And across the shore, the people from Minnesota had quitted their weathered redwood deck for perhaps the first time since they'd moved in, so there was no one to watch Tina as she took her first tentative step on that glassy river, or her next, or her next....

It was difficult to keep her footing on those cruelly-jutting glassy peaks and stiff ripples, but the rocks lay only a few yards away, adorned with their patina of mirror fragments...pieces which weren't dislodged by the steady pattering rain of tiny, tiny mirrors.

But the pile-up of reflective rain was enough to stop Tina: it made the already uneven terrain underfoot impossibly slippery while the broken shards worked their way into her shoes, bloodying her feet. Sniffing back sobs of disbelief and indignation, Tina had to make for the hillside once more, scrambling up the sloping, sphere-covered ground almost on her hands and knees, until she finally reached her neighbor's backyard and was able to cross over his property until she found herself in her own backyard She wasn't able to use the flagstone walkway— too well-covered with a miniscule cobblestoning of pearl-size mirrors—but the lawn was long enough to give her some traction as she stumbled and staggered toward the kitchen door.

Once Tina was inside, she slammed the door shut and hurried

for the downstairs bathroom in search of some bandages and peroxide for her torn feet and knees, splattering the bottom halves of the hallway walls with flecks of bright blood as she ran.

The cleaning lady will kill me for messing up the walls, kept running though her mind while the woman's own words, *Comes back to haunt another day*, provided an eerie descant to Tina's thoughts of woe.

The bandages and the peroxide were inside the medicine cabinet, but after Tina entered the bathroom, she found herself unable to simply open that door and take what she needed from the metal shelves within...for the mirror on the cabinet wasn't reflective anymore.

All Tina could see was a placid, depthless, moist surface like that of a quiet, quiet river on a hazy summer's day—and this time, she knew better than to so much as touch those peaceful waters.... Let alone defile them as she'd done that morning, before the river had returned her bad luck to her—one crystal-line droplet at a time.

And as she stared at the just barely rippling half-reflection of her own sobbing, twisted features in what had once been her mirror, all Tina could do was wonder if the river would be content with a mere seven years of retribution...while the first droplets of her mirror *plashed* with a soft, liquid echo on the pristine cleanliness of the sink below.

PART FIVE
AFTERDAMAGE

DEBRIS

(September 2, 2002)

Later, she discovered that she was one of those people who never heard the train-whistle roar of the tornado as it slammed through her town. The first sound she did hear, aside from the pummeling rain which slammed her windows, was the sudden sharp smash-crash-glassy jangle of something bursting through her beveled glass door insert in the vestibule.

She'd been heading for the door leading to the vestibule when it happened, had her hand on the old brass knob, but hadn't yet turned that smooth orb. After she heard the sound, she didn't want to open the door, didn't want to see, but sick curiosity got the better of her.

At first, all she could think when she looked at her glass-strewn vestibule was *That doesn't belong here*. A white rectangular wooden sign, covered with green painted lettering, was jammed halfway into the layers of jackets and winter coats hanging on the coat rack just in front of her.

The corners of the alien rectangle of painted wood were jagged, raw, showing the unpainted core of the sign itself. As if it had been ripped off its moorings. Where did this come from?

There were no such signs near her house, no slim white rectangles announcing days and times in fluid hand-painted green letters and numbers—The days. The times. This thing jutting in her shattered front door came from over three quarters of a mile away, down Highway 8, from that open patch of grass (once covered with scruffy spruce trees, all of which came down back in 1997, when the first bad storm blew through town, later covered with some sort of broad leafed trees, most of which had been broken down by the worse-than-'97's storm which tore through the town just last June) where the Farmer's Market was held each Wednesday and Saturday during harvest season. It should have been hanging between two white wooden posts, from hooks, she thought. There were no hooks on her vestibule rug, just jagged shards of thick beveled glass.

The sign was entangled in the semi-sheer green curtains she'd hung across the ruined glass insert, along with the painted wooden crow with the coiled wire legs she'd hung there just that morning. Beyond the mess of sign-glass-curtains-dangling crow figure, she could see just what had happened to her town... but it went beyond the *deja vu* of seeing storm damage like that of '97 and '01.

The long chain-link fence which separated the middle school parking lot from her street was twisted like a crepe paper streamer, and once she yanked the wooden sign out of her doorway, slicing open her right ring finger, and was able to poke her head through the doorway, she saw that her front lawn was littered thickly with glass, tufts of soggy pink and yellow insulation, scraps of roofing shingles in colors she didn't recognize from any of the roofs in her neighborhood, jagged tree limbs (their pulpy cores fleshy beige or sickly white with green edges), frayed squares and rectangles of plywood, limp wallboard fragments, still more glass, some of it green-tinted, some pieces smokey grey, parts of plastic store front signs from Ewert Avenue, and a wind-curled aluminum attic vent. And that only covered the building materials, the scraps of houses and fences and car parts that once made up what passed for her block, her neighborhood. Once she'd opened her ruined door (the edges of the two-by-five-foot broken insert were too jagged, too maw-like to pass through even with bent head and rounded back), and stepped down to the sidewalk, to see one of her three locust trees bent at a stiff 45° angle over her neighbor's lawn, she saw the rest of the debris, all the things which belonged... elsewhere, not on her lawn...not on any lawns at all.

Dolls, some stripped naked and decapitated, tucked in low-lying tree branches, wind chimes and baskets and wet *National Geographics* and bent pieces of what might have been kitchen utensils and strange curtains and pieces of crockery, over-laid with limp personal checks from one of the banks close to the center of what had been town, endorsed but not yet paid out, And every house on her block had broken windows, hers included—she recognized some of the shards from her own windows, the edges touched with paint smears from the broken mullions, lying on her neighbor's lawn—and torn shingles. But she still couldn't figure out where the dappled pieces of shin-gles resting on her lawn, the ones with the mottled mix of grey, raspberry-red and charcoal pigments over the underlying black, came from. No one in the neighborhood had a roof that color, nor did she recall anyone, anywhere, having a roof with shingles like that. Somehow, figuring this out seemed important, even as she zombie-stumbled over the debris sprouting from her lawn, watching all her neighbors (those who were at horne, on this Labor Day afternoon) come out and stare at the afterdamage, the abrupt change left behind.

She was holding a piece of the strange shingle material in her hand when her neighbors came home, the parents and the kids and the mulatto girl who was apparently fostering with them, or something (she was always there lately, going to school with their kids in the morning, coming home with them at night), she didn't know the neighbors well enough to ask, or even care, really. They leaned out of their truck, shouting to each other that all the windows were gone, and the siding shattered, again, as she stood next to the broken locust which covered half their front yard, waiting for them to get out of the truck so she could ask them about the shingle she held in her bloody fingers. That she'd never liked them was a moot point, in this time of debris and damage and inexplicable change. People were stopping in mid-street, in running-but-stopped vehicles, to talk to each other, to compare damages, to marvel at their survival, so it didn't seem strange to now talk to her neighbors, after years of stony stares over the wooden fence she'd put up between their yards after they'd strayed too far onto her grass with their set-too-low mower, punctuated by her occasional shouts at the kids when they strayed on to her property while playing ball at night.

They didn't demand that she get her tree off their yard, nor did they know where the stray varicolored shingles came from. Just as they couldn't figure out where their garage had blown off to, along with all the power tools and the boat inside. The guy did say he wanted to go move to Iceland, after having had so much damage to his house during these last three storms. His siding was shattered where limbs and whatnot hit it, revealing the old asphalt siding hidden under the layers of green foam insulation and beige vinyl siding, and long strips of siding flapped and slapped against the back of the house, where his electrical mast had been torn away from the house, after the main power pole in the alley snapped in two. This was the second time in as many years that his mast tore away from his house, and she couldn't really blame the man for suggesting the move to Iceland—she didn't think they had tornadoes there, and the guy said he could ice fish there year round, which seemed comforting to him, at least.

Wondering what had happened to her own power line, she went around her house, and saw her own mast bent like one of those ribbed straws, a smooth right angle in painted metal, while her power lines snaked across the leaf-glass-shingle-frag-ment-and-plywood-dotted grass. No power, which meant who knew how many days and nights with only a battery radio for company, sitting in the candle or flashlight-lit darkness, just as she'd done for five days last June, when the power had gone out, only that time, she didn't have to worry about getting someone to fix her mast...later, she was sure that that was the moment when the impact of the tornado really hit her. Even if the power was restored elsewhere, if she couldn't get that mast hooked up, she'd be even further isolated. Not wanting to think about the dark, silent house waiting for her, she began walking, across her own back yard, and straight across her neighbor's yard, reflexively picking up whatever debris she recognized as coming from her house, her porch, her own life.

Although she hadn't heard the tornado, she could hear the helicopters already circling overhead, like metallic buzzards buzzing the dying town below. And the droning beepbeepbeep of rescue equipment snaking cautiously through the downed trees and tossed cars and ripped-away front porches, which formed an eerie descant to the mingled shouts and cries coming from the ruined blocks which lay parallel to the river which had attracted the tornado's twisting force in the first place. The alleys were blocked by downed power poles and uprooted trees, so she had to move onto the street between the houses as she moved west, pockets filled with small personal items of hers she'd picked up from lawns dozens of yards away from her house. The rounded old porch columns from one old Victorian lay scattered like anorexic bowling pins on a neighboring lawn, while across the street, a cement slab garage floor sat exposed after the garage itself had blown away cleanly, leaving no outward sign of its existence—not a shingle, not a strip of siding.

Black-tinged glass from the courthouse windows sparkled in the late afternoon sunlight as she continued to make her way westward, toward the caved-in ruins of what had been Ewerton. Brick façades were pulled off the sides of stores and apartment houses, aluminum vertical siding over storefronts now hung down like thick strands of wet hair over the shattered windows fronting blown-in pieces of furniture and merchandise, and everywhere were moist blobs of insulation, somewhat fleshy and weirdly meaty-looking in the slanting sunlight. Firetrucks blocked her way near the far end of the business district; she heard someone say there were gas lines ruptured, although she couldn't smell it. But already, the slightly wet, punky odor of soggy wood was filling the air, that strange half-rotted odor which was somewhat food-like, somewhat inorganic, but inescapably pungent.

And while what had happened not quite a year ago in New York, the whole 9-11 thing, was still relatively fresh in her consciousness, this was a totally different landscape...a cross between a war zone, and an out-take from the mall-trashing scene in *The Blues Brothers*. No billowing clouds of dust, no orange-black balls of flame...just more broken glass than could be accounted for given the number of windows and doors in town prior to the tornado, and shingles everywhere. And...stuff. Things which belonged There, Inside, which were now Here, Outside, lying on the street getting wet and dirty. Children's toys, clothes from the stores, plants from desk tops, papers pertaining to businesses now gone from existence and even memory (funny, how she could not remember how town had looked just a few hours ago, how the ruined buildings suddenly seemed alien, without prior form or function) a business card from that small employment agency down the street, on one of the blocks now bright with the flashing lights from the fire trucks parked side by side the wrong way in the street.

Forced to walk back toward her own neighborhood, she took a side street, one slightly less damaged than the main section of down-town, then crossed over to a parallel business-zoned street, where the damage was more random and minor. But there was still debris on the sidewalk, the ubiquitous shards of glass, the sodden clumps of insulation...and as she walked past one of the bars, its door propped open and a piece of cardboard marked "FREE FOOD" covering the broken window which once sported neon beer signs, she saw the ledger book. At first, she thought it was the one from her own house, from one of the upstairs rooms whose window had been broken, the long thin dun-colored book with the maroon fake leather corner guards and the pseudo-antique geometric-and-leaf design surrounding the old-fashioned type font which read "Day" on the front cover. The book she'd picked up just this spring from the annual Catholic church rummage sale, for 5¢. She'd been writing her personal expenses in it, long columns of bills paid, check numbers, and dates. But after she'd bent over to pick it up, losing half the contents of her pockets in the process, she noticed that the pages in this book were covered with far more writing than hers was, in a hand not her own. And there were pictures, pen and ink drawings of houses and trees which should have looked familiar, given their general layout and shapes, but...weren't. Figuring that it had to be someone's book, even if it wasn't hers, she picked it up, and—after putting all her own things back into her pockets—tucked it under one arm, before walking back to her own block, and her own house. Her neighbors were still outside, still circling their house, picking up glass and wood and that mushroom-like insulation, so she doubted anyone had tried to go inside her house. After asking the guy if he'd call her an electrician on his cell phone, she went inside, to the darkness and the silence, while the helicopters continued to circle, circle, overhead....

Once she'd found a radio that worked, and lit some candles, she looked inside the ledger book for a name, and address, but there was nothing written on the cream-colored paper which lined the insides of the cloth-colored cardboard covers. But there was plenty of writing on each page, done by someone left-handed, from the slant and flow of the letters (as well as the occasional left-to-right smudging of some of the inked letters), the script fairly easy to read, once she figured out some of the slight idiosyncratic quirks in the handwriting, like a backwards lower loop on the "f" and "p". Whoever started this journal did so last June, during the storm which was supposedly straight-line winds, but was more like a lower-grade tornado, probably an F0 or an F1, judging by the way the trees in the park across the river were broken down in circular patterns, or the way the damage skipped over small sections of some blocks.

"Could this town be a new tornado alley? Over fifty years since we were hit with a real Dorothy-over-Kansas twister, then within five years, we get two major 'weather events' as the Shitty Council likes to call them, given the fact that no one thought to sound the sirens before the last Big One in '97. No sirens means no asking for state aid later on, since no proper warning was sounded, so what was obviously a mini-tornado becomes what they call 'straight-line winds'...*my butt*, straight-line winds don't make the water in the river lift straight up out of the riverbed. I saw it happen, just like I saw the trees swirl around in a circle, and fall like stacked dominoes, after you start the whole laid-out pattern of them to falling. Nobody is going to convince me that we didn't have a tornado."

As if to prove his or her point, the writer supplied a drawing of the fallen trees on the page facing this brief rant; pen and ink, mostly cross-hatched, with some pointillism used to show the bark patterns on the fallen tree trunks. She thought she recognized the group of downed tress as a cluster of pines which had fallen in the park, but there seemed to be either too many of them, or not quite enough in that circle of jagged-edged stumps and pick-up-sticks scattered trunks. Maybe whoever did the drawing was as bad at math as she was. Maybe he or she was looking at a different group of trees...so many had fallen in '01, in so many places, but wasn't that the small house just past the tennis courts in the park she knew, roughly sketched in the background of this drawing? The shape of the tiny house seemed right, and there was the unmistakable diamond-shaped cross-hatching meant to represent the fence surrounding the court itself. But the number of trees just didn't gibe with her memory of the storm, or the prolonged clean-up, which had given her and anyone else interested more than enough time to look at the downed trees before they were chain-sawed into neatly stacked logs....

Flipping the page, she read the next passage:

"What is perhaps the strangest thing of all is how I cannot remember how things were before whatever ripped through town did its thing. I mean I know there were trees here, or a roof there, but what kind of tree was it before the top got chopped off and hauled away, leaving just the tuber-like roots lying on the horizontal, exposed and reaching out across what's left of the sidewalk? What color were the shingles on the roof that was blown bare-to-tarpaper? The skyline along the river looks like tattered Scherenschnitte when I go jogging in the mornings, all backlit black cut-paper outlines of trees, only totally asymetrical and jagged, with weird gaps between the branches and leaves. And I know I should remember what it looked like before, only the newness of the Now has torn away the shapes and silhouettes of the Then, as if those straight line whatevers blew the memories right out of my head, cleaning my brain via the ears, side-burn to side-burn."

Whoever wrote this was a he, at any rate. She tried to remember if she'd seen anyone jogging in the early morning hours, near the river which was only one street away from where she lived, but even though she'd worked the early shift at the convenience store down Highway 8 for the last six years, she'd never seen any man jogging that area. She did see two women joggers, the bony one with absolutely no body fat who ran with five-pound weights in each skeletal arm, and the snotty shrew with the two dogs who once scolded her for "scaring" the puppy running along side her when she walked up from behind the woman and the dogs, but no male jogger ran along any street near the river.

Outside the house, she could hear the drone of helicopters, more than one of them by the sound, and the rescue vehicles continued to beep-beep their way down the streets, accompanied by the rending crack of wood hitting the ground after the chainsaws bit through half-broken limbs and trunks. A sound she half-remembered from last year's storm, and a sound the writer of the journal had also found both annoying and comforting:

"Odd, how the usual sounds of a week-day—car tires kissing the asphalt, truck doors slamming shut, birds chirping, squirrels barking and chattering, the metallic whump of a mailbox lid slamming down after a delivery—are wholly masked during the aftermath of a storm like this. Suddenly it's chainsaw time, trucks backing up, Dumpsters being dropped onto side streets, wood rending as it breaks free of the rest of the downed tree, and over all of it, the hum of voices, never letting up, people telling other people what to do, where to put it, when to move it. An alien background hum, but still the sound of things reluctantly jerking back to normal, after being displaced by the abnormal. The kind of sound that keeps up and keeps up, until you get used to it, then suddenly everything is chopped up, hauled away, and re-roofed and re-sided, and you have to get re-used to the old sounds, the formerly normal life sounds."

On her radio, there were words about the tornado, distant expressions of disbelief, warnings about when everyone was to be inside, when everyone could emerge from their ruined homes, if they did, indeed, still have a home. She realized from brief glimpses via the side-streets that the next street over, the one parallel to the river, was a complete disaster—roofs blown clean off, windows exploded, curtains hanging outside sashes, to flap wetly against the peeled-away vinyl or aluminum siding, chimneys broken to Lego-shaped bits scattered across roofs, one whole house just gone. And the trees...so many gone, that the very sky above them looked naked, with nothing between the ground and the houses still standing. Just gaps, in the skyline, and in her memory, even after so short a time following the disaster. As the music coming from the radio was interrupted more and more frequently with word of the tornado, she kept on reading in the flickering yellow-bright light:

"Each time we've had a storm, I take pictures, of what's left, but not having any before photos, all I get is a sense of cease-less change, of reality altered and then altered again, with no residual sense of what Was, Before. I can't even remember what used to be in any given spot. Once the houses are torn apart, the siding ripped away like great gaping wounds showing the underlying insulation and tar-paper muscles and viscera, I can't imagine what they used to look like. I try to remember, but I'm not sure if my memories are any more real or surreal than what is left behind."

There was another sketch, this one seemingly colored-in afterward with what looked like a wet fingertip rubbed with a colored marker, of a row of houses that she almost recognized, perhaps on the next ruined street over, or maybe, just maybe, over in that section of town out by the hospital...some place where the houses were older, square in general shape (not like the newer rectangular ones, which sometimes came down the street in two doll-house like halves, on those big trucks fronted with the "WIDE LOAD" signs), and mostly two-storied. The four-to-a-block configuration seemed right, and she thought she recognized a couple of porches and one house with a uniquely mullioned window next to the front door, but there were so many little details which were off-kilter, she found herself more puzzled than disquieted as she peered at the drawing. That the trees he'd roughly sketched in along the boulevards (quickly scratched onto the paper in long, wiggling strokes, topped with horizontal amorphous blobs which resembled the clumps of insulation sprouting on every lawn, and nesting in almost every still-standing tree) were somehow wrong was also obvious; either there were too many or too few to correctly correspond with the houses she thought he might be trying to depict. But still, the houses seemed so familiar, and the dates of the storms he was referring to corresponded to the storms here...so why didn't the houses and trees match up the way she thought she remembered them? Were both of their memories that faulty, that mixed up? He was a good enough artist for her to realize he was trying to be specific, not generic, in his depiction of what must have been his block of houses...so why couldn't she figure out which four houses he had drawn in this journal?

He'd roughly sketched in the pole with the street signs, but it was foreshortened, and too small to read, even if he had written anything on the two tiny signs jutting out from the top of the post itself. But the color of the signs was right, a smear of green over the inked rectangles.

Telling herself that it wasn't important, or at least any more important than the source of those strange shingles littering her lawn, she reluctantly turned off the radio, to save her batteries, and curled up on the couch in the living room, listening to the chopper and truck sounds until an uneasy sleep overtook her. And when she dreamed, it was of houses murky-dark against cross-hatched clouded skies, house after house set up much too high on lawns which rose up two feet or more above the sidewalks fronted by boulevards with too many trees....

Things had already changed by the time she woke; four wheelers driven by volunteers, law enforcement officers and National Guard members were the only vehicles able to get through the mess of tree limbs and building debris lining the streets, and every few blocks there were drop off stations for boxes of bottled water, and bags of chips for the volunteers and work crews. The radio had said everyone had to go up to the courthouse, or more rightly to a tent pitched across the street from the courthouse, for a wristband, before anyone would be allowed to go into town itself, so once she'd dressed, she left her house, not caring if anyone got into the ruined door or not, and picked up her wristband, a neon-orange Tyvek band left over from the previous year's county fair.

It was difficult to make it over to the highway, where the convenience store she should have been working in by now was located, thanks to the need for police and sheriff's officers from just about every neighboring town, city and county to hand-direct traffic, as well as serve as railroad crossing guards, now that the red and white striped poles which had fronted the rail lines had been broken off in the tornado. She passed by the spot where the wooden Farmer's Market sign had hung, now reduced to one support pole bent on a twenty degree angle in the grass. The rest of the trees planted after the '97 storm had been blown over.

Her convenience store's pumps were blown to a permanent leaning angle, and the windows were all blown to jagged shards in the store beyond...no one was around, so she assumed she was unemployed. That fact simply merged in with everything else that had happened, another unwanted change, another bit of past memory to be permanently made unreliable. She found that she could hardly remember what the inside of the store even looked like anymore, on the walk home, past the place where the watertower was now a crumpled mass of silver legs and what was once the tank that held the water, like a squashed metallic spider.

The old Carnagie library was all off-kilter, the roof partly blown off, only to resettle a few degrees off to one side over the walls. The new brick-walled garage built next to the building, after the current owners began turning it into a bed and breakfast, was totally gone, but a small wooden town hall for a neighboring township was still standing,..the wood siding pieced in one spot by a tree limb, but the walls remained plumb, the roof intact. She thought that was something the writer of that journal she found would find ironic, or possibly even amusing.That little town hall was situated mere yards from the water tower, the missing brick garage, as well as an insurance agency and an apartment house/beauty shop (both buildings formerly mostly brick) which were now little more than rubble.

Yes, her unknown left-handed journal writer would definitely see the unspoken truth behind such a weird twist of fate...something which defied all logic, all Three Little Pigs moralizing, and probably some principle of physics she herself couldn't hope to understand....

The rest of that day was a blur of pay phone calls to insurance agencies, contractors, electricians and too many other people she only would have to either pay or hit up for money in the coming weeks; volunteers came by with plywood for her broken windows, and left tarps for her damaged roof, with the promise that someone would come by to put them up once the lightning let up—after the tornado, which in itself had failed to get rid of the high humidity and heat which had plagued northwest Wisconsin all summer, they'd gotten still more storms— until evening came, bringing the eight o'clock curfew, a strict one, prohibiting even being out on one's lawn...so all she could do was sit and read that journal she'd found, hoping to find a name, an address, some clue as to who wrote the damned thing in the first place. That she'd found it uptown meant nothing— she still hadn't figured out where those shingles came from, either—the guy could live anywhere in town, but judging from his comments, and his sketches, he most likely lived quite close to her:

"You'd think in a place this small, that these damned storms would leave damage everywhere, in every neighborhood, but as Belushi used to say, 'But nooooooooooo—'

Seems like those of us near the river get hit worst, which would be natural if the Town (Fat)hers' would admit we did have a tornado, but straightline winds should be more democratic. I've seen my neighbor's insulation so often, it's like I'm a peeping Tom. His siding is getting to look like lace, so many holes in it you can start to see a pattern if you stare at it long enough. Yet, out by the hospital, in the crappy section of town, the houses remain pristine in their inherent Ticky-Tacky ugliness...."

He had to be old enough, close to her age, to remember that "Ticky Tacky Houses" song, about all the ugly houses that all looked the same, save for the different colors. The line about Belushi, that could've been from watching reruns of SNL on cable, but nobody but nobody ever sang or even mentioned the "Ticky-Tacky" song nowadays.

Unfortunately, it ended up running through her head before she fell asleep, that numbingly cheerful little tune about all the houses that all looked so much alike....

Before she left the house the next day, to mail a bill she hoped against hope would get down to Milwaukee on time, since she'd intended to mail it the day before, before what happened Happened to her town, she purposely listened to the radio, to make sure she heard the latest about the wristband situation. Word was, people coming into town today would need new bands, but the old ones would still be in effect for residents. So she walked into town, envelope in hand, and kept on walking past the courthouse, crossing an intersection where a female police officer from some neighboring county waved her through while directing traffic, and she was about halfway down the block when she heard a voice behind her:

"Hey lady, where do you think you're going?"

Turning around, she saw a strange woman, not a local, of that she was positive, striding behind her, blonde head of Harpo-style permed curls bobbing like little saggy balls on her head with each pounding step of her white sports shoes, her blue plaid flannel shirt open and flapping like crow wings over her white tank top, while her thin tan legs scissored sharply forward in a pair of too-tight light blue shorts.

"I said where do you think you're going?—without the right wristband?" The woman's voice was still as strident and crazed as it first sounded. Raising the letter in her hand, she tried to explain that she was just going to the post office, that she already had a wristband, but the harpy with the Harpo hair would have none of that—"I don't want your excuses, I've been up twelve hours straight, you stupid wimp, so get your frickin' *ass* over to that courthouse, now...."

She tried to tell the woman there was no reason to swear at her, but in answer, the woman lunged at her, fists up and balled, and she ended up running back to the courthouse, where the volunteers under the tent assured her that the wristband she was wearing was *OK,* but just in case she ran into the crazed woman again, they gave her a second band, this one orange and white striped, and wrote the words "Post Office" on it for good measure, an amulet against the blue-shirted freak stalking the streets. She found out that the woman wasn't one of the volunteers, and before she left for the post office, she saw the woman, and pointed her out to one of the real volunteers—and once the man from the tent approached the woman, asking her what her problem was, she lunged at both of them, shouting that she hadn't had any sleep in over forty-eight hours, and that she'd had to have the National Guard posted outside her rental property, and how much she hated "wimps" who wouldn't obey the rules, and then she began lunging at them again.

The woman was still shouting and gesticulating when the man told her to just go on to the post office, that he'd handle the situation. On the way to the post office, she saw several people roaming around uptown with either the old wristbands, or even no wristbands, and for the first time since the tornado hit, she felt a sense of damage, of violation...the tornado, that had been a dumb, mindless thing, a swirl of wind and debris and pure speed, but that woman—that woman was damage. She didn't care that people saw her crying as she walked, she had plenty of company in that regard, but for different reasons.

Who had slept well these past two days? Who hadn't had damage to their homes, their businesses? Who wasn't faced with this mess? And while some houses and plywood-boarded businesses now sported spray-painted messages of "Thank You," "Thank God—We'll Be Back," and "Thanks Volunteers" all she could wonder was which rental property belonged to that freak who stalked her from the east, and how she might get around the evening or morning curfew, to set fire to it, take away everything that the woman had just taken away from her....

The next morning, she ventured out of her house well before the morning curfew was over, and stole a whole case of bottled water from the drop point near her house. It made up for the assault, for a while. Not that she was alone in her mode of thought; while waiting for the curfew to end in earnest, a few hours later, she kept on reading:

"It pisses me, how some people manage to get all the storm perks, while the rest of us get nothing—seems they announced on the local station that the Salvation Army would be giving out free food, to everyone who lost stuff during this week-long power outtage...only they announce it once, so those of us who have to work get nothing, even if we lost all the stuff in our fridges. Plus they turn around and get insurance for what was already replaced with S. A. food! It's like the way it used to be here, back when they still had half the kids go to elementary school in that building across the river—all the businessmen's kids—while all the rest of us had to go to the regular elementary in town, and once the river kids came here for the fifth grade, they lorded it over the rest of us until the twelfth grade. Because their school building was fancier than ours, because they were richer. In a way, I was rather glad when this storm hit that part of town so hard this year—blowing the roof off that old elementary building did have a way of making my day. Although it's lucky for all those preschool kids there now that this happened on a holiday—

She read the last two sentences twice, just to make sure they said what she thought they said. She knew what building he wrote of, the big brick two-storied chocolate brown school house which now housed a Tender Learning Center, ever since the late 1980s. And she remembered when all the rich snots went there up until fourth grade, but the thing with the roof... the radio said it had just happened, this year. Not last year, last June...but since when were there holidays in June?

As if to prove his point, as if anticipating her future questions, he had made a sketch of the damaged building...and it was the TLC, as she remembered it from earlier this year, when she'd gone there for a rummage sale sponsored by the preschool. Same sign with the building blocks out front, same chain link fence surrounding the playground, only he'd drawn a gaping jagged roofline, where the roof had been. There was no sign of it in the sketch, though.

The only holiday in June she could think of was Father's Day, and that wasn't a weekday holiday...could he have meant Memorial Day? That was in late May, not June. And he mentioned the June storm, had been specific about it, saying that it was two months past the time when April showers were supposed to bring those May flowers, only the nursery rhyme didn't mention anything about June tornadoes. There were no week-day holidays in June, and the preschool would've been closed on Father's Day as a matter of course.

Maybe he was confused...it happens, she tried to equivocate, but that did not explain the roof being off a building when no roof had blown off last June. When it did blow off this year, this September.

Not wanting to read any more, yet feeling compelled to keep touching the ledger, to maintain whatever contact she could with this man who somehow felt so much of what she was feeling now, she paged through the long thin book, glancing at the sketches he'd made of the houses in town...which just didn't look right, as opposed to that drawing of the old elementary school. That she recognized easily...but these houses, those she should have recognized, but just couldn't. It was like someone had taken the same basic black dress, only used different accessories, until the entire effect was wholly different. The wrong shape windows, siding that was too fat or too thin, doors that had side lights when they shouldn't have.

Either he was a bad artist, or had a sloppy eye. But he seemed to be a good draftsman, apart from that left to right smearing problem. Everything was recognizable for what it was, even if nothing looked the way it was supposed to look. Then, toward the back of the book, she found some thumb-nail sketches, small architectural doodles of damaged portions of buildings and houses...a roofline with a bit of gingerbread trim torn away, a set of iron stair rails twisted into a fantastic curled shape, like an underwire bra left in a dryer for too long, a wall whose brick outer skin was ripped away—

Things she'd seen, right after this tornado. The handrails were the ones leading up to what remained of the Congregational Church...she was sure of it. She'd mainly been staring at the ruins of the nearby water tower, but she'd seen those twisted iron rails. The remains of the old cross design within the circular decorative details inside the left-hand rail was unmistakable. And she'd seen the brickwork on that one apartment house hours after the tornado. The sketch was too small for her to be sure-sure, but it did look like what she'd seen.

Drawings of storm, maybe tornado damage, from a weekday June holiday storm, which happened last year...maybe here. If not this here, perhaps another *Here*. She may not have gone to the fancy-ass elementary school across the river, where all the rich kids went, but she was more than vaguely familiar with the concept of all the potential variations of any given act, any given event, turning out just a little bit differently, only every variation did happen, just not here, just not now. But in a place where now would become then, only not the now or then she happened to know about.

There was a word, a phrase, to describe all the different nows and thens and maybes which could happen before or after any given event, but she didn't know it. She guessed that whoever wrote this journal knew it, though; he wrote much better than most people she knew talked, so whatever Here he lived in was just a bit more refined, perhaps a bit better educated, than her Here. How his book got into her Here was another story; maybe the guy who wrote those Oz books had the right idea all along. Only a place called Oz wasn't waiting for you at the end of the twister, just another Here. Different enough to be called There, but not so truly different from Here.

Maybe the mottled roof shingles she still needed to rake up out of her grass came from There, too. You never really could know where any given bit of debris came from, after a tornado. They still hadn't found the roof from the TLC, according to the radio. The realization that she might never figure out just where the owner of this book was came with a leaden sinking sensation, deep in her bowels; for all she knew, he could literally be in his version of her Here, maybe even in what passed for the same house. Maybe he had black broken shingles from her house on his lawn. And some of those geraniums which blew off her porch, never to be found. Or they could be somewhere in the river, or across it. That she wouldn't, that she just couldn't know, was a fact more sad than mystifying, or even frightening to her. For the places he drew were far more appealing, far better appointed, even in their ruined state, than her town could or would ever be....

Walking down the street which also formed Highway 8 a month later, she was hit with a realization far more insidious, far more hurtful, than either the tornado, or that crazed nit-wit in the flapping plaid shirt could ever have been—this town wasn't going to be able to rise up again from this tornado. So little had changed; plywood still covered most of the building windows, only now some of the buildings smelled horrible, a funky mixture of mildew, rotting wood, still-soggy insulation, and standing water; garbage was still piled knee- or hip-high behind too many buildings, most businesses torn apart by the tornado were still open-walled, their interiors exposed like forgotten doll houses, the exposed toilets and bathtubs and cashier's counters and sinks and store rooms all sadly vulnerable, to both the weather and to the effects of sun and wind erosion, while too many houses were still sporting Civil War colored blue and silver-grey tarps, and plywood windows and doors, some painted with pitiful messages and supplications to God, or offered thanks to the volunteers who'd left weeks before, leaving additional water bottle and pop can debris on the streets, dropping the cans and bottles where they stood, before moving on to the next boarding-up job. One house on the street behind hers offered up a huge blue, black and white spray-painted "ISIAH 52:10" while another—before it was torn down—had announced "ELVIS HAS LEFT THE BUILDING" along with the usual thanks to God and Volunteers. Another house had two signs, each more baffling and disquieting than the other—

GOD Bless America
One nation under GOD
In the beginning GOD
In GOD we trust
THANKs
GOD BLESS
NORTHLAND INSURANCE
ALL VOLUNTEERS
AND EVERYBODY

EVEN THE PACKERS

—given the fact that no work at all had been done on the place, and there was a "FOR SALE BY OWNER" sign in the porch window, surmounting a pair of phone numbers, neither of them local. What she found so sad was that despite all the food, water and pop they consumed, and all the Dumpsters full of debris they'd loaded during the weeks they had been in town, the volunteers' efforts seemed to be for nothing—most of the homes and businesses still remained damaged, or had been torn down (or should be torn down, including the apartment house where someone's smoke alarm battery was giving out, and kept whining and buzzing day and night), the city council and the local business men couldn't agree whether to tear it all down and start over, or try to salvage what they could, or *what*. Right after the disaster, the mayor had made statements to the paper to the effect that he was sure this tragedy would bring the usually fractious town together, but so far, all she noticed was that those who had damage were jealous of those who didn't (home owners included), and those who did get insurance settlements right away were hated by those whose companies didn't come through...the tornado ripped apart the physical town, and the people were carrying through with the damage.

One gas station's price sign carried the message "JUST SAY NO TO TORNADOS" as if they were a form of drugs one could avoid...not that this place wasn't already in the throes of tornado addiction. No one could stop talking about it, stop complaining about it, stop thinking about it, even after a month had gone by. And it was the same in wherever-the-hell that ledger book she'd found had come from, that other Here-but-not-Here...after not looking at it for a few weeks, she'd finally grown curious again, even after her power and cable had been restored (but not her job; she was getting aid created for just such contingencies, but that had to run out sometime, probably before any businesses reopened), and she really had no excuse to go reading that other person's *journal*...but there was a lack of warning, either from the weather bureau, or from the people in charge of sounding the sirens in the first place, and she was dimly aware that the cars on the highway were starting to pull into whatever parking spots they could find, while the drivers hunkered down in their seats, but still she kept on walking, thinking of that journal writer who could only jog and jog in the afterdamage time, in whatever other Here he was from. Something hard and heavy smacked into her back from behind, but she kept on walking, even as the wind started to whip her pants legs around her, pulling her forward, forward, and as she saw the swirl of debris surround her, she told herself, *Not again. No sitting in the dark, waiting for the power, no more wristbands, no more being chased by nut-jobs in bad perms, no more volunteers, no more God bless and thanks to the Packers on plywood, no more stink of rotted wood and standing filthy water and wet asbestos in buildings no one can tear down for fear they'll contaminate the whole damn town no more no more no more looking at the same debris sitting in the same places for over a month, no more of this. No more.*

The wind set her down before she knew she'd been up in the air, and as she hit the sidewalk, she almost collided with a middle aged man in grey and blue jogging sweats, his wavy brown hair flopping over his broad, sloping forehead as he huffed his way toward her. By the time she'd steadied herself, she was looking up into his face, into blue-grey eyes and a somewhat long but narrow nose, over a mouth pulled into a quirky little smile. Reaching out with his left hand, he pulled her all the way to her feet, and said, his words coming out in out-of-breath spurts, "Way the wind was blowing, I thought for sure we were going to have another tornado—you OK?" Looking past his concerned face, she saw her damaged town...*or* something very close to it, even as the very nature of the partly cleared debris was different—the loose piles of bricks and broken wood she now dimly remembered were cleaned up, and yellow and red plastic fire line and crime scene tapes were gone from buildings now neatly boarded up, their interiors no longer gaping like open mouths of decayed teeth. And on the highway, cars were moving at a reasonable pace, not rolling forward slowly as the drivers rubbernecked and gawked at the lingering damage...no one had pulled off the road to avoid a coming storm, either. There were clouds in the sky, but they weren't low-scudding, just high, well-rounded, and slightly gold-tinged from the descending sun. To her left, the railing of the Congregational Church had been replaced, with a new rounded hand-hold, while the structure itself, while obviously damaged during the latest storm, was under repair, with no flapping sheets of opaque plastic covering gaping holes in the windows or roof. Turning her head to look over her left shoulder, she saw that old small wooden building, the one she'd somehow thought was recently covered over with ugly plastic siding, had instead been repainted, with one board on the front replaced where a branch had pieced it. And as she looked back at her unexpected benefactor, she noticed a small pad of notepaper and a pencil sticking out of his right jacket pocket. Why she should find that comforting was just beyond her mental grasp, but in reply to his question, she turned to look at him, saying, "Yes, I'm OK...thanks for asking. Uhm...do you mind if I jog along with you? I could use the company...."

RUBBERNECKS

"NEVER UNDERESTIMATE THE enduring appeal of plywood, is what I think," Drew replied, in answer to my question about why people kept corning back to see Tornado Town, years after the last of the real thing actually touched down.

If the rubbernecks who continued to drive to this patch of ruined landscape dotted with broken trees and half-demolished buildings had a jones for plywood, this has to be bud-board heaven. Thing was, you could tell the original, after-damage-era plywood from the newer stuff Drew and his fellow carnies nailed up, even though Drew, Lamar, Niles, Rand and Garvan, the head prop-master, did their darndest to capture that small-town-ain't-we-grateful-we-didn't-up-and-die sense of humbled gratitude toward their volunteer-saviors when it came to spray-painting stuff on the squares and rectangles of plywood nailed over the windows and doorways of the made-for-the-tourist demolished houses and businesses. The genuine boards, back from the first decade of the century, had these quirky slogans, things like "Just say no to tornadoes" and "Thanks, God Bless, all volunteers and even the Packers." Rand told me that one of the houses which was later torn down had "Elvis has left the building" written on it, but that seems awfully generic. Either that, or the guy was like the Wizard of Oz, traveling around in tornadoes. Which might account for why he seems to favor the midwest and the southwest....Garvan's crew, they do try their best, and they get the misspellings right and all, but "It's alive!" and "Gone but not forgotten" just doesn't sound like something a town of high-school-or-less educated northern Wisconsinites would come up with. Word was, there used to be a lot of churches here, before the '02 tornado blew the Baptist one clean away, and did a lot of hurt to the rest. Supposedly the mangled iron hand rails leading up to what used to be the Congregational Church are from the real tornado, although they do look a bit contrived to me. But when you get down to it, they did a whole lot of thanking God for something He or She or Whomever might've sent to touch down in the middle of their little burg in the first damn place. Like licking the salt of the boot that's just kicked you in the nuts.

"You'd think people could buy their own piece of plywood and nail it up, look at that...this place is a hell of a ways away from anything else half-way interesting, and I wouldn't drive all that way to look at this—" I handed him a fresh-but-distressed roll of yellow "CRIME SCENE STAY CLEAR" tape, the edges pre-scored and ragged with my Swiss Army knife's small blade, which he began winding in sloppy circles around a rusted street light pole, before walking, unrolling plastic tape trailing behind him, to attach a loop of it around one of the many battered sawhorses straddling the middle of the cracked sidewalk in front of a particularly smelly corner building.

"Go ask Niles 'bout it. He was one of the real volunteers, back when it happened-happened. Once he 'tole me that every week-end, the roads were jammed bumper to tailpipe with rubbernecks, mostly from Minnesota. Most every car had them Land of 1000 Lakes license plates.Once they hit town, they'd do this crawl up and down every damn street, heads craned out the windows, which was rolled down on 'count it was a real bitch of a hot summer that year, and stared their eyeballs out."

Bending over, Drew ripped off the end of the tape with his teeth, then tossed me the rest of the roll, adding, "Niles claims that was what finally decided the folks here on what to do with what was left of this place. Don't take a fool to realize that build-ings this old, they's gonna have asbestos in 'em, and what with more than half the businesses and the accompanyin' tax base wiped out, no one had the dough for a real hazmat team to come in and clean up the mess proper, so...'cording to Niles, who was from some town not too far from here to begin with, it was getting to be a bone of contention among the city council—"

"'City council'? Even before the twister hit, what was this place, around four, five thousand people tops? That's a *village*, for—"

"Don't look at me, kiddo. They was incorporated, and had a city style government. And Niles says they never did top over four thousand souls, least not in the 2000 census. *Any*who, they had them a city council. Which couldn't agree on what to do with all the mess on 'count of winter coming on, and them being faced with a hell of a lot of brick and wet insulation and broken-apart houses that nobody wanted to pay to have torn down on 'count of them being owned by out-of-town slum lords who were mostly behind on their taxes anyhow...so some towns people sat, and says, 'Why don't we just turn the whole thing into a big haunted house come this Halloween?' Once folks got done laughing, some of 'em got to thinking, put the current state of ruin together with the long lines of cars clogging the roads come week-ends, and added in all them out-of-state-plates and...after figuring the cost of repairing versus actually tearing down and starting over, 'specially with no actual guarantee that any new businesses would want to come to a place that was turning into a tornado alley after three bad storms in five years, they eventually come to *this* conclusion," Drew finished grandly, extending his chewed-down nailed hands up and down the now-empty streets for emphasis.

The *"this"* Drew spoke of was the carnival-cum-theme-park-cum-pseudo-historical-exhibit known for the last five or so years as Tornado Town. The place still officially carried its original name, Ewerton, which was what was stamped on any outgoing mail at the post office located further down the perpetually ruined main street. The stamp for outgoing mail also had a little twister motif on it, sort of like those specialty logos they use come Christmas time, featuring the Grinch or whatever. They sold special post cards showing the genuine, from Labor-Day-2002, tornado damage, too.

Rand had a whole set of the Tornado Town postcards, back in his tent pitched behind some of the ruined-house façades over on that street which was hit hardest by the original twister. The plywood-fronted and blue or grey tarp-roofed "houses" were really three-sided things, which shielded the carney workers' tents and small RV's from the view of the rubbernecks. While he was showing me his set of postcards, Rand told me that people still living in the untouched part of town, all those houses south of the by-the-river damage, didn't want "nothing to do with" the whole Tornado Town set-up, instead preferring to shop and work and play on the weekends in some of the neighboring towns, mostly out of the county, but "they sure do like the money this set-up brings in come tax time each January. Then we's good enough for the likes of *them*."

Back when I first came here, in late July, I pitched my tent next to Rand's, since he was easily the biggest, meanest-looking, and worst-mannered of the carnies, and I figured if I was bunking down next to him, anyone who bothered with my stuff would eventually have to bother with *him*, and he didn't even like for people to look at his postcard collection, unless he offered first. So he had me sit down on what he called his "guest suite" which was really one of the biggest pink rocks I'd ever seen in my life, and showed me his collection after I'd been camping out next to him a couple of days. Once I'd balanced my ass on the squat rectangular rock ("took me two days of diggin' to get that thing, and when I leave it goes with me, so don't go farting on it"), he unwrapped his collection of postcards shoved under his sleeping bag in a wad of those brown paper towels that come in gas station washroom dispensers, and handed them to me, while he sat on yet another huge rock (this one mottled grayish) and watched me flip through his collection. He did have more postcards than what was sold in either the post office lobby or the various convenience stores which lined Highway 8 coming into town, including ones taken from pictures snapped minutes after the tornado ripped through Ewerton just around 4:20 P.M. on that terrible Labor Day afternoon. Wet pink insulation hung from maple and oak trees like mutant Spanish moss, while fist-sized hunks of plywood and sprinkles of shattered green and clear and smoke colored glass covered the shiny green grass, and everywhere, just everywhere, were houses and buildings with broken-out windows, the curtains inside hanging limp and lopsided on the outsides of the sturctures, like a dog's lolling tongue, and store fronts were blasted, signs broken into hundreds of jigsaw fragments, to be scattered for blocks in either direction. A sign reading "Dean Motel" was lying on a residential lawn, far from the actual two-storied motel itself, whose one side was just gone, revealing a double-stacked doll's house of just-bedrooms. Cars were flipped upside down, or wrapped around power poles. What was left of the old water tower looked something like Dr. Loveless' big iron tarantula in that 1990s *Wild, Wild West* movie, only less rusted.

"Once you've been post-carded, you've hit the big time," Rand told me, before lighting the Camel he'd shoved between his lips. "I heard tell they sell these cards in the Metropolitan Museum of Art...not the ruins ones, but the graffiti ones, from the houses. Me, I likes the one from that gas station out on the highway...'Just Say No to Tornadoes'...that's a hoot. My sister's boy, he bought her a copy of that one when he was in New York City. That's how I knows it's sold there. She sent me the receipt and everything. So I'm not bullshitting you, boy. This place, it's post-*carded*. Like the Mona Lisa or all them places on a European tour you never gets the time to go to when you're there, but can say to your friends you saw it for real-real through the bus window."

Some of the buildings Drew and I were "distressing" for the coming weekend's shows were pictured on those postcards in Rand's collection, and darned if he wasn't right...this place was post-card worthy, if only for the fact that it was the only small town in all of America which put all its post-tornado efforts into staying just as ruined, just as moldy-looking (sprayed-on flocking, though, the real stuff was a health hazard), and just as stinky (weird how you can literally get any kind of funky odor in a can nowadays...John Waters would surely dig this place, if he had a mind to come to the upper buckle of the Bible Belt any time soon) as it was in the sorry weeks just after the disaster, when the streets were crawling with volunteers and out-of-town cops and deputies and Red Cross workers and ambulance-chaser contractors and roofers with photocopied flyers in canvas sacks slung under their arms, ready to be shoved in the mailboxes of those with the worst structural damage to their houses and week-end rubbernecks and news crews from as far away as Milwaukee and the Twin Cities and National Guard members and the out-of-town slumlords who hauled ass into town for a change to guard their precious rental properties and towns-people who took to just wandering around in a sleep-deprived daze for days, then weeks, and once the worst of the debris was hauled away, they were still left with a sorry looking wreck of a town, and no way to properly fix it up, so...they left it that way. On purpose. And, eventually, for money.

Drew took a hammer out of the loop on his carpenter's pants and started whacking on one of the plywood sheets covering what used to be the window of a place called (according to the after-images left behind once the wooden letters spelling out the name of the store were removed) "Len's Bottom Dollar," saying between ringing thwacks! of the hammer head against bud-board, "Thing is, it ain't cheap to keep a town lookin' so weather-blasted...which is why some of them buildin's is shrink -wrapped with that plastic-shell stuff. Them's the ones with the worst asbestos in 'em. Go on, look behind the plywood on that corner shop we was standing by—"

While Drew continued to hammer up the flapping rectangle of plywood, I walked back to what had once been a Hallmark store, a shoebox configuration tan brick rectangle fronted with loosely-applied sheets of plywood over what had been the windows. Peering into the gap between the plywood and what had been a window beyond, I saw the dull shine of taut-pulled plastic underneath…. Feeling the brick surface of the walls, I noticed that the texture wasn't as rough as it should have been, but was instead semi-smooth…damned if Drew wasn't right. What they couldn't decontaminate, they shrink-wrapped and left to rot from within. Two doors down was one of the faked-ruined buildings, an attraction, actually—judging by the sun-bleached flyers still taped to the insides of the unbroken windows, this had been a carpet and shoe store ("From sole to floor, we've got you covered!"), but now, it was a combination fun-house and obstacle course and mini-maze, all rolled into one 50¢ a pop attraction. Guy named Calder ran this one, stood outside the door, wearing one of those blaze orange tie-on vests the rescue volunteers used to put on during the aftermath of the real twister, and "let" people go in, two at a time, and just do their thing amid the fake, sanitized and safety-first rubble and falling ceiling tiles and candy glass covering the floor. They had extra support poles and rolls of carpeting and what-ever else might constitute enticing junk in there, and for half a buck, anyone with a mind to could root around in the mess, in search of a hidden goodie (small plush animals like they usually give as prizes in rifle shoot booths, souvenir pairs of little shoes stamped with the saying "I Survived Tornado Town!" and gift certificates for free cones of insulation yellow or pink cotton candy) among all the funk-in-a-can scented debris inside.

I'd seen Calder (he was an RV guy, didn't do much talking to us tent guys, in some sort of carny pecking order I didn't quite understand yet) prancing around in his hard hat and his flimsy orange vest, practicing his spiel, but hadn't had the nerve to ask him what the attraction *was*, letting people cross over a velvet rope of droopy red "Fire Line Do Not Cross" tape, to go crawling around in the half-dark of a phony ruined shoe and carpet store, so Drew explained it to me one morning, while we were waiting for a free spot in one of those blue port-a-potty's lined up right in the street near the reconstructed residential disaster area near the river (just as they'd been lined up on the sidewalks on the less-damaged side of the street all those years ago, next to the big buckets of ice water holding bottles of spring water meant for the volunteers, sitting right on people's lawns):

"Who don't want to go pokin' thru a building that's fixing to fall down on your head? The combination of shredded insulation, bust glass and broke wallboard can be mighty tempting, 'specially when the whole unsteady shebang is wrapped up with yellow and red crime scene ribbons."

"Well...I wouldn't, for one," I'd started to say, to which Drew replied, "And I suppose you never played with big cardboard boxes when you was a kid, neither?"

I shook my head, and luckily someone emerged from the port-a-potty nearest to me, so I never did hear what Drew thought about kids who didn't play with discarded cardboard boxes. I knew it would be colorful, if not hurtful.

Today, though, Drew seemed to have forgotten about my appalling childhood disdain for things shapeless and discarded, so intent was he on giving me the Tornado Tour—my history lesson for today:

"Then they noticed how people reacted when the big machines was in town, cranes and cherry pickers and bull-dozers...big crowds would assemble to watch, 'course, most folks didn't have jobs for a long time afterward neither, so this was something to do 'sides fight with their insurance carriers over settlements, or sit talkin' to the FEMA people in their trailer parked in the IGA parking lot. Hell, they've made a fortune out of those video tapes for young'uns, showin' all the big monster trucks and whatnot doin' their thing, so why not have the same stuff for the big kids? Maintenance on a cherry picker or a crane is less expensive than a Ferris wheel or a tilt-o-whirl, and the insurance is about the same—all you need is extra safety harnesses for the rubbernecks. The wind machines, and the buildings on gimbals, that came later on, once some money started rollin' in from the first two Tornado Town days they held. That was when they started to get us real carnies involved, once they improved the attractions, made 'em more complex. That's where Lamar came in, he used to work over in

La-La Land, doin' some sort of back stage work for some syndicated TV science fiction show. Only he said they didn't use no
gimbals under the sets, to make 'em rock when the space ship got
hit. The people was just real good at rocking in their seats, and
pretending to get alien-hit. Gimbals cost the big bucks, which
is a sure sign this place is makin' some serious bucks, even if it
don't trickle down to us workers. 'Course, 'cording to Niles, this
town's always been famous for not spreadin' whatever wealth it
did have around. Real caste system oriented, he says. Like when
the twister hit, and they was askin' for donations. Money came
in, but most of the locals never saw one Abe's head worth of it.
Business men kept it for themselves, mostly. Went and bought
some new Christmas decorations, to hang over the main street
come Thanksgiving. Like a big plastic ornament with a light-up
center is gonna improve the tax base.

"So...once they hit on this Tornado Town idea, and started
workin' to make it a reality, most of the common folks, includin'
them that lost most of the houses they've re-created near the
river, they didn't get squat. Least that's what Niles tole me. You
ask him, he'll tell you what's what with this place."

Niles may've been smaller than Rand, and less talkative than
Drew or Calder put together, but in many ways, he scared me
more than all three of the other men squeezed together. One
of those smallish, thin, grey haired guys with a haircut that's
always a bit too short, and clothes that are just a little too clean
and tucked in, always. The kind who doesn't talk much, but
when he does, watch out. Anyone who stays bottled up for that
long at a time almost surely will spew out like a shaken soda
bottle once you do try to open him up. Niles was in charge of
the gaffed houses, the ones designed to seemingly blow apart
when the tree and false-house-fronted wind machines were
turned on at precisely 4:20 P.M. each day that Tornado Town
was open for business. Everything strung together like a mari-
onette, with wires and pulleys attached to just about every piece
of insulation, wallboard and shingling, so everything would fly
out precisely come the magic twenty-past the appointed hour,

then magically pull back in place once all the rubbernecks were gone for the evening.

I had no real reason to talk to the man directly, until the afternoon when the place was full of gawking tourists, most whooping it up while riding the cherry pickers, or pretending to crawl around in what had been someone's house years before, until the town took it back in lieu of taxes owed, or wandering around aimlessly, nibbling foot long Disaster Dogs (covered with tons of mustard and dyed pink pickle relish, plus tossed on corn chips to simulate wall board or some such hunk of debris) or licking cones of pink or yellow cotton candy—and Lamar got himself a royal case of the trots from actually eating some of the swill sold to the rubbernecks. (The rest of the carnies, even newbies like me, knew better than to eat that local-yokel crap.) So he was there, sitting in one of those little blue plastic port-a-pottys (or as Rand called them, Crap Castles), saying through that little black mesh screening along the top of the potty, "Man, you gotta cover for me—no way no how can I do it today. Just go tell Niles it's OK with me—"

I didn't stick around to listen for the rest of the sound effects, but pressed through the crowd, looking for Niles. He was fiddling with the piano wire and fishing-line rigging attached to the break-away window mullions in one of the Twister Homes, as they were called in the official Tornado Town brochures ("See a real home blown to bits by the simulated F3 twister!") when I walked up, and all he needed to see was my approaching shadow before he asked without looking up, "Lamar can't make it? You know *anything* about gimbals? I'm not in the mood to—"

I'd seen enough of those Discovery Channel "Movie Magic" shows from the late 1990s to know what a gimbal was, and basically how it was worked via remote controls to be able to hunker down near him and say, "Enough to know what to do if you show me once. It's this house, right? Rocks about ten degrees to the southwest, no?"

"Twelve degrees, and yes, it is to the southwest. The control box is in that port-a-potty over there...the one marked 'Broken.'

Don't wrinkle your nose, there's no seat in there. The town owns it, along with these houses. You're smaller than Lamar, so it should be a more comfortable fit for you. There's a riser built in, so you can see the house through the mesh around the top. I'll show you what to do once I get this done...you been here long, kid?"

"Not nearly as long as you have, according to Drew...about three weeks, give or take a few days."

"Rand show you his postcards yet?"

"Few days ago."

"Get to sit on his rock?"

Niles tied the free ends of the fishing line attached to the mullions to a control board inside the house, speaking over his shoulder as he worked.

"As long as I didn't cut one on it. He's a cool guy, though."

"Yeah, they're all cool guys, compared to the locals. And the locals look like saints, next to the rubber-necks," he said with a disdainful prissiness that all but shouted the hyphen between "rubber" and "necks."

"Niles...why do they call the tourists 'rubbernecks'?"

"Come on, you're a college boy, aren't you? Went to college at least? Thought so. Didn't you read *Nightmare Allley*? See the movie *Freaks*? Of course, I'm not sure if they defined rubber-neck in there, but it's so obvious...necks like rubber. Bend in either direction, so they can take in every damn thing. Gawkers, with no sense of decorum or style, just...rubbernecks. Back when this all happened for real, I was one of the first volunteers on the site, I lived only eight miles away, in an even smaller village than this place, but we had the sense to call it a village, so it was a short drive for me. I was off from school—I used to teach, close to retirement, but I was still a science teacher—and when I heard it on the radio, I was in my pick-up and down the road before the station had time to repeat the news. I worked the tents set up by the court house, giving people bottled water, handing out wristbands, signing in the other volunteers who came later. For weeks afterward, the sight of a metal tub filled with icewater and bottled spring water made me nauseous. You can't imagine what it was like. This circus freak show has nothing on what really went on. Helicopters droning up above for hours on end, streets backed up with cars and trucks, cop cars from towns and cities even I'd never heard of, including some from the Indian reservation to the south, that yellow and red disaster tape wrapped around just about everything, people with wristbands, like a hospital had exploded, dumping out all the patients...just hellish. I'd never seen so many loose bricks in my life, or so much wet insulation.

"For the most part, the people were all right, townies and lend-a cops, and the Red Cross people, that's their job to be OK, but there was this one bitch, The Wicked Witch of the East, I called her, that made me want to tie a bunch of wristbands together, and strangle her with them...she blew into town two days after all this happened. Skinny shrew with less brains than body fat, running around on a hot as hell day with a god-damned flannel shirt on over another shirt, and this stupid head of sprayed curls, all bobbing like yo-yos on her damned head, and she's marching around, terrorizing the locals. One gal, I used to see her around here when I'd come into town, but I haven't seen her since not long after all this happened, she comes to the tent, crying, barely able to talk, saying that this whacko had come running after her, telling her she had the wrong wristband...like there was really such a thing as a right wristband, since we were using left-overs from the county fair, and they came in about five different colors to *begin* with. Anyhow, this over-dressed nutso started harassing her, wouldn't let the woman go to the stupid post office. Like this little woman—she was maybe five two at the most, just swimming in the shirt she was wearing, had these little tiny hands, like a hamster or a raccoon—was going to shove half a building under her shirt and run off with it. Or climb into an open window and start looting. I saw she had a letter in her hands, for Chrissake! You don't carry a stamped envelope in your hand if you're planning to go loot a building. So we ended up giving the woman another damned band, like we really had any more to spare, and then I agreed to help her find this weirdo. Damned if the bitch wasn't coming over to the cop shop on the west side of the court house, maybe to tell the cops how to do their job. The gal she'd screamed at points her out, and damned if she doesn't come tearing across the sidewalk, ready to tear all four of our eyes out. Damnedest, nastiest thing I saw all the while I worked there. Don't know what sort of bug was up her crack, but it had to be a big nasty one with pinchers and feelers. I told the shorter woman to get going, and I tried to steer Miss Crazy Legs of 2002 over to the inside of the cop shop, but she's shouting about how she hadn't slept in forty-eight hours, how the National Guard was keeping watch over some rental property of hers, which I knew for a damned lie, since the Guard wasn't watching any private property, but patrolling the streets, and how she hated that other woman for being so "wimpy"—and I just told her to get lost, and out of my sight. We were so busy, I didn't have time to kick her ass from the tent down to the river...but God, I wish I had. After things settled down, I kept trying to look out for that other woman, the one she'd attacked, but I never saw her again. And I'm sure she was a local, too. Someone else driven out of town, and not even directly by the tornado. Damn shame....

"Ok, you see this control panel?" We were trying to both squeeze into the *faux* port-a-potty, where Niles was showing me the remote controls for the gimbal-mounted houses by the river. House One (the place whose windows he'd been rigging) was to tilt in one direction, while House Two (a low slung ranch, with an attached garage that was rigged to fly off toward the river) was to rock in place for exactly fifteen seconds, then settle down slowly once the wind machines stopped. I retraced his instructions on the turned-off keyboard, just to show him I understood, before he went on, "It's gotten to the point where I dread the sight of a car with Minnesota plates. If you ever find yourself on the highways in or out of Minnesota, don't ever get stuck behind any old geezer from that state wearing a hat, and driving a big whale of an older car. Guys like that, they never go faster than forty in a fifty-five-mile zone, and if they do want to make a turn, they'll never signal. We had dozens of them come into this town every weekend after the tornado, to survey the damage. And they kept on coming, even when everything was covered with plywood, and tarps, and reasonably cleaned up. The same damn people, too—I started to recognize their vehicles. They were worse than a guy wearing a Packer jacket on a Sunday morning, not stopping at the stop signs because he can't wait to get home for the pre-game show. Same sort of bad, no, ignorant driving. God, no wonder this place has become the Disneyworld of the northwoods. How some people will pay to look at anything—"

I wanted to ask him more about the town itself, the things Drew told me to ask him, but after hearing the rage in his voice as he recounted the story of that curly-haired Wicked Witch of the East, I decided against it. The man would be working high powered wind machines in a few hours, and I didn't want to get him even angrier than he already was....

"Kid, you got a radio on you?" Drew's sun-weathered face was blanched under the leathery hide, his eyes darting strangely under his bristling gingery eyebrows, as he sat down next to me during our lunch break. I knew that the pseudo volunteers who roamed the few blocks of Tornado Town open for the public routinely handed out small portable radios (freebies emblazoned with various sponsor logos, right on the bodies of the things), mimicking the real volunteers who'd handed out radios donated by Wal-Mart during the '02 twister, so I motioned to one of the gals wearing the requisite orange nylon vests, and asked her to throw me a radio. Once I got it out of the plastic shell (no easy feat, since I had to use my Army knife), and put the batteries in, Drew grabbed it from me, and started tuning it to one of the area stations. He listened to some classic rock for a few minutes, while I ate my sandwich, until a voice came on from the station's "live radar update" center, announcing that there was a severe storm warning for all of Polk, Wright and

Dean counties, until three thirty that afternoon. It had seemed awfully hot and humid that day, especially for September, and while I'd been too busy to notice before, the clouds in the hazy sky did look rather weird...low scudding and sort of limp. And there wasn't much of a breeze....

"Kid, you have anything you gotta be doin', like *now*?"

"I have to take over for Lamar come four twenty—"

"Don't go worryin' about no four-twenty. I don't think Niles's gonna need you...go find Rand, he's workin' the cherry picker. Tell him to get his ass down to the cop shop down the street, into the basement. Then *you* follow him. I'll get Calder and Lamar if he's done crappin' his guts out yet."

"You don't really think...."

"Thinkin's got nothing to do with it. Just go *do*. I'll get Niles, too. Garvan's on his own, he don't let nuthin' get to him. Go, would'ja?"

"Go" is what I did, even as I realized that Drew hadn't said anything about me warning the locals or the rubbernecks. There wasn't any rain, but darned if you couldn't feel that something was coming. In the distance, down the residential streets, where Tornado Town rubbernecks were no longer welcome, I could hear dogs barking and howling, and I saw squirrels running around without nuts in their mouths, just running for the sake of running somewhere that wasn't where they were.

I found Rand, and he was quite willing to lower the basket on that cherry picker in mid-ride after he heard the words "*Drew said to go*—" even as the woman riding in the basket, a wiry meatless skinny thing with a head of blonde permed curls and skinnier legs jutting out from under a pair of denim shorts began ragging on him, shouting, "I just paid for this ride, you goon! You put me back up there, now—get your fat ass back in that cab"—and I've never been much of a believer in serendipity before, but that just had to be Niles's Miss Crazy Legs of 2002. She had to be, I felt it in every molecule of my body. And I knew just the man she'd need to see about that ticket price she'd just paid, too....

Rand and I met up with Drew and Lamar and Calder in the elevator leading down to the cop shop/court house basement; the way we were dressed, I suppose the cops thought we were janitors or something, and never asked us where or why we were all piling into that little elevator clowns-in-a-car fashion, and frantically jabbing the button marked "B." Once we were down there, we felt sort of stupid, sitting on folding chairs next to this huge furnace, smelling the slightly wet basement odors, and looking at the black mottled grey cement walls, not saying anything to each other, not needing to, either, and I don't think any of us felt any real guilt over not saying anything to anyone as we came down to the basement. This was Tornado Town, after all—free battery radios were just being handed out like Mardi Gras beads. You didn't even need to show anyone your pecs or your tits to get one. And the cops above all should've been listening, too—

After a while, I did ask Drew where Niles was, but he just said, "Them wind machines, they're bolted down real good, and Niles is a strong little sucker. He'll do OK. He'll still be up there." And so we sat, like those kids in that *Signs* movie, all of us in a row on those beige folding chairs. All we needed were those little silver foil caps on our heads, to make sure the locals and the rubbernecks didn't read our thoughts. I wondered how Niles was, but he was a wiry little sucker, he'd make it. I just hoped that nut-case bitch found him, and stayed long enough to make my efforts worth while in sending her there.

Some people say that tornados make a train noise, they have something like that on the speakers mounted near the houses on gimbals down that river-front street, but I thought the sound was more like giant lips whistling across a Paul Bunyan-sized bottle. Just this low rumbling *whoosh*, then you could hear glass breaking, heavy stuff falling, and that terra-cotta tinkle of bricks falling. Then, it got quiet. Trouble was, the power went out, so we had to find the stairs leading back up to the court house proper in the dark. Drew was first, then Calder, then me, then Lamar and Rand brought up the rear, and all Rand kept saying all the way up those dark steps was, "Don't you go letting them go on me, man. I needs my oxygen—"

Ironically, the place didn't really look all that different once we got topside, oh power poles were down, and more than the windows were broken in the court house this time around, as in not only the wooden shield in front of the giant air conditioner was gone, but the A/C unit was blown halfway into the parking lot of the thirty-minute women's fitness center across the street but the folks who had designed Tornado Town more or less got it right. This time, there were bodies, which I suppose is natural with an F4 tornado. Which is what I later learned this one was... what hadn't been flattened the last time sure was flattened this time. I looked over at the riverfront where the Tornado Town false houses used to stand...nothing but open skyline, now. My tent was gone, as were the RVs parked back there, too. Rands' two rocks were still there, though. His sleeping bag and the post-cards were long gone, confetti in the twister. If he was lucky, he might find them on some local's lawn, later on.

But over at the end of the street,where the wind machines were, Niles was still there, arms wrapped tightly around the base of the wind machine, his skin bloody, and his face pierced in countless places by small shards of glass, but when I reached him, all he did was smile, and say through puffy lips, "Go look over there...that's why they call them rubbernecks," before letting go of the steel framework, and slumping to the ground, that weird smile still creasing his face.

He was OK, despite the bleeding, so I walked through the fresh, wet debris, over to what remained of House One, the two-storied gimbal fun house. It had fallen over twelve degrees, to be sure, but it didn't just get blown over. It had fallen on some trees, but also on someone...white sneakers and too-thin legs were just visible, resting in a pool of blood that kept spreading outward, toward my own boot sales before I jumped back a few feet, and started laughing, my eyes watering, especially after I realized that that bitch's neck, hell, her whole body, would sure be rubbery after a damned house fell on her. From where he lay by the wind-twisted scaffolding of the wind machine, Niles said, "I think this house was a rental property...."

Me and Drew and Niles and all the rest of the carnies, we left the next day. Volunteering wasn't our job, and even though Niles had been one, he already had gotten the amusement he was seeking after all these years, so as far as he was concerned, his real job here was over, done with. I hitched a ride out of town with Drew, and Rand (who took along his big rocks, because "I dug them things out of the ground with these two hands, and they's going with me!"), who sat in the back of the pick-up with his big pink and grey rocks and all the rest of our gear.

"Think they'll ever have another Tornado Town?"

"Once all the free action is gone, and the helicopters and the fourwheelers are out of here, yeah, sure, people are gonna start getting the jones for that nailed up plywood. Once the rubber-necks from Minnesota clear out, the roads should be free again. Give 'em time. We'll be back. It'll go back up again. Only this time, Tornado Town's gonna be a Tornado *City*...gonna be more of us carnies. I'm thinkin' about buyin' me a bunkhouse—you know what one of them is, right? One of them long, long trailers, sub-divided into renting rooms? Well, I'm gonna get me one of them, be a travelin' slum lord. Beats a tent, cheaper than your own RV. Wanna get in on it? I know where I can get one third-hand, down in G-town in Florida."

While I thought about it, all I could hear was the drone of helicopters, criss-crossing over our heads as we waited on the clogged highway for the cop from the Indian reservation up in Hayward to let us cross the intersection.

AFTERWORD
EWERTON DEATH TRIP

Perhaps the best way for me to approach an afterword for this collection is in increments, bits of background for each story by an overview of the real_Ewerton... *aka Ladysmith, Wisconsin.*

"Night Skirt"

Many years ago, a hardcover short story collection called *Masques* came out, and in it was a story from the well-respected horror writer Jessica Amanda Salmonson, plus a brief tale of a story she didn't write, based on an idea she had during the night, scribbled down, then looked at the next morning and discarded...something called "Night Skirt." Well, at the time I had her address, since I belonged to a writer's organization with a membership list, and I wrote and asked her if she'd be willing to allow me to write a story based on her idea...she graciously agreed, albeit somewhat bemusedly. For her, the words were meaningless, but for me, they immediately conjured up a tale of a most magical skirt...one which those who have read the book *The Amulet* will recognize as the prologue of that novel (albeit in somewhat different form). Personally, I like the *way* the story turned out better than the novel itself..

Many years ago, there used to be an A&P store (which later became a Super Valu, then was bought out by Fairway Foods, then it became a Sears outlet, then it morphed into a combination of Curves, a tanning salon and a big-vehicle storage unit) which had a window with a ledge along the bottom. Upon which, one very cold morning, I happened to see several empty baby food jars lined up in a row. Just looking at those abandoned empty jars lined up on that window ledge made me wonder where the baby who'd consumed the food was...and this story came into being. I also knew a woman very much like the evil Inez, who also popped up briefly in *Amulet*, who'd caused me a bit of grief, and I just couldn't resist tweaking the shrew in the story. Plus, I honestly am not into kids or babies, nor do I think they're always a good idea in a marriage already tainted by poverty. There was one line in the story which the editor cut out prior to publication, in which the husband says that there's nothing worse-looking than a pregnant woman, which in turn helps to fuel the wife's decision to abort. Ironically this same basic idea (what may have been the first in a subsequent wave of stories dubbed by some editors "The Revenge of the Aborted Fetus") also came to an author up in Canada, Augustine Funnell, who wrote and submitted a story called "Tiny Feet" to the same publication "Four Days..." was published in, at virtually the same time I did, only his story took a bit longer to reach the New York office of the editor...who liked both stories, and actually asked me over the phone if I'd mind if he printed the other story, even though it had a few minor similarities to mine. I said, Hey, why not? so Funnell's version came out a few issues later. And it was a better story than mine, so I'm glad he got his version of this same basic theme into print, too.

"The Holiday House"

One night, I had this dream about a group of boys who were daring each other to enter a haunted, empty house, and the dream cut out just as one boy was about to enter this room which was extremely *green* inside, as if sunlight was reflecting on intense, lush vegetation, but I never saw what was in the room itself. I actually ended up doing three versions: this one, "Double Dare Ya," and "Not a Haunted House At All," each of which had a different "haunting." At one point I tried to work a revamped version of this tale into my novel *Dark Journey*, but it didn't work out, and I ended up cutting it out. The "Holiday House" itself was based on a (then) sage green house in my town, which was rather huge...and visually arresting, in a late Victorian *way*. The house did survive the tornado of September 2, 2002, although some of the gables *were* damaged, and badly repaired, so the roofline was messy and bumpy, plus the new owners turned it into a duplex, and for some reason stuck a huge wooden cross on one front gable, and ripped out the stained glass windows upstairs. The house is now grey with white and purple trim, and an incomplete front porch, which lacks horizontal railings.

"Simon Says"

I don't like to think about this one too much; much of what little Charlie went through was based on things my mother and grandmother used to do to me, and how they loved to make me squirm and cry. One side note; when I was subbing this to the editor at *Night Cry*, he actually called and asked me if Andy raped little Chuckie when they went upstairs—it was bothering him, and I could tell by his voice that if I said Yes, the sale would be off. So I lied.

"Garbage Day in Ewerton"

This one was literally a dream, one which haunted me for years, and eventually spawned a couple of other stories, "Just Another Bedtime Story" and "The Last Bedtime Story" which *were* published in a couple of magazines (*Night Cry* and *Grue*), back in the 1980s. But the bare bones of what happens here came to me in the dream, including the last thing the little girl says to her mother. And as I said before, I'm not into kids, so I have no idea *why* I dreamed that. It was so horrible, it woke me up, and unlike most dreams, this one's details stayed with me upon waking. It was so utterly vivid....

"When the Bad Thing Comes"

The origin of this one is so silly, it's almost unbelievable, but it did happen to me—back when Rubik's Cubes *were* the rage, I was working at this one motel/bar, and the owner's son had a knock off cube which was bigger/had more rows than the usual Rubik's Cube. One day while I was cleaning up the bar, I took the thing down off the back shelf and tried to play with it, and somehow I had my hand too close to it while I was turning it, and (how I have no idea save that I'm an incredibly clumsy person!) a bit of my flesh got caught between the moving rows, and it pinched me hard enough to feel as if it bit me. That is how I came up with this story. I actually based the two brothers on the two sons of the motel owner (which was necessary, since I'm an only child and have no real experience with sibling rivalry), plus I tossed in some characters from the novel I was working on at the time, *Dark Journey*. And my mother did have a cousin who literally did try to saw down the two-by-fours holding up some relative's house. Why he was doing that, no one knows. Apparently the kid was a total brat, into everything. But at one time I was hoping to expand this novelette into a novel; I had a third novel option on my contract with Bantam, but my editor hated the first two novels I'd turned in, she hated me, and she was in the process of starting to hate her husband, my editor at *Night Cry*, and on top of all that negative feeling toward me, Bantam was being sold to a German company, and a lot of writers' contracts weren't being honored all the *way* (I know of one writer whose trilogy was suddenly turned into a two-book series), so I guess I was lucky to get both contracted books published at all.

"Street Coffins"

One day during the city-wide clean-up days in the fall, this one house in the neighborhood where I was living at the time actually did put out a steel coffin (one of the folks in the house worked for the coffin factory which used to be located here). But I couldn't quite come up with a complete storyline for this, so I started a story, and sent it to my long-time pen-pal and former small press magazine editor John S. Postovit, for expansion. He added in the part about the body of the dead little girl from "Garbage Day..." and the ending. By the time it was written, *Night Cry* was pretty much dead, so it ended up being published in a one-off small press magazine. **Note by John S. Postovit**: "A. R. sold this story to *Bone-Chilling Tales* as a package with an illustration I did of it. By an odd coincidence, the figure in the illustration bore a strong resemblance to A. R., yet I'd never seen a picture of her. And this was also before I was aware of her Ewerton stories as a fictional-autobiographical set."

"Trick or Treat!"

This was published on the first try at *The Horrow Show*. Around the same time, on the short lived syndicated TV show, *Tales from the Dark Side*, there was an episode which bore only the very slightest passing resemblance to this tale which also ended with some Halloween visitors to a very nasty old man turning out to be supernatural beings...and unknown to me, my then-foreign agent in Germany, a fellow later found out to be a story thief (who printed stories overseas and pocketed the money on his clients to payoff gambling debts), who did steal at least one reprint fee from me, had offered my story to a German film magazine, claiming it was the basis for the DARKSIDE episode (which it was not). I ended up asking someone in a writer's organization about the matter, since I'd never seen the episode in question, and we determined that my story was not the same one televised (much later I did see the specific episode, and it is not a rip off of my story at all, so they didn't lift my idea), but the whole episode left a bad taste in my mouth.

"Scrap When Empty"

Many years ago, the Soo Line Rail Road used to pass through Ladysmith, and the cars were decorated with some marvelously imaginative chalk sayings and drawings, many of which I included in the story. A simple idea...but one which I still enjoy, perhaps more so than all the rest of the Ewerton stories.

"Does It Ploop?"

Lots of people really like this one, judging by the sales of it on an e-book publisher I sold it to a few years ago. The old guy was based loosely on a couple of old pain-in-the-ass coots I knew at the time. The magazine *Bloodbath Quarterly* was inspired by *Night Cry*, and I do recall that this one was a lot of fun to write, but at the time my life was going a whole lot better than it has been for a long, long time, so I honestly don't think I could write anything this giddy/funny again.

"The German Lady"

I wrote about this at length in the afterward of the other short story collection in which it appeared, but since I've more or less written that collection off for various reasons (none of them very happy), I'll do a nutshell recap—this was written for a young adult antho about Green Men, but rejected for not being something a young person could relate to. It was based on some things which happened to my mother while she was working as a personal care giver in the mid-1990s/early 2000s; a lot of the old ladies she looked after were anorexic, sometimes alarmingly so. Plus there was this one WWII war bride living in town who was from Germany (although she was nothing like this woman at all; she loved to cook and eat), and I borrowed elements of her accent. It's also the next-to-last Ewerton story I've written.

"Redeem My Soul from the Power of the Grave"

This one is based on something which actually happened—a preschool teacher died, and her relatives placed little pictures of all her students in the coffin with her, including that of a Hmong child, not knowing that their beliefs prohibit such actions, due to their belief that the picture is part of the child's soul. Lawyers for the woman's family claimed there was no legal reason to dig up her remains, but the family eventually decided to have her exhumed, so the picture could be removed from the coffin and returned to the child's family. I was taken with the concept, but realized right off that I needed help on this; a pen pal of mine, James B. Johnson, served in Southeast Asia during the Vietnam War, and I knew he'd be the best person to help flesh this one out—about 60% of the writing here is actually his. I thought his work meshed beautifully with mine, and my only regret is that the story wasn't more widely known as part of the Ewerton cycle.

"This Is the Way..."

Another dream, this one very brief, totally horrible, and unspeakably weird—I used other parts of the same nightmare in a section of *The Amulet*—and the only way I could shake it was to use part of it in a story.

"The Wi'ching Well"

One of those ideas which just comes to a person all of a piece—I really can't add anything more to that, save that the "Dean Motel" was modeled on the real Davis Motel, which was destroyed in 2002's tornado. I used to work at the Davis, as a maid.

"Bringing It Along"

I was going for an Urban Legend feel here; the sort of thing which seems like it may have actually happened to someone, but didn't. The part about the bird-calls was based on something nasty my grandmother used to say to taunt my mother, when she heard Killdeers chanting what sounded like her first name. The cat was based on my own Tweetie Pie, who looked like the cat in the story, and who lived to be about sixteen years old.

"Rigent-Double Agent and the Shopping Cart Bump"

This is what happens when a person spends too many hours poring over Kenneth Anger's *Hollywood Babylon*. The stories about the dead actors and actresses are true. I was also toying with different approaches to a basic vampire theme, using age instead of blood.

"Dear D. B...."

This one started out as a story called "Initial Appeal" and in it, D. B. literally turns into a man as she writes her stories. The editor didn't like it, and I did a lot of rewriting and changing to make it into what turned out to be *Night Cry*'s final issue with this; I still think it needs work, and I'm not terribly happy with it, but people still seemed to like it, so there *you* go....

"Hunger"

This is a story I just can't write about; too much of it actually did happen to me, and they are things which are still too painful to write about—pure fact vs. slightly filtered fiction. But the opening paragraph is actually a slight rewrite of a passage from an introduction in an issue of *Night Cry*—I'd told the editor that I wanted to do a co-written piece based on that bag lady, for which I'd give him half credit, but he said no, just use it with his blessing, so I did. So even the bag lady was real. One thing I can say with only mild discomfort is that the window described in New York City (the one with the rags and air conditioner stuffed in it) was something I saw from a bus window when I was in the city in November of 1979, accompanying the college concert chorale as a paid rider on their tour bus. I was haunted by the sight of that window in an otherwise abandoned-looking building. That's all I can say about this one, for now at least.

"From the Far Away Nearby"

Yet another dream, this one of the two brothers applying the puffy pipe-A/C thingie to my then-living room window. Very vivid, but for a change, rather fun; I never could sell this story, since it was too cross-genre, but I always loved it. I actually lived in the house described, only as an adult. And one neighboring house was a trailer which looked like Will and Bill's place.

"The Cat with the Tulip Face"

The four cats in this piece were actually named Sassy, Little Guy, Puff, and Pumpkin; they're all gone now, but they were exceptional animals. Sassy did have huge ears, but he was definitely earth-bound. Arlene is based partly on myself, and partly on a woman I used to know in town here, who also used to go around early in the mornings looking for cans on the streets and in trash-cans and Dumpsters. She had numerous animals, too.

"Oksa's Children"

I actually did have a teacher in high school who'd let his icicles grow to gargantuan size one winter; as I recall, the local rag which calls itself a newspaper ran a picture of them, plus a short article. Not long afterwards, somebody broke all of them, and the teacher—who did call them his "children"—was heart-broken. I assume kids did it, or drunks—either *way*, he never let the ice build up like that on his house again. It was rather a shame; the guy was so proud of those damned things....

"Soft"

This is a story which a lot of editors didn't "get"—I don't know if it was the deliberately slow, quotidian pacing, or the lack of an eventual "reveal" of what was in the can (or even what the can was to begin with) that put them off, but this story did generate perhaps the weirdest, most bizarre "rule" of writing I've ever heard of—this one editor informed me that "only hard words" can be used to describe something soft, and that I needed to completely rewrite the story, using "hard" descriptive words *only*, no soft-and-fuzzy language, *period*. I've never heard of a "rule" like that before, but I suppose that the next time I write about a f*l*u*f*f*y cloud in the sky—I'd better describe it as knife-edged and jagged...yeah, right-Not!!!

The car wash where some of this is set exists in my town, as does an apartment house much like the one described (back in 2006, a guy who was trying to augment his income as a house painter tried to cook some meth and burned out his apartment, and nearly took down the whole building). We also used to have a gift shop with the dreamcatcher logo (and name), but that's gone now, too. And I actually did find a dead puppy in a municipal parking lot trash can, still slimy from amniotic fluid, and wrapped in a clear plastic bag—from the size of it, it was a fairly big breed. I do a lot of Dumpster and trash bin diving, looking for cans, mostly, but you never know what will show up there, especially during the summer, and throughout hunting season. (I'm a freegan, too, for those who know what that means—for those of you who don't, you probably don't wanna know how I put food on the table.) I've found a lot of neat stuff—books, garage sale stuff people buy then dump, clothes (some stuff literally new), small gifts still in their gift bags, small electronics, and once—ironically at the same car wash I used in this story—someone left thirty-two pounds worth of potting soil, all in unopened bags, next to one of the vacuums. I had a diving buddy with me that day, and yes, we took every last bag of that stuff. And by the way, I don't drive, so all my treasures come home the hard way, by hand, in bags. Which is why folks look down on me, both for looking and for hand-hauling the stuff home every early morning, but hey, if you haven't done it, don't knock it.

"River of Glass, Mirror of Water"

I wrote this story for a Romanian high school newspaper called *The Blue Danube*—which was the project of the students of a long time pen-pal and translator of my work, Petru Iamandi—the paper was named for the river which runs through his city, and he wondered if I could come up with a new story for the publication, which somehow tied in with a river. Right after it appeared there, I also placed it in a very small press magazine here in the states, since I felt the story would also be of interest to an American audience, so it was almost a simultaneous publication on two continents. The Romanians enjoyed it greatly—I have no idea what the reaction here in the States was like.

"AFTERDAMAGE"

"Debris"

On September 2, 2002, at around 4:30 P.M., an F3 tornado ripped through a small portion of Rusk County, affecting Gilman, Tony, and most significantly, the County Seat of Ladysmith. Some people, including my mother and a neighbor of ours, saw two twisters, side by side, which worked their way in tandem down Miner Avenue and Lake Avenue—one seemed to have been weaker, since the houses on one street were damaged, but many of those on the other were destroyed outright. Downtown Ladysmith was hit the hardest, with twenty-six businesses wiped out. To this day, there are still gaping holes in the downtown, and many businesses are barely hanging on (something which has been harder to do since the town let in a Wal-Mart Supercenter, which has been leeching business away from just about everything in the immediate area). But the thing that struck me the most after I left my house—once I was able to extricate the big wooden Farmer's Market sign out of my front door's former beveled glass insert—was the sheer amount of debris *everywhere*. And some of it wasn't even familiar debris, either—I still haven't figured out where those grey-red-pink specked shingles came from. For months, the whole town was discombobulated, which was odd in that the town wasn't as severely damaged as some other Wisconsin towns had been in the past (Siren's tornado literally wiped out damn near everything in sight). But this is a mean-spirited, clique-oriented, super unfriendly town and I suspect that played a part in the slow recovery—people were quick to scam FEMA (people who weren't even affected by the twister ran to claim money for imaginary damages, while people like me, who can't drive, were unable to collect so much as a dime of aid that first week), supposed volunteers in the city government and law enforcement turned around and kept monies which were paid to them in error (including the sheriff), the mayor quit his job over a dispute over some property he'd razed, then filled in without first removing "flammable" materials (a damp ceiling beam from the former basement) from the fill, and in an act of head-scratchin' weirdness, someone actually hired an Elvis impersonator out of Vegas to perform at the block party for those affected by the tornado, only instead of holding a true block party on those two most-affected streets, they held the party out at the fairground miles away from town, so again, I wasn't able to attend due to having no car. I have no idea how much it cost to pay *faux*-Elvis's plane fare and performance fee, but I do know he didn't do it for free (something the Real Elvis would've done as a charitable act!).

And I was attacked by a woman who'd gone nutty; she was the sister of a businessman, and as such, nothing was done to her, even though I did complain to the police. Out here, nothing is done to businessmen, or their kin, lest they pick up stakes and take their money with them. Over eight years later, the town still hasn't fully recovered, and I suspect it never will.

"Rubbernecks"

Clean up here took so damned long (and got so terribly smelly, with all the wet, rotting, molding wood behind stores, and the buildings which literally sat for months and even years virtually untouched) that I got to thinking that the town should just preserve the post-tornado look, and charge ticket fees to all the yahoos who drove slowly up and down the damaged sections of town, unabashedly rubber-necking, and getting in the way of the sporadic clean-up efforts. This story is specifically inspired by one editor I dealt with right after the tornado; I had a story in an anthology of his, and since he was based in Minnesota, he decided to combine my having to sign a shitload of signature sheets for the antho with some sightseeing—right after the tornado, he got word to me that he was coming into town that weekend, bringing the pages, and expected them signed before he left town. Now this was over 500 pages, and he wanted them done in a few HOURS. I begged with him to please wait, and let the other people sign the sheets first, but oh no, he wanted to not only meet me, but *see* the town while it was still freshly uprooted. Plus...I was supposedly the last one to sign that particular sheet, and this just couldn't wait. Well, I was in no shape at all to play host to a rubbernecker, so what I ended up doing was locking the plywood repaired door, and putting a big sheet of paper out on the porch railing, with a message saying, basically, I'm in no mood for you, so leave the box by the door and I'll sign the sheets in two hours. Which is what happened—the guy never did get to meet me, and I made sure I signed *every* damn one of those sheets (which, surprise, surprise, still had two-to-three other empty spaces for other writers to fill in—I was not the last one to sign the sheets, and if he had time to send them out of state, twice, he could've waited...but didn't dare risk missing out on all the fresh damage!)...even tho I felt like my hands were about to fall off when I was done. And I hurried them outside and then went back into the house and shut the door before he had a chance to *see* me.

And the irony was, the antho didn't do all that well anyhow. Served him right for pulling that crap on me.

The Real Ewerton, aka Ladysmith, Wisconsin

Even though it calls itself a city, Ladysmith (afterward referred to as LS in this essay) is actually more like a very small town/largish village with illusions of city-hood...ultra clannish, narrow-minded, bigoted, culturally backwards (although in its early days, at the turn of the last century, the "city" actually did have an opera house, a roller rink, and far more cultural perks than it does now; the population peaked at around 5,000 back in the 1930s or so, but after WWII, it began a slow, grotty decline: fervently religious, sports-hunting-fishing-oriented to the exclusion of most of the more intellectual pursuits...in short, the type of place which is just begging to be looked down upon and ridiculed. Or as a character played by the wonderfully funny actress Jane Lynch, in the Christopher Guest film, *A Mighty Wind*, described her just-outside-of Chicago home town, LS is a place pretty much "peopled with pure unadulterated white trash."

Back when the town was still named Warner, over a century ago, the town fathers were trying to get some out-of-towner with Big Bucks to settle here, so they renamed the city after his wife...who could barely stand the place, and urged her husband to leave as soon as humanly possible.

Smart woman. So LS is stuck with what is essentially a *suck-up* name, designed to lure the powerful and rich into a place that was (and still is) little more than a roughshod river town. Back in the early days, LS's whorehouse, which was located close to the railroad tracks, was infamous for its drug-and-dump practice of spiking the loggers' drinks, then stealing their pay, and dumping them onto whichever train was stopped near the whorehouse that night, and letting the boxcars take the unlucky horny-toads where ever the train was headed next. One mother was pimping out her teen-aged (as in all of thirteen years old) daughter to various businessmen, until she was finally caught and arrested.

During the Depression, a WPA artist was assigned to do a mural in the Carnegie Library, only this person had the misfortune to be 1) a woman sent to a rigidly patriarchal lil' burg, and 2) highly imaginative in that she tried to incorporate a symbolic over-sized ear of corn in among a Thomas Hart Beaton-like design of a logger straddling a river, which the local cluck-heads couldn't understand as being symbolic, and not literal...they proudly took turns standing around the scaffolding she used to paint the mural above the Postmaster's office door, heckling her, until she was so fed up she left the painting unvarnished, so that when a Postmaster in the early 1960s bowed to public pressure and painted over the mural (an offense which should have had him removed from his job, if anyone had cared enough to notify the USPS, which of course they didn't), and the layers of paint sunk into the mural, and it was unsalvageable years later, when some art teachers at the now defunct Mount Senario College were interested in at least trying to recreate the mural from existing photographs, but their efforts came to naught when all the oldsters who'd originally tortured the poor artist begged the then-Postmaster not to restore that "hated" mural! (Needless to say, the wall above the office is still bare and white.)

In the early 1990s, a representative from some major industry came into town, scouting LS as a possible site for a new factory, but after he spoke to a few people, and realized what a dump this place is, he told the mayor that he was withdrawing his offer to possibly consider LS as a worksite, and cited the facts that the people were unfriendly, the town had no culture to speak of, and that he simply didn't think any of his supervisors would want to move their families to this place. When the Mayor got word of this, he immediately called the man out of a business meeting, not only demanding to talk to him about the pull-out, but also formally requesting to know the names of those traitorous folks who'd dared to tell the man that they didn't like living here, and that they didn't think the factory folk would, either. The fellow claimed not to know who said what, but the Mayor nonetheless reported the entire rather embarrassing and pitiful incident in his weekly column in the local paper. Which is how most folks here heard about it…and the mayor actually did brag about how he forced the fellow's secretary to call him away from a business meeting.

I wish I'd had a chance to speak to that representative from the Unknown Business—I would have loved to have told him what was said to me a couple of decades earlier, when I attended the Wisconsin Junior Academy of Arts and Sciences' annual Wordsworks writing Workshop, which was held during the first week of June down in Madison, Wisconsin. Only twenty students were chosen to attend each year; you had to submit a portfolio of either fiction or non-fiction, which was sent to the WJAAS, and judged—I was the first student from LS to make it there, ever, and one of the few from North-West Central Wisconsin; most of the rest of the kids came from downstate, where the schools are admittedly better, and the cities are bigger for the most part. On the first day there, they held a picnic for the attendees, and while I was sitting on the grass with a couple of girls with whom I'd just ridden down to Madison with that morning (I couldn't drive and had no one to drive me, so I went with two other attendees from the area, in the car driven by one girl's parents), marveling at the gigantic ants which were nonchalantly climbing all over my legs *en route* to the paper plate on my lap, and the hot dog in a bun sitting on the plate—those things were about half an inch long and had heads like round push-pins—a couple of guys who were on the board of the Academy came around to speak to everyone, and one of them said to me, "I never thought I'd ever see anyone from *Ladysmith* attending this workshop!" During the rest of that week, his sentiment was echoed over and over again by the rest of the kids in attendance, most nastily by a couple of girls from the Milwaukee/Madison areas, who informed me that I came from 1) a "stupid school" whose students regularly washed out of the major universities within a semester, and 2) a "stupid county" which I soon learned was nothing but a laughing stock down in Southern Wisconsin, and 3) "one of the dumbest towns in the state." LS was deemed to be "behind" academically, and a dirty, sleazepit of a burg to boot. No one had any positive thing to say about the town, or the county. Most of the other attendees marveled that I was even able to write, let alone write fiction and poetry. Which is why I wasn't the least bit surprised by what that Unknown Factory Rep had to say about the town, but since the Mayor was born and bred here, he was flabbergasted by the man's candidness and clarity of perception.

As *you* may well guess, my family and this town have never been a good fit; if I had been able to get a driver's license back in 1976, I would have left town decades ago, but since no one in *my* family could drive, and that meant no one to drive with for practice between Behind the Wheel lessons, I ended up failing the test three times (the BTW test, not the actual driving test), due to not having any depth perception, and thus always missing the curb by more than a few inches when parallel parking. Other than that, I was able to do all the rest, but I was repeatedly told that I had to practice, but with no one to accompany in the junker car my mother had bought for me second hand that summer, all I could do was drive up and down the long driveway of the hideous wreck of a house out in the country my grandmother had bought back in 1969. I wasn't legally able to drive on the real roads with a learner's permit and no licensed driver beside me.

From the first time we came here, we were outcasts—we didn't belong to any church, there was no man in the family, none of us could drive, we weren't related to anyone in the vicinity of Rusk County, we were from Illinois originally (LS natives despise people from that state, and especially loathe people from Chicago, even though the town has quite a few former Windy City residents...all of whom are equally disliked), and my mother was, horror of horrors, a divorcée, which in the northern reaches of the Bible Belt meant she was some sort of terrible sinner. I was openly accused of being illegitimate due to nobody having seen my father, and because my grandmother, who'd come here a few months before we moved, looking for a house, was an indiscriminate flirt and somewhat man-crazy, she made a major play for the Realtor, in front of his wife, we were soon dubbed "The Three Whores of Agnes Avenue" by the woman and all the other members of her church, many of whom I went to school with. In high school, I was denied membership in National Honor Society despite being in the top ten of my class and a High Honor student because 1) I was an atheist, and the advisor for the organization called me a "devil worshipper" in front of my English class, and 2) I didn't date, which in that old crone's eyes made me a lesbian—something else she openly accused me of being, in front of my peers. I was the only student in the Honors bracket who was denied membership...and I was the only student in the school who never went to the Prom and/ or Homecoming, Sadie Hawkins, et al (and anyone who says that a *guy* cannot refuse a request for a date for Sadie Hawkins is full of it—I was soundly turned down twice in one day!). In an effort which pre-dated Stephen King's *Carrie*, one teacher did try to get a guy to take me to the Prom my junior year...and he told her he'd rather stay home than be seen with something like me. To her credit, the teacher was terribly upset by what he said to her, but that still didn't stop a group of his buddies from cornering me and threatening to beat the shit out of me for what the teacher did on my behalf.

One of my teachers asked me if I was capable of "walking and chewing gum at the same time" while another asked me "did your parents have anything that lived?" And while I could have graduated early, I wasn't able to, due to missing a quarter-credit of phys ed—I'd been unable to learn how to swim (I literally cannot float; every time I tried it I'd sink feet first to the bottom of the shallow end), nor could I do gymnastics due to a bad back/sloppy hip joints, so I ended up taking Freshman/Sophomore phys ed when I was a senior...luckily, the girls in the class were far nicer than my own classmates, and didn't treat me unkindly, and while I never did learn how to swim, I did get an eye infection from an unclean swimming pool right before graduation, so rather than risk having my mother sue the school for my medical expenses, they passed me with a "B" for the quarter, and I was able to graduate, and not merely receive the ubiquitious "Certificate of Attendance" many of my classmattes received (which was a piece of paper saying in essence that they had spent four years in school and didn't learn enough to get a diploma!). As it was, though, the school refused to tell me if I was graduating or getting the C of A—I had to go through my ceremony not knowing what was up (we received empty diploma cases on stage and were all ordered not to touch our tassles on our hats, since "most of you aren't actually graduating" as the one guidance counselor put it at the rehearsal!) until I turned in my cap and gown, and got the envelope which contained my diploma...with High Honors. By that time, my elation over graduating had been thoroughly negated, so I just went home with my family (needless to say, I was *not* invited to anyone's graduation parties).

But I think the thing about LS which to me represents the

sheer nastiness of this place was something which happened to me back in 1992—two years earlier, I'd moved into the house I now live in, and had the very ancient boiler replaced with one of those steam-generated high efficiency ones. Only thing was, the guy who installed it—a friend of my mother's—botched the job, badly, by venting the thing into an unlined brick chimney, which caused all manner of interior cosmetic problems, including badly blistered/cracked plaster on the wall of one bedroom. I informed my insurance company, seeking damages from his insurance, since the boiler itself was also defective, and had been badly installed. Well, my people contacted his people, who also contacted the maker of the boiler, and when the guy from the boiler company saw the installation, he immediately fired the guy as one of their reps, and forbade him from working on their boilers in the future. I had another repairman install a plastic venting pipe, but there was more wrong with the boiler than even the maker realized—the first guy had manually enlarged the orifices, since he'd gotten the smallest boiler possible, and needed to make it put out more heat for a house which was basically too large for the unit—and on October 17, 1992, carbon monoxide began flooding the house, only I had the flu, so I didn't notice the symptoms of the poisoning, and my mother was out of the house most of the time, so she didn't notice it, either, but on the morning of October 18, she didn't get to her part-time job, and even though her bosses kept calling the police (the station is literally only about four *blocks* from my house), they refused to come over here, and ignored the dispatcher's requests for a welfare check because they said they were "afraid" to go...all because the father of one of the deputies was the same doofus who'd installed the boiler, and got canned by the maker because of my insurance claim (which by the way was never cashed by me, due to a wicked estoppel clause attached to the thing which said, according to my lawyer, that if I were to cash the check, the guy would have the right to not only sue me for the amount of the claim, but also sue me for additional damages due to him losing his repairman job with that company, as well as loss of reputation).

The dispatcher eventually told my mother and me about this, ten years after it happened (she'd been worried about the Sheriff—who is now our Chief of Police—firing her if she told us that the entire cop shop's staff had refused to do a due diligence check); as it was, only two officers, a policeman and a deputy, both of whom were coming off duty, were willing to come to the house, by which time I'd finally been able to literally crawl out of bed, terribly sick and literally deep cherry red all over, to answer the phone, so I was able to let the two officers into the house—and as soon as they saw me, they expressed disbelief that anyone as red as I was could possibly be alive, let alone walking and talking, then ran into a house full of carbon monoxide and carried out my unconscious mother, then dragged me out, too. I wanted to stay with my cats (miraculously, none of them died, and none ran away while the fire department aired out the house) but I had to be hospitalized, too. Once there, my mother and I were treated like dirt—the wife of the deputy whose father was fired was the head of the critical care unit, and I don't know if it was sheer incompetence on the part of the hospital staff, or something else, but neither my mother or I were taken a mere forty-five minutes away to a nearby hospital which had a hyperbolic chamber, nor were we given empathetic treatment—with only one exception among the nurses, they bombarded us with repeated comments like "We can't figure out why you're still alive," "You (meaning me) must've caused the accident," "She (me, again) must've been trying to kill *you* (said to my mother)," and, repeated over and over to me during the eleven hours I was there, before signing myself out AMA, "You really should be dead."

Plus the entire time I was there, my oxygen mask was so steamy/drippy I was literally gagging and choking—they refused to allow me a cannula, even though I did better for the brief half hour or so they allowed me to wear one while I ate lunch, claiming it wasn't "giving me enough oxygen" even though it was the only time I could breathe without feeling like

I was inhaling dense foggy dew—and the staff had the nerve to tell me that they'd had to call down to Madison's poison control center, since they had "no idea how to treat carbon monoxide poisoning"!! That they said that with a straight face was all the more sickening.

And after the accident, there was no mention of it in the weekly paper at all, as if it never happened—ten years later, the same dispatcher who took the repeated calls asking for a welfare check on us told my mother and me that all the officers involved were ordered by the sheriff not to make any written reports about it, so that "she can't go filing any more insurance claims." The incident was literally buried, and while the policeman who rescued us just retired soon afterward, the deputy was soon fired for having "too much facial hair" to fit under a rescue mask...a claim the deputy tried to fight, to no avail. Eventually, he did try to run against the sheriff several times, but every time he did so, the city crew (by the way, one of the sons of the boiler installer I inadvertently got fired had a wife who was on the city crew...nepotism does run rampant out here! !) would remove his signs from all the yards and lawns... you'd see them in a heap in back of the building which housed the fire trucks every couple of years. Our sign among them.

Ever since 1992, we've been harassed by either the police department or the city crews, and whenever I try to complain about what happened at the hospital (which displayed a stunning lack of medical ethics all around that day), either the city or the police start in on us, usually within a day of my complaint to the hospital. Once, a few days before Christmas of '05, two city worker goons came knocking, demanding to go down to our basement to inspect the "tampering" we'd done to our indoor water meter, because we hadn't been "using enough water" (we're into conserving in a big way), and despite our protests, marched down to the basement...and found out we'd done absolutely nothing to the meter. Did I get an apology when I asked for one? I was told that the next time, they'd bring along a cop "for our protection" from me, and a "search warrant." Really *lovely* Christian behavior right before their most significant holiday.

Due to this incident from 1992, I'm firmly convinced that if anything bad ever happens to me or my house, no one will lift a finger to help me or try to save the house—it's just the way this town works. If you're related to at least one Important Family who's been here since the glaciers, you're OK...otherwise, you're an eternal outcast. While moving is not an option for me, mainly due to not being able to drive myself and my belongings out of here myself, I do take small comfort in knowing that my continued presence is a major thorn in the side of the Powers That Be here. And over the years, for various reasons, I've written my tales of a lightly fictionalized Ladysmith, just to get the real word out, and set the myth of this place being a nice little place to live on its scabrous ass. But my fictional creation pales in comparison to the real place, which is far more vicious, underhanded, petty and festeringly putrid than anything I can come up with.

Before I sign off, here's a little anecdote for the road: The first time I went to get myself a non-driver State ID card, I was repeatedly asked by the fellow working at the local DMV (a rather portly specimen with a lank, greasy black comb-over and a dour expression) "What kind of a retard are you? You're too young to be getting a non-driver ID, so...what kind of a retard *are* you?" My mention of learning disabilities and a lack of a car fell on deaf ears; before I left with my new card that day, I'd been asked the "r*e*t*a*r*d question no less than four freaking times. Now, I know what I *should* have said to Mr. Greasy-Comb-Over:

"Gee, Mister, what kind am I" The kind who has stayed in this butt-wipe of a town *way* too long. The kind who would've left decades ago, *if* she'd been able to."

Hope you enjoyed the collection. It often wasn't as much fun living parts of it as it was writing it, but it was just something I needed to do…or go crazy.

A. R. Morlan (and cats)
September, 2010

ABOUT THE AUTHORS

A. R. MORLAN WAS born in Chicago, IL on January 3, 1958, and moved with her family to the Los Angeles area in 1961, where she lived until 1969, when her family moved to Wisconsin, where she still lives.

Morlan has a BS degree in English (Liberal Arts), *Magna Cum Laude* from the now defunct Mount Senario College, which folded shortly before a F3 tornado tore apart her place of residence in 2002. She has been a free-lance writer since 1983, and has had fiction and non-fiction published in over 123 different magazines, anthologies, collections, and e-zines in the US, Canada and parts of Europe, in addition to two novels, *The Amulet* and *Dark Journey* (both available from Borgo Press), a Romanian-language collection called *Femia Coperta* (*Cover Woman*) which came out in 2004, a couple of upcoming collections from Borgo Press, a co-edited (with Martin H. Greenberg) anthology called *Zodiac Fantastic* (DAW, 1997), and assorted introductions for various short fiction collections by other authors.

She is single and childless, but a proud pet-parent of a varying number of cat-children.

JAMES B. JOHNSON has written five novels: *Trekmaster, Habu, Mindhopper, A World Lost*, and *Daystar and Shadow*. *Mindhopper* was optioned twice for a movie, and two books were translated into French and German. He has also written numerous short stories and articles. Jim has sold advertising, worked for the Post Office, and spent eleven years in the Air Force. He lives in Sarasota, Florida, with his wife Beverly.

JOHN S. POSTOVIT was born on December 18, 1962 at Grand Forks, North Dakota. He published several of A. R. Morlan's stories as editor of *Alpha Adventures SF*, and has been an occasional collaborator on several of her stories. He currently lives in Boulder Creek, California, and makes his living as a teacher and gallery artist.